Sophie Hannah is twenty-eight an[...] Oxford. She is a fellow of Wolfso[...] teaches part-time at Manchester M[...] Writing School. This is her second novel.

Praise for Sophie Hannah's first novel *Gripless*:

'Hannah's first novel is a prize contender' *Times Metro*

'Hannah has a wonderfully down-to-earth style . . . This book is sure to be loved by all those out there who love a good love story' *Irish Times*

'Absolutely brilliant' *19* magazine

'A thoroughly enjoyable read, it tackles the serious theme of morality' *City Life*

'A comic heroine so possessed by lust that she makes Bridget Jones look listless' *Observer*

'Funny, audacious, well written – guaranteed to breathe life into your day' *Prima*

'If you have ever been in love, read *Gripless* by Sophie Hannah. You'll giggle, you'll laugh and you'll chortle' *B* magazine

'Funny and original' *Buzz* magazine

Sophie Hannah

Cordial and Corrosive

An Unfairy Tale

ARROW

Published in the United Kingdom in 2000 by
Arrow Books

3 5 7 9 10 8 6 4 2

First published in the United Kingdom in 2000 by Arrow Books

Arrow Books Limited
The Random House Group Ltd
20 Vauxhall Bridge Road, London SW1V 2SA

Random House Australia (Pty) Limited
20 Alfred Street, Milsons Point, Sydney,
New South Wales 2061, Australia

Random House New Zealand Limited
18 Poland Road, Glenfield,
Auckland 10, New Zealand

Random House (Pty) Limited
Endulini, 5a Jubilee Road, Parktown 2193, South Africa

The Random House Group Limited Reg. No. 954009

www.randomhouse.co.uk

A CIP record for this book is available from the British Library

Papers used by Random House are natural, recyclable
products made from wood grown in sustainable forests.
The manufacturing processes conform to the environmental
regulations of the country of origin.

Typeset in Sabon by MATS, Southend-on-Sea, Essex
Printed and bound in Great Britain by
The Guernsey Press Co. Ltd., Guernsey, Channel Islands

ISBN 0 09 9280361

For Dan with love

Acknowledgements

I would like to thank Suzanne Davies, Chris Gribble, Norman, Adèle and Jenny Geras, Lisanne Radice, Jane Gregory and Victoria Hipps, all of whom helped to improve this book. Thanks also to Ian Tomlinson and Rachel Hanlon for the Pizza Express debate which provided part of the inspiration, and to Ben Shift, Morgan White and Julian Murphet, all of whom contributed to the ideas for the novel. I am grateful to Paul Barratt and Guy Martland for answering some crucial questions and to Janet Hazzlewood, a memorable driving instructor. The following people gave me general support and encouragement while I was writing the novel: Dan Jones, Michael Schmidt, Tony Weir, Johnny Woodhams, Isabelle Thomas, Peter Salt, Hilary McDonald and Gaynor Hodgson.

Last but not at all least, I would like to thank all my colleagues at Trinity College, Cambridge, which is in every way a brilliant place and gave me the inspiration for all the good things about Summerton College and none of the bad.

Cordial
and
Corrosive

Prologue

Demolishing the Consolations

Let me correct a few popular misapprehensions.

When you apply for a job you really want, get as far as the interview stage and are then rejected, these are some of the things you say to yourself:

1. It wasn't meant to be.

Wrong. This implies a grand plan beyond human comprehension. There is none.

2. I must not have been the best candidate.

Wrong. This assumes that justice governs our lives and takes for granted the existence of a moral world order. There is none, as proven by the number of people who do their jobs badly. Several weeks ago my husband Sebastian and I were at the Cine City Cinema in Cambridge, missing the beginning of the film we had gone to see because the two young men on the Häagen-Dazs counter took a full fifteen minutes (I timed it, to use against them in evidence) to get the ice-cream into the tubs, the tubs into our hands and my money from my hands to their hands to the till. In a fair universe, those men would not be purveyors of cinema snacks, although perhaps I have been spoiled by spending my formative years in Manchester, where the unemployment statistics are much higher and most people on ice-cream counters have PhDs.

1

The I-must-not-have-been-the-best-candidate consolation – although resignation to one's innate inferiority can hardly be thus described – is also based on the incorrect assumption that the people who interviewed you are sane, sensible and trustworthy. This may not be the case. An appointments committee is an unknown quantity, often comprising a shocking assortment of social inadequates, brain-dead bureaucrats and lunatics, chaired by some greying husk who is eminent to the point of imbecility.

3. There are people worse off than me.

Right, but at best an irrelevant and at worst a dangerous philosophy. Taken to its logical conclusion, this means that only one person, the most unfortunate person on earth at any given time, has the right to suffer without being ashamed of it, or to protest about his or her lot in life. By this token I should not have complained that the Häagen-Dazs vendors' inefficiency caused me to miss the first quarter of an hour of *Sliding Doors* because some people have neither ice-cream nor films to watch and spend their days being speared in the eye with a sharp stick. This consolation is regularly offered by those who espouse large political causes and whose concern for injustice on a global scale makes them strangely insensitive to less newsworthy instances of misery. When my first car, an Austin Maestro that I had saved for over a year to buy, was cruelly disfigured by a particularly vicious band of local toddlers, my neighbour, who encountered me sobbing beside it in the street, told me to think about those worse off than me, citing the example of babies born near Chernobyl who were growing extra limbs. Luckily I was well aware that she was a fervent member of CND (it was her only topic of conversation) and knew from previous experience that she would remain unmoved by anything short of total nuclear devastation.

4.   I ought to count my blessings.

Futile and sneaky. There is a silent clause in this consolation, stating that you should be satisfied with your total, whatever it may be. But how can you, when nobody gives you a fixed point of reference by which to measure your score? Unless we know what is the average number of blessings per person, how will we be able to tell if we have been short-changed?

5.   If I keep trying, I'll get something eventually.

Wrong. You may or may not get something eventually, but there is no cumulative effect in operation. Every job for which you are interviewed is a discrete case and each time the odds are one in x, x being the total number of interviewees and one being you. It is equally untrue that if you are really good you will at some point succeed (see refutation of consolation 2 above). You may be so embarrassingly superior to those interviewing you that they will have no choice but to reject you for the sake of their self-esteem.

6.   There's no point letting it get to me because there's nothing I can do.

Wrong. There is always something you can do.
    Why am I telling you this? To ruin your day and make you feel a bit worse about everything? On the contrary; I am stripping you of your hackneyed consolations in order to furnish you with better ones, ones that actually work.
    To do this, I have to tell you a story. I'm glad to say murder plays no part in what I'm about to relate. It very nearly did, which is why I refer to it at all, but it doesn't and I'm glad. In addition to obvious personal reasons, I'm glad because I think a disproportionate number of books are

3

written about murder, given how small a part it plays in most of our lives.

I am going to tell you a story about a job interview. Job interviews play a vital role in almost all our lives. My question is this: why do more people want to read about murder than about job interviews? Your answer is this: because we are interested in extreme events, extreme emotions. These are more likely to surround a murder than a job interview. My response is this: oh yeah? Wait and see.

Chapter One

Kate Nunn – Curriculum Vitae

Name
Kate Nunn. I used to be called Kate Cahill until I married Sebastian Nunn. This surname is more appropriate for him than it is for me, because it reflects the number of jobs he has been offered since he finished his PhD in June 1997. He has applied for twenty-two, been interviewed for eleven and got none. I changed my name, although it is unfashionable to do so, to avoid a Scarlett Skinner predicament (see address section below for further details).

Address
Flat 1, Noble House, 14 Renshaw Road, Cambridge. This is off Hills Road, south of the town centre. Noble House is part of a complex of buildings which together make up Summerton College's married accommodation for its graduate students and fellows. I don't like the word 'fellows', but I'll let it pass for the time being. Most of these buildings are large late-Victorian town houses, except for Noble House, which was added in the early nineteen seventies and is an angular three-storey brick-and-glass affair. The bricks are caramel-coloured and the door and window frames are chocolate-brown. When Sebastian and I first came to look around – light years ago in 1994, when his surname represented the number of his failures, not his successes – we weren't sure we liked Noble House's peculiar shape. It reminded us of a deformed fudge cake. It

consists of a central corridor from which three wings branch off, each containing three flats, one per storey. The nine flats are mirror images of each other, rotating around an imaginary central axis.

Every flat in Noble House has white walls and grey-green carpets. Ours is on the ground floor, with french windows in the lounge that open on to the large, well-tended garden and that, when closed, create an impression of there being a whole wall of window. This is our flat's best feature, although all of its features are pretty fantastic. It has a brand-new, fully fitted kitchen and a bath that slopes down gently from the wall on one side so that you can lie back and read without getting a sore neck. We have lemon-meringue-coloured chairs, sofa and bed linen, as do the other flats in our wing. In the other two wings, the chairs, sofas and bed linen are red and navy-blue respectively. This is because, when three representatives of Summerton's buildings committee were sent to choose furnishings, they couldn't agree on the best colour and so compromised by taking a wing each upon which to inflict their chosen hue.

This was not the first time a decor-related issue had caused controversy at Summerton. In 1987 a block of college flats had to be completely overhauled because it was deemed to be too luxurious. The buildings committee had got a bit carried away on the interior-design front and when the Master went to look at the property he decided that anyone who lived there would become accustomed to a degree of luxury that, on leaving Summerton, they would never find again. This would present them with a grave real-world-adjustment problem, the Master argued, and so thousands of pounds were spent redecorating the building, making it a bit less attractive, a bit less comfortable.

Noble House is named after Edmund Noble, the famous sixteenth-century painter. Renshaw Road is a homage along similar lines to Tobias Renshaw the physicist. Both of these men were students at Cambridge's Summerton College. Now that they are long dead and legendary, now that accommodation is named after them, it is hard to imagine them running around Summerton's grounds, all those centuries ago, saying 'Bollocks, my essay's due in this morning and I haven't even started it', but presumably they must have done.

Noble House is set back from the road at the end of a long, beige and rather regal-looking strip of driveway. All the buildings in the complex share a vast garden the shape of an artist's palette with a sandpit area for children, two large, tree-shaded car parks and a small, free-standing caramel-brick laundry room, also with chocolate-coloured window and door frames. This must have been designed by the same architect and built at the same time as Noble House; it looks like its baby brother. The laundry room contains two washing machines and an industrial-strength drying machine that is larger than the bedrooms provided for undergraduates in most university accommodation.

Sebastian is no longer a graduate student at Summerton College – he finished his PhD a year ago – but the Junior Bursar kindly allowed us to keep the flat for an extra year as there is no shortage of accommodation. We are not the only people who live in Noble House under false pretences. Flat 3, across the corridor from us on the ground floor, in the navy-blue chairs, sofas and bed linen wing, is occupied by Joe Fielding, his wife Terri Skinner the feminist – she is a feminist more than she is anything else, including a person – and their daughter Scarlett Skinner. A Scarlett Skinner predicament, as mentioned above, is a situation where belief in an abstract principle has absurd concrete consequences. Scarlett Fielding is clearly a less risible name than Scarlett Skinner and, if all three of them were called Fielding, nobody would need to feel like the odd one out, like the lone Fielding in a flatful of Skinners. Skinner, incidentally, is a surname Terri inherited from her father, a grumpy, loudmouthed old curmudgeon who sometimes comes to visit. This makes no sense. As you get to choose your husband but not your father, it would surely be more in keeping with the feminist ideal to take the name of the former rather than the latter.

I don't know if Joe Fielding objects to being marginalised on the surname front. I see his torso and limbs all the time but his face hardly ever. If the legs were the windows to the soul, I would know an awful lot about Joe Fielding's state of mind. His top half is almost always obsured by a flurry of laundry bags, Tesco bags, briefcases, soft toys, folding pushchairs and a shrieking Scarlett.

He is the son of Professor Daphne Fielding, Summerton's main authority on film and media studies. Her specialism, aside from securing college flats for her close relatives, is black-and-white cinema. Joe is a marketing consultant who, despite his title, was not consulted before being transferred by his firm from Oxford to Cambridge. Terri, at that point, had just completed a D.Phil at Oxford University so moving to Cambridge with her husband and daughter did not disrupt her career, as indeed nothing but a geological catastrophe could. On the contrary, she has indicated to me on several occasions that, having conquered Oxford, she is keen to add Cambridge to her academic empire.

What is Terri Skinner doing in my CV? Well, people do not exist in a vacuum, independently of one another. What goes on one CV necessarily comes off another; it is a zero-sum game. At the moment, Terri and my husband Sebastian are both competing for the same job at Summerton, as if it isn't bad enough that we have to live opposite her. If she gets it – a possibility I won't rule out, since her mother-in-law is a professor there – it will go on her CV and not Sebastian's, which will affect mine, so I'm putting her in right from the outset.

Age
Thirty.

Marital Status
I have been married to Sebastian for four years, although

8

we lived together for four years before that. I adore him and would do anything to make him happy. Also, I do not regard him as a failure, as I might accidentally have implied earlier. I don't want to give the wrong impression; Sebastian has won a major prize and is having his doctoral thesis published as a book. It is not his fault that university department after university department is unable to recognise his obvious merits. We have no children.

Employment History

I am a driving instructor. I am self-employed and refuse to team up with BSM or any of the bigger operations. It is important to me to be my own boss and to be able to choose with whom to spend my professional time. I have a trial session with every prospective pupil and if I don't like them after that, I ditch them. I call myself 'The Red L Driving School'. There is a sign to that effect, in the shape of a Toblerone tube, stuck to the roof of my Nissan Micra.

I hate it when one of my learners fails a driving test, but at least it's sort of fair. Driving tests, to a certain extent and leaving aside nerves, do actually test a person's ability to drive, unlike most job interviews, which test one's ability to be interviewed rather than to do the job itself. I once had a student who was a brilliant driver but fell apart every time she took a test. She told me tearfully after failing her fourth that the only way she could ever pass was if she downed a few Valium tablets, which of course I couldn't allow her to do. Instead, I charged her a hundred pounds, went to North Wales where no one knows me and took her test for her. I'm happy to report that she passed easily. Not fair, do I hear you say, as if without my tampering it would have been? How touchingly naïve. People who protest about specific instances of unfairness are, by extension, implying that there is a background of fairness against which these unfair acts are taking place, or else why mention them?

When I learned to drive in Manchester, my driving instructor used to insist I call the handbrake 'Knickers'.

'First on, last off,' she would cackle. I tell my pupils to call the handbrake 'Suspicion' for the same reason.

Driving instructors get a bad press and are assumed by most to be obese, brash, bigoted chain smokers. This is why the Red L School is so popular, particularly among Cambridge undergraduates, who make up the majority of my clientele. I am more refined and educated than many in my profession and I try to teach my pupils a bit about life as well as driving, so they get real value for money. I work long hours, usually from eight in the morning until seven at night, because Sebastian is not earning any money.

Between university and training to be a driving instructor when we moved to Cambridge, I worked as a publicity assistant for the Theatre Royal in Manchester. This was an awful job – we worked for a pittance in a basement with no windows – so I tried to do it as ineptly as possible. Unfortunately there are very few excellent jobs in the world and so most of us at some stage have to accept dreary ones. The only compensation for this is that great satisfaction can be gleaned from doing a bad job badly, which is something I always tell my learner drivers. Whatever your occupation, I tell them, your performance should be as impressive, mediocre or downright appalling as the job itself.

Qualifications and Education
BA Hons (IIi) Combined Studies – History and French – from the Victoria University of Manchester, where I met Sebastian. A levels and O levels, which I remember only as an unwelcome distraction from chip-eating and boy-chasing.

Strengths and Weaknesses
My strengths are determination, an optimistic and cheerful temperament, intelligence, good organisational and inter-personal skills. My weaknesses include stubbornness, grudge-holding, vengefulness, ruthlessness and a tendency to develop a crush on any man with a steady job. This has

10

nothing to do with the men themselves; it is simply the difference principle in operation. They have the one thing Sebastian does not have, therefore I am attracted to them as a form of escapism. Luckily I am aware of this and the reasons behind it so I can control it quite easily. Over the past year, I have resisted the temptation to embark upon affairs with my postman, a lorry driver I met at a Little Chef, and Zac Hunt, the Master Manager of Kwikfit on Newmarket Road. He has proved the hardest to banish from my mind, partly because of his title and partly because I see him so often, every time one of my pupils severs the exhaust from my Micra. Sometimes I wish that Sebastian were Master Manager of a branch of Kwikfit, but of course he'd hate it. He would hate most jobs and who can blame him for that?

Other Information
I am tall, thin and flat-chested with long blonde hair that is as straight as a ruler. I have a square jaw and rather masculine features. My hobbies include reading, going to the cinema and plotting hideous revenges on everyone who has ever decided not to give Sebastian a job. Soon there may be more of these than there are films and books.

Chapter Two

The De La Wyche Enmity

Beware of all jobs, that's my advice, but beware particularly of those that call themselves 'fellowships'. The word is misleading and designed to lull innocent applicants into a false sense of security. 'Fellowship' sounds amiable and cosy, whereas the reality of applying for a job is anything but those things. Only after you've succeeded in getting one of these elusive wonders – which may never happen – can you bring yourself to call it a fellowship without having a sense of startling linguistic inaccuracy. But at the advertisement in the newspaper stage, when who will be welcomed and who banished is still unknown, I think it should be called an enmity. 'Enmity in European Law at King's College, Cambridge' the *Times Higher Education Supplement* should say.

At three o'clock on Thursday 4 June I was waiting, as I had been all day, to hear whether Sebastian had got the Summerton College De La Wyche Enmity, which is the most prestigious post-doctoral research position in the country, as well as the most lucrative. Those lucky enough to get elected do not have to pay tax and receive their salary in the form of generous donations. The Enmity is named after the long-dead Grimshaw De La Wyche, world-famous economist and expert on the ways in which taxes could be dodged, who was Master of Summerton at some point in the distant past. The Enmity is Grimshaw De La Wyche's legacy to Summerton. Every three years the college selects some fortunate baby intellectual upon whom to bestow its late Master's generosity. The person must be under thirty-five at the time of appointment and no one may hold the position more than once. Applicants can come from any subject area and have to submit a detailed proposal outlining the research they would undertake. Sebastian's was all about totalitarian states, but if he didn't get the Enmity I knew he would shortly be undertaking an in-depth practical examination of a severely depressed state, and by extension so would I.

I had just returned a pupil to his house on Sterling Road after a lesson through which I had struggled in a demented haze. I took his money, waved him away absent-mindedly and pulled over by a spare stretch of kerb, unable to think about anything apart from when my mobile phone might ring.

We were supposed to find out yesterday, but when I forced Sebastian to phone and enquire the panel still hadn't decided. Why the bloody hell not, I wanted to know. Surely a full day's discussion was enough. No explanation was offered and Sebastian said they sounded guilty when he asked. They had probably forgotten which interviewee was which, or something equally cretinous.

I switched my phone off and on again for the eighth time, to check that it was working. I was tempted to phone home and ask Sebastian if there was any news, but I didn't want to agitate him with a false-alarm phone call and besides, I knew there was no point. He would have let me know if he'd heard anything. I tried not to imagine him anxiously pacing the flat, only metres away from where Terri Skinner was presumably doing the same, possibly with slightly less desperation, as the interview panel had been chaired by none other than Daphne Fielding, her mother-in-law.

I fumbled in the glove compartment for my cigarettes and wound the window down, noticing as I did so that 'No Parking Here' had been daubed on the pavement just beside where my car was parked. The writing was yellow and wobbly, as if the painter had been shaking. I realised I was blocking a wide driveway, flanked by two white gateposts and with a white-doored garage at the end. The garage did not suit the large detached house on to which it had been grafted. All the houses on Sterling Road were terraces except for this one on the junction with Huntingdon Road which looked like a small castle in comparison. There was a gold plaque on one of the gateposts and I stuck my head out of the car window to read it. 'Mr Vincent Strebonian' it said. 'Cosmetic Surgeon'. Terri Skinner would be in need of his services, I thought, if she got Sebastian's job.

But then so many jobs over the past year had been Sebastian's job, in my head at any rate, until they turned out not to be. I sighed and lit a cigarette, trying to convince myself that the De La Wyche Enmity was not his last chance, although it had a feeling of finality about it. Sebastian had not helped to dispel this impression. Ever since the interview two days earlier he had been marching around the flat yelling, 'This is it! Death or glory! My last chance!'

I stuck my arm out of the window to flick ash and came into contact with unexpected human flesh. There was an excessively tall, thin man with grey hair and a grey paintbrushy moustache bending down next to my car so that his head was level with mine. His face and hands were wrinkled and leathery brown. He was wearing a cream linen suit that was as crumpled and cross-hatched as his skin.

'God, sorry,' I muttered. 'Did I burn you? I didn't see you there.'

'Whether or not you burned me is not the issue,' he replied gravely. 'What is very much the issue is that you are blocking my driveway. You are parked directly in front of my gateposts, where I have explicitly indicated that parking is forbidden.'

'Sorry. I'll move.' I smiled at him, proud of my verbal

economy, which stood in marked contrast to Vincent Strebonian's lack of the same. I switched on the Micra's engine and prepared to move off. I nodded politely and was about to lower Suspicion the handbrake when Mr Strebonian's creased hand tapped me on the shoulder. 'Kindly switch off your motor car's engine,' he said.

I sighed and did as I was told, eyeing my mobile phone that still lay dormant on the passenger seat. 'What?' I asked.

'May I ask why you deliberately chose to disregard my instruction and block my passage, regardless?'

Resisting the temptation to tell Mr Strebonian to stick it up his passage, I reiterated my apology and assured him I would avoid making the same mistake again.

He ignored my contrition and continued to tick me off. 'Supposing an emergency occurred while you were parked there and I needed to get out in a hurry? I would be unable to get my motor car out of the garage and on to the road, would I not?'

'No,' I told him bluntly. 'I've been sitting here all the time waiting for a phone call. If you'd needed to get out I would have moved straight away, as I will now if you'll let me.'

'You young people think you know the answer to everything.' Vincent Strebonian shook his finger in my face. Most of his forearm was inside my car at this point. 'In an emergency situation, even if you were inside your vehicle, vital seconds might have been lost. Once you add up the time it would take me to tell you I wanted to get out and the time it would take you to . . .'

'Hey,' I interrupted him. 'If your life is so full of emergencies, how come you can afford to waste time having a go at me? I've said sorry. You're quite right, I shouldn't have parked here. I didn't see the "No Parking" sign, I've got a lot on my mind at the moment. I'll move. Can't we just leave it at that?' I picked up my mobile phone to check I still had a signal. Why wasn't Sebastian ringing? Surely they must have let him know by now.

'Kindly put your telephone down when I'm speaking to you, young lady.' Vincent Strebonian's voice was quiet but threatening. 'You ought to pay more attention. If you have a lot on your mind then you are in no condition to drive, nor fit to give instruction to others.'

I noticed a young blond man with round wire-rimmed glasses and a small triangular beard peering out of a ground-floor window across the road. He seemed to be watching our exchange with interest. 'The irony,' I said to Dr Strebonian, 'is that you are now preventing me from moving the sodding car and prolonging my parking offence by keeping me here against my will.' I wondered whether irritations sought out the already irritated, whether my anxiety about Sebastian radiated from my body, attracting further misfortune. Vincent Strebonian seemed keen to cast himself in the last-straw role. The shape of his body was not dissimilar to that of a straw, so perhaps he had done a De Niro *Raging Bull* in reverse.

'I am merely trying to make my point,' he said. 'The least you can do, after thoughtlessly impeding my path, is allow me to have my say.'

'I did, but your say appears to want to go on all fucking afternoon,' I yelled. 'Look, just leave me alone. Go and surge cosmetically.' I heard footsteps and turned to see the young blond man from the window running across the road towards us, rubbing his beard anxiously. A sheen of sweat appeared to cover his entire face. He must be seriously unfit, I thought, if he can't even cross the road without becoming shiny. 'Are you okay, Mr S?' he asked as he approached. His voice was soft and genteel. I wondered if he was landed gentry or had been to finishing school.

'No, I am not. This young lady is being extremely rude to me.'

'No I'm not.' I sighed and leaned back in my seat, lighting another cigarette.

The bearded man inserted his head into my car through the open window. He smelled strong and rich, like cake mixture. 'You mustn't be horrible to Mr Strebonian,' he said, staring at me earnestly. 'He gets very upset when people block his driveway.'

'You don't say,' I said angrily. 'I've apologised several times but he keeps moaning at me.' My phone, which I had temporarily forgotten as a result of the ensuing turf war, started to ring. My breath caught in my throat. All Sebastian's rejection letters to date flashed before my eyes: *wish you every success in your search . . . unfortunately on this occasion . . . other candidates had skills more suited . . .* The blond man still had his head in my car and was blinking his concern at me from behind thin spectacle lenses. 'Move!' I yelled and pushed his forehead with my fingertips. It felt as slippery as it looked, but its texture was more creamy than sweaty. He gave me a hurt look and retreated.

I wound up the car window, vowed that if Sebastian got the De La Wyche Enmity I would immediately give five hundred pounds to Save the Children and pressed the green button on my phone. 'Hello? Sebastian?'

'Yeah,' he said mournfully. 'I've just heard. I didn't get it.'

I clutched the steering wheel in agony, waiting for the awfulness of this news to subside to bearability level. It didn't. Why did this have to keep happening? I wasn't sure how many more times I could go through it. 'Oh no,' I said, and then again for good luck, in which I no longer believed, 'Oh no. I'm really sorry.'

'That's it.' Sebastian's voice shook. 'It's over. I've had enough, I've fucking had enough. I've got a book coming out, I won a prize, for fuck's sake! Why will nobody give me a job? Why will nobody give me a chance?'

'It's not over,' I said calmly, forcing myself to sound more cheerful than I felt. As one of the main good things in Sebastian's life I have an obligation to wear a mask of resilient jollity at all times. He would be even more miserable if he knew how much all this was getting to me.

'We'll sort something out. Everything will be all right in the end, you'll see.'

'No it won't. Everything's shit. They offered the job to Terri fucking Skincrawl and she doesn't even know if she wants it!' Terri Skincrawl is Sebastian's nickname for our esteemed neighbour. That or Terri Skinflick, which he finds particularly funny, given her feminist leanings (lurchings would be more accurate). His hatred for Terri dates back to long before she got his job. He once said that her treatment of Joe, her husband, should be a matter for the UN Sex War Crimes Tribunal. 'I wanted it, I definitely wanted it,' he went on. 'Why didn't they give it to me?'

'What do you mean, she doesn't know if she wants it?' I asked.

'She's asked for two weeks to think about it. Apparently she's had another job offer from Reading University. It's not fair! Why does she get everything and I get nothing?' Why indeed? I had long ago given up trying to find reasons for things. Rationality is useless, as my recent exchange with Vincent Strebonian had proved. Nobody acts in a particular way because there is a good reason why they should; people simply do as they please and invent reasons afterwards to justify their impulsive behaviour. This is why no one ever follows another person's advice unless it happens to tie in with their own subconscious inclinations.

'Reading?' I said incredulously. 'Most people would find it fairly easy to choose between Cambridge's richest and most famous college and Reading.'

'Not her, obviously.'

'But Sebastian, that means she might not take it . . .'

'Forget it.' He sighed. 'I'm not even first runner-up. If Terri doesn't take it they're going to offer it to Rod Firsden, their second choice.'

'Oh.' I clutched the wheel harder. 'Who's he?'

'I don't know!' Sebastian yelled. 'What does it matter? He's someone they preferred to me. Why does nobody ever want me? What's wrong with me?'

'Nothing,' I said firmly. 'There's something wrong with them.' Vincent Strebonian and his do-gooder neighbour were still standing on the pavement beside the Micra, no doubt waiting until I was free to be lectured again. If they thought my attitude was bad before, they were about to get a shock. I'd make them wish they'd quit before it was too late.

'Do you know anything about this Rod Firsden?' I asked wearily. 'Like whether he would take the job if he were offered it?'

'I don't know. If both he and Terri turned it down, I'd get it, but what fucking chance is there of that happening?'

'How do you know that?' I asked. 'Are you their third choice?'

'Don't sound so excited,' said Sebastian. 'There are only three of us. Yeah, I'm their third choice, their last choice.' Bitterness dripped from his every word.

'I thought they interviewed four people.'

'They did. The fourth dropped out yesterday. If she hadn't, I bet they'd have chosen her over me as well.' Sebastian was not a bouncer back by nature. He tended to take on the properties of Dead Sea salt in the presence of even the mildest wound. He was also intelligent enough to be able always to find new damaging things to say, each one sharper and more original than the last, and with more power to hurt us both. It was at times like this that I wished I was married to Zac Hunt, the Master Manager of Kwikfit, who probably had a well-worn, meaningless phrase that he produced for every bad patch, something like 'These things are sent to try us'.

'She dropped out? Why?'

'I don't fucking know, do I?'

'Sebastian, who phoned you?'

'Valerie Williams. She said something really odd.'

'The doctor?'

'Yeah.'

'What the fuck is the college doctor doing on an

19

interview panel anyway? She shouldn't be there and neither should the mother-in-law of one of the applicants, the one who coincidentally gets the job. It's such a stitch-up.'

'I've had enough. I can't go on,' Sebastian murmured. I winced, wishing I could say something that would make it all right. I noticed Vincent Strebonian was no longer standing next to the car. The blond bearded man was waiting alone, peering at me rudely.

'Sebastian,' I said calmly. 'I'm coming home right now. What did you mean about the doctor saying something odd?'

'She said something like "you very nearly got it". But how can I have done? I mean, I wasn't even second.'

'She said that?'

'Something like that, yeah.' Sebastian sighed. 'What does it matter? It's all over. My life, my career, it's finished.'

'Will you stop saying that?' I shouted, trying not to burst into tears. 'Nothing is finished. Look, wait for me to get home and then we can talk about it properly. Will you be okay until I get back?'

'I'm not okay. I won't be okay unless someone gives me a job and no one will.'

I massaged my temples, realising too late that my fingertips were still greasy from having touched Blond-beard's forehead. I raised my left hand to my nose and sniffed: coconut lotion or cocoa butter or something similar. No wonder his face was shiny if he covered it with that stuff. 'Sebastian, don't forget that the last De La Wyche fellow disappeared,' I said. 'Maybe it's jinxed.' I didn't really believe this but I would have said anything rather than allow silence to creep in. Silence gives you time to think, to draw conclusions. And it was true, the last person to hold the position, Fernando Rose, did vanish in a most mysterious fashion, if college legend was to be believed.

'I wish the whole college'd disappear,' said Sebastian. 'I'm sick of the lot of them, ungrateful bastards. Haven't they got any loyalty? I was there for three years, three fucking years! My PhD won a prize and what do I get for it? Nothing, not a bloody sniff at a chance. There's no way I'm going to tomorrow's feast now, not after this.'

'We have to go,' I said, although I too was dreading it. 'Otherwise we'll look defeated.'

'We are defeated,' Sebastian wailed. Every so often Summerton laid on a banquet for its fellows, students and recent ex-students. These feasts always took place in the Great Hall, under the vigilant painted eyes of all the college's ex-Masters whose portraits lined the walls. A feast usually involved seven or eight courses, a grace chanted in Latin, songs from the choir, toasts to the Queen, exquisitely printed menu cards embossed with Summerton's crest and more alcohol than a person could reasonably be expected to consume. Fellows and graduates wore gowns for such occasions, long black loose garments that covered them from neck to toe. The first time Sebastian had taken me to a feast I hadn't been able to stop laughing at the sight of a large hall full of people who looked as if they had scarpered from Vidal Sassoon midway through a haircut.

The last thing I wanted to do was socialise with Summerton fellows, people who not only had academic jobs but who took the fact that they had come by them so easily entirely for granted. There was no evidence of surprise or enthusiasm on their faces when goose, rabbit and swan were placed in front of them. Most of them didn't even glance at their menu cards; Sebastian and I, on the other hand, collected ours.

Blondbeard was still standing beside my car, stooping from time to time to wiggle his fingers at me. I made a dismissive gesture with my left hand, indicating that he should sod off.

'We aren't defeated at all,' I said. 'Look, don't be too depressed. I'm on my way home.' I pressed the red button on my mobile phone and threw it on to the back seat in disgust, resenting it for bringing me bad news. I switched on the engine and was about to release Suspicion when there was a knock on my window. I wound it down impatiently.

'Look, just fuck off, will you?' I spat at Blondbeard. 'Your friend was in the wrong, I was in the right.'

'It's not that. I . . . I wanted to ask about driving lessons. The Red L Driving School. I like that. It's a more interesting name than most.' He pushed his glasses up his shiny nose. The smell of cocoa butter wafted towards me.

'No,' I said.

'No?'

'I mean, you can't have any. Not with me, anyway.'

'Why?' He looked puzzled.

'Because I don't like you.'

'You don't like me? You don't even know me. Is it because I interfered in your fight with Mr Strebonian?'

'Look . . .' I restrained myself from adding 'Dickhead'.

'Rod,' he said helpfully. 'Rod Firsden.'

I stared at him in disbelief. Surely not. He couldn't have said what I thought he'd said. This was some kind of joke. 'What did you say?' I mumbled through numb lips.

'Rod Firsden,' he said. 'That's my name.'

Chapter Three

Studying the Understudy

Every nerve in my body was jangling as I invited Rod Firsden to get into the car. You know that feeling you get when something happens and you know it's important even though you haven't yet had time to work out why? That was how I felt. This is the first reserve for the De La Wyche Enmity, I chanted to myself, trying to calm down. This is the person to whom it will be offered if Terri Skincrawl turns it down.

Could this man be lying, I wondered as he climbed into the passenger seat beside me, rubbing his shiny nose in apparent agitation. Maybe he'd heard me through the car window saying the name 'Rod Firsden' to Sebastian and decided to pretend that it was his name. No; why would anyone do that, unless they were mad? It must be him. I was still unsure as to what this meant but I was beginning to feel a soaring light-headedness which suggested that its significance was positive rather than negative.

I realised the first thing I had to do was backtrack from my original hard-line position. Thank God I hadn't called him Dickhead. I cleared my throat. 'So,' I said hoarsely. 'You want driving lessons?'

I was not at all prepared for what happened next. Rod Firsden took off his glasses, balanced them neatly on the dashboard, put his glossy face in his hands and burst into loud sobs. I sighed, thinking that this was exactly the sort of behaviour I could do without. It was hard enough to cope with Sebastian's distress without having the anguish of a total stranger to contend with.

There is an unspoken convention that dictates that crying people must be hugged, but I was reluctant to touch Rod Firsden so instead I just looked at him, taking in his black polo-necked jumper and black jeans. Today wasn't exactly boiling but it was too hot for what he was wearing. He had also tucked his sweater into his trousers, which looked ridiculous.

'Look,' I said, 'I'm sorry for saying I didn't like you . . .'

'It's not you.' He gulped, wiping his eyes. 'It's not that.'

'Oh.' I leaned back in my seat, feeling slightly irked that my nastiness had not been the cause of his tears.

'It's unbearable,' Rod went on mysteriously in his precise, clipped, finishing-school voice. 'I'm sorry. I shouldn't be burdening you with this. I just . . . couldn't help it. I seem to be losing my sense of perspective. My whole future is hanging in the balance.' It was when he made this last comment that I realised he had to be referring to the De La Wyche Enmity. I couldn't believe my luck. Here we were, getting straight down to business with almost no social preamble. That's the advantage of hysterical people: you don't have to wait too long before they say something interesting. With people whose emotions are under control, on the other hand, you sometimes have to know them for years before getting so much as a whiff of good gossip.

'What do you mean?' I asked encouragingly. Rod wiped his eyes, sniffed a couple of times and lifted his glasses from the dashboard with both hands. There was a neatness about his movements that reminded me of a mime artist.

'I'm terribly sorry,' he said. 'Listen, you don't want to hear about my problems. I really meant it when I said I wanted driving lessons . . .'

'I do want to hear about your problems,' I contradicted him.

'You do? Why?' He blinked at me suspiciously.

'Well, it's not every day a total stranger bursts into tears in my car.'

'That's not a reason,' said Rod.

'Well . . .' I searched my mind for something more convincing. 'If I'm going to give you driving lessons, I need to know what's wrong with you . . . if you know what I mean . . . otherwise there'll always be this mysterious thing between us and . . . I won't be able to concentrate on teaching you.'

'Fair point.' He nodded. I smiled at him with relief. My explanation had sounded absurd to me, and I was terrified he'd change his mind and get out of the Micra, never to share an enclosed space with me again. I knew I needed to keep him there, although I still wasn't sure what I hoped to achieve. Shadowy ideas were beginning to form at the back of my mind. 'Have you heard of Summerton College?' he asked me.

'Of course I've heard of Summerton,' I said huffily. 'I've lived in Cambridge for four years. I may be a driving instructor but I'm not totally ignorant.'

'Oh.' Rod seemed surprised. 'Have you, by any chance, heard of the De La Wyche fellowship?' His voice shook as he mentioned the Enmity.

I considered whether it would be wise to answer yes. It was plausible that a local driving instructor might have heard of Cambridge's most famous college, but perhaps not so credible that she would also know its research fellowships by name. 'Vaguely,' I muttered, deciding on a compromise solution. 'Oh – isn't that something to do with that guy who disappeared? You know, what was his name? Fernando Rose, wasn't it? It was in all the tabloids.' I permitted myself a small self-congratulatory grin that I'm sure Rod didn't notice. To mention the tabloids was a stroke of genius, as it would surely tie in with what my new shiny unhappy pupil would expect from a driving instructor. I was convinced I'd got my facts right as well; I distinctly remembered a headline in one of the more preposterous papers saying something like 'Cambridge Fellow Abducted by Aliens'.

'Yes, it's that one,' said Rod. 'Although it's slightly frustrating that that's its main association now, in most people's minds. It's Oxbridge's most competitive, most highly regarded research fellowship. Several ex-De La Wyche fellows have gone on to win Nobel Prizes.' He said 'Oxbridge' in the way I might have said 'the world' and I guessed that he made no distinction between the two.

'Do you know anything about that? Why he went missing, I mean?' I thought I'd play the scandal-seeking ignoramus for a bit longer, to keep Rod talking while I worked out a strategy. Once I had been genuinely interested in the disappearance of Fernando Rose, along with everyone else who was connected to Summerton, but unsolved mysteries, which always seem so fascinating at first, become dull after a while during which no new facts emerge. I'd never met Fernando, and Sebastian hardly knew him, although they'd been jointly involved in college drinking sessions once or twice. Unless the person at the centre of a mystery is a loved one, your desperation to know turns, given long enough, into acceptance that you never will.

It had happened early last year, while Sebastian was writing the final draft of his thesis. His hypothesis at the time was that Fernando Rose had run off with Martine Selinger, the wife of Damian Selinger, another Summerton fellow. I frowned at the thought of him; he was on the offending panel that had two days ago interviewed and today rejected Sebastian, and he was supposed to be his friend. Damian had relied heavily on Sebastian's support, both emotional and practical, on several occasions over the past few years when he and Martine had been going through the sequence of bad patches they optimistically called their marriage.

'No,' said Rod crossly, breaking into my resentful reverie. 'I'm not interested in gossip. Do you want to know why I'm upset or not?'

'Yes. Sorry.'

'I was interviewed for the De La Wyche fellowship, the next one, starting this October. The interview was two days ago. I don't think I can possibly explain how much I wanted it. It's what I've been working for all my life.' He paused to stare at me solemnly and I nodded with equal seriousness. 'I did everything I possibly could to ensure that I would get it,' he went on.

'Like what?' It was worth knowing whether there were any aspects of his approach that I could poach for Sebastian, if he ever got another interview. If he ever applied for another job, I thought miserably, remembering his insistence that his career was over, not to mention his life.

'What?' Rod blinked at me. 'Well, you know, I did all the necessary interview preparation.'

'Okay. Go on.'

'I thought that the worst thing that could happen to me was that I wouldn't get it. That would have been unspeakably awful – I had no idea how I would deal with it if it happened, how I would survive – but something much, much worse has ... oh, God!' He whipped his glasses off again, put them in my glove compartment this time and began to howl like a wounded cat. If he hadn't been so distraught I would have told him sharply to keep out of my car's intimate crevices. There were documents in the glove compartment that had my name on them, but fortunately he was too upset to notice. I didn't know whether Rod knew Sebastian's name, or even that Sebastian had also been interviewed for the De La Wyche Enmity, but I knew I couldn't let him find out that his new driving teacher – and psychiatric nurse, it seemed – was the wife of a rival De La Wycher. I needed to make up a false name for when he asked me – if he ever did – what I was called. I could keep the Kate part, but the Nunn would have to go. I decided to revert to my maiden name, Cahill.

'What's the something much much worse?' I asked.

'I came second!' Rod wrung his hands in despair. 'That would be excruciating enough in itself – almost succeeding is far more painful than clear failure – but there's more. The person who came first – Terri Skinner, her name is – has asked for two weeks to make a decision, the sort of decision that makes a mockery of the word: between Summerton and Reading, can you imagine?' He might have said 'Broadmoor' with equal disgust. 'Summerton should reject her outright, for having the audacity to think Reading might be better. But they've said yes, they've given her her two weeks!' He threw his head back and yowled. 'Two weeks of torment, teetering on the borderline between heaven and hell and not knowing which way it's going to go!' I stared at shiny Rod Firsden in amazement. He was, if such a thing were possible, even more melodramatic than Sebastian. A disloyal thought occurred to me. Perhaps Terri Skincrawl had been chosen for the Enmity because both Rod and Sebastian had brought too much performance angst to their interviews. On the surface Terri is all poise and charm, unlikely to come out with anything eccentric. Nobody knows that she's got a little white slavery thing going in flat 3, Noble House, least of all the white slave's mother, Professor Fielding (I'm guessing, you understand). Joe Fielding doesn't look the type to complain. In fact, based on the few sightings I have had of his face, I would say he seems remarkably happy, given his Rochesteresque situation. I'm talking about being lumbered with a grim wife, not falling in love with a nanny. Joe Fielding hasn't got one to fall in love with; he is the nanny.

Rod was still weeping beside me. I yearned suddenly to be in the company of Zac Hunt, the Master Manager of Kwikfit, someone strong and capable as I assumed he was. I needed another man to comfort like I needed a lecture from Vincent Strebonian. Still, I feigned patience, feeling I was close to a breakthrough of some kind.

'So,' I recapped, 'if Terri Skinner turns down the En . . . the fellowship, you get it?'

'Yes! But I can't stand it, I'll die before then, I can't wait two weeks. I've got to do something,' Rod squealed pitifully.

'What, you mean do something to Terri? To get her out of the way?' My mind clicked into gear as I said this. Was Rod deranged enough to consider violence as a means of removing a certain human hurdle from his career path? If he was – and judging by his behaviour so far, I wasn't ruling it out – that meant one obstacle fewer for me. It was difficult not to think in terms of obstacles. Terri and Rod were all that stood between Sebastian and the best job in the world, possibly even a Nobel Prize, if Rod was to be believed.

'Don't be ludicrous,' he snapped. 'What do you mean, get her out of the way?' He opened the glove compartment and put his glasses on again.

'Well, I don't know.' I tried to shrug it off. 'You sounded fairly desperate. I thought you might have been . . .' I shrugged, hoping his imagination would fill in the gaps.

'No!' he said vehemently. 'You can't just . . . get rid of people.' He looked at me as if I were mad.

'But you've thought about it, haven't you? Come on, you can tell me. What did you mean when you said "I've got to do something"?'

'I meant,' Rod said self-righteously, 'that I need an activity to throw myself into, to take my mind off the waiting. Like learning to drive.'

'Oh,' I said glumly. Why did he have to turn sane when I most wanted him to be a maniac?

'Am I so transparent?' he asked unexpectedly.

'What?'

'I feel as if you're reading my mind. I have thought about . . .' – he swallowed – '. . . that sort of thing, but it's just a sick fantasy. I know it's terrible of me, it makes me a bad person, but if I had a choice . . . well, I don't know what I'd choose.' I knew immediately to what choice he was referring, despite his cryptic delivery.

'You mean, if God came down and said either Terri dies and you get the job or she lives and gets the job?'

'Exactly!' Rod panted enthusiastically into my face. His breath was warm and moist. 'You're amazing,' he said. 'You're so . . . wise. How did you guess that?'

I cleared my throat, feeling the need to get the conversation back on a more normal level. Now that Rod was showing more enthusiasm for Terri's possible death, I was starting to feel a bit spooked. 'God doesn't come down and offer choices, though,' I said. 'Not in the real world.'

'I know.' Rod sighed. 'And I'd never really wish for anything like that, I'm just so . . . frustrated. Will you teach me to drive? Can you do it in a fortnight? I mean, full-time, all day, every day . . .'

'Hang on,' I interrupted. 'I've got other pupils, you know. And it takes a bit longer than a fortnight to learn to drive. Are you starting from scratch?'

'Yes. But please, you've got to see me at least every day. I love talking to you. I really connect with you.' He leaned towards me, beaming, as if he'd forgotten that he was supposed to be miserable. How could he love talking to me, or have any opinion about it? We'd met less than half an hour ago.

'Are you not working at the moment, then?' I asked. It was vital that I steered him away from the subject of our 'connection'. I couldn't afford to get too close to this human impediment to Sebastian's happiness.

'I can't work now, in this condition,' Rod snapped. Clearly he thought I'd made an improper suggestion and now he was glaring at me when only a few seconds ago he'd been beaming. I had known a few changeable people in my time but no one whose moods overthrew each other so quickly. Talking to Rod made me feel as if I was sinking in quicksand. I decided that to disregard both his speech and his actions was the only sensible way to proceed. 'I'm sorry,' he said tearfully. 'It's just that . . . I can hardly function, since the interview. You know, stress, depression.

30

Well, maybe you don't know.' He didn't wait to find out. 'Normally I do odd bits of casual work. I stuff envelopes for a T'ai Chi school.'

'You're joking?' I giggled, realising as I did so that he probably wasn't. I'd seen no evidence of a sense of humour since he'd got into the car. At least Sebastian took some time off from gloom-mongering occasionally to make me laugh.

'Why would I be joking?' said Rod, confirming my impression of him as a humourless neurotic.

'Well, I don't know. I thought you were the academic type.' I had been about to say that most academic types I knew would not consider taking any other kind of job, even assuming they could function outside a university, which many of them could not. When Sebastian used to take me in to dinner at Summerton as his guest, we would often pass some old begowned gentleman or other who would shudder and make a strange noise that sounded like 'Gughugh' when Sebastian introduced me. I came to recognise this as the sound of a Cambridge don reeling from the shock of being expected to converse with a layperson.

'I suppose you're the sort of person who sneers at T'ai Chi,' Rod said crossly. 'You probably think it's a load of new age hippy rubbish.' I found it hard to believe this was the same man who had called me wise only minutes ago.

'Excuse me!' I protested. 'Why are you being so aggressive?' Coincidentally I did think T'ai Chi was a load of new age hippy rubbish but I could tell Rod thought all my opinions came straight from the driving instruction bigotry wholesalers and I wanted to dispel this impression. What I don't like about T'ai Chi is that it leads to Buddhism in the way that marijuana leads to heroin. Buddhism is all about inner peace, which is a naïve and ineffectual emotional state. No amount of inner peace will get Sebastian the De La Wyche Enmity.

'I'm sorry,' said Rod, 'but you keep questioning me.'

31

'It's called making conversation,' I said sarcastically.

'All right.' He exhaled slowly. 'I'm sorry. When I finished my doctoral thesis, I couldn't find a job at first. I desperately needed some money and this place needed envelope-stuffers. It's just the odd day, cash in hand.'

'So how long have you been there?'

'Look, what is this?' He turned on me furiously. 'Twenty questions?'

'For God's sake, what's the matter with you?' I had had just about enough of this head case. Still, he was prepared to do menial work to earn money, which was more than could be said for Sebastian. He understood the concept of economic necessity. 'Let me explain,' I said. 'Within the framework of a friendly conversation, it's customary to show an interest in the other person. That's all I'm doing. You ought to try it some time and stop being so self-obsessed. My name, in case you were wondering, is Kate Cahill.'

'You're right. I am self-obsessed. I can't help it. But I'd rather not talk about work. It's boring. Envelope stuffing!' He snorted contemptuously. 'If I got the De La Wyche fellowship, then I'd be doing work that was worth talking about.'

'Oh?' I said casually.

'Yes. My research proposal was on the poetry of George Herbert. Have you heard of him? Seventeenth-century poet?'

'No,' I said truthfully.

'No?' Rod looked shocked. 'But he's sublime! He's one of the greatest poets that ever lived. You must buy his *Collected Poems*.'

'Well . . .' I tried to think of a tactful way to say that I had more pressing needs and that the *Collected Poems* of George Herbert was fairly low down on my shopping list, but Rod wasn't paying attention. He was staring straight ahead through the windscreen with a fervent glint in his eye.

'He's my hero. If I get the fellowship, I'm going to write

32

the definitive book on him, you know. It's about time someone did.'

'Mm,' I said with feeling, as if I too were deeply concerned about the inadequacy of the George Herbert literature to date.

'But if I don't get it, if this Terri Skinner accepts it . . . I don't even know what her subject is. I'm sure it can't be as important, how can it be?'

It certainly isn't as important as Sebastian's research into totalitarianism, I thought, still unconvinced that the world would be a sorely deprived place without Rod's musings on some sixteenth-century poet of whom I'd never heard. As Terri Skincrawl's neighbour, I knew a moderate amount about her work, although of course I couldn't tell Rod I knew. Fishes' teeth. No, that's not a euphemism for an obscene phrase, that is the foundation upon which she has built her career. The teeth of fish. This is what she thinks about, sitting in Summerton's library, to which her mother-in-law the professor has thoughtfully given her a key, until sometimes nine or ten at night, while poor Joe collects the child that doesn't share his surname from nursery, makes her dinner and puts her to bed at the same time as doing the shopping, the washing and the hoovering. Mackerels' molars. Goofy goldfish. Whichever way you put it, it sounds absurd.

'Kate?' Rod put his hand on my arm. 'I'm sorry if I've been snappy. Will you forgive me? Will you teach me to drive? We could start straight away,' he said hopefully.

I hesitated. Sebastian would be expecting me home by now but I wasn't ready to let Rod go. If Terri Skinflick didn't take the job they would offer it to Rod, who would. Unless I could see to it, somehow, that he didn't. 'Go on then, let's swap places,' I said.

As we got out of the car, I realised we had been blocking Vincent Strebonian's driveway all this time. 'Serves the bastard right for giving me aggro,' I muttered to myself.

'Are you talking about Mr S?' Rod asked, climbing into the driver's seat.

'Yes. What an arsehole. He's not even a proper doctor. He's only Mr Strebonian.'

'All surgeons are called Mr. And he isn't . . . what you said, he's just highly strung. People always ignore his "No Parking" sign. He's an old man. You shouldn't be so hard on him.'

'Whatever.' I shook my head dismissively. Some people, in their dealings with others, practise the opposite of victim support, listing the good points of your attacker before you've even struggled to your feet. Privately, I reacted to Rod's defence of Vincent Strebonian as an apple would react to a mercy plea on behalf of William Tell. 'Right, there are three pedals at your feet,' I said, launching into my first-lesson spiel. 'Accelerator on the right, which we'll call "gas" because it's quicker, brake in the middle and clutch on the left.' Rod nodded and stared absent-mindedly at a tree by the side of the road. 'No, don't take my word for it,' I said. 'Look at the pedals. You need to know where they are because you're going to put your feet on them in a minute.'

Never in all my professional life had I had a more obtuse pupil. It took me nearly fifteen minutes to teach Rod which pedal was which, where the different gears were and how to switch on the ignition.

Once he had absorbed all that, I said, 'This is the handbrake. We call it "Suspicion".'

'"Suspicion"?' Rod looked puzzled.

'Yes. First on, last off.' I explained about my driving instructor and 'Knickers'.

A smile broke out across Rod's shimmering face. 'That's great,' he said. 'I like that. Suspicion! Knickers! You've got a way with words. The Red L Driving School – did you think of that?' I nodded modestly. 'Have you ever tried writing poetry? I bet you'd be good at it.'

'Nah,' I said. 'But then I bet Jim Herbert never taught anyone how to drive.'

'George Herbert.' Rod chuckled. He looked quite endearing when he relaxed a bit and suddenly I felt desperately sorry for him. He's in the same boat as Sebastian, I thought. Then something happened to remind me that, in a more literal and life-threatening sense, he was in the same car as me. Rod lowered Suspicion, slammed his foot down on the gas pedal and we shot forward at about sixty miles an hour. 'Rod, there's a woman . . . !' I yelled, slamming my foot down on the dual control brake. We skidded to a halt, inches away from a large, pear-shaped figure who was crossing the road. She seemed hardly aware of us and continued to lumber on regardless. I noticed she was crying copiously, walking in a sort of trance, with heaving shoulders and a bowed head. She was wearing a dark coat with a hood, even though it was summer. She turned to look at us briefly, then walked on.

Rod was shaking beside me. 'Oh, Jesus!' he said. 'See what happened? I felt happy for a moment and now God's punishing me, he's punishing me. I was feeling a bit better and then this! You see, he won't let me be happy, not even for a minute. Oh, I'm a bad person,' he wailed, plucking at his jumper with distraught fingers.

'Rod, that didn't happen because you felt better and God punished you,' I explained patiently. 'It happened because you pressed the accelerator too hard.'

'But . . . her!' Rod pointed at the back of the woman he had nearly hit. 'Oh, God.'

'She's fine,' I said impatiently, 'fine' in this case meaning that Zac Hunt of Kwikfit would not finds parts of her body in my exhaust pipe, not that all was right with her world, for it clearly was not. Her shoulders rose and sank as she stomped away like a heavy ghost. I shivered, glad I didn't believe in them. Rod was in too severe a state of shock to continue with his lesson, so we made another appointment for the following day and I went home, stopping at Heffers on the way to buy George Herbert's *Collected Poems*.

Chapter Four

Sebastian Nunn – Curriculum Vitae

Name
Dr Sebastian Gregory Nunn.

Address
Flat 1, Noble House, 14 Renshaw Road, Cambridge.

Age
Twenty-eight.

Marital Status
Married to Kate Nunn (née Cahill) since February 1994.

Employment History (post-BA, MA and PhD)
JUNE 1997–PRESENT
Unpaid: turning his PhD into a book for Scholars Press. No other employment, unless applying for jobs can be counted as a job. Firm belief that there are only two professional avenues open to Cambridge residents: academia or working in a bun shop. Extends bun shop category to include everything that isn't based in a university faculty or college. Advertisements for posts such as library assistant, editorial assistant for local newspaper and part-time bookseller at local academic bookshop, when spotted and pointed out by wife, are rejected on bun shop grounds, meaning beneath dignity of high-calibre intellectual.

Employment History (in two years between A levels and University)

JUNE 1989–JULY 1989 – SALES ASSISTANT, OUR PRICE RECORDS
Sacked after three weeks for unexplained absences due to boringness of job and insufficient mental stimulation from colleagues, for telling customers that the CDs they wanted to buy had gone into a time warp and for treating the question 'How much is it?' as an existential conundrum rather than a consumer enquiry.

MARCH 1989–JUNE 1989 – SALES ASSISTANT AT DILLONS' BOOKSHOP
Fired after three months for general unfriendly and unhelpful temperament due to tedium of daily routine and specific refusal to move a pile of Terry Pratchett novels from one part of the store to another on the grounds that, in the grand scheme of things and on a global scale, it did not matter where the Terry Pratchett books were positioned.

JUNE 1988–MARCH 1989 – UNEMPLOYED
Much time spent lying on sofa. Tried to get on to an agency's books for part-time office work but fell at the first typing test. When asked to type his name, forgot how to change lower case to upper. Asked, and was directed to the 'Shift' key. Then typed what he thought was his name but what in fact was the name of his administratively challenged alter ego, Sebastian Shift.

FEBRUARY 1988–JUNE 1988 – WAITER AT PIZZA HUT
Fired for interfering in customers' conversations, particularly ones about current affairs, and for being caught spitting into the food of those with abhorrent political views.

Fired for constant administrative cock-ups, and for
refusing to dress up in a beaver costume and walk around
the streets of Manchester singing 'Be a busy beaver, be a
high achiever' while handing out leaflets promoting the
agency.

Qualifications and Education
PhD – 'Lenin: From Seal to Steel' – Summerton College,
Cambridge, September 1994 to June 1997. MA (with
distinction) Political Theory, Victoria University of
Manchester. BA Hons History and Politics, University of
Liverpool (Grade IIi. Should really have been put up to a
first, since precise mark was sixty-nine and a half per cent,
but three most influential members of History Department
at relevant time were involved in bitter and sordid love-
triangle situation, so were all feeling edgy and mean-
spirited.)

Publications/Achievements
Doctoral thesis to be published as a book entitled *Lenin:
the Sealed Man* by Scholars Press (Cambridge and New
York) in March 1999. This also won the Lord Entwhistle
Prize, awarded by the Political Studies Association, for the
best thesis of the year on a political subject. Two articles,
one on the Mensheviks and one on Stalin's Five Year Plans,
published in the *European Political History Review* and
International Affairs respectively.

Strengths and Weaknesses
Strengths include intelligence and occasional brilliance,
dedication and commitment (when interested and if
activity is considered worthwhile), ambition, originality
and ability to write things about the Russian Revolution in
general and about Lenin in particular that are better than
anything anyone else has ever written on the same topic.

38

Weaknesses (personal) include unwillingness to compromise integrity by doing anything but own research, irrespective of monetary considerations, and tendency to assume wife will provide financial support until university position is secured, although to be fair this assumption has been substantiated by much factual evidence. Weaknesses (professional) include flying into violent rages when work is going badly, losing crucial documents, deleting essential files from computer, having first put back-up floppy disc in trouser pocket and trousers in washing machine. Overriding weakness is inability to lie at interviews, for example, in answer to the question 'What impact do you think your research will have?' saying 'None, same as yours, I expect', and thinking this is a good and accurate response, since everybody knows that books and articles produced by academics hardly affect the real world, being so rarely read by its inhabitants.

Other Information
Height: five foot eleven inches tall. Weight: twelve stone. Hair: dark-brown and wavy, short. Eyes: brown. Interests: politics and modern classical music, much to regret of wife, who regularly complains that most of CDs in household sound like a musician and several instruments being kicked downstairs.

Chapter Five

I Am a Rock

I parked the Micra and walked up the driveway to Noble House, thinking how beautiful the garden looked with the lawn neatly trimmed in dark and light stripes and surrounded by the pink and white blossom of the trees all along its border, and how sad it was that our enjoyment of it should be spoiled by constant harrowing insecurity about Sebastian's future. I hurried as I approached the front door, fumbling in my handbag for my key. This was the part I hated, coming back to the flat on days when Sebastian had found out that he hadn't got a particular job. Or waiting at home for him to return from an interview. I dreaded the sound of his key in the lock on these occasions because I knew how closely it would be followed by the sight of him in his exquisitely tailored interview suit that belied his dejected expression, looking like the living symbol of wasted effort.

I let myself in, shouting his name as I stumbled through the door. There was no reply. I ran into the lounge. No sign of him. Oh my God. I ran into the kitchen. He wasn't there either. He had said his life was over, those were his very words, and I had wasted the last hour with Rod Firsden when . . . I ran into the bedroom and there was Sebastian. He was stretched across our lemon-meringue-coloured double bed, face down, with a green towel wrapped around his midriff. His hair was wet. He looked dead.

'Sebastian!' I shook him violently. 'Are you okay?'

'Ow,' he muttered. 'Get off. That hurts.'

'Are you okay?' I demanded, relieved that he was alive and angry with myself for suspecting he might not be. He had had a bath, I realised. That had to be a good sign. Sebastian often says that if it weren't for me, he would be a tramp by now. Once we were walking across the Coe Fen and I caught him peering under a bridge. When I asked him why the sudden interest in the undersides of bridges, he said that he always kept an eye out for places he could live if he were ever homeless. A faint odour of Yves Rocher's Bourbon Vanilla bath oil emanated from his immobile body now, though, which surely meant that he was not yet desperate enough to consider vagrancy as an option.

'As okay as someone without a job can be,' he replied.

'What are you doing, lying there like that? Get up. I want to talk to you.'

He yawned and hauled himself into a vertical position. The left-hand side of his face was covered in lines from where the crushed duvet had dug into his cheek. Judging by the depth of the marks, he must have been lying there for ages. I felt a mixture of tenderness and impatience. I couldn't help thinking that his lack of success on the job front was not altogether unconnected to his being the sort of person who can happily spend an afternoon lying prostrate on the bed with his face pressed into a quilt.

'What's there to talk about?'

'I want to know everything,' I said. 'All about what Valerie Williams said on the phone, all about the interview, the panel members, the other interviewees, everything. I want to know about the last De La Wyche fellow who disappeared and Damian Selinger's wife and . . .'

'Why?' Sebastian interrupted me. 'Why do you want to know all this?'

'Because we've got two weeks,' I said bluntly. 'I don't know whether there's anything we can do in that time, or whether I'm completely mad to consider it, even, but I need to know everything, just in case.'

41

'Don't be ridiculous,' Sebastian snapped. 'Of course there's nothing we can do. I mean, what did you have in mind? Abducting their first and second choices so that they give the job to me?'

'Believe me, I would if I thought I could get away with it.'

'What am I going to do?' He ignored me. 'I'm nearly thirty and I've never had a proper job. I've just had my mum on the phone as well, telling me I should give up and work in a fucking bun shop.' After translation this meant that Sebastian's mother had made the mistake of suggesting that he consider alternative careers. 'I can't do that!' he yelled. 'I'm shit at everything else. I did enough menial jobs before I went to university and I got sacked from every one of them. There's nothing else I can do. What's going to become of me?'

Sebastian had a knack of saying the things I least wanted to hear. I felt as if someone was squeezing my heart. Contemplating what might become of him was too tricky and potentially dispiriting an activity, so I decided instead to focus on gathering facts, for what purpose I wasn't quite sure.

'Get dressed,' I said firmly, throwing open the double doors of our fitted wardrobe. The first thing to catch my eye was Sebastian's grey Armani interview suit. I bared my teeth at it in a silent snarl, grabbed an old pair of his jeans and a rugby shirt, and threw them at him. He began to get dressed without saying a word. The air was heavy with disappointment and failure. I couldn't bear it. Part of me wanted to turn and run, go somewhere far away from Sebastian's problems, but a bigger part knew that his problems were also mine. In fact, in a way I saw them more as mine than his, because if I'd had to put money on one of us to solve them, I'd have gone for me every time.

'So, come on, tell me all the details,' I said brightly. I'm a great believer in filling the air with random words at times of difficulty.

'Like what? I've told you already.' Sebastian looked at

himself in our full-length mirror and sighed.

'Who was on the interview panel?'

'You know!' he yelled at me.

'Tell me again,' I said, grabbing a notebook and pen from the drawer of my bedside cabinet. 'I'm going to write it down.'

'Why? What good will that do? What good will anything do, come to think of it? It's all a joke, having to answer stupid questions like where do I see myself being in ten years' time!' After a brief limbering-up period, Sebastian's moaning muscles were back to their full strength.

'What was your answer?' I knew I wouldn't like what I was about to hear.

'I said "It depends on you. If you give me this job and the chance to carry on with my research, I'll probably have a personal chair in ten years' time. If not, I'll probably be in prison or a mental hospital."'

'Oh, Sebastian, what did you say that for?' I felt my energy begin to drain away.

'Because it's the truth. I refuse to lie just to impress them.'

'No wonder you didn't get it. That's the worst answer you could possibly have given. It makes you sound arrogant and manic depressive at the same time. You'll never get a job if you don't change your interview technique.'

'Exactly! This is what I've been trying to tell you. I'll never get a job. I'll never get one! I'll never get one!' He grabbed his discarded bath towel and started to slam it against the wardrobe doors, gnashing his teeth in a way that made him look psychotic.

'Sebastian, stop it.' I stood up and wrestled the towel from his hands. 'I don't know about you, but I'm not prepared to curl up and die just because of . . . what's happened.'

'Can you think of a better option?'

'Yes. I'm going to get you the fellowship.'

43

'What?' His expression was half-dismissive sneer, half-hopeful smile. His eyes pleaded for good news. I folded my arms defiantly. We both wanted to believe me. I realised I had sounded more convincing than I felt.

I must be a rock, I told myself. Somehow I would have to get Terri and Rod out of the way. What with that and being a rock I would really have my work cut out. How does one go about removing prospective Cambridge fellows from the scene in an igneous manner?

'I'm going to get you the De La Wyche fellowship,' I repeated with confidence.

'How?' asked Sebastian.

'By seeing to it that Terri and this Rod Firsden both turn it down.' I referred to Rod in a way that made it sound as if I'd never met him. For some reason I didn't want to tell Sebastian he'd just been in my car.

'But . . . there's no way you'll be able to do that. What will you do, threaten them? Plead with them?'

'I'll think of something,' I said. Sebastian smiled tentatively and the atmosphere in the room suddenly seemed lighter, jolly almost.

Chapter Six

The Trojan Bear

'So come on, then.' I waved my notebook and pen at him. 'Tell me. First of all, what did Valerie Williams say on the phone? As close to word for word as you can.'

'She said I very nearly got it. No, hang on. She said there was a point yesterday when I very nearly got it, but then they had to adjourn the meeting, or something. That's why they didn't make their final decision yesterday like they were supposed to.'

'Why was the meeting adjourned?'

'I don't know. I didn't ask.'

I sighed. 'Did you ask what happened in between your nearly getting it and not getting it?'

'No.'

'Sebastian, you're so . . .' I blurted out in frustration.

'Crap. Pathetic. I know.' He nodded emphatically. That's the trouble with criticising Sebastian. The minute you start, he joins in, and then you feel mean and have to take back your original admonition.

'No, you're not. Look, I'm sorry I said that, but why don't you phone Valerie again and ask her? It'd be useful to know.' Would it? I wondered. I had to pretend we were working towards something. Even if our new and very possibly false hope only lasted for the next two weeks, it was better than nothing. My attitude resembled that of a heroin addict: anything to delay the agony, to make me feel better right now. I am a procrastinator of pain.

'No way. I'm not going crawling to those bastards, begging them to tell me why I didn't get the job. It's demeaning.'

'But Sebastian, we need to find out what went on . . .'

'Even with a so-called friend on the panel I didn't get it,' said Sebastian indignantly, ignoring my attempt to persuade him. 'That's the last time I help Damian Bastard Selinger.'

'Tell me about the panel,' I said, pulling the lid off my pen.

Sebastian sat down on the edge of the bed and ran his hands through his hair. 'There was Damian, Professor Fielding, Valerie – the fucking college doctor for Christ's sake – and Emily Lole, Fernando Rose's ex.'

My ears pricked up. 'Fernando Rose? You never told me Emily Lole was his girlfriend.'

'You never asked.'

'Isn't she the worm scientist Damian was always slagging off – the wet one?'

'Yep.'

'Well . . . tell me more about her.'

'Apparently she had a sort of breakdown after Fernando and Martine Selinger ran off together. She never got over it. She studies microscopic worms – fascinating or what? That's all I know about her.'

'Do you really think they ran off together?'

'Probably. They both went missing on the same night. And it was very shortly after she came round here brandishing a knife, looking for Damian. I should have given him to her, let her stab him, the bastard.' Damian had frequently used our flat as a hiding place when he and Martine had had an exceptionally vicious row. Their fights usually involved one of them chasing the other through the streets of Cambridge with a lethal kitchen utensil.

'You don't know that Damian didn't support you,' I said. 'Maybe he was outvoted.'

'Of course he didn't support me, none of them did! Even

though I'm the only internal candidate, the only one who did my PhD there. They were happy to bask in the reflected glory when I won my prize. They shouldn't have advertised the fellowship. They should have just given it to me.'

'They would argue that would be unfair,' I said mechanically.

'It's no more bloody unfair than everything else,' said Sebastian bitterly. 'It's no more unfair than making a random choice on the basis of having talked to each of us for a measly half-hour, asking their pathetic formulaic questions. What's fair about that?'

'I agree,' I said patiently, 'but Sebastian, this isn't getting us anywhere. Let's stick to the facts. Okay, the other candidates. Apart from Terri Skincrawl, who were they?' I glanced at our open bedroom window to check that I had not been overheard disrespecting my neighbour.

'Rod Firsden and some woman. Bryony somebody.'

'Did you meet them?'

'I met him, briefly. We sat on a sofa outside the interview room together.'

'What was he like?' I wanted to ask Sebastian if Rod had been as shiny then as when I'd seen him, but I couldn't. I considered admitting to my Rod encounter, but decided against it. If Sebastian knew, he might be tempted to interfere in some way, which could only be a hindrance.

'I didn't speak to him much. We just introduced ourselves. He seemed really uptight, though. He kept . . . chewing this copy of the *Spectator* that wasn't even his.'

'Whose was it?' I asked, puzzled.

'The college's. You know, they'd laid out a few magazines for us to look at while we waited, and Rod Firsden just rolled up the *Spectator* and stuck it right in his gob. When he took it out it was all wet and gooey, right to about a third of the way down. He must have had it half-way down his throat. And he kept making disgusting slurping noises.'

'Hm,' I said, pondering the strange ways of my latest

driving apprentice. 'What about the woman, Bryony?'

'Never saw her. She dropped out, anyway. I have no idea why, before you ask.'

'Okay. Anything else? What about the interview itself? You haven't really told me much about that.'

'It was a farce, like most of the ones I've been to. Damian was in an unusually good mood. He kept grinning and giggling, and asking me nonsensical questions.'

'Like what?' I had trouble linking the words 'grinning' and 'giggling' with Damian Selinger. Whenever I had seen him he'd been grumpy and almost offensively surly. Sebastian had always told me not to take it personally. Damian found it difficult to be civil around women, apparently, because Martine had prejudiced him against our gender.

'What was it again?' Sebastian frowned, trying to remember. 'Oh yeah. He asked me whether I believed in love at first sight.'

'What? Why?'

'I don't know. The others seemed a bit embarrassed when he asked that. Emily Lole spent the entire interview looking as if she was about to burst into tears. The whole thing was a ridiculous charade. Professor Fielding kept glancing at her watch and hardly listened to anything I said. Valerie Williams was the only one who seemed to be concentrating.'

'Is she going to be at the feast tomorrow? If she is, we can chat to her then. Find out what she meant about you nearly getting it.'

'Oh God, the feast,' Sebastian groaned and fell back on the bed, staring at the ceiling in despair. 'I'm not going! It'll be so humiliating.'

'Sebastian, stop whingeing. I've told you, I'm going to sort it out.'

'Yeah, right, I'll believe that when I see it.' He allowed his body to slide on to the floor and lay there motionless.

'Get up, Sebastian.'

'No,' he said petulantly. 'What's there to get up for?'

I marched out of the bedroom and into the kitchen, in severe need of an alcoholic drink. I poured myself a large glass of whisky and tried not to cry. One of our neighbours, a Chinese man who lived in flat 9, walked past the window and waved at me before disappearing inside. Our kitchen window is just by Noble House's front door, so everyone going in and out gets to peer in at us. I forced a smile. He was wearing a suit and carrying a briefcase. Another person with a job. There were so many of them out there. Why couldn't I have one, I thought, allowing a tear to roll down my cheek. Why wasn't my man coming home from work in a suit instead of lying on the bedroom carpet like a pair of dirty underpants?

A few moments later Joe Fielding walked past, also in a suit and carrying a briefcase. Fortunately I didn't have to pretend to be happy for his benefit as well, because his face was, as usual, camouflaged by a pile-up of several large shopping bags. If he pierced his ears and wore hook earrings, his load-bearing capacity could be increased yet further. I was surprised Terri hadn't thought of it. I wondered why Joe didn't object to doing all the shopping after a long day at the office, while his wife, who had just finished her PhD and had nothing to do apart from receive numerous job offers, spent all her time in Summerton's library reading about fishes' teeth in scientific journals. Probably for the same reason that I didn't complain about supporting Sebastian, both emotionally and financially – love, what else?

'Come on, Scarlett, come and help Daddy do the laundry,' I heard him yell. His daughter ran down the driveway after him, dropping her teddy bear as she followed him through the front door. Joe was too busy being a beast of burden to notice. I sighed, wondering whether I should go and rescue the cuddly toy, save Joe a bit of work.

Sebastian appeared behind me and put his arms round

49

my waist. 'Sorry for being foul,' he said, in his best cute voice, the one he knows I can't resist. 'I'm only worried about my future, that's all. I want to feel like a proper person.'

'I'm just going to pick up Scarlett's bear,' I said, pointing at it through the window.

'Okay,' said Sebastian. 'I'll see what's on telly.' I hoped that he would find something interesting to watch that would keep him if not happy then at least quiet for a while.

I strolled outside and picked up the teddy bear. It was chubby and dark-brown with big black eyes and a red bow tie round its neck. There was a label neatly sewn to its back that said 'Muffy Skinner'. Even the toys in that household colluded in the surname hegemony. I thought the bear would have suited the name Muffy Fielding much better, myself.

I took it inside and was about to ring flat 3's bell when Joe opened the door. Scarlett was standing behind him, clinging to his legs. She was a small, doll-like child who looked suspiciously ornamental. Her hair was almost black and naturally curly, hanging around her pink-and-white face in ringlets. She looked much more like Terri than Joe, who was blond with a more ruddy complexion.

'Hi, Kate.' He grinned at me. He was carrying the biggest shoulder bag I had ever seen, which was stuffed full of dirty washing. You could have fitted at least three human bodies in there. Joe stooped under its weight. 'Guess what?' he said. 'Just when I need to do our washing, the machine in the laundry room breaks down. Now I've got to go to the launderette and Scarlett's not even had her supper yet.'

I smiled understandingly, omitting to point out that if Terri ever got back from the library at a reasonable hour, her daughter wouldn't have to starve until the laundry was done. 'You forgot this.' I tried to give him Muffy, but he didn't have a spare hand. One was being pulled by Scarlett and the other was helping to support the gigantic sack on his shoulder.

'Just throw it in there.' He nodded towards the doorway. I threw the bear over Joe's head. It landed on the navy-blue sofa, which was a darker-skinned carbon copy of our meringue-coloured one, upon which Sebastian was probably now reclining, watching something comforting on television.

I asked him how work was going as he ushered Scarlett out of the flat and checked his pockets for all the necessary equipment: wallet, car keys, house keys. His answer was the same as always: 'tiring'. I didn't know much about what marketing consultants did, but I couldn't believe his working life was more tiring than his home life. Maybe he was projecting, in denial about what his real problem was.

We exchanged a few more pleasantries, and I waved goodbye to him and Scarlett as they headed for the car. I was about to go back home for an update on Sebastian's mood, when I noticed Joe had forgotten to close his front door.

I reached out to pull it shut, then stopped as a wicked thought lodged itself in my brain. What time was it? Seven o'clock. Terri rarely got back before nine, and Joe and Scarlett would be gone for at least an hour. My heartbeats began to trip over each other. I looked over my shoulder to check no one was watching me and, once I was sure it was safe, tiptoed into Joe and Terri's flat, quietly pulling the door shut behind me.

Chapter Seven

Terri Skinner – Curriculum Vitae

Name
Teresa Jane Skinner, known as Terri. This, Joe told me during one of our many laundry room chats, annoys her dad, who thinks that Terry is a name for pot-bellied pub landlords and who specifically chose for his daughter the lovely, feminine name of Teresa. Much of Terri's life has been devoted to annoying her father (whom I think of as Grumpy Skinner, since his lower lip wraps around his chin in a permanent expression of disgruntlement). I once overheard the two of them having a conversation in Noble House's car park and he seemed determined to dismiss whatever she said. I noticed that he started to shake his head half-way through every sentence Terri uttered, then followed up the head-shaking with a sort of swishing hand gesture that looked extremely patronising even from a distance of several metres. A good reason to ditch his surname, if you ask me, but at some stage in Terri's development her grudge against her father transmuted into feminism, at which point the behavioural codes must have become confused.

Address
Flat 3, Noble House, 14 Renshaw Road, Cambridge. This is on the ground floor, directly opposite flat 1.

Age
Twenty-eight.

Place of Birth
High Wycombe.

Physical Appearance
Glossy black naturally curly hair that hangs in ringlets. Five feet three inches tall, eight stone light. English rose white-and-pink skin, masking hidden thorns. Big blue eyes with long dark lashes. Strappy, revealing clothes and scrupulously shaved armpits and legs (but to please self, not men – very important distinction). Cutesy smile permanently plastered across face, to conceal the inner viper.

Marital Status
Terri is to her marriage what Captain Bligh was to the *Bounty*. Joe is Fletcher Christian after too many T'ai Chi sessions, possessed by an inner peace that could turn even the fiercest mutiny into a midday nap. Terri was dubious about marrying Joe, apparently, because her father approved of him, but she went ahead for two reasons. First, Joe was soft and controllable, in contrast to her father, who was rigid and harsh. Second, marrying Joe would mean an immediate exit from Grumpy's house with no opposition from him to impede her escape.

Employment History
Has been offered two jobs, Summerton College's De La Wyche fellowship and a lectureship at Reading University. Whichever she chooses, it will be her first paid employment. Until now, Joe has provided all the financial backing for the Skinner-Fielding household.

Qualifications and Education
D.Phil on some obscure aspect of fish dentistry from

53

Pembroke College, Oxford. Now plans to undertake further research in that area, as if three years were not enough. BSc (first) in Zoology from Merton College, Oxford, before fish were singled out from the rest of the animal world for special attention. During time at Oxford University, was Students' Union Women's Officer, Head of the Graduate Women's Group and Chair of the 'No Means No' Committee, and did voluntary work for a battered women's refuge. Four 'A's at A level, nine 'A's at O level, from Thorndene College, a private school for girls in High Wycombe. Always worked extremely hard, because from an early age she had heard Grumpy complaining that he was the only member of the family who didn't have a pea for a brain. During Terri's teenage years, Grumpy encouraged her to trawl the nearby private boys' school for boyfriends who might later become suitable husbands, but Terri instead pursued the school caretaker, a tattooed, tobacco-stained man with a rough voice, and Colum Monahan, her parents' gardener, both of whom she knew her father would loathe.

Achievements
Many articles on fish published in scientific journals. Duke of Edinburgh Award for worthwhile and gruelling countryside activities, for which slinky dresses had to be abandoned and muesli socks donned instead. Fluent in Spanish and French. Grade eight piano and stopped there only because there were no more grades.

Strengths and Weaknesses
Key strength is ability to focus single-mindedly on career, to work seven days a week and twelve hours a day without needing a break. Primary weakness is tendency to neglect family in the process, also failure to understand concepts such as enjoyment or relaxation. Strength: ability to manage without friends and instead make do with 'contacts' who might prove professionally useful. Weak-

ness: carelessly allowing neighbours to witness exploitation of husband, thereby undermining effort that has gone into flashing pearly grin around pretending to be a nice person.

Other Information
Makes regular financial contributions, via standing orders from her bank, to charities including Womanaid, Fempathy and Survivors of Domestic Cruelty. In the case of the last, she could dispense with bureaucracy and give the money straight to Joe. Presumably it's his anyway. Sometimes, when caught unawares and unprepared for contact with humans, smile is not present and scary, harsh expression is seen instead, for such a fleeting moment that the viewer wonders whether he or she has imagined it.

Chapter Eight

Neighbourhood Watch

The first thing I did in Joe and Terri's flat was panic. What was I doing here? Had I gone mad? What if Joe had forgotten something and came back? I had often seen him from our kitchen window, rushing out of the door only to return a few minutes later, cheerfully yelling 'Forgot Scarlett's gloves!' or 'Did you see me drop a hoover bag?' I decided I couldn't cope with the fear of being discovered and was on my way to the door when an unusual sight stopped me mid-stride. I may be cowardly, but when it comes to a competition of characteristics, nosiness wins hands down every time.

Neat white bookshelves, divided into small boxy sections by vertical and horizontal planks of wood, covered the top half of an entire lounge wall above the desk area. This was the same as in our flat, but what had caught my attention and interested me sufficiently to stop me from leaving was the peculiar use to which Terri and Joe had put their shelves. Out of a total of sixteen little segments, only three contained books. One was piled high with videos, both shop-bought and home-recorded, and the rest were crammed full of framed photographs. I had never seen so many photos in a living-room before. There were about fifty of them. Their shapes and sizes varied enormously, as did their frames – some were gold and heart-shaped, others were plain black cardboard – but there was one constant, one thing that all the pictures had in common: they all contained Terri Skinner, and in none of them, not a single one, did either Joe or Scarlett feature.

My mouth tasted sour and I found it hard to swallow. I felt the way I feel when I'm leafing through a magazine and I catch a glimpse of something frightening or horrific. I know that if I examine it more closely I'll regret it, but as soon as I know it's there I have to look, even though part of me doesn't want to.

I walked up to the bookshelves and started to pick up the photographs one by one, to check that my initial impression had not been a mistake. If I got closer to the display and surveyed it more carefully, I would be bound to find Joe and Scarlett in there somewhere, I thought. But no, all the pictures were either of Terri alone, or Terri with people who were definitely not her husband and child. Even the one wedding photo, a large glossy print in a thick brass frame, showed Terri standing next to Grumpy, with Joe nowhere in sight.

I could feel myself grimace like the father of the bride as I stared at Terri's sugary fake smile and white frilly dress. How did she reconcile frills with her feminism, I wondered. She ought to have got married in a white trouser suit, like Richard Gere's outfit at the end of *An Officer and a Gentleman*.

There were a couple of other pictures of Terri with her parents and a few in which she looked a lot younger – probably about sixteen – and was surrounded by a cluster of giggling girls. Were they proper friends, or had Terri had only contacts even as a teenager? Sebastian and I had noticed shortly after they moved in that Joe and Terri never had any visitors of their own age. We never saw them coming in or going out in a chatty, laughing group of their peers. Joe was permanently shackled to Scarlett and Terri seemed to make no effort to spend time with any creature that lived on land. When they first moved to Cambridge from Oxford, we did the neighbourly thing and invited them round for a meal. I still remember vividly the way

Joe's eyes lit up when I asked him. 'Oh, that would be so nice,' he said. 'But Terri's snowed under with work at the moment, I don't know whether she'll be able to come.' She had come in the end, only to leave an hour and a half later, seconds after we'd finished eating, to get back to her books, dragging an apologetic Joe after her. 'Stay if you want to, Joe,' she'd said, but I knew she didn't mean it. 'Stay and I'll make you suffer' was what she was really saying, I could tell from Joe's reaction. 'No, no,' he'd answered hurriedly. 'It's not fair if I stay out when you have to work.' What kind of warped training programme had she put him through, I wondered, and why did someone who had just finished her PhD have to work at ten o'clock on a Friday night?

I hurried through the photographs as quickly as I could, aware that I had an entire flat to search and time – safe time, at least – was running out. There were two graduation pictures in which Terri was holding a rolled-up degree certificate, wearing a black gown and smiling a wider, more self-satisfied smile than usual. I felt a twinge of resentment as I recalled Sebastian's account of his graduation day: three years of hard work ruined by the department's refusal to put his mark up by half a per cent so that he could get the first class degree he so obviously deserved. This was now years in the past, but I was still filled with bitterness every time I thought about it. Sebastian had had two graduations since then, for his MA and PhD, but he still had never quite got over this earlier disappointment.

I stepped back from the shelves and looked at the total photographic display. There was something extremely sinister about this. Three people lived here and yet the lounge was overflowing with images of only one of them. Why? Was Joe so in love with Terri that he insisted on putting nothing but her face in every available frame? Even so, why were there no pictures of the two of them, not to mention the three of them, together? That couldn't be the explanation. It was far more likely, I thought, that Terri's photo gallery reflected her priorities. But what sort of parent would not include a picture of her own daughter?

I looked at my watch. It was seven fifteen. I wondered where Sebastian thought I was. He probably assumed I was chatting to Joe after returning the bear, Muffy Skinner. I've often told him that when I bump into Joe I feel obliged to stop and have a substantial chat because he's so clearly starved of adult company.

Seven sixteen and the seconds ticking away. I clenched my fists in frustration. I had to make good use of what little time I had, and it would be foolish to stay beyond eight o'clock since Joe and Scarlett could arrive back any time after that, but the pressure I was under was preventing me from thinking straight. This was Terri's flat and therefore a good place to gather information about her, information I could then use to . . . to what? I had no idea.

I walked back over to the bookshelf and picked up a few of the video tapes to read their labels. Apart from some tedious scientific programmes that Terri had preserved for posterity, they had home-recorded copies of *Thelma and Louise* (a film that purports to be a celebration of sisterhood but is really about it being okay to kill people if they annoy you and are male), *Beaches* and something I'd never heard of called *My Brilliant Career*. Maybe that was Terri's home movie, assuming she has ever been at home for long enough to make one. Their shop-bought videos were mainly children's stuff: *Pinocchio*, *The Jungle Book* and *Teletubbies*.

There was nothing on the video shelf that I would have attributed to Joe, nothing that looked like his equivalent of Sebastian's grainy black-and-white war film collection. Poor Joe. Perhaps if he watched *Cross of Iron* or *Das Boot* he would be inspired to stand up to Terri. One thing was for sure: no tyrannical regimes were going to be overthrown if *Beaches* was his only influence; Bette Midler cooing over a dying Barbara Hershey is hardly the stuff of which heroes are made.

59

I moved over to the three shelves of books. There were three by Daphne Fielding, and the sight of them made me feel sick. I had to force myself to stand still and read their titles – *Fantasy and Femininity: Deconstructing Dietrich, The Popcorn Polemic: Class and the Cinema* and *Shades of Grey: the Ambiguity of Black-and-White Cinema* – instead of backing away and retching, which was my instinctive reaction. How dare this woman not give Sebastian a fellowship? He had important things to say about politics, about things that affected all our lives. The same clearly could not be said for this esteemed Summerton professor. It occurred to me, looking at the three slim volumes, that books written by academics always have colons in their titles. I wondered whether any university would give me a forty-five-grand-a-year professorship if I published a collection of my own cinematic ponderings. I could call it *The Häagen-Dazs Dichotomy: Ice-Cream and Inefficiency at the Cambridge Cine City*.

I pulled the book on Marlene Dietrich off the shelf and, in doing so, dislodged something that had been balanced horizontally across the top of it. Whatever it was fell down and landed on my right foot. 'Ow!' I yelled and then remembered I should be quiet because I was an illegal presence in somebody else's flat. I picked up the offending object and saw that it was a copy of the film *Witness for the Prosecution*. On the front of its case there was a still from the movie, a picture of Charles Laughton and Marlene Dietrich standing face to face in an otherwise empty courtroom.

I smiled nostalgically, wondering whether I could steal this film without arousing suspicion. I hadn't seen it for ages, not since I was a kid, and I would have loved to watch it again. If that and nothing else went missing, Joe and Terri would be unlikely to think they'd been burgled. What sane burglar would take a classic courtroom drama and leave behind the television, video and music system? I decided not to pinch it, though, just in case it was one of Joe's treasured possessions. He might well have inherited his mother's passion for black-and-white films and/or Marlene Dietrich.

Maybe I could pop round another time, 'happen to spot it' and ask to borrow it then. I had never thought about it before, but *Witness for the Prosecution* was a turning point in my development as a film buff, I now realised. It was the first film I ever saw which had a twist and it remains one of the best. In a lot of contemporary thrillers the twist is that you expect the film to be good and then it isn't.

I leafed through the index of *Fantasy and Femininity: Deconstructing Dietrich* to see if there was a reference to *Witness for the Prosecution*. There were several. I looked them up and was both disappointed and heartened to discover that I couldn't understand what the Prof was on about. The sentences were long and pretentious, and bore no relation to the movie I knew and loved. If this idiot could get a chair, so could Sebastian, I thought. I settled happily into despising Daphne Fielding. If she'd been a decent person, she would have stepped down from the De La Wyche panel as soon as Terri was shortlisted.

I decided that, instead of adding theft to my list of crimes against my neighbours, I would try to get *Witness for the Prosecution* out of Heffers' video section. I especially wanted to watch it now because I knew it would remind me of Sebastian's and my situation.

The film is about Christine Vole (Dietrich), a woman who loves her husband Leonard Vole so much that she would forgive him anything. When he is arrested for a murder that she knows he's committed, she wants to help him get away with it. No one would believe her if she appeared as a witness for his defence, because she's his wife and therefore obviously biased in his favour, so she convincingly pretends to loathe him and appears as a – you've guessed it – witness for the prosecution. She gives evidence in court that suggests Leonard did it and it looks as if he will be convicted. No one in the courtroom likes her, but they appear to believe her. This is where the twist comes in. Christine cunningly disguises herself as a bizarre old slapper with a Cockney accent, arranges to meet Leonard's barrister, Sir Wilfrid Robarts (who fortunately doesn't recognise her) and gives him some letters she has written to an imaginary lover, Max, that prove she was lying when she testified against her husband. Sir Wilfrid produces these letters in court the next day, Christine is revealed to be a liar and Leonard is acquitted.

What did this have to do with me and Sebastian? Well, I loved him enough to break the law, didn't I? Okay, he wasn't a murderer – I'm sure he would look down his nose at assassinhood and view it as yet another demeaning bun shop occupation – but there I was, trespassing on Joe and Terri's property in order to find some way of getting Sebastian the De La Wyche Enmity.

Thinking about this old favourite film of mine had reminded me that appearances could be deceptive. Terri Skincrawl seemed, on the surface, to treat her husband badly, but then so had Christine Vole and she had a good reason for it, a loving reason. Could I be wrong about Terri? Reluctantly I admitted to myself that I did have a tendency to make snap judgements and that I ought to keep my mind open a bit more, give people the benefit of the doubt. On the other hand, Joe Fielding was not on trial for his life and films were obliged to have twists in a way that life was not. I wanted to carry on thinking badly of Terri, so that I would find it easier to . . . what, exactly? It was now half past seven and I hadn't even explored beyond the lounge, let alone defined my aim in being here. Useless, I scolded myself. I made a move towards the bedroom, stopping as I heard a sudden noise.

It was the sound of a key turning in a lock.

Chapter Nine

Name in a Dress

Thank God for the architect of Noble House, who had put six internal fireproof doors in each flat; huge, solid, soundproof slabs which slammed shut automatically, so that if any sort of blaze broke out it would be contained within the room in which it had started. The only thing that saved me from being spotted instantly by Terri Skinner was the door between what Summerton's property agents call the 'outer lobby' and the lounge.

At first when I heard someone coming in I assumed it was Joe and Scarlett returning from the launderette. I stood rooted to the spot with fear, desperately trying to think of a good excuse. Then, through the small rectangular glass panel in the internal door, I saw Terri's black glossy ringlets as they emerged from under her bicycle helmet. What the hell was she doing back so early? Had there been a bomb scare at the library? Luckily she didn't see me; she was standing with her back to me, facing the coat pegs, taking off her neat fitted jacket and hanging it up with great care, as if it were a priceless item.

I realised no excuse was going to get me out of this one. Joe might have fallen for whatever lame story I cobbled together, but there was no way Terri would. Moving faster than I had for years, I hurled myself into the 'inner lobby', which is too grand a name for the few square metres of carpet between the lounge and the rest of the flat, and ran into the master bedroom – probably known as the mistress bedroom in this establishment – but not before I'd noticed a rectangular pottery sign on the door with a picture on it of a curly-haired, rosy-cheeked girl holding a bunch of flowers beside the words: 'Terri's room'.

A double bed dominated the room. There was a large pink heart-shaped cushion on the navy-blue duvet that looked as if it was made of satin. Was this proof that Joe and Terri loved each other, that they both slept here despite what the sign on the door said, or simply poor taste in home furnishings?

I heard another door opening. It sounded like the one between the lounge and the kitchen. Living in an almost identical flat myself, I found it easier than I would otherwise have done to interpret noises. After taking off her jacket and cycling helmet, Terri had probably gone straight to the fridge to get a drink. That's what I normally do when I get in from a long day's work. I estimated that this would take her perhaps twenty or thirty seconds, but then what did I know? Maybe she wasn't getting a drink at all, maybe she was at this very moment heading towards the bedroom. I needed a place to hide, quickly. I wished I'd stayed in the lounge and invented some lie; getting caught in the bedroom would make me look even more guilty.

I pulled open one door of the fitted wardrobe and saw a few grey suits and a long black woollen coat on the far right-hand side. The coat marked the end of Joe's cupboard entitlement. Terri's clothes took up at least three-quarters of the available space, which didn't surprise me. A balanced wardrobe equals a balanced marriage. I can proudly say that Sebastian and I share all our storage space fifty-fifty.

I heard a metallic sound and spun round to see the door handle twisting downwards. My thinking time had run out. I jumped into the wardrobe, pulling the door shut behind me with my index finger. It slid gently into a closed position a fraction of a second before Terri pushed open the bedroom door and walked into the room.

I crouched uncomfortably on top of a pile of Joe's shoes,

arranging the long coat so that it covered me as completely as possible. I didn't really know why I was bothering. If Terri opened the wardrobe, the chances were she would spot me immediately, whatever I hid behind. I would just have to pray she didn't want to get changed.

I held my breath and listened. I heard a zip being undone – or done up, I couldn't tell which – and then the sound of shuffling papers. Was she getting some work out of her bag, I wondered. Unlikely. I would have put money on Terri being the sort of person who would only work at a desk.

Something clicked, sounding familiar. I was almost sure it was a phone being picked up. Sebastian and I didn't have one in our bedroom, only in the lounge, which was why the noise sounded out of place. Terri probably had a telephone extension in the bedroom so that she could ring through to Joe in the servants' quarters and order breakfast in bed.

She cleared her throat. 'Um, yes, hello, can I speak to Gary Conley please?' She sounded positively timid, I thought. Where was her usual smarmy confidence? 'He what? When? Oh. Oh, I see. Well ... have you got a contact number for him? Oh. I don't suppose you know whether he's still working for NEG? No, I didn't think he would be. Okay, um ... I don't suppose you know where he went?' Terri sounded increasingly disappointed as the dialogue progressed.

My legs were starting to ache and I needed to go to the toilet. I adjusted my position slightly, taking care not to make a sound. I could see nothing but a thin slice of light where the wardrobe doors met. The next time Terri left the room, my plan was to rush to the larger of the two bedroom windows and climb out. When Sebastian and I had first moved in, we had been offered a choice between flat one and flat three. We had chosen flat one because it was at the front of the house, and any intruder trying to climb in or out of a window would have to do so right beside the driveway and front door to the building.

Joe and Terri's bedroom faced on to the back garden, so

I could be reasonably sure no one would see me emerge. I listened hard and for a while didn't hear anything. Then the bed creaked and the phone clicked again. Damn. She was making another call.

'Er, yes,' Terri's voice cut into my thoughts. 'The name's English, E-N-G-L-I-S-H, like the nationality, and the initial's R. I'm afraid I haven't got an address. I only know it's in Reading. Yes, Reading. I'm sorry I can't be more precise.' As soon as I heard the word 'Reading' I forgot all about my cramped legs and aching bladder. These didn't sound like business calls, and yet Terri was considering taking a job at Reading University. Could it be a coincidence? I wondered what NEG was, where Gary Conley, whoever he might be, apparently no longer worked. Perhaps it was in Reading and connected to the university in some way. Maybe Terri was making business calls after all.

'Is there?' Terri sounded more cheerful, as though she had received some good news. 'It must be that one, then. Can I have it please?' I heard the sound of a lid being taken off a pen. 'Mm-hm, mm-hm. Thank you.' Two more clicks followed and some pressing of buttons. I guessed that Terri was now phoning R English, so I was surprised to hear her say, 'Excuse me, I don't know whether I've got the right number, but I'm trying to get in touch with Gary Conley.' Aha. So R English was merely a means to an end, the end being to locate the elusive Gary. 'You are?' Terri exclaimed joyfully. 'Oh . . . what good luck! I hope you don't mind me phoning, it's just that I'm a friend of Gary's and . . . well, I haven't been in touch with him for a while, not since he lived in Wokingham. I just phoned his old number and Owen said he didn't live there any more. Can I have his new address, please?' Why was it so urgent, I wondered, for Terri to contact Conley all of a sudden? This was certainly no casual enquiry. Her breathing was becoming heavier by the second.

'Oh,' said Terri after a long pause. She sounded disappointed again, quiet and timid. This was not the harridan I knew and hated. I remembered Marlene Dietrich and *Witness for the Prosecution*, and resolved not to make up my mind about people too quickly in future. 'Well, do you know how many YMCAs there are in Reading? Maybe there's only one.' Terri seemed almost to be pleading with her interlocutor. There was another substantial pause. 'No, no, no message. Thanks anyway. 'Bye.'

I kept myself busy in the wardrobe memorising facts, so as not to forget any of the new information I'd gathered before I reached pen and paper. I was convinced Terri's search for Gary Conley had to be relevant to her possibly taking the Reading job. Why would someone so career-obsessed consider Reading University as a serious alternative to Summerton College, Cambridge, unless there was something else at stake?

A loud, shrill cry – spontaneous like an animal's but unmistakably human – pierced the silence just as I was beginning to wonder what Terri was doing now. I jumped, insofar as one can jump when one is hunched in a ball over one's neighbour's shoes, stuffed into a corner of his cupboard. The wardrobe doors shook. I gritted my teeth, expecting Terri to throw them open any minute and expose me for the eavesdropping housebreaker that I was. Instead, she continued to howl vociferously to an accompaniment of creaking bed springs. I imagined her bouncing up and down on the bed, beating it with her fists. Eventually the howls turned into stifled groans, then juddering sobs. She was making so much noise that I was able to clear my throat without giving myself away. I was amazed. Aside from the spy in her wardrobe, I couldn't see that Terri, with her two job offers, had anything to cry about.

Finally she stopped yelping. I heard footsteps, then the metallic ping of the door handle. She was leaving the room at last. I waited for the reassuring thud of the door slamming after her exit. Sebastian and I both hated the way all internal Noble House doors did this automatically. We preferred to keep ours open and had bought little wooden wedges for this purpose as soon as we'd moved in. I was grateful that Terri and Joe hadn't done the same; I would have been even more scared with nothing between me and Terri but open space.

As soon as I heard the thud, I stuck my head tentatively out of the wardrobe. I didn't want to get too far from my hiding place in case Terri decided to come back, so I thought I'd give it a few minutes before heading for my escape window.

Now that I'd let in some light I could see Joe and Terri's clothes more clearly. His were all suits – those of us with no leisure do not need leisure wear – or separate smart jackets and trousers sharing hangers. Terri's clothes wouldn't have looked out of place in a lap-dancer's wardrobe, except that the lap-dancer would have worn them in an unenlightened way that pandered to male expectation, whereas Terri would claim – I'm guessing, but I'm sure I'm right – to use them as a means of empowerment. She appeared not to be coming back, so I stood up, wincing with pain as my knees creaked out of their bent position, and took a closer look at her collection of revealing dresses.

The start of Terri's wardrobe territory was marked out by a short black sequinned shift. I lifted its skirt to see if there was any sign of a designer label. Terri had once boasted to me about her expensive tastes and Joe's eagerness to indulge them. Sebastian, on the other hand, wouldn't let me buy him new clothes even when he desperately needed them. Dressing scruffily, he claimed, enabled him to prepare gradually for his inevitable decline into tramphood.

There was a label sewn to one of the inside seams of Terri's black dress, but not a designer one. It was exactly the same size and shape as the label that had identified Muffy Skinner, Scarlett's teddy bear, and its inscription was in the same handwriting. 'Gordon and Maxine Fleming, 4th February 1997' it said.

I frowned, confused. The Muffy Skinner label had made perfect sense, identifying the object to which it was appended, but I had trouble believing that Terri, even in peculiar wailing mode, would call one of her dresses 'Gordon and Maxine Fleming'. And what was the significance of 4 February 1997?

I moved along to the next garment, a sky-blue silky strapless number. When did Terri get the chance to wear something as fancy as this? It was hardly suitable for the library, which was the only place she ever seemed to go. This dress had two labels, one from Versace that confirmed my suspicions about Terri's extravagant use of Joe's money and another baffling handwritten one. 'Tim and Bettina Elworthy' it said. '24th May 1997'. What on earth was going on here? I raced through the remaining dresses. They all had labels sewn into them on which were written the names of two people and a date. The earliest date was Gordon and Maxine Fleming's, February 1997, and the latest was April 1998. Terri and Joe had moved to Noble House in December 1996. My brain felt swollen, stuffed full of frustratingly uninterpretable facts. I tried to remember as many of the names as possible so that I could write them down later.

I was about to make a dash for the window when I noticed a red evening dress that had slipped off its hanger and on to the floor. I looked for a label and found one, also in the familiar handwriting. My mouth went dry as I read it: 'Keith Cobain and Ethan Handley, 15th March 1998'. I knew these people, they were Summerton College fellows. Sebastian and I had been to the pub with them a couple of times. We referred to them as Keithanethan, because they were the sort of inseparable friends that one comes to regard almost as a single person, or a two-person fusion with a single character. They certainly weren't a couple though; those two were about as heterosexual as it was possible to be. But then perhaps Tim and Bettina Elworthy weren't romantically involved either. Maybe they were siblings, and Gordon and Maxine Fleming father and daughter.

What was Terri Skinner's connection to Keithanethan? It was bad enough that one of the college professors was her mother-in-law. Now, lo and behold, here were the names of two more Summerton fellows sewn into one of her dresses. I detected a faint whiff of corruption, and hoped that it was serious and that I would somehow succeed in exposing it. Then Sebastian would be one step closer to the De La Wyche Enmity. I didn't want to think about how the hurdle of Rod Firsden might be removed. Still, it was hard to imagine what the precise nature of the corruption might have been. Keithanethan put in a good word for Terri and in exchange she . . . sews their names into her evening wear? What a tempting offer for them.

Music drifted through the closed bedroom door, some kind of turgid ballady stuff that was probably just what Terri wanted to hear in her present distressed state. If she'd put on a CD, she couldn't be planning a return to the bedroom in the near future. I decided now was an opportune moment and left the relative safety of the wardrobe, tiptoeing briskly across the floor to the window. I fiddled with the catch and opened it to its full extent. This was quite a tricky manoeuvre, but I'd had lots of practice opening ours at home, usually when I wanted to evict spiders, so I knew I could do it in a hurry.

I tumbled out on to the grass and ran around the building to the front entrance. Sebastian waved at me from our kitchen window, where he had started to prepare dinner. He had a new strange wavy-lined pattern down one side of his face, from which I concluded that he had fallen asleep on the sofa while watching TV.

He looked pleased and relieved to see me. 'Where have you been?' he shouted as I rushed past him to the loo.

'Chatting to Joe,' I lied. I was really tempted to tell him about my adventure and peculiar discoveries, but I resisted the urge. Sebastian was both tactless and a bad liar. All I needed was for him to blurt out something to Joe.

'Kate?' Sebastian called out. 'Do you think everything'll

be okay? I mean, you know, my career and my future?'

'Yes!' I yelled from the toilet. 'I've told you, I'm going to get you the De La Wyche fellowship.' I didn't feel quite so dishonest saying this now as I had before. I'd gathered so much information in the past hour that I was sure some of it could be used to our advantage.

I went through to the bedroom, got my notebook and pen out of my bedside cabinet, and made the following list:

Peculiar Things re T.S.
1 Photos only of self, not Joe or Scarlett
2 Sign on bedroom door saying 'Terri's room' – not also Joe's bedroom?
3 Who is Gary Conley? (Used to work at place called NEG, maybe now lives in a YMCA in Reading.) Who is R English? Obviously knows Gary C.
4 Is Terri's desire to contact Gary Conley linked to her possible preference of Reading job over De La Wyche Enmity?
5 Public vs private face of Terri – why was she so upset? Is her smiling confidence just a mask?
6 Labels in clothes – what do they mean? Who are Gordon and Maxine Fleming, Tim and Bettina Elworthy, etc?
7 Why are Keith Cobain and Ethan Handley's names there? – v. dodgy – what's their connection to Terri?

Satisfied that I had jotted down all the main areas of interest, I switched on my mobile phone and proceeded to cancel all the driving lessons I had booked for the next day except Rod Firsden's. I couldn't really afford to lose the money, but I needed to concentrate wholeheartedly on the Enmity. I only had two weeks and there was a lot to be done. First thing tomorrow I would go and see Valerie Williams, Summerton College's doctor.

71

Chapter Ten

Valerie Williams – Curriculum Vitae

Name
Dr Valerie Bronwen Williams.

Address
Room D4, Tyndsall Court, Summerton College,
Cambridge. Fellows and senior members of college staff
who live alone are given what is known as a 'set' in college.
A typical set consists of a bedroom, bathroom, kitchen and
lounge. D4 is slightly larger, boasting two lounges, one of
which is used as a surgery. Tyndsall is generally agreed to
be the most attractive of Summerton's courts, of which
there are three: Queen's, Tyndsall and Old. It is a
rectangular limestone quadrangle, framing a neat green
lawn. At the top end there is the Great Hall, where both
fellows and students eat – though not, of course, the same
thing – and at the bottom is the library, Terri Skincrawl's
stomping ground, or perhaps chomping ground would be
more appropriate for someone who studies fishes' teeth.

Age
Forty-seven.

Place of Birth
Swansea.

Marital Status
Single. Never married, nor cohabited. Was once engaged, but broke off engagement after fiancé confessed to one-night stand with another woman while drunk.

Employment History
1988–PRESENT:

Summerton's doctor, attending to medical, and often emotional and psychological, problems of college population. Feels guilty occasionally, or so the college gossip would have it, for working in what is arguably a privileged community and thinks that it would be more moral, somehow, to attend to the ailments of the underprivileged, but is confronted with regular evidence that social, intellectual and financial advantage do not necessarily bring with them superior physical and mental health, particularly not the latter. Deals regularly with people whose academic success in getting to a place like Summerton has sent them into a state of paranoid terror in case they can't keep it up. Once you have been a success, the prospect of failure is too awful to contemplate. Look at Sebastian. If he hadn't got into Summerton as a graduate student, his expectations would never have been raised so high. He would probably have done a diploma at the Boringstead Institute of Boringstead Institute Studies and then settled happily into bun shop management of some description. Sympathy for the plight of the fortunate, therefore, provides Dr Williams with the justification and motivation necessary to combat their symptoms: stress, insomnia, bulimia and clinical depression.

1979–1988:

General Practitioner, Barlow Rise Health Centre, Bristol. This involved working mainly with people who were too ill to think about success or failure and concentrated instead on matters such as rheumatoid arthritis, cardio-vascular disease, emphysema and osteoporosis. Sebastian suffers

73

from none of these complaints, but remains unconvinced by the argument that everything is all right as long as you've got your health. He has his health, but would also like a good job. Those who raise our expectations have an obligation to fulfil them, in my view. I don't think we should let this unfair world wear us down to the point where happiness and the avoidance of lung cancer become one and the same. If everybody asked for too much, perhaps more of us would get enough.

Qualifications and Education
MRCGP and MB B.Chir. Clinical Medicine, Addenbrooke's Hospital, Cambridge. MA (BA) Pathology (IIii), Summerton College, Cambridge.

Took education and training seriously. Worked hard and did not participate in kidney-throwing contests or any of the other japes contemporaries got up to. Did not behave disrespectfully towards those good enough to leave their human remains to science by making crude comments about the fatness/ugliness/deformity of the bodies up for dissection. Made a point of shunning all male medical students who made jokes about their intention to specialise in gynaecology.

Strengths and Weaknesses
Strengths include punctuality, social conscience and dedication to job. Weaknesses include occasional medical incompetence, ridiculous notions of duty above all else, moral self-righteousness and a tendency to think her own judgement is infallible.

Another weakness is her conviction that the following of rules and the doing of duties leads to a situation of fairness. Strong belief in fairness, which might count as a strength if such an idyllic condition were possible to achieve. It is a weakness because, without the co-operation of God, nature, coincidence and all the living beings on the planet – and many of these either don't exist or do not have

74

consciousnesses with which to agree to co-operate – we will never make life fair. The most we can hope for is effective counter-unfairness to balance things out.

In trying to get Terri Skinner and Rod Firsden out of the way so that Sebastian can have the Enmity, I am not tampering with justice, only with custom. Is it fair that Terri has been offered the job, or that Rod is the runner-up? Of course not; it has simply come about in the usual way, via a standard application and interview procedure. Unfortunately, many people are too dim to distinguish what is merely habit from what is right.

Other Information

Member of a reading group called Cambridge Readers Circle that meets on the first Wednesday of every month to discuss a particular book. Also a member of Friends of the Earth. Attends service at Summerton chapel every Sunday morning and works as a volunteer for the Botanic Gardens every other Sunday afternoon. Likes classical music, the proper tuneful kind, as well as hiking, canoeing, cooking and knitting.

Physical Appearance

Short and plump. Hair fair (ash-blond with the odd streak of grey) and square (cut in angular page-boy style). Always wears long white doctorish coat when on duty, so dress sense cannot be commented upon, except for shoes which are always flat-heeled with laces. Never wears make-up or perfume.

Chapter Eleven

Doctors, Appointments

I woke up early the next day and set off for Summerton, having reassured Sebastian as best I could that I had a workable plan for getting him the Enmity. Although this wasn't yet true, I felt strangely hopeful that it soon would be, partly because of what I'd seen and heard in Terri's flat the night before and partly because of George Herbert. I'd only bought his *Collected Poems* to get some insight into what made Rod Firsden tick, but I'd become hooked as soon as I started reading. There was something hypnotic about the verses, even though there were quite a few I didn't entirely understand. I spent all evening trying to memorise a poem called 'Jordan', reciting it to myself over and over again under my breath, much to Sebastian's irritation.

There was no doubt that George Herbert had contributed to my good mood this morning. It was the sound of the poems that I liked; I found them almost addictive and, strangely, they made me feel anything was possible. Perhaps Rod Firsden's research, if he got the chance to do it, would help to explain exactly how a load of words in a particular combination could have this sort of effect.

As I turned off the main road on to Summerton Lane, I shook my head to banish the disloyal thought that Rod's work might be interesting. Besides, poetry shouldn't be analysed, it should simply be read and appreciated. I didn't think its essence could ever be pinned down, on the basis of my one evening as a George Herbert fan. Still, as hard as I tried to fight it, I knew that my attitude to Rod Firsden had changed ever so slightly now that we had this small thing in common. I thought of him crying in my car, taking sick leave from the T'ai Chi school because he wanted the Enmity so much and had to wait two weeks to find out whether he would get it. Poor Rod. Poor Sebastian.

I drove slowly up the lane, noticing the well-groomed fields on either side of me, through the college gates that had Summerton's crest at the top, and into Old Court. This was the parking area for fellows and visitors. It was a square courtyard that enclosed a circular lawn, the central point of which was a large oak tree. The grass was fuzzy and neatly trimmed. It reminded me of the back of Sebastian's neck when he's just been to the hairdressers, apart from the greenness, obviously. Sebastian had once told me that Summerton employed more than thirty gardeners and judging from the grounds they all did their job extremely well, far better than the De La Wyche panel, who not only didn't make their decision when they said they would, but compounded that error by making the wrong decision. Perhaps the gardening team could be put in charge of future Enmity committees; they would be bound to do a better job, if the perfectly colour-coordinated flowerbeds I could see were anything to go by. No wonder everyone wanted to work here, I thought. The place was so beautiful.

I pulled into a parking space near a little arched doorway – all Summerton's doorways are arches – and got out of the car, wondering whether my Red L Driving School sign would attract any new customers. I knew where Valerie Williams's surgery was from when I'd had to bring Sebastian in once with a sprained ankle. 'There's no point showing it to Valerie,' he'd protested at the time, hobbling along with his arm pressing down on my shoulder. 'She's crap. She prescribes the same cure whatever's wrong with you – Strepsils.' I had said that surely this couldn't be true.

I was naïve in those days, before Sebastian's many job rejections, and believed that most people in really important positions, like doctors or lawyers, must be good at their jobs or else they would not be allowed to continue to do them. 'I'm not joking,' Sebastian had insisted. 'Whatever you've got, from diarrhoea to diabetes, she gives you Strepsils. The only people who think she's any good around here are the ones who've been to see her about nothing but sore throats.' As it happened, she did not give Sebastian Strepsils for his ankle, but I did spot a huge jar full of them on the shelf.

I walked across the cobblestones and under the tall archway that led from Old Court to Tyndsall Court. If I remembered rightly, Valerie's rooms were immediately to the left.

I stopped in front of the 'Doctor's Surgery' sign. I didn't want to knock in case she came to the door, asked who I was and refused to see me when she discovered I was neither ill nor a member of the college. On the other hand, I didn't want to antagonise her by being rude and barging in, so I settled for a compromise solution: I knocked and walked in at the same time.

The surgery was a cramped room with a grey ribbed carpet. Peeling wallpaper that had once been white provided a shabby backdrop to five or six health warning posters, which were unnervingly bright and cheerful-looking given their subject matter. There was one about smoking, one about HIV, heart disease, unwanted pregnancy – all the gang were there. Valerie Williams was sitting at her desk, which was pushed up against the far wall of the room under a high window, filling in some kind of form. She was bending over it and frowning with great concentration. She didn't see me at first, so I coughed loudly and regretted it immediately. I didn't want to be fobbed off with Strepsils like all the other suckers.

She turned to face me and smiled a caring doctorly smile. I felt physically sick, just as I had when I'd seen Daphne

Fielding's three books in Joe and Terri's flat. The taste of regurgitated Corn Pops filled my mouth and I swallowed hard. Perhaps Dr Williams could suggest some treatment for my new allergy to De La Wyche panel members.

'Hello,' she said warmly. 'Have you got an appointment?' Her voice was low, almost like a man's, and leisurely. One word seemed to roll into another. I imagined it would be a good voice for telling people they only had a few months to live.

'No,' I said. 'Do I need one?'

'Well . . . I usually like people to make appointments, but I suppose it doesn't matter. I'm free now, anyway. I haven't seen you before. Are you a student or a fellow?'

She sounded kind and friendly, and for a minute I wanted to burst into tears and hurl myself into her plump arms to be comforted. I had to force myself to think harsh thoughts. 'Neither,' I said, sitting down uninvited on the only spare chair. 'I'm a driving instructor. My name's Kate Nunn. I'm Sebastian Nunn's wife.' I was expecting a regretful sigh followed by a platitude along the lines of 'I'm sure Sebastian will find a job eventually' and maybe a few Strepsils thrown in for good measure. What I got was a bland, blank expression.

Valerie Williams's warm manner had vanished so quickly that I wondered whether I'd imagined it. Looking at me now, her face was a cautious podgy mask. 'What can I do for you?' she asked.

'I wanted to ask you a few questions about the De La Wyche fellowship, the interviews, Sebastian . . . that sort of thing,' I said, forcing the sort of smile I thought a reasonable person in my position might put on her face.

'I can't tell you anything. The discussions of the fellowship committee are confidential.' Valerie smiled back frostily.

'I know that,' I said. 'But sometimes it's possible to get a bit of feedback, you know, find out where you went wrong so that you can improve for other interviews.' I thought a spot of mock-deference might win her over. Went wrong, indeed. It was she and her sidekicks who had gone wrong, not Sebastian.

'If Sebastian wants to ring up and ask . . .' Valerie began.

'I'm asking. I'm his wife. He knows I'm here, so why can't you tell me? You said on the phone that Sebastian nearly got the fellowship, but he didn't even come second. How is that possible?'

'Perhaps you should have a word with Professor Fielding.' Valerie smiled again, tightly.

'You were the one who rang and told Sebastian he hadn't got it,' I pointed out. 'Why can't I ask you? Why were you on the panel, anyway? Isn't it a bit unusual for the college doctor . . .'

'It's in the rules.' Valerie patted her knees with both hands. I got the impression she found rules reassuring. 'The panel that appoints the De La Wyche fellow must contain one member of non-academic staff. The Dean of Chapel and the Chaplain were both on holiday, which left me.'

I suppressed a scowl. Valerie's use of the order-obeying defence made her more guilty in my eyes, not less. I would refuse to be on an appointment committee, if I were ever asked, whatever the rules said. I couldn't live with myself, knowing that a decision made in an hour or so by little fallible old me and a few other people with equally flawed judgement was going to create lasting misery for several people. As I tell my learner drivers all the time, anyone with imagination knows that the only rules you should follow are the ones you make for yourself, and that right and wrong cannot be administrated. The way I see it, the world divides neatly into two categories: interviewers and interviewees. Forget distinctions of race, class and gender; this is the stratification system that really counts. The fact is that if you're an interviewer, you're probably going to have a prosperous and contented life, whereas if you're an interviewee, you are trapped in a cycle of rejection from which it is hard to escape. Of course, all interviewers are ex-interviewees who have sold out and joined the bad guys. The only way the interviewees will ever beat the interviewers is if successful interviewees unite and refuse to go over to the other side. Then the whole system would come crashing down and society would be forced to allocate jobs in a different and, I hope, more sensible way.

Watching Valerie Williams shuffle her ample behind around in her chair and repel my questions with her all-form-no-content smile would have been enough to convince me, if I had needed convincing further, that she was unfit to serve on the De La Wyche committee and should not have been put in charge of anything more controversial than Strepsil allocation. My frustration erupted. 'This whole thing has been so unprofessional,' I blurted out. 'Professor Fielding's daughter-in-law was one of the candidates, the successful one, would you believe it? The decision was delayed by a day with no explanation. You refuse to answer my questions. I say it's a stitch-up.' I folded my arms and waited for a reaction.

Chapter Twelve

A Jolly Good Fellow

'I can assure you that Terri wasn't chosen because of any nepotism.' Valerie's features remained impassive. 'In any case, she and Professor Fielding don't get on. They're certainly not close.'

'Not close?' I couldn't believe what I was hearing. 'They're in-laws! Why wasn't Daphne Fielding removed from the panel as soon as Terri applied?'

'It's in the rules.' Valerie recited her favourite phrase again. 'There must be a college professor on the panel and none of the others was available on this occasion.'

'Sounds to me like you need better rules,' I said in my best scathing voice. 'Why didn't you make your decision the day after the interviews, like you said you would? Why did you need a whole extra day to think about it?'

Valerie looked at her watch. 'I don't remember the precise details,' she said.

'You mean you won't tell me.'

'There's nothing to tell.' She turned away, as if I was an item of business she'd dealt with and dumped in her out-tray. 'Now, I'm extremely busy . . .'

'Fine.' I pursed my lips. 'If you can't remember I'll ask the other three panel members. Maybe their minds are a bit more successful on the old fact-retention front.'

Valerie sighed. 'Well, I suppose I can't stop you,' she said, 'but could I ask you to go easy on Emily, please? She's going through a difficult patch.'

'What sort of difficult patch?'

'I really can't talk about that.'

'Look, Dr Williams,' I made a point of not calling her by her first name, 'I'm not inclined to go easy on anyone. I don't feel that any of you have gone easy on Sebastian, particularly now, with your refusal – and we both know that's what it is – to let me in on what should be public knowledge.' Her cheeks reddened slightly, so I continued with added vigour. 'If you want me to handle Emily Lole with care, you'd better tell me why. Otherwise I might lay right into her.' I bared my teeth to show I meant business.

Valerie expelled a disapproving gust of air through narrowed lips, making a whistling noise. I could hardly believe she was the same person as the smiling woman who'd greeted me a few minutes ago. 'Emily's found life a struggle since Fernando disappeared – do you know about that?' I nodded. 'She's had two serious breakdowns. I've had to put her on antidepressants and her pills have given her eczema. And I should warn you that Damian Selinger is not the easiest of people to deal with . . .'

'I know Damian,' I interrupted impatiently.

'He has a temper and a half, that man.' Valerie's mouth twitched. 'I would advise you to accept the panel's decision and go home. There's nothing you can do about it now. The decision's been made.'

'So, let me get this right,' I said, ignoring her advice. 'The interview panel was made up of yourself, who, on your own admission, can't remember precise details a mere three days after the event, Professor Fielding, whose daughter-in-law was one of the candidates, a pill-popping unstable neurotic and an unapproachable maniac with a raging temper.'

'Everyone has personal problems.' Valerie frowned. 'That doesn't make them unprofessional at work.'

'Yeah, right. So what about this woman who dropped out, then?'

'Bryony James?' Valerie sounded surprised, as if she hardly remembered the fourth candidate. Perhaps she really did have a bad case of amnesia, one that no amount of Strepsils could cure. 'I don't know why she did that. You'd have to ask her.'

'Where did she come, in the pecking order? Would she have beaten Sebastian as well, if she hadn't dropped out?'

'You shouldn't think of it in terms of winning and losing.'

'Really? In what terms should I think of it, then?'

'It's not a battle. Nobody's won and nobody's lost.'

'Except Fernando Rose,' I reminded her.

'Look, I'm very busy and I'm afraid I can't help you.' Valerie looked upset. I decided to try and build on my advantage. If the subject of Fernando distressed her, that might be a way of wearing her down.

'Do you know anything about that? Where he went?' I asked.

'Nothing.' Valerie shrugged. 'Only that Grimshaw De La Wyche's portrait went missing on the same night.'

'What?' Sebastian had never mentioned this.

'Yes, from Great Hall. The college was devastated. It was priceless, an original Edmund Noble.' So the man after whom Noble House was named had painted the creator of the Enmity. Sometimes the whole of Cambridge felt like an extended family. 'The painting disappeared on the same night as Fernando,' said Valerie.

'He probably pinched it before he ran off with Martine Selinger,' I said.

'Ran off with Martine Selinger?' Valerie chuckled in spite of the irritation my presence was causing her. 'Of course he didn't. Who told you that?'

'That was the rumour at the time,' I said with as much confidence as I could muster.

'Well, it's not true.' Valerie shook her head at the ludicrousness of my suggestion. 'I don't know what happened to Fernando Rose but it certainly wasn't that.

Fernando loved this college. It meant everything to him. For the first year and a half of his fellowship he came in every day, and I mean every single day. Everybody thought he was wonderful, especially compared with some of the other De La Wyche fellows who never showed their faces from one year to the next.'

'What do you mean?' I interrupted. 'They disappeared as well?'

'No, they just never came into college. They went off gallivanting, having a good time, happy to take Summerton's money but not willing to give anything back in return.'

'Hang on a second.' I sat forward, trying to make sense of this new information. 'What do you mean they never came in? In most jobs when employees don't show up for work they get sacked. Why didn't the college fire all these De La Wyche fellows who absconded?'

'Well, because strictly speaking it was within their rights,' Valerie explained. 'They weren't breaking their contracts. The fellowship doesn't have any obligations or specific duties. If you want to you can take the money and run, as all these people did. But Fernando was different.' Her eyes clouded over wistfully as she indulged fond memories of the one decent De La Wycher who had bothered to turn up, for one and a half years out of the three at any rate.

'I'm sorry, I don't get it,' I said bluntly. 'What do you mean, no specific duties? I mean, I know it's a research fellowship and there's no teaching requirement, but I thought the person at least had to . . . go into college and do research every day.'

Valerie shook her head. 'It isn't in the rules,' she said, placing particular emphasis on her favourite word. 'They don't have to make a single appearance in the whole three years if they don't want to. Obviously we hope the De La Wyche fellow will participate in college life, but we've been disappointed many times.' I wasn't at all surprised to hear this. I imagined that most employers who merely hoped their employees would pop in occasionally, without putting any retributive muscle behind this aspiration, would be disappointed on a fairly regular basis. The injustice of it struck me temporarily dumb. Sebastian, had he been successful, would have participated in college life. He would have gone in every day, I was sure of it, and contributed as much as he possibly could, if only he'd been given the chance. The thought of all the money Summerton must have wasted on these undeserving, ungrateful con-merchants made me feel nauseous.

'Maybe Fernando Rose was just another disappoint-ment,' I said, trying to take my mind off this latest insult.

'Not at all,' said Valerie. 'He was one of the few I approved of. He loved it here. He used to say he'd stay for ever if he could. That's why it was so strange when he suddenly . . . went, when he still had half of his time left.'

'What was his subject?' I asked.

'English Literature. John Donne. He used to publish articles about him in journals all the time, but since he vanished we've not seen a single piece by him anywhere. Emily was devastated. We all expected the two of them to get married.'

'Obviously he fancied a go at Martine Selinger,' I said. 'He was with her on the night he disappeared.'

'Fernando would never have left here by choice,' said Valerie stubbornly. 'He was out with Martine among other people. Keith Cobain and Ethan Handley were there too. They all went to that nightclub on King's Parade.'

'The Jive Hive?'

'Yes, that's right. Keith and Ethan were a bit tipsy and . . . well, I think they'd met up with some girls, so they didn't really keep track of Fernando and Martine.' That sounded like Keithanethan, I thought. Wherever they went they 'met up with some girls', or, to be more accurate, girls flocked adoringly around them. Even some men had a go, against the odds. The catchment area of Keithanethan's attraction had few limits, in fact it seemed only to exclude male heterosexuals. Everyone else, it was well known, fancied either both of them or at least one of them. Occasionally a person would come along who claimed to fancy neither of them, but this was generally regarded as an affectation.

Keith was gorgeous, dark and enigmatic, and Ethan was gorgeous, blond and enigmatic. Together they sauntered around the streets, pubs and clubs of night-time Cambridge, breaking hearts unintentionally in darkly and blondly enigmatic ways.

'At the end of the night the two of them had disappeared,' Valerie went on. 'Keith and Ethan looked everywhere. We never saw either of them again. Unfortunately, Keith and Ethan were too inebriated to remember anything that might have given us a clue.'

'So what do you think happened? Surely you don't agree with whatever paper it was that said he was abducted by aliens?' I laughed bitterly.

'Of course not.' Valerie tutted. 'I don't know. We couldn't even find out if he was still drawing on our donations, not without police help. We're still paying the money into his bank account even now. The Master, Sir Noel Barry – he's not Master any more but he was then – informed the police, but they didn't seem to feel it was worth investigating, especially when we told them about the precise nature of the De La Wyche fellowship.' I nodded, imagining how the police would react to the news that someone with a job that didn't involve turning up had not turned up.

'Did you ring any of his relatives?' By 'you' I meant the college, not Valerie specifically. Still, the usage struck me as apt. Valerie seemed to be more of a functionary of the institution than a person in her own right.

'No,' she said with an undertone of defensiveness. 'We didn't know anything about his family. Even Emily didn't.'

'Isn't that a bit odd?' I asked. People who were on the

verge of getting married usually knew a bit about each other's backgrounds.

'Many things are odd,' said Valerie unhelpfully and with evident impatience.

'If you don't think Martine ran off with Fernando, what do you think happened to her?' I demanded.

'I have no idea and I don't wish to speculate.' Valerie began to shuffle papers on her desk. 'I know her marriage to Damian was a difficult one, though, and in situations like that, people sometimes leave. It isn't unheard of.' Was this a feeble attempt at sarcasm on Valerie's part, I wondered, or did she simply think I was an imbecile?

She was certainly right about the Selingers' marriage. I could still remember a driving lesson I had conducted near their flat about two years ago, with my pupil valiantly attempting to reverse round a corner against an aural backdrop of Damian bellowing abuse and Martine shrieking like a banshee as each threw the other's most prized possessions out of the window. It was no wonder my pupil kept mounting the kerb; we were both understandably distracted by the sight of televisions, stereos, radios and the occasional rather beautiful vase or small sculpture tumbling out of the Selingers' third-floor window and smashing on their concrete front yard. 'You bitch, you fucking bitch!' Damian shouted, not caring if the whole neighbourhood heard.

'Help, help, he's going to kill me!' Martine blared in panic.

'Do you think we ought to do something?' my pupil asked me.

'Oh, no,' I said. 'It's okay, I know them. They do this all the time, it's their hobby.' I genuinely believed the Selingers revelled in their misery, otherwise why would they have let it drag on for so long? It struck me as most unlikely that Martine, after nine years of plate-throwing, knife-wielding marriage, would suddenly decide to do a runner. From what I'd seen of her socially, I got the impression that her fights with Damian gave her a much-needed purpose in life and something to talk about. Martine was the sort of person who told you the most intimate details within a minute of meeting you. The first time we'd met she had dragged me into the ladies to show me a scar on her left buttock – Damian-inflicted, naturally. Her other topics of conversation – hair care, nail care, skin care, suntanning, the latest fashion – did not attract nearly so many listeners.

'That's too much of a coincidence,' I said to Valerie. 'They're hardly likely to disappear on the same night, unless they went off together.'

'There's no point in speculating.' Valerie sighed heavily. 'Look, I must get on with . . .'

'If Fernando Rose's subject was English Literature, how come you've picked a first reserve this time who's also an English Lit person? Rod Firsden's research is on George Herbert.'

'How do you know that?' Valerie asked suspiciously. 'I didn't tell Sebastian that.' I decided not to tell her the truth about how I met Rod because I doubted she would believe me. It would seem too much of a coincidence. Like Martine, Fernando and the painted Grimshaw De La Wyche all vanishing separately on the same night.

'I know more than you think,' I said, impressed with how confident I sounded. 'And I'm going to find out the rest. I don't for one minute believe in your loss of memory. You seem to remember Rod Firsden and his work well enough. Do you really think it's fair to appoint one literature fellow straight after another?'

'We didn't appoint Rod,' Valerie said wearily. Her round shoulders slumped and she fiddled with her watch. 'We appointed Terri Skinner.'

'Yes, but if she doesn't take it, I mean. How long is it since a politics person has had the De La Wyche fellowship?'

'I can't remember.'

'Well, it looks like I've got a bit of research to do, then, doesn't it?' I said, standing up. 'Maybe Summerton'll give me a fellowship to investigate its appointment procedures.' I turned and marched out of the room, slamming the door after me so hard that the 'Doctor's Surgery' sign shook. I heard Valerie cry out in shock at the loud noise it made. It served her right, I thought, lying Strepsil bitch that she was.

Chapter Thirteen

Fernando Rose – Curriculum Vitae

Name
Fernando Rose BA, MA, PhD. According to some of the bitchier Summerton fellows, and unbeknown to the man he calls 'Dad', Fernando is the child of a Mallorcan waiter by the same name, with whom his mother had an affair. Sid Rose objected strongly to the name Fernando on the grounds that it was poncey and foreign, but his wife Doreen insisted and eventually they struck a deal: if Sid would agree to Fernando, Doreen would leave the naming of any subsequent children they had (Carolette and Rocky) entirely to him.

Address
At present unknown.

Age
Thirty-one.

Place of Birth
Guildford, Surrey.

Nationality
British.

Marital Status
Single, or was when last seen in March 1997.

Employment History
OCTOBER 1995–PRESENT
De La Wyche fellow at Summerton College, Cambridge, although it could be argued that this term of employment ended with sudden disappearance on 21 March 1997. Specialism: the poetry of John Donne.

OCTOBER 1988–JUNE 1995
Part-time cashier (ten hours a week during university term time and twenty-five hours a week during holidays) for Victoria Wine, Seven Sisters Road, London. Specialism: selling cider and Berkely cigarettes to under-age but threatening teenagers. Also, at the opposite end of the age spectrum, selling cheap sherry to bad-smelling old women with cracked faces.

Qualifications and Education
PhD: 'The Heart and the Spirit: The Poetry of Andrew Marvell', King's College London, October 1992 to June 1995. MA with distinction on Poetry and Phonetics, King's College, London, October 1991 to June 1992. BA Hons English Literature (IIi), King's College, London, October 1988 to June 1991. Four A levels: English Literature (A), English Language (A), Theatre Studies (A) and Psychology (B) from Crowhill Sixth Form College in Guildford. Eight O levels: five 'A's, three 'B's, one 'C' from Grimbley Comprehensive School in Guildford.

Publications
The Heart and the Spirit: The Poetry of Andrew Marvell (Routledge, London, 1996). Article entitled 'John Donne's Imagery' in *Poetry and Metaphysics* (ed. Michael Schmidt, Oxford University Press, 1996). Occasional reviews of contemporary poetry books in the *Times Literary Supplement*, the *London Review of Books* and *Poetry Review*.

Strengths and Weaknesses

Friendly, helpful, diligent. A pleasure to work with, everyone agrees, be it in an off-licence or a Cambridge college. Sensitive to the needs and feelings of others and renowned for generosity, financial and emotional, towards friends and colleagues. Kind and charitable, notably to people encountered in daily life, as opposed to Terri Skinner, his possible De La Wyche successor, who is charitable to those who quietly cash her cheques and don't interfere with her blatant self-promotion programme, while being vile to her immediate family. Extremely popular with both employers and employees. Always got glowing reports at school and references brimming with the highest praise from people as diverse as Professor Neville Bernard, Head of the English Department at King's College, London, and Sheila Golightly, manager of the Victoria Wine shop in Seven Sisters. Overcame great odds to get to university, since family was of the what-the-fuck-use-is-a-degree-you-want-to-get-down-that-job-centre-son ilk. Was therefore always appreciative of educational opportunities and made the most of them, as opposed to many of his contemporaries at King's who saw university as a liver challenge of three years' duration. Minor weakness – minor because it harmed no one but himself – was extreme susceptibility to stress and tension about anything pertaining to his work. On several occasions during his time at Summerton, Valerie Williams had to talk him through hours of relaxation exercises, without which he couldn't unclench his teeth and fists. Another weakness is that nobody knows where he is, although whether this should be counted as his deficiency or the rest of the world's is a matter for debate.

Other Information

Member of the Poetry Society 1991–1997.

Interests: poetry, *The Times* crossword (for the successful completion of which he won prize money occasionally), architecture, walking, cycling.

Chapter Fourteen

Sighs and Groans

No matter how angry I am, I never take it out on my car. I love cars, always have. Okay, so they pollute the atmosphere, but they don't mean to. They are not cruel or negligent in the way that people are. They do not arrogantly set up committees in which they then lord it over their vehicular comrades, making them fail their MOTs. So I did not thump the steering wheel or kick the bumper. I mentally kicked Valerie Williams instead.

What made me furious was not so much my certainty that she was withholding pertinent information for some devious and malignant reason – on the contrary, that gave me hope, because if I could find out what it was, perhaps I could use it to Sebastian's advantage – but the thought that people like her and Damian Selinger and Daphne Fielding were in positions of authority at Summerton despite their obvious personal failings.

There is something wrong, is there not, with a man who cannot distinguish between marriage and nine years spent shouting 'You bitch, you fucking bitch' at a woman who shouts 'Help, help, he's going to kill me' in response? With a woman who justifies sitting on an interview panel when one of the interviewees is her own daughter-in-law by saying she doesn't like her much anyway? With a doctor who claims not to remember things she said and did three days ago? And yet these people felt they had the right to play with Sebastian's future, Sebastian who was scrupulously honest – more honest than interviewees were supposed to be – and who knew how to conduct a happy and healthy relationship.

I was more determined than ever to eliminate Rod Firsden and Terri Skinner, and to get Sebastian the Enmity, and more worried than ever that I would not be able to. I sat in my Micra on Summerton Lane, under the shade of a large tree's leafy canopy, and cried until it was time to go and pick up Rod Firsden for his second lesson. A porter walked past and tipped his hat at me through the car window. It was a rather peculiar way to react to a sobbing woman, I thought, but it made me laugh, so perhaps it was an expert porterly counselling technique that I just didn't know about.

I was in the process of wiping my eyes and pulling myself together when my mobile phone started to ring. I was seized by a sudden fear that it might be Rod, phoning to cancel his lesson, but then I remembered he didn't know my mobile number, not unless he'd been very crafty and memorised it from my Red L Driving School car sign. I realised I was looking forward to seeing him, partly for plan-furthering reasons but also because I was keen to discuss George Herbert with him. Ideally, he would agree to turn down the Enmity within the first two minutes of the lesson and we could spend the rest of our hour together talking about 'Jordan', the poem I'd memorised last night. Some hope.

I picked up the phone with a hand still damp from tears. It was Sebastian. 'I've got some good news,' he said. I stretched my mouth open to its full capacity and shook my fist in the air. The panel had changed their minds. Valerie Williams had just phoned to say it had all been a mistake and to offer Sebastian the Enmity. Another porter chose this moment to walk past. I must have looked extremely peculiar, with my mouth wide open, gyrating in my car seat. He tipped his hat at me, just as his colleague had done. Were porters trained to execute this manoeuvre in response to any display of female hysteria?

'What?' I asked, holding my breath.

'I've got two more job interviews. I just found out this morning. Sheffield and Canterbury.' I felt my face crumple and tears prick the insides of my already sore eyelids. Two more job interviews. Two more opportunities for Sebastian to be rejected by a bunch of pompous, scruffily dressed, undeservedly tenured idiots, many of whom would be less well qualified than he was, if past experience was anything to go by. When he was interviewed for a lectureship at the Surrey West University College in Farnham, there hadn't been a single person on the panel with an MA, let alone a PhD, let even more alone a prizewinning PhD. He'd been irate when they wrote to tell him he hadn't got the job. 'Academia's a fucking joke!' he yelled, breaking a CD case or two. 'I mean, it's like fucking Delia Smith being interviewed for a head chef job by a group of primary school dinner ladies.'

As usual, I didn't share my negative thoughts with Sebastian. He had enough of his own to contend with and if he was going to go to these interviews he needed to be as upbeat as possible. Must be on our best behaviour for the people who are going to ruin our lives. 'When are they?' I asked.

'Sheffield is on the nineteenth of June and Canterbury's the twenty-second. They're both okay jobs as well. I mean, not as good as the De La Wyche, obviously, but not bad. One's a two-year research . . .'

'That's after Terri's two weeks,' I interrupted, brightening up a bit.

'What?'

'Terri asked for two weeks to think about the De La Wyche. That was on the fourth of June, so two weeks from then is . . .' – I worked it out – '. . . the eighteenth.'

'So?' asked Sebastian impatiently.

'So, I said I'd get you the fellowship by then, didn't I? And if I do, you won't need to bother going to these interviews.'

Nothing would have made me happier than the knowledge that Sebastian would never again enter the portals of a university, assuming that was what he wanted, of course. Why couldn't he have a sudden, unexpected change of vocation and decide that his dream was to work at Kwikfit? I trusted Kwikfit in a way that I did not trust academia. One only needed to compare slogans to see the superiority of one over the other. 'You can't get better than a Kwikfit fitter' is alluringly catchy and alliterative. In the seventies, when university lecturers were protesting that their salaries were not increasing at the same rate as those of other professionals, their slogan was 'Rectify the anomaly'. Really rolls off the tongue, doesn't it? Axe the tax, kill the bill and, er, rectify the anomaly, if you would be so kind.

'Come on, Kate. We both know that's just a fantasy. There's no way you're going to get me the fellowship.'

'What?' I screamed down the phone at him.

'Well, you aren't, are you? That was just a stupid, false hope that we were both clinging on to when there was nothing else. These two interviews are real chances. Even though they'll probably come to nothing like all my other interviews,' he concluded glumly.

'It is not a stupid, false hope.' I started to cry again. 'It's a real hope. You don't know the half of it. I'm making progress on it already.' This would be true, I thought, if only I could put my suspicions about Terri Skinner and Valerie Williams to good use.

'Whatever,' said Sebastian dismissively. 'Anyway, it's good that I've got two more interviews, isn't it?'

'Yes, of course it is, although it's no less than you deserve, so don't feel too grateful to the bastards. And it'll be even better when I get you the De La Wyche fellowship and you can turn Sheffield and Canterbury down.'

'God, you're in a really angry mood, aren't you?' Sebastian sounded impressed. 'Are you okay?'

'Fine,' I said. 'Listen, I've got to go. I've got a busy two weeks ahead of me.'

'Are you really serious about this business?'

'I wasn't at first,' I admitted. 'But now I am.'

'Why? What's changed? You haven't ... have you spoken to Professor Fielding?' Sebastian sounded awestruck.

You can't get lesser than a Summerton professor, I sang in my head, inventing my own slogan. 'No,' I said. 'But I will. Leave it to me.' Thankfully Sebastian let me off without further questioning.

I switched off my phone and headed for Sterling Road where Rod Firsden lived. It occurred to me that I could brighten up my day considerably by provoking another clash with Vincent Strebonian, he of the hypothetical driveway emergencies.

I parked on the stretch of pavement beside his 'No Parking Here' sign, leaned back in the driver's seat and closed my eyes. It took him all of thirty seconds to bang loudly on the roof of my car. I pretended to wake up, stretching lazily, and wound down the window. 'Ah, good morning, Mr Strebonian,' I said. 'Long time no irritating repetitive harangue.' He was looking even more wrinkled than he had the previous day. Perhaps his particular brand of cosmetic surgery involved actually swapping skin with his sagging patients.

He glowered at me fiercely, sucking his brushlike moustache with his lower lip while he worked out how best to commence today's invective. 'Are you deliberately trying to infuriate me, young lady?' he asked.

'Yes. On a scale of one to ten, with one being crap and ten being excellent, how am I doing?'

'Would you please move your vehicle this instant? Or else I shall move it myself. I shall call the police, do you hear?' He bent down and started to claw at the Micra's tyres with his fingernails. 'I'll pull your confounded wheels off!' he spluttered.

'More emergencies, hey?' I asked breezily. 'What do you do, sit at the window all day checking no one parks on your precious spot? Shouldn't you be looking at your patients instead of the road, or do they not mind coming out with three noses each?'

'How dare you . . .' Vincent Strebonian's chin puckered in fury. It reminded me of a peach stone. He was still fumbling with the tyres and seemed indeed to be attempting to pull the wheels off the car.

'Kate, Kate!' I heard Rod Firsden yell, rushing across the road. 'What are you doing, parking across Mr S's driveway again? Move, quickly.'

'Is this offensive woman your driving instructor?' Vincent Strebonian shouted at Rod.

'Erm, yes.' Rod dipped his head deferentially. 'I'm really sorry. I'll sort it out, I promise.' He climbed into the Micra and stared at me sternly as I pulled away from the kerb, waving at his officious neighbour as we moved off. 'You're so cruel,' he said. 'Leave the poor guy alone. Why are you trying to make his life a misery?'

'Because he did it to me first,' I explained. 'And I've just had enough of . . . everybody and everything.' Antagonising Dr Strebonian was merely displacement, I realised. It was the De La Wyche panel I wanted to harm.

'What's wrong?' Rod leaned forward. His face wasn't quite so shiny today, but I could still smell cocoa butter. 'You've been crying.'

'Nothing,' I said.

'Yes something is.'

'I'd rather not discuss it,' I said. 'It's personal.'

'I'm a good listener,' said Rod, rubbing his beard in apparent concern over my emotional state. 'And believe me, I know all about suffering. There's nothing you can tell me about torment that I haven't experienced first-hand.'

This was such an extreme statement, delivered so earnestly, that it made me giggle. 'You've been reading too much George Herbert,' I said. 'Look.' I opened the glove compartment to show Rod I'd taken his recommendation seriously. My copy of the *Collected Poems* was tucked in between a Nissan Micra manual and a pile of old service receipts. I'd taken out everything with my name on it and stuffed it in the boot before I'd set off this morning.

'You bought it!' he gasped. 'Oh . . . that means so much to me!' He gazed at me adoringly.

'It does? Well, I mean, I just thought I'd, er, give poetry a try, you know.'

'And?'

'Well, I think it's really good. Especially "Jordan".'

'Hm,' Rod frowned. 'That's not his best. "Sighs and Groans" is my favourite. Do you know it?'

'No, I don't think I've got to that one yet.' The title didn't sound promising. I wondered whether George Herbert had travelled forward in time and eavesdropped on one of Sebastian's and my interview post-mortems.

'Listen.' Rod pulled the book out of the glove compartment, handling it with great care. 'I'll read it to you.'

'Shouldn't we get on with your lesson?' I said. 'Remember, you're paying me.'

'I don't begrudge either you or George Herbert the money,' he said seriously. 'Some things are more important than . . . clutch control, you know.'

I laughed. 'Okay, then,' I said, driving down Huntingdon Road with no particular destination in mind.

' "O do not use me",' Rod began, booming portentously.

> 'After my sins! Look not on my desert,
> But on thy glory! Then thou wilt reform
> And not refuse me: for thou only art
> The mighty God, but I a silly worm:
>   O do not bruise me!
>
>   O do not urge me!
> For what account can thy ill steward make?
> I have abused thy stock, destroyed thy woods,
> Sucked all thy magazines: my head did ache,

Till I found out how to consume thy goods:
　　O do not scourge me!

　　O do not blind me!
I have deserved that an Egyptian night
Should thicken all my powers; because my
　　　　　　　lust
Hath still sewed fig-leaves to exclude thy
　　　　　　　light:
But I am frailty and already dust;
　　O do not grind me!

　　O do not fill me
With the turned vial of thy bitter wrath!
For thou hast other vessels full of blood,
A part whereof my saviour emptied hath,
Ev'n unto death: since he died for my good.
　　O do not kill me!

　　But O, reprieve me!
For thou hast *life* and *death* at thy command;
Thou art both *Judge* and *Saviour, feast* and
　　　　　　　rod,
Cordial and *Corrosive*: put not thy hand
Into the bitter box; but O my God,
　　My God, relieve me!'

'That's brilliant,' I said, feeling goose-pimples rising on my arm. 'I'm not sure I understand it all, but I love it. The rhymes and the rhythm . . . I don't know. How did he write it? It's weird to think someone just . . . made up something as good as that. '

'I recited part of it in my interview for the De La Wyche fellowship. I made copies of it and gave one to each panel member.' Rod sighed. 'They always ask you if you've got any questions or anything you want to say. I wanted to convey to them how desperate I was to get the job, and the last verse of "Sighs and Groans" summarises my feelings on the matter far more effectively than any words I could come up with. You see,' he said, turning deliberately towards me as if he had something crucial to say, 'the interview panel has replaced God in our society. They are, as Herbert says, "both Judge and Saviour, Feast and Rod, Cordial and Corrosive".' Rod was so enthusiastic about his theory that he'd begun to pant. I felt less alone, suddenly, realising that I wasn't the only person in the world who was obsessed with interview panels. I'd never elevated them to a spiritual level, though. 'They have "both life and death" at their command, in a metaphorical sense,' Rod went on. 'My life certainly won't be worth living if Terri Skinner decides to accept the fellowship.'

'Don't be silly.' I parked in a pay and display space on Chesterton Road, since the petrol gauge was pointing to low and we weren't really going anywhere. 'You must have other things to live for. Friends, family, girlfriend?' He frowned and turned away so that I couldn't see his face. 'Well?' I prompted.

'I meant what I said,' he almost whispered. 'Without the fellowship, I'll have nothing.' I wished I hadn't contradicted him. How did I know what other areas of his life were like? Maybe I'd put my foot in it and reminded him of additional misery-inducing items. Perhaps Rod was even more unfortunate than Sebastian, who would at least admit that he had me to live for, irrespective of his job situation. Did this mean Rod needed the Enmity more? I admonished myself for this inconvenient sympathetic impulse. Never mind Rod; there was Sheffield and Canterbury rejection to be avoided now, and I saw only one way to do that: eliminate the De La Wyche obstacles.

'You shouldn't allow ... one thing to become so important to you,' I said. 'There must be other English Lit jobs coming up all the time.'

'So? I want this one. It's the best. It's what I've been working for all my life. I . . . I have to get it.' He looked at me and shrugged apologetically. 'It might sound stubborn to you, but . . . nothing will change the way I feel. I don't want to work anywhere but Summerton.'

'But even if you do get it, even if Terri Skinner turns it down, it only lasts three years.'

'I'm aware of that,' Rod snapped.

'So eventually you'll have to work somewhere else.' I wasn't sure why I was wasting my energy trying to talk him round. I often had to do this with Sebastian when he adopted particularly extreme positions, but Rod Firsden's attitude to life was none of my business.

'Possibly,' he said enigmatically, scratching his neat beard so that the hairs stuck out horizontally.

'No, definitely,' I corrected him. 'Unless you're planning an extremely early retirement.'

'My plans are my own business,' he said, then winced as if he was already regretting his rudeness. 'Ignore me,' he said. 'I didn't sleep at all last night. I'm just tired and tense.'

'Why didn't you sleep?'

'Because I'm an insomniac,' he blurted out. 'There! You've got one more fact out of me, are you satisfied?'

'Look, I don't mean to be nosy,' I said, although my intention was basically irrelevant, since I clearly was nosy whether or not I meant to be. 'I'm just trying to help.'

'Thank you.' Rod simulated a smile. 'But I don't think you can.' We sat in silence for a while and gloom seemed to fill up the car until I felt as if I could hardly breathe.

'Listen,' I said. 'I've got something to tell you that'll cheer you up. I broke into Terri Skinner's flat last night.' I regretted the words the second they were out of my mouth. I quickly grabbed a contingency plan that I hoped might salvage the situation. I hadn't intended to share my espionage anecdote with Rod, but now that I'd gone this far, perhaps I could turn it to my advantage.

'You . . . you *what*?' Rod looked at me as if I were a total nutcase. 'You broke in? But . . . how did you know where she lived?'

'Oh.' Shit. If I admitted to being her neighbour Rod would wonder why I had failed to mention this yesterday. 'I looked in the phone book,' I improvised, thankful for once that Terri wore the trousers in flat 3. I had once needed to phone Sebastian, who'd left the phone off the hook by accident, and I'd had to look up Joe and Terri's number. The Fielding-Skinner clan were indeed in the telephone directory under Terri's name, since to be listed under 'Fielding, J' would represent phallic oppression at its most pernicious.

I told Rod about the one-sided telephone conversations I'd overheard while hiding in the wardrobe. He listened in stunned silence as I recounted Terri's questioning of R English in order to track down Gary Conley, shaking his head occasionally. I didn't bother to mention the labels in Terri's dresses. Too much information might confuse Rod, and I needed him to be focused if I was going to use him as a pawn.

'But ... but ...' he spluttered when I'd finished my account. 'I don't understand. What if you'd been caught? You were taking such a risk! You would have been arrested.' I sneered cockily at the prospect of incarceration; living with a depressed unemployed person who grew sadder and more defeated every day was infinitely more upsetting. If I could survive that, I could survive bullying by butch women prison guards with bad hairstyles. 'What were you hoping to achieve?' Rod continued to question me.

'I don't know, really,' I said honestly. 'I don't know exactly why I did it.'

'But thank God you did.' Rod grabbed my hand and squeezed it. 'Do you realise what this means?'

'No. What?'

'Gary Conley lives in Reading. If she was crying like that she must care about him a lot. That must be why she's considering taking the Reading job, it's the only possible explanation.'

'Well . . .' I thought that was going a bit too far, but Rod wouldn't let me get a word in. At least I had put an end to his trappist sulk.

'You say she hadn't been in touch with him for a while?' Rod asked eagerly. I nodded. 'Well, that's it, then. They must have been having an affair and . . .'

'Why?' I asked, extracting my hand from between his sweaty palms. 'There's no evidence for that.'

'The crying!' Rod yelled impatiently. 'She wouldn't cry over him if he were just anyone, would she? They were having an affair, I'm telling you. She's trying to make it start again,' he said, as if relationships were cars. 'That's why she's considering Reading.'

'You're pulling this out of thin air!' I laughed.

'Well, what else could it mean?'

'Okay. R English is Gary Conley's bisexual ex-boyfriend. Terri had an affair with R English and Gary, a violent and vengeful bruiser, has threatened to kill her if she ever goes near Reading again. She was ringing to try and find out whether Conley's still in the area because if he is, she can't accept the Reading job for fear he might kill or maim her.' I smiled, pleased with my alternative interpretation of events.

'Don't be absurd,' said Rod. 'I'm right, I know I am. I've got to go to Reading, as soon as possible. I should go now, right now!'

I gave myself a mental pat on the back. This was exactly how I'd wanted him to react. 'And do what?' I asked calmly.

'Find Gary Conley. I'll start with all the YMCAs. I'll go to NEG, whatever it is, and ask questions. I'm sure I can find him.'

'And if you do?'

'I don't know.' Rod clutched his head with both his hands. 'This is so exciting, I can't reason clearly.'

'Well, you'd first need to find out his precise relationship to Terri,' I said encouragingly. 'Which might help you to

105

work out how his behaviour might affect Terri's decision about Reading.'

'Yes, of course!' His eyes lit up. 'You're so clever. You're so brilliant. I can't believe you did that, broke into her flat, just to help me!' He gawped at me in admiration and I had no alternative but to accept this erroneous compliment. 'I've got to set off now. Can we rearrange this lesson? Give me your phone number, I'll ring you when I get back from Reading.' I gave him my mobile number and told him to leave a message if it was switched off. I'd have to make sure I didn't have it on when Sebastian was around.

Rod opened the passenger door, then closed it again. He grabbed my face with both hands and kissed me on the lips. It was a quick, smacking sort of kiss. 'What would I do without you?' he said reverentially, before leaping out of the car and running off down the road.

Chapter Fifteen

Insect Morality

After Rod's sudden ecstatic departure, I sat in the car on Chesterton Road for nearly an hour, having neither paid nor displayed. It was lunchtime, but my stomach felt too unstable for me to risk eating anything. I knew what was causing my biliousness: Sebastian's forthcoming Sheffield and Canterbury ordeals. The first ten or so interviews he attended, I'm happy to report, didn't adversely affect my health in any way. It was round about number eleven or twelve that my symptoms first appeared: inability to sleep, nightmares, night sweats, vomiting, diarrhoea, headaches, panic attacks, tickly coughs – all of these would start to plague me as each interview date approached.

I didn't bother to go to my doctor, since there's not a lot that can be done about illnesses of psychological origin. Besides, I knew she wouldn't be able to understand. How do you explain that feeling of encroaching despondency to someone who has probably never experienced it?

I distracted myself by concentrating on a few minor worries, like Rod Firsden saying, 'What would I do without you?' I hoped he wasn't getting too attached to me. He didn't seem dangerous and I would have described him as eccentric rather than out-and-out mad, but you could never tell for certain. I found his occasional unprovoked displays of aggression alarming, but they were probably brought on by the stress of De La Wyche uncertainty, with which I could identify only too well.

It occurred to me that there might be certain advantages to being the object of Rod's obsession. If he transferred his desire from the Enmity to me, perhaps I could persuade him to withdraw his application, leaving the field free for Sebastian. How else could I eliminate him from the competition? There didn't seem to be a Gary Conley equivalent in his life, from what little I knew about it, someone with the power to affect his career decisions.

I wasn't sure whether I regretted sending him off to Reading in search of Gary Conley or not. The chances were he wouldn't be able to find Gary, but what if he did and made a hash of it? I wished I'd forced Rod to stay in the car a bit longer, until we'd had a chance to work out a rough strategy.

I was sure it would be a wasted trip, which is why I didn't want to make it myself. We didn't know for certain that Gary Conley was significant. What if he was a random friend of the family and Terri was crying because one of her fish had toothache?

I treated myself to a heavy nicotine lunch, ideal for someone with Rejected Husband Syndrome, and drove back to Summerton. There were three panel members I had not irritated beyond measure and I scolded myself for being so remiss. I decided to tackle Damian Selinger first. At least I already knew him, so we'd be able to cut out any introductory small talk.

After Martine Selinger had run off with Fernando Rose (I was sticking to my original hypothesis, despite Valerie Williams's protests), Damian had sold his flat on Bateman Street and moved into a college set. He was able to do this easily because it was his flat rather than theirs. I remembered Martine telling me once that she had wanted them to get a joint mortgage on it, but Damian had been sure, even before the wedding, that they would split up one day and said it would be less complicated all round for him to buy the flat and her to pay him a monthly rent. I lost all respect for Martine when she admitted, with no shame, to having agreed to this.

I wasn't sure exactly where his set was – in Damian's case the term was appropriate, since he wasn't much taller than a badger – so I headed for the porters' lodge and made enquiries. The head porter, whom I recognised as hat-tipper number two, advised me not to go to Dr Selinger's rooms without an appointment. Apparently Damian was renowned for his vicious verbal attacks upon unexpected visitors. The head porter chuckled as he said this, as if a tendency to dish out slanderous tongue-lashings to all and sundry were an endearing quirk rather than a serious character flaw. I supposed college porters had to believe in the innate wonderfulness of their allotted dons, otherwise they would surely object to calling them 'sir' and 'ma'am', and patiently teaching them how to use the college fax machine.

I assured the head porter that I could cope with whatever profanities Damian saw fit to inflict on me; I was, after all, a driving instructor. His set was in the largest court, Queen's, at the top of one of the corner towers. I panted as I ascended the long, winding staircase, trying not to think of Alfred Hitchcock's *Vertigo*. I thought I was reasonably safe, since my friend Hat-tipper hadn't included the hurling of unwelcome guests off the roof in his list of Damian's amusing idiosyncrasies. I knew that it was possible to get on to the roof if you had a fellow's key; this was one of the perks of belonging and traditionally all new fellows make a point of walking on the roof just because they can. If Terri or Rod got that far, I might just push them off myself, I thought, but then I remembered I didn't have access to a fellow's key; I was the wife of one of the excluded.

When I reached G12, I stopped and caught my breath before knocking. I didn't want to be sweaty and red in the face when Damian first saw me. I needed to look composed, cool as a Cambridge winter. I leaned against the wall and read Damian's door. 'Dr D Selinger' was painted half-way down and above it there was a lime-green poster advertising a one-day moral philosophy conference at which Damian was apparently giving a paper entitled 'Me, Me, Me: Embracing Selfishness'. To give him credit, this sounded marginally more interesting than the other two talks advertised on the poster: 'Insect Morality' and 'Is Evil a Valid Concept?'. The proponent of this latter waste of everyone's time was a Dr Patricia Gerraghty from the University of Central Lancashire. I could have saved her a lot of research, I thought, by simply telling her that it was. I felt evil welling up inside me every time Sebastian came back from an interview with that look of hope-turned-to-rage in his eyes and slammed his briefcase down on the table. I found it easy, in fact, to see how people become murderers. But then perhaps in Central Lancashire everything's just hunky-dory, and Dr Patricia Gerraghty and her colleagues are fluffy and pastel-coloured, and romp around the campus like oversized Care Bears.

When I was ready, I knocked on the door and waited, preparing myself for a hostile reception. Surprisingly, it was a beaming Damian Selinger who threw open the door with a broad smile splattered across his face. 'Kate!' he said, as though I were his dearest friend. 'How nice to see you. Do come in.' I had forgotten how short Damian was. He couldn't have been more than five foot three. His hair was blond and shaggy, almost shoulder-length. Whenever I'd seen him before he had had a crew-cut. This new style suited him much better. In his previous incarnation he had resembled a militaristic peanut.

'What's got into you?' I asked before I could stop myself. 'I've never known you to be so cheerful.' I quickly scanned his lounge. It was tidier than the flat he had shared with Martine, but that was probably because a bedder came in every day to do his cleaning – another perk of fellowship. The floor creaked loudly as we walked in. All the wooden surfaces shone from recent polishing. Even the dark, wooden, slightly crooked beams on the ceiling gleamed. I imagined a varicose-veined bedder leaping up to reach them. I noticed Damian's taste in posters had changed. The flat on Bateman Street had been full of grimy industrial scenes and unsettling surrealist stuff, Dalí's dribbling clocks and the like, whereas the new long-haired Damian seemed to prefer big, colourful abstracts. In the centre of the room there was a mahogany coffee table with legs shaped like those of a poodle.

'Of course I'm cheerful,' he agreed, attempting a pirouette. 'I'm in love, isn't it marvellous?' I didn't reply. Nothing seemed marvellous to me at the moment.

'Is that why you asked Sebastian if he believed in love at first sight in his De La Wyche interview?'

'Oh, that.' Damian stopped dancing. He adjusted his beige sweater awkwardly. That was one thing about him that hadn't changed, his appalling dress sense. It wasn't so much the clothes themselves that were offensive as the fact that he wore exactly the same thing every day. He had several versions of one outfit – a white shirt, beige slacks, a beige V-neck pullover, white socks and brown slip-on shoes – that he alternated between, but it amounted to his wearing the same clothes every day. I had always maintained that this had worrying implications for his personality. If I were ever on an appointments committee – and as you know I would never agree to participate in this particular form of institutionalised barbarism – I would make a point of asking the candidates about the contents of their wardrobes. Sebastian has an exemplary wardrobe. It is sane and well-balanced, comprising jeans, suits, rugby shirts, T-shirts, sweaters of all colours, both hand- and machine-knitted. He does not have mysterious names and dates sewn into his clothes, nor does he dress as if he may at any moment need to camouflage himself in a box of Werther's Originals.

'Do sit down.' Damian pointed at a narrow, high-backed chair that looked extremely uncomfortable. I recognised it from the Bateman Street flat. Most of Damian and Martine's furniture, in fact, had reminded me of things I'd seen as a child in the dungeons of Lancaster Castle, where my parents took me on a day trip. The torture instrument chair he was offering me seemed to be the only item he'd kept as a souvenir from the Martine era. Everything else in the set was wide and deep and soft – provided by Summerton and specially designed, no doubt, for the voluptuously privileged. I perched on the skeletal chair and Damian stretched his short body out across the plump-cushioned sofa opposite. He folded his arms up behind his head. 'Yes, I'm sorry Sebastian didn't get the De La Wyche,' he said. 'I can't quite understand what happened, myself.' His tone was jocular, as if we were discussing the latest events on *Coronation Street*.

'What's there to understand? You chose Terri Skinner.'

'Well, not at first. At first we chose Sebastian.'

'What?' This made it even worse, if they'd decided in his favour, then changed their minds. Damian clearly didn't care in the slightest. He scratched his nose and stared at the uneven beams on the ceiling. I resisted the urge to shake him to get the information out of him at greater speed.

'Well, on the Wednesday we'd practically made up our minds to give it to him. But then Professor Fielding insisted on ending the meeting . . . look, I don't know whether I'm allowed to tell you any of this. Ah, fuck it, they're a bunch of wankers anyway.' Having resolved his ethical dilemma, Damian continued amiably. 'Professor Fielding said she had to go and that we'd have to meet again the next day, Thursday. Yesterday.' He seemed to struggle to get his head round the chronology of events.

'Why?' I asked. 'I thought the decision was definitely supposed to be made the day after the interviews?'

'It is. It's even in the rules,' said Damian. Aha, I thought. So Valerie, with her enthusiasm for Summerton rules, had omitted to mention that one had been broken. Did the Master know? Perhaps he had the power to declare the whole process invalid if even a minor ordnance had been contravened. 'None of us knew why she did it. Her mind wasn't on the job, though. She was in a world of her own.

Kept looking at her watch as if she had somewhere important to go.' This rang a bell; Sebastian had also mentioned Professor Fielding's distracted behaviour. 'And then there was that head case Emily Lole,' Damian continued, 'who kept crying and insisting we give the job to the greasy-faced poetry guy . . .'

'Rod Firsden.'

'Yeah, that's his name. How did you know?'

'He came second. Valerie Williams told Sebastian.'

'I was against that, I really was.' Damian shook his head. 'We'd just had a poetry guy, Fernando Rose was a poetry guy. And he fucked off.'

'With Martine, according to college rumour,' I couldn't resist interjecting.

'No way,' said Damian. 'He was an intelligent guy, Fernando. There's no way he would have saddled himself with a shit-for-brains tart like Martine. No, he fucked off with a bloody expensive painting, the Noble portrait of De La Wyche.'

'Do you really think he took it?'

'Course he did. It vanished the same night he did. Those portraits are easy as anything to nick. This place is ludicrously old-fashioned. Proper security measures are regarded as somehow crude and ungentlemanly.'

'From what I've heard, Fernando doesn't sound like the thieving type. Do you think he was capable of it?' I asked.

'Anyone's capable of anything if there's enough in it for them. Talking of which, that's the subject of my new book. *Me, Me, Me: Embracing Selfishness*, it's called. The launch is on Monday. You and Sebastian'll be getting an invite. Anyway, I'll wager Fernando felt guilty about stealing the painting and that's why he's not shown his face since.'

'Neither has Martine,' I reminded him.

'For which relief much thanks. Now there's a countenance I simply could not countenance.'

'You obviously don't miss her, then.'

'I miss her money. It was hard to adjust to having no

purse to steal from. Not that I was short myself, you understand.' I assumed he meant he wasn't lacking in money, since he unequivocally was short in the literal sense. 'But it was more fun to steal hers.' He grinned and I smiled my best approving smile. I couldn't afford to antagonise him, since the number of beans he seemed prepared to spill would have bankrupted Heinz. 'She never even realised she was being robbed, dim bitch. Well, it wasn't really theft. Alimony in advance was how I liked to think of it.'

'You must have loved her once,' I pointed out.

'I suppose there was a time when I didn't dislike her,' he said. 'I don't think I knew what love was until I met . . .' He broke off suddenly and blushed. 'Anyway, we're supposed to be talking about the interviews,' he said quickly.

'Yes,' I agreed. I couldn't have cared less about his latest girlfriend, not unless she was in a position to employ Sebastian.

'Well, I don't know what I can tell you.' He shrugged casually, making no attempt to hide how little my predicament mattered to him. 'We'd almost decided to give it to Sebastian on the Wednesday, as I said. Then Professor Fielding ended the meeting suddenly, didn't explain why. None of the rest of us knew what was going on. The next day, for no apparent reason, the Prof and Val Williams were supporting Terri. Well, Val had been all along, but the Prof was agreeing with her. I asked why she'd changed her mind, but she kept avoiding the issue. Val knew what was going on, I could tell, but me and Emily hadn't got a clue. Emily was getting hysterical about giving it to Rod – poetry man – and by that stage I didn't give a shit any more because . . .' He stopped, as if he had changed his mind about whatever he had planned to say next. 'Well, I didn't care, I'd had enough. I abstained, in fact, and Emily was outvoted two to one, so Terri came first and Firsden came second.'

'But . . .' So many questions were competing for priority in my mind that I was at a loss for words. 'Did you support Sebastian originally?' I asked.

'Well . . .' Damian turned to face the window.

'You didn't, then.'

'No, to be honest, I didn't, but he was my second choice. I would have been quite happy to see him appointed, I like the guy a lot. Anyway, he didn't need me – Daphne was rampantly supporting him. At Wednesday's meeting, that is. All four legs of her professorial chair were pointing in his direction.'

'I thought you said she wasn't paying attention.' I was getting confused.

'She tuned in and out,' said Damian. 'During her brief spells on the planet, Sebastian was her number one man. She'd worn us all down by arguing so convincingly in his favour. That was where we were at when she adjourned the meeting. Then on Thursday, yesterday, no explanation but she's supporting Terri all of a sudden. Which is fucking weird because those two loathe each other. On Wednesday, the Prof said Terri's research was "empty and lacking in direction". Those were her very words. And that Terri was "a woman of dubious character". So God knows what happened. Terri's references were a bit suspect too. Sebastian's were infinitely superior. One of his referees said he was – what was it? – a truly great . . . a truly great . . . oh, something or other.' This rather unsatisfactory conclusion to Damian's statement was lost in the noise the door made as it swung open behind me. I turned and saw a tall, thin woman with light brown braided hair and a set of keys in her hand. One look at me drove the smile from her face and a pinched, anxious expression took its place.

'Hello.' She looked me straight in the eye. 'I'm Bryony. Are you Martine?'

'No,' I said. 'Bryony? As in the De La Wyche candidate who dropped out?'

'Yes,' she said, looking at Damian uncertainly.

'Oh, shit,' he groaned, covering his face with his hands.

Chapter Sixteen

Damian Selinger – Curriculum Vitae

Name
Dr Damian Selinger.

Address
G12 Queen's Court, Summerton College, Cambridge.

Age
Thirty-three.

Place of Birth
Barnstaple, Devon.

Nationality
British.

Marital Status
Married Martine Selinger (née Odams) on 11 March 1988. As a teenager, Damian was extremely unattractive and no pretty girl would go near him. Securing one became the pinnacle of his ambition and when he became a Summerton fellow, when his status finally outweighed his peanut features, he married the incredibly pretty Martine, not because he loved her, but just to prove he could. Union noteworthy on two counts:

1 sudden, inexplicable disappearance of wife in March

1997, at the same time as equally sudden and inexplicable disappearance of the then De La Wyche fellow, Fernando Rose and indeed the portrait of De La Wyche himself, and

2   commonly agreed to be most warped and destructive conjugal situation ever observed by its observers, of whom there were many, owing to this couple's inclination to try to kill each other in public.

Marriage also remarkable in that it was even worse – time to stretch those conceptual categories to breaking point, folks – than the Fielding-Skinner farce, as the latter only involves appalling behaviour on the part of one party. It has at least fifty per cent of the necessary ingredients for a good marriage, those brought home in the shopping bag of Joe Fielding. On the other hand, maybe appalling behaviour from both spouses is preferable, because then at least no innocent party is made to suffer. Peaks of Selinger wedded bliss include: the time when Damian asked Martine's parents to buy him a cricket bat for Christmas, then bashed his wife over the head with her parents' gift on New Year's Eve, causing severe concussion. Martine retaliated with the time when she stayed out all night, then got her friend to phone Damian in the morning pretending to be a police officer bringing sad tidings of her death. This ruse backfired horribly; Damian was thrilled to discover Martine was dead. The unwelcome news that she was still alive inspired him to further 'times when', too numerous to list here.

Employment History
1996–PRESENT
Fellow of Summerton College, Cambridge. Teaches moral philosophy and political and moral theory to undergraduates and graduates, as well as pursuing own research in those areas. Much prefers research to teaching, and, in fact, has come to resent the intrusion of students upon his

time to such a great extent that he has taken to adopting the following tactics:

1   hiding behind locked door when students arrive for supervisions until they conclude he isn't there and go away;

2   when in a bolder mood, simply shouting 'Go away!' in the faces of students, often reducing them to tears,

3   cutting down hours wasted on double-marking of exam scripts by opening first marker's envelope and allocating random marks, which never differ by more than two or three per cent from those of the first marker, without reading the scripts. This is a particularly effective time-saving device. And finally

4   avoiding all graduate students: never phoning them to enquire about how their PhDs are going, never reading their work, never meeting them to discuss work, responding to chapters submitted in draft form by simply returning them with not a single comment written on them, except for own publications added to bibliography. The beauty of this tactic is that it allows one to take on loads of PhD students – after all, does it matter how many you have in theory if in practice you help none of them? – and then ask to be given fewer administrative duties on account of excessive number of supervisees.

Qualifications and Education

D.Phil, 'Ethics and the Human Animal', from St John's College, Oxford. BA Hons Philosophy, Politics and Economics (IIii) from St Johns College, Oxford. Three A levels and eight O levels from the Grange Grammar School in Exeter, where in spare time was school bully. This phase was the origin of his interest in moral philosophy. Once avoided expulsion for persecution of younger pupils by inventing the Cause–Effect Proposition. This was the theory, put seriously to a puce and trembling-jawed

118

headmaster, that the layperson's understanding of the cause–effect relationship is oversimplified and that, philosophically, we cannot prove that effect doesn't cause cause as much as cause causes effect. Damian argued that his actions (punching, pummelling and toilet-dunking) were, in part, caused by the so-called effects experienced by others (being punched, pummelled and having one's head rammed into a lavatory). His theory was that if Jeremy Pulford from form 3B had not had his school blazer set alight, then he, Damian, would not have set fire to Pulford's blazer. This claim was apparently just as valid as the claim that if Damian hadn't applied a naked flame to Jeremy's uniform, it would not have ignited and burned the poor boy almost to a crisp. The two boys were therefore equally responsible for the incident, according to Damian, although not by any means equally burned. The head-master, enraged but confused by the Cause–Effect Proposition, issued a suspension rather than an expulsion and signed-up for night classes in philosophy. It was then that Damian decided moral philosophy was his vocation, since it was the only field he could think of where you could (a) build a successful career on theories that were staggeringly moronic and (b) justify your own more unpleasant personal characteristics with these nonsenses, once formulated.

Publications
Me, Me, Me: Embracing Selfishness (Scholars Press, Cambridge and New York, June 1998). This work aims to demonstrate, using theory and case studies, that everybody is selfish, even those who appear not to be, and that by demonising selfishness we are creating an unhealthy society. *Long Pig: Ethics and the Human Animal* (Castle Press, London 1997). Adaptation of D.Phil thesis. The book's central tenet is that humans are no more capable of morality than animals and therefore should not be held ethically accountable for their actions. The author

119

confused a conclusion (correct) based on own behaviour with a workable theory (incorrect) for the whole of the human race. In other words, just because Damian has the integrity of a centipede, it doesn't give him the right to generalise. His editor at Castle Press should have told him to speak (or bleat, or bark) for himself. How could anyone have let such bobbins get into print? The fact that I will not shortly be sued by an angry centipede collective proves, surely, that humans and animals are vastly different.

Physical Appearance

Wears same beigeyfawnycaramelly clothes every day, has extremely short body and shoulder-length blond hair. Used also to wear an ugly scowl every day but has recently fallen in love – with one of the De La Wyche candidates, would you believe it? – and taken to grinning maniacally, so now looks like Little Lord Fauntleroy after a magic-mushroom binge.

Strengths and Weaknesses

Ability to fall in love has to be applauded, especially in someone who was previously so hostile and emotionally wizened. It may turn him into a better person in the long run; in fact, promising signs can be seen already. Bryony James has no cricket-bat-shaped dents in her skull. Not yet, anyway. To list all his weaknesses would use up too much paper, so much, in fact, that even the most conservative estimate would be certain to contain the phrase 'tree genocide'.

Chapter Seventeen

De La Wyche Drop-out

It's always a good idea to seize control of a situation straight away, otherwise you can find yourself permanently on the back foot. I tell my more hesitant learners this all the time, the ones who like to dither behind parked buses while forty or fifty passengers shuffle on and off.

What I should have done, immediately, was demand an explanation for the fact that the De La Wyche drop-out had a key to Damian's set and follow up the demand with a few searching questions: how long had they known each other? Were they sleeping together at the time of the interview? What with Daphne Fielding being Terri Skinner's mother-in-law and Bryony James turning out to be the new love of Damian's life, I was beginning to get a seriously inbred feeling. Did Sebastian represent the lone stranger in town? That would be an irony, I thought, since, on paper at least, he was the only internal candidate, the only one who had done his PhD at Summerton. Next I would find out that Rod Firsden and Valerie Williams were once Siamese twins, until she severed their connection with a sharpened Strepsil.

Before I had a chance to adjust to this new development and react accordingly, Bryony hogged the limelight by collapsing at the foot of the sofa and burying her head in Damian's short, bony shins. 'Oh, for a terrible moment I thought you were Martine,' she whispered into his toffee-coloured trousers. 'I thought you'd come to take him away from me.' Her accent sounded faintly Liverpudlian.

'Don't be stupid.' Damian smacked the back of her neck affectionately. 'If Martine came back I'd spit in her face.'

'You say that now, but you don't know how you might feel.' Bryony looked up at him for further reassurance. It reminded me of the way disciples look at Jesus in old religious paintings. Perhaps Bryony had cataracts in both eyes, I thought, since to me it was inconceivable that such a radiant gaze should be directed at an egregious beige runt like Damian Selinger.

'Yes, I do,' he said. 'I love you, not her.'

I coughed to draw attention to my presence, and Bryony turned round and smiled at me. 'I'm so sorry,' she said. 'It's just that . . . well, we've only just got together and you know how insecure you are at the beginning of a relationship.'

'How long has this been going on?' I asked brusquely, furious that they were so preoccupied with their alleged love that they didn't even attempt to volunteer an excuse for this highly questionable situation. 'Did the rest of the panel know that you were involved with her?' I barked at Damian.

'No.' He sighed.

'Damian, what's going on?' Bryony clung to his shins.

'This is Kate Nunn, the wife of one of the unsuccessful candidates.'

'Oh.' Bryony's voice dropped an octave and she stared at me with big round eyes. She was reasonably attractive but a bit frayed at the edges. She looked as though she'd spent a lot of time getting blown around on clifftops, but not in a healthy, wholesome way. Her hair was coming out of its braid, falling in wisps all around her face, and her eyes and skin looked weather-beaten and diluted. She was wearing a long black skirt with tassels at the bottom and a black tunic top. 'I'm terribly sorry,' she whispered to me, as if spies were all around. 'I know how awful it can be.'

'I doubt you do, if you can afford to drop out of the competition on a whim. Why did you, by the way?'

'You don't have to tell her,' Damian chipped in, in a valiant attempt to protect his feeble woman. He could be quite chivalrous when he wasn't hitting people over the head with cricket bats. 'Listen, there's nothing corrupt about this, if that's what you're thinking,' he said to me. 'Bryony dropped out so . . . there's nothing wrong with us being together.'

'So I can tell the other panel members, can I? The Master?'

'Well . . . I'd rather you didn't.' Damian dusted down his old scowl and tried it on again, briefly, for size. 'Although the Prof wouldn't have room to talk, as Terri Skinner's mother-in-law. But she'd claim this is different because she doesn't like Terri, whereas I more than like Bryony.' He stroked her face as he said this.

'I'm so sorry for you and your husband,' said Bryony. 'I wish there was something I could do to help.' I tried not to be moved by her reaction. Of all the people to whom I'd mentioned Sebastian's predicament, she was the first and only one not to churn out the customary consolations.

'Help?' Damian gave her a puzzled look, as if she might have to explain that one to him later on.

'There is,' I said. 'You can tell me why you dropped out. Was it because of you and Damian, because you knew it would look dodgy if you got it?' Bryony bit her lip and looked away, as if my question had made her uncomfortable.

'Yes,' said Damian quickly.

'Damian . . .' She yanked at his toffee trouser-leg. 'It wasn't.'

'Shut up!' he hissed at her.

'What's going on?' I demanded. I would have to have an in-depth session with my notebook very shortly, I decided. I was being bombarded with so many peculiar, jarring incidents that if I didn't write them down I might forget some of them.

'Damian doesn't want me to tell you something,' said

Bryony. 'Although I can't think why not.'

'Because it's none of her business,' he snapped.

'But Damian, she's just like me. She'd understand.'

'In what way am I just like you?' I asked. As hard as I was trying to loathe Bryony, I found that I couldn't. Genuine concern is easily recognisable, particularly after you've spent time around the likes of Damian Selinger and Valerie Williams. I believed Bryony would have helped me if she could.

'I'd better not say, if Damian doesn't think I should,' she said regretfully. It's lucky Terri Skinflick isn't around to hear this, I thought. She would see a comment like that as grounds for execution.

'So you didn't drop out for ethical reasons, because of your relationship with Damian,' I concluded aloud.

'No,' said Bryony. 'Look, I really can't say any more, but . . . it's nothing to do with the De La Wyche fellowship or your husband. I dropped out for . . . a personal reason.'

'Can't you bugger off now?' Damian grinned. This was him in love, then. He was still obscene, only now he swore more cheerfully.

I stood fixed to the spot. I would leave when I was good and ready, not before. 'How long have you two been . . . seeing each other?' I asked.

'Since Saturday,' said Bryony, stroking Damian's kneecap.

'What? Less than a week?'

'Bry, do you have to keep blabbing all our personal stuff?' Damian whined.

'Where did you meet?' I demanded.

'In the Mitre Tavern, a pub on . . .' Bryony began.

'I know the Mitre,' I said. 'What were you doing in Cambridge four days before your interview, if you didn't already know Damian?'

'Look, I really can't . . .' She sighed. 'Oh, God, I really wish I could help you. Maybe . . .' She turned to look at Damian, who simply shook his head. 'I'm sorry,' she said.

124

'Really, I am, but I can't tell you anything else.'

'Why not?' I asked. 'I can tell you want to. Do you just do what he says automatically?'

'Oh, don't start with that bra-burning lesbian shit,' Damian sneered.

'Damian, don't!' Bryony scolded him mildly, perhaps to demonstrate to me that she could be relied upon for an uprising if necessary. I wasn't impressed.

'Where are you from, anyway?' I asked her. 'What's your research on? Have you got another job?'

'No, I haven't. I've just finished a PhD at Edge Hill University College in Lancashire. On the Cultural Theory of Antarctica.' She smiled. 'I'm from St Helens. But Damian and I are getting a place together . . .'

'Why don't you just tell her how often we fuck and have done with it?' Damian said sarcastically, sending Bryony into peals of laughter.

'You're so witty.' She patted his elbow, then turned back to me. 'I'm truly, truly sorry,' she said. 'I can sense that you're in pain.' Bryony stretched out her hand towards me. I wasn't sure what I was expected to do with it. Damian picked his nose, oblivious, and flicked its contents across the room with his thumb and forefinger.

I concluded that their compatibility stemmed from the fact that they were both barking mad. Feeling suddenly threatened by their compound unsavouriness, I mumbled an excuse and left, running down the grey stone steps of the tower like a person who knows there is a chopping block looming at the top.

Chapter Eighteen

It's All Gone Pear-shaped

I ran back to the Micra in Old Court and switched on my mobile phone, hoping that a normal, well-adjusted person might have left me a message. Even the half-electronic, half-human voice of my Callback service would be reassuring after Bryony's eerie solicitation of my friendship. A little envelope symbol on my phone's screen told me I had one message. I dialled Callback and smiled as I heard Rod's voice tell me that he was at Cambridge station, about to get on a train. He sounded breathily enthusiastic. I could picture him rubbing his beard.

The phone rang as soon as I put it down on the passenger seat. It was Rod again.

'You can't be in Reading already,' I said.

'I'm not. I'm at King's Cross, just about to head for Paddington.'

'Oh. Is there a problem?'

'No, no. I just ... well, I just wanted to tell you something. I don't think it's something I could tell you face to face.'

'Oh.' I crossed the fingers of my free hand, trying to ward off any new trouble. In my experience, when people say they have something to tell you rather than simply telling you, that something usually ends up ruining your day. 'What?'

'Well, it's ... I really like you. That's all. I just wanted you to know. The way you've ... joined in this De La

Wyche business, you've really entered into the spirit . . . no, that sounds wrong, it's not some sort of game, I mean, it's the most important thing in my life!' His voice rose in volume and I had to hold the phone a few inches from my ear. 'What I'm trying to say is, you've taken it all so seriously, even breaking into Terri Skinner's flat, and helping me to . . . take positive action instead of sitting around moping. If it wasn't for you I wouldn't be in Reading now.'

'You aren't in Reading now,' I pointed out. 'You're at King's Cross.'

'Ha! You're so literal.' He laughed. 'Well, I will be in Reading soon enough and it will be thanks to you. No one's ever cared about me this much before.' I opened my mouth to query this statement but he rattled on breathlessly, 'Oh, I'm not saying you care about me in *that* way, I'm not that presumptuous, I just mean you've really . . . got involved and helped me even though this whole mess is nothing to do with you. You're so unselfish.'

'Oh,' I said uncertainly. 'Well, I think you might be overestimating me. I don't think I'm as unselfish as you think I am.' I paused to consider what I'd just said. Was I doing this for me or Sebastian? Perhaps the two couldn't be separated. If he was unhappy, I was unhappy. So for me to devote the next two weeks to trying to get him the Enmity was both selfish and unselfish at the same time, I concluded. One thing was for sure, though: I wasn't doing any of it for Rod Firsden.

'I'd better go now,' he said. 'I just wanted you to know how much I appreciate you.'

'Well . . . it's nothing.' All this praise made me feel distinctly uneasy.

'Can I see you tomorrow? I don't think I could bear to go a day without seeing you.'

'Why?' I asked tactlessly. I needed to assess the damage. Was this just gratitude for my philanthropic Terri-spying or was it something more?

127

'I'm coming on too strongly, aren't I?' Rod's voice trembled. 'Anyway, you have to see me,' he added petulantly. 'You promised me a driving lesson every day.'

'Yes, yes, of course. Ring me when you get back from Reading,' I said wearily. Nice one, Kate, I told myself. Now you've got two emotionally draining men in your life and they're both after the same job. Could things be any more complicated?

'Kate?' said Rod, in the tone Sebastian always used when he asked me to promise I'd never make him work in a bun shop. 'Is this mad, I mean, going to Reading? What if Gary Conley's got nothing to do with anything? What if I can't find him? And what am I going to say to him? It'll sound absurd.'

'Okay, then, forget it,' I said. 'Come back to Cambridge.' I often used this psychological tactic on Sebastian.

'No! Of course I can't do that, I can't just give up! I've got to try, haven't I?'

'Well, go on then, go, before you miss any more trains.'

'Okay. I'll ring you as soon as I'm back. 'Bye. 'Bye. 'Bye, 'bye. 'Bye.' His 'byes' got progressively shorter and quieter. After the fifth one, I pressed the red button and put an end to the call, just in case he intended to go on into the night.

I looked at my watch. It was two o'clock. I could easily fit in some more snooping before I had to go home and get ready for this evening's feast. I shuddered as I thought about it. How would Sebastian cope with seeing all those happy, successful fellows the day after he'd been rejected by the college? I would have to bolster up his ego by promising the Enmity would be in the bag in a matter of days and I would have to say it with conviction.

I got out of the car and asked the nearest porter – who was quite impressively near, as porters seem always to be at Summerton – where Emily Lole's rooms were.

'Tyndsall Court. K9,' said the porter, who was neither of the hat-tippers. Bit of a dog, then, is she? I restrained myself from asking. Not everyone would be able to identify with my desire to inflict pain and nastiness of varying degrees of severity on the De La Wyche panel members. 'Are you family?' the porter asked. He was a short, barrel-chested man with a heavy Glaswegian accent.

'No.'

'Friend?'

'No. I just ... want to ask her something.' I smiled benignly.

'Well, you know she's ill?' His brow knotted with concern, as if he was afraid my visit might cause her health to deteriorate. I hoped it would.

'No, I didn't,' I said. 'I mean, I know she's had a few problems since Fernando Rose disappeared, but . . .'

'Oh, yes, of course, there's that,' said the porter, as if it was old news. 'But she's been seriously ill since lunchtime. She collapsed in Great Hall.' Lucky cow, I thought. Why should she get to collapse in Great Hall when poor Sebastian would have to settle, if he were ill, for conking out on the steps of a bun shop? No he wouldn't, I resolved. There was to be no bun shop ignominy for him; I wouldn't rest until he had the Enmity. As I made this resolution, I feared I might be kidding myself; defiant vows were all very well, but I still lacked a workable plan. The twin hurdles of Terri Skinner and Rod Firsden were yet to be surmounted.

'What sort of seriously ill?' I asked.

'I'm not sure, I only heard it from Dr Williams. But I don't think she's in a fit state to receive visitors.'

'Well, I won't stay long.' I grinned merrily and walked away before he had a chance to detain me further. The K wing of Tyndsall Court was in the top right-hand corner, just next to the door to Great Hall. Conveniently positioned for those who chose to lose consciousness during banquets, I thought bitterly. I climbed up the stairs to K9, singing 'Apartment Number Nine' by the late and, in my view, great Tammy Wynette. The maudlin lyrics applied quite well to the Emily Lole–Fernando Rose situation.

I knocked loudly on Emily's door, making sure to create enough noise to rouse her from whatever comatose state she might be in. Remembering what Valerie Williams had told me about Emily's antidepressants and eczema, what Damian had said about her hysteria and the porter's news of her recent collapse, I prepared to be greeted by a scabby, frail waif with a deathbed aura. Instead, the door was yanked open by a big, hefty woman with blond curly hair who looked as if she could be captain of the college hockey team. There was something very familiar about her, but I couldn't work out what it was.

'Are you Emily Lole?' I asked doubtfully.

'Yes.' She looked at me with dull eyes and didn't ask who I was. We stared at each other for a while.

'I'm Kate Nunn,' I said. 'Sebastian Nunn's wife.'

'Yes,' she said again. Either she was exceptionally dense or some kind of mood-controlling drugs were pumping their way round her buxom body. I thought the latter was more likely.

'I heard you were ill,' I said. 'Are you well enough to talk to me for a few minutes?'

'Yes. Dr Williams gave me some pills,' she mumbled slowly, blinking at me. 'I suppose you can come in.' I followed her into her set, which was almost pitch-black because all the curtains were drawn. Emily made no move to open them or switch on any lights. Her rooms were less attractive than Damian's, from what I could see of them: a narrow hall led through to a tiny L-shaped kitchen and a cramped, low-ceilinged lounge sprouted unnaturally from the bottom bar of the 'L'.

I followed Emily's slow progress through to the lounge, wondering whether she'd ever been on television. I was sure I'd seen her somewhere and yet I knew we'd never met before. 'Sit down,' she druggily drawled. Whatever Valerie Williams had given her must have been pretty powerful stuff. Perhaps if I'd asked the college doctor one more tricky question this morning I too would have been sedated.

I sat on the sofa and Emily sank heavily into an armchair opposite. There were a lot of framed photographs in her lounge, although not as many as in Joe and Terri's flat. I glanced at the two on the table by my end of the sofa. They were both of a young man with white-blond hair and a nose and chin that curved towards each other, a bit like a cartoon profile of the moon. He was oddly attractive, in an ugly sort of way. 'Would you mind opening the curtains?' I asked Emily, hoping to get a better look at the pictures.

'I don't like the light,' she said.

'That's silly, light's good for you,' I told her. 'You don't want the sun never to shine on apartment number nine.'

'What?' She blinked at me.

'You know, like the Tammy Wynette song.'

'Who?'

'Tammy Wynette. You know, the singer? The Queen of Country?' Emily shook her head. 'Never mind,' I said. 'Look, please open the curtains a bit. I can't see a thing.'

She sighed and lumbered over to the window. I thought her definition of 'a bit' erred on the side of not at all, but she did allow a small shaft of light to enter the room and it was enough to illuminate the photographs. They were all of the same man, Mr Moon Profile. Whoever he was – and I was pretty sure I knew – he was clearly as important to Emily Lole as Terri Skinner was to Terri Skinner.

'Is that Fernando?' I indicated the picture nearest to me.

A jolt of life flooded into Emily's eyes, as if she'd suddenly been given an electric shock. 'Do you know him?' she asked me quickly, abandoning her slow drawl.

'No, I . . . I've only heard of him,' I said. 'I know he disappeared and that you were his girlfriend.'

'He didn't leave me, you know. He didn't leave me by choice.'

'Urm . . . could I please have a glass of water?' I asked, hearing my voice crack in my parched throat. Neither Valerie Williams nor Damian, I realised, had offered me a drink and now Emily had also failed in her duties as a host.

Damian could always blame it on his 'embracing selfishness' research and Emily on her assorted plagues, but what was Valerie's excuse? I was forgiving none of them; Sebastian would never forget to offer a guest some refreshment. All these people's fellowships should be confiscated and given to him, I decided. And Rod could have one as well – a minor one, I thought magnanimously.

'Help yourself.' Emily nodded towards the kitchen. 'I shouldn't move too much. I've been ill. I keep haemorrhaging.'

'Oh dear,' I said over my shoulder as I escaped to the kitchen. That was a bit more detail than I needed. 'What's wrong with you?'

'My body's collapsing,' she said. 'It started when Fernando left. It's only a matter of time.'

I filled a glass with water, noticing that there were three more photographs of Fernando Rose in the kitchen. I felt a tremor of desire pass through me and recognised it as an instance of my weakness for employed men, except that in this case it was even more powerful because Fernando had not had just any old job – he had been the De La Wyche fellow, he had the job of all our dreams. Compared with him, even Zac Hunt, Master Manager of Kwikfit, paled into insignificance.

I went back to the lounge with my glass of water. Emily had been crying in my absence and as I appeared she grabbed the edge of a curtain and wiped her eyes and nose with it. 'Sorry,' she said. 'Run out of tissues. I thought . . . when you mentioned Fernando, I thought you might have had some news.'

'No. Sorry. I'm actually here to talk about my husband's interview,' I told her.

'When will I find him again?' Emily whispered, completely ignoring my explanation.

'Do you think there's any chance he ran off with Martine Selinger?' I asked. If I'd realised how perilous a question it was I would never have asked. Emily began to cry.

'I wasn't saying he did,' I amended hastily. 'I was just asking.'

'Everyone "just asks" that.' She sobbed bitterly. 'As if I'm not miserable enough already. Of course he didn't run off with her, he loved me. Me!' Emily grabbed the curtain and folded it around her head. It was the same one she'd used as a hanky. She looked like someone in a Magritte painting: a torso topped by a fabric-wrapped face.

'I'm sorry,' I said. 'I didn't mean to upset you. I just want to ask you a few questions about Sebastian's interview.'

'Sebastian?' Her muffled voice emerged from behind the curtain. She sounded as if she'd never heard of him. This wasn't feigned amnesia, Valerie Williams style; this was the all-consuming self-obsession of a deeply miserable person. If it didn't involve Fernando Rose, there was no room for it in Emily's head. It was the same with me and Sebastian's job situation, the same with Rod and the De La Wyche Enmity.

'Why were you so strongly in favour of Rod Firsden?' I asked, trying a different approach. Damian had implied that her support of him had verged on hysteria. 'Is it because his subject is poetry, like Fernando?'

Just as I was congratulating myself on my perceptiveness and comparing Emily with James Stewart in *Vertigo*, who wants to spend time with Judy purely because she reminds him of Madeleine, the woman he loved and lost, Emily made a strange wheezing sound and pulled the curtain away from her face, clutching it like a turban round her head. She stared at me in horror. 'You know where Fernando is, don't you?' she said slowly, as if this terrible, wonderful realisation had only just dawned on her. 'You know, don't you? Please, you've got to tell me.' She shuffled closer to me in her chair. I ignored her, trying to work out where I had seen her before and sensing that I was getting closer. When she'd pulled the curtain round her hair like a headscarf, she'd reminded me of a Plymouth Breth, or whatever the singular form of brethren is, and I felt a jolt of recognition, a flash of subliminal insight that went almost as soon as it came. I trawled my memory for religious associations, wondering whether Emily could have been one of a religious group that had turned up on my doorstep at some point. I doubted it. I got the impression that Fernando Rose was the only deity in her life.

What on earth could have given her the idea that I knew where he was? She'd made me feel almost guilty. I subjected myself to stringent internal questioning on the subject, to confirm that I genuinely had no idea of Fernando's whereabouts.

Emily's head dropped low suddenly, as if her neck could no longer bear its weight. I knew where I'd seen her before: on Sterling Road. She was the hooded pear-shaped woman with the sagging head that Rod had nearly driven into. She had been crying then as well, so much that she didn't notice her narrow escape from vehicular annihilation.

The solution of this small mystery didn't put my mind at rest in the way that I'd expected it to. On the contrary, I felt an odd chill as I conjured up my first image of Emily Lole, how pale and ghostlike she'd looked. Another coincidental connection, this time of Sterling Road to Summerton. The edges of my world were curling inwards, like Fernando Rose's nose and chin, to shut out the light and air. It's just because Cambridge is so little, I thought, trying to comfort myself, but it didn't work.

Chapter Nineteen

Emily Lole – Curriculum Vitae

Name
Dr Emily Lole.

Address
K9 Tyndsall Court, Summerton College, Cambridge.

Age
Twenty-nine.

Place of Birth
Ilkley, Yorkshire.

Marital Status
Single although, according to Damian at his most evil, has spent much of her life forecasting marriages that never happened. Everyone at Summerton thought she was going to marry Fernando Rose, including her, but then he went missing. Everyone at Cambridge's Trinity College, where she did her undergraduate and post-graduate degrees, had thought she was going to marry a Mr Robert Stock, including her, and although Mr Stock did not disappear, his intention to marry Emily certainly did. Everyone at St Joseph's High School in Ilkley thought she was going to marry Billy Metcalfe, including her, until his parents, Dr and Dr Metcalfe, got wind of this plan, panicked and sent Billy off backpacking around the world instead. The Drs

Metcalfe were an academic couple who thought that for their son to marry so young would have been embarrassingly 'C2' and conventional, and how would they have justified it to their friends, whose children were all protesting against the building of motorways or being arrested for drug-smuggling?

Employment History
1995–PRESENT
Fellow of Summerton College, Cambridge. Researches the various facets of microscopic worms. Teaches Natural Sciences, supposedly for fifteen hours every week, but in fact this target has not been achieved for a long time, owing to ill health. Usually manages to teach for four or five hours each week before passing out, haemorrhaging, bruising internally, bruising externally, inflaming, itching, swelling or choking. Natsci colleagues (Natural Sciences, not National Socialist) were at first sympathetic but are growing increasingly intolerant of the aforementioned health problems and the extra work these create. A few people have dropped hints that, as more than a year has elapsed since Fernando disappeared, Dr Lole ought to be pulling herself together by now, which just goes to show that psychological sophistication counts for nothing when there is a surfeit of exam scripts to be marked.

Qualifications and Education
1989–1995
PhD (with distinction) on microscopic worms and BSc Zoology (first) from Trinity College, Cambridge. Ability to monitor the minutest movements of microscopic worms must have made mislaying of large research fellow all the more painful, in an ironic sort of way. Four grade 'A' A levels from St Joseph's High School in Ilkley: Maths, Biology, Chemistry, Physics. Eight grade 'A' O levels: Maths, English Literature, English Language, Biology, Chemistry, Physics, Home Economics, Art.

Publications
Several articles on microscopic worms published in scientific journals, some single author, some co-written with members of research group, on which occasions poor worms must have felt seriously outnumbered. Either that or part of a big family.

Strengths and Weaknesses
Has been strong when there has been a prospective husband on the scene and weak otherwise.

Physical Appearance
Heavy and bulky. Pear-shaped (so has her life gone. Perhaps if Fernando came back and married her, her body shape would change to that of a less metaphorically doom-laden fruit). Blonde curly hair in a bob. Appears healthy and strapping until you hear her speak. Then comes across as sluggishly delirious.

Other Information
Thinks I know where Fernando Rose is. Why? Rod Firsden nearly ran her over in my car – was that God giving me a great opportunity for revenge on a De La Wyche panel member that I missed? Had I used my dual-control brake to go against destiny? Driving instructors can't afford to be fatalistic, particularly when what is meant to be includes the constant bashing of their cars into hard, unyielding surfaces by incompetent pupils. Hobbies include crying, being bedridden, suffering, sitting in darkened rooms, indulging insane impulses, wiping nose on curtains. Revolting. Sebastian would never do that.

Chapter Twenty

Marlene on the Wall

I couldn't get anything else out of Emily Lole, at least nothing that made any sense, so I cut my losses and left, stepping over her on my way out. Fernando Rose's disappearance no longer seemed quite so mysterious. Having met Emily, I could well imagine why he might have been keen to prolong his bachelorhood. Perhaps she'd hoped Rod Firsden would step into Fernando's shoes and become her next almost-husband. I had the satisfied sensation of something clicking logically into place. What with Terri Skinner and Bryony James both being women and Sebastian being married, Rod was the only one of the four into whom Emily could have dug her amorous claws. The old me, the one that used to exist before Sebastian started applying for jobs, would have argued that there was no way an interviewer from a respected institution like Summerton would support a particular candidate simply because she fancied him. Now I know that interviewers are capable of anything. I'm not just making slanderous accusations here; I can prove it. At Sebastian's interview for a job at the University of the South Downs in Brighton, he had been asked what three books he would recommend to a politics undergraduate. He said he didn't know what the three best political books were. It was too serious a question to answer so quickly. Over a subsequent sandwich lunch, Sebastian happened to ask another candidate, a woman called Dominique who had no publications and had not yet completed her PhD, whether she had been asked the same question. She had and she had named three books straight away, each one by a member of the interview panel. 'Actually, all three are shite, but I thought it might get me the job,' she confided cheerfully to Sebastian and she was clearly a bright girl because it did indeed get her the job. Shakespeare must have turned in his grave. 'I write *King Lear*,' he must have thought, 'and no one takes the blindest bit of notice.'

I went back to the car, got out my notebook and pen, and redrafted my list of things I considered to be peculiar or in need of explanation. There were numerous additions to be made and it took me about ten minutes in total. When I'd finished it looked liked this:

Weird Things surrounding the Enmity
1   Fernando Rose's disappearance
2   Martine Selinger's disappearance
3   Grimshaw De La Wyche portrait's disappearance
4   Why did Prof Fielding seem distracted and keep looking at her watch during Wednesday's meeting?
5   Why did Prof Fielding end meeting on Wednesday and delay decision until Thursday?
6   Why did Prof support Sebastian on Wednesday, but Terri on Thursday?
7   What did Prof and Val know (according to Damian) on Thursday that they wouldn't tell Damian and Emily?
8   Why are there no photos of Joe or Scarlett, only Terri, in flat 3, Noble House?
9   Why does the sign say 'Terri's room' – isn't it Terri and Joe's?
10   Why does Terri have names in her dresses, including those of Keithanethan, Summerton fellows?
11   Who is Gary Conley, who is R English and what bearing do they have on Terri's Reading/ Summerton choice?

12 What was Terri crying about while I was in her wardrobe?

13 What was Valerie Williams lying about and why did she pretend to have forgotten everything about the Enmity?

14 Why didn't Emily know anything about Fernando's relatives, even though she was virtually engaged to him?

15 Why did Bryony James drop out of the Enmity competition?

16 What was Bryony James doing in Cambridge on Saturday, when the interviews were on Tuesday, if she wasn't already involved with Damian?

17 What is it that Damian won't let Bryony tell me and why?

18 Why did Emily seem so convinced I knew where Fernando Rose was?

19 Why is everybody and everything so totally abnormal?

I thought I'd pretty much covered everything, but instead of making me feel as though I had things a bit more under control, my list had the opposite effect. I stared defeatedly at the plethora of questions I would probably never be able to answer, feeling as if I hadn't made any progress at all. All I was doing, it seemed, was getting drawn deeper and deeper into the den of freakishness that was Summerton College. Meanwhile Rod was probably having experiences in Reading as pointless as the ones I was having in Cambridge and none of it was getting us anywhere near an Enmity for Sebastian.

And tonight was the dreaded feast. I closed my eyes and was about to devote the next few minutes to indulging my self-pity when I heard the sound of raised female voices. I wound down the car window and tried to locate the source of the din. This proved to be no great challenge: there was an open window on the other side of Old Court, beside the big arch that led to Summerton Lane. I realised I would have to pass the room in question on my way out, so I decided to do so in a leisurely manner. If I was lucky I might get to hear a scandalous student brawl that would distract me from my problems for a few seconds.

I turned the key in the ignition and allowed the Micra to creep around Old Court. As I approached the open window I saw something that made me forget altogether about leaving. I stopped the car, put on Suspicion the handbrake and switched off the engine. From my present position I had a clear view of one whole wall of the room and most of it was occupied by a large black-and-white poster of Marlene Dietrich. I recognised it instantly as a still from the film *Witness for the Prosecution*. It could have been a coincidence, but I didn't think it was.

Apart from the poster I could see an old-fashioned wooden writing desk with a chair behind it, a mirror and a bookcase. 'If you weren't happy you shouldn't have agreed to it,' said a loud, lisping voice whose owner was clearly angry. 'I don't appreciate you coming and landing this on me now. I thought it had all been sorted out.'

'So did I, until this morning,' said a deep female voice. My eyes widened; it was Valerie Williams. 'I've done nothing wrong, Daphne. I'm not going to wait around for some . . . driving instructor to start throwing accusations.' My brain jolted as I jumped to the conclusion that I was the subject of discussion. How many other driving instructors could Valerie have spoken to today?

'Look, we've been over this,' the lisping voice boomed. 'I know you haven't done anything wrong, quite the contrary. You righted a wrong. It's all dealt with now, so let's just forget about it. For God's sake, Valerie, I haven't got time to keep going over this. My life is hell at the moment, what with exam marking and the new punts to be launched.' I shook my head in disbelief, wishing I could ram a punt up her professorial posterior. Hell, indeed. She didn't know the meaning of the word.

141

I heard footsteps as somebody crossed the room and suddenly I could see Daphne Fielding clearly, framed by her office window. She had the same features as Joe and was also blonde with a ruddy complexion. She was considerably less attractive than her son, though. Her teeth protruded slightly and both her ears poked out through the curtain of her hair, like Shelley Duvall's do in *The Shining*. I guessed that Daphne was in her late fifties. She was wearing a greeny brown tweed jacket and brown slacks.

'I don't like dishonesty,' said Valerie intransigently, unmoved by the hell Daphne claimed to be going through. 'It's always better to have things out in the open. How many more people are going to turn up asking questions?'

'Oh, great! Well, thank you very much,' said Daphne Fielding sarcastically. 'You mean you want to tell tales on me!'

'No, but I don't see why I should lie . . .'

A loud beep behind me drowned out the rest of Valerie's sentence. I turned round and saw a large black Mercedes with an angry driver. I was blocking his exit. There were no parking spaces available on this side of Old Court, so I had no choice but to switch the engine back on and head for Summerton Lane. I sighed as I left the college grounds; my eavesdropping had left me feeling dissatisfied. Although it was gratifying to discover that my visit to the college had caused a stir, there was no way of knowing what they were arguing about and I hadn't even been able to root for one or other party in the dispute. I hated both Valerie and the Prof in equal measure, although perhaps the punt-lauching hell comment tipped the scales slightly. It was like watching the Wimbledon final when you've never seen or heard of the finalists before. Even now, I long for the Borg–McEnroe days, when I really cared who won. I always supported McEnroe; while other people condemned his ungentlemanliness, I admired his world view. Who says umpires know best?

I wished I had a bit of his energy and fighting spirit now. I was feeling dangerously inclined to give up after my tiring and confusing day. I decided to head back home, see Sebastian and prepare, both physically and psychologically, for the feast.

I drove out of town, admiring the view as I cruised past the college backs. I always check that my driving pupils know how lucky they are to live in Cambridge. Many of them don't and on those occasions it falls to me to enlighten them. I personally believe Cambridge is the best place on earth. I would have been willing to bet a year's salary that there was nothing as beautiful as Trinity's Wren Library or the King's College Chapel in either Sheffield or Canterbury. I consoled myself with the thought that I wouldn't have to move to either of these places because Sebastian never got the jobs for which he was interviewed.

Another thing I love about Cambridge is the flatness of the land, although I know from my learners' complaints about the county's topographical dullness that I'm in a minority. I've got a theory about the Cambridge boring landscape allegation: I think it's one of those things that someone said once and now everyone feels they have to agree or else they will be flouting convention. People say 'Oh, it's so flat and boring' in the same way that they say they don't like mobile phones and Jimmy Hill; there is no good reason for it, they've just sensed that this is the opinion they're supposed to have on the matter.

I can't understand why a hill is thought to be superior to a field. Is it because it sticks out? Surely this would also mean pot-bellied people were more interesting to look at than those with flat stomachs and no one seems to think that. The thing about hilly or mountainous landscapes is that you often can't see very much sky. I like my sky to start low and then go up and up to the top, wherever that is. The Cambridgeshire landscape is nature's equivalent of an open-plan office, and psychologists have found open-plan offices to be beneficial to employees' morale because everything is visible and, well, open. It gives you a sense of perspective, whereas walls and steep rocky ridges divide things up so that one person can't see what another is doing. It makes me feel calm to look around and be able to see everything for miles into the distance, instead of having my view obstructed by a large heap of rock.

I parked in Noble House's car park beside Joe Fielding's car (which Sebastian calls the Terri-ferry because Joe mainly uses it to ferry her around), wondering what it was doing there at this time. Joe didn't usually get back from work-nursery-school-Sainsbury's until after six. Perhaps he had such vast amounts of domestic skivvying to do today that he'd had to take an afternoon off work in order to manage it all before Terri returned.

I pulled George Herbert's *Collected Poems* out of the glove compartment, picked up my handbag and mobile phone, and headed for Noble House. As I walked up the driveway past the laundry room, I heard whirring and saw steam pouring out of the ventilation shafts at the side of the building. One day, I thought, Joe will fall into the washing or drying machine in his eagerness to purge a wifely bra of accumulated library dust, and he'll spin round and round until steam is all that's left of him. I had said this to Sebastian once and he'd said, 'I'd rather be steam than married to that viper.'

I glanced in through the laundry room window and saw Joe, Scarlett, a man I'd never seen before who was wearing a tennis shirt and shorts and a little boy, probably about Scarlett's age, who was concentrating hard on picking his nose. Joe gestured frantically at me to come in, indicating that he had something to tell me. If he wanted me to testify in his favour at the custody hearing, he only had to ask. The trouble was, I didn't think he ever would.

He hadn't yet been transformed into steam, but pearls of sweat stood out on his brow and upper lip. At his feet was the giant bag he'd been taking to the launderette on the night I sneaked into his flat.

I doubled back, stuck my head round the door and said, 'You're back from work early.'

'The woman who runs Scarlett's nursery was ill, so I had to go and collect her. This is William' – he indicated the bogey-hunter – 'who goes to the same nursery and this is Gordon Fleming, one of my colleagues from Spectrum.' Spectrum was the company for which Joe marketed.

'Pleased to meet you.' Gordon Fleming walked towards me, holding out his hand. I shook it dutifully and tried to contain my excitement. I suffered no Emily Lole-style memory delay this time. I had seen the name Gordon Fleming recently and I knew exactly where: in the pages of my Enmity notebook. His was one of the names that had featured on Terri's dress labels. 'Gordon and Maxine Fleming, 4 February 1997,' I recited to myself.

Joe held up a green sock. 'This is Sebastian's, isn't it?' he asked rhetorically. Most of the residents of Noble House enjoyed a surprising level of intimacy with Sebastian's smalls. He was incapable of bringing all the washing back to the flat, always leaving behind exactly one item, usually a sock or pair of boxer shorts. I felt especially guilty when Joe was the person who rescued the stray garment; too much of his time was taken up with knicker transportation as it was, without Sebastian adding to the problem.

'So, you work with Joe?' I said to Gordon, wondering if there was any way I could ask him, in a subtle and unobtrusive manner, if 4 February 1997 meant anything to him. He was a short plump man with thick dark hair, balding on top, and a beard.

'Yeah, and our kids go to the same nursery,' said Gordon. 'Small world, hey?' Yeah, and his wife has your name sewn into her dress lining. Very small. 'We're just off, actually. Got to get this one home and to bed.' William Fleming continued to pick his nose, oblivious to the plans that were being made on his behalf. I restrained myself from pointing out that if Gordon and Maxine (who I assumed was his wife and a surname-sharing wife at that – some guys have all the luck) forced William to go to bed at such a ridiculously early hour, they would only create problems

145

for him in later life. My parents used to put me to bed early and as a result I now stay up until two every night in case I miss out on something. What with that and anxiety over Sebastian's future, I'm permanently knackered.

'Give my love to Maxine,' Joe said to Gordon and I beamed with satisfaction. This was no coincidence, then. The man who stood before me in tennis garb was undoubtedly he of Gordon and Maxine Fleming fame, and she had to be his wife. I wondered who Tim and Bettina Elworthy were, the other dress-label couple. Was one of them a Spectrum person too? Not necessarily. Neither of Keithanethan was, and they too were immortalised in the Skinner wardrobe.

'He's a great bloke,' Joe said after Gordon and William had left. 'And his wife Maxine's a scream. We'll have to have you and Sebastian over with them one night for dinner.' I made polite noises. 'But Terri's so busy,' he went on. 'I don't know when she'll next be able to spare an evening.'

'Not as busy as you, surely,' I said. 'I thought she wasn't working at the moment?'

'Oh, well, I mean, she hasn't got a job but she's working. In the library, doing her research. Terri, not working!' He laughed. 'What an idea! She works all the hours God sends. I wish she'd take it easy, but ... well, her dad's always undermining her work and it drives her round the bend. I want to be supportive. He's continually mocking the fact that she studies fish. But ... you know, they make her happy.' Joe smiled benignly, as if Terri's well-being were all that mattered to him. She had married the right man for her purposes, that was for sure. Joe Fielding was a saint. He was the saint of the laundry room, so benevolent that he couldn't recognise the evil forces at work in his wife's mind.

'Still,' I said. 'Who'd have thought fishes' teeth would be so ... time-consuming.'

'I just wish she'd slow down a bit,' said Joe. 'We haven't seen any of our friends for ages. I'm sure it'd do her good to take some time off work and have a bit of fun.'

'It'd do you good as well,' I said. He smiled blankly, as though he wasn't quite sure what I meant but didn't want to offend me. I got the impression that he was so unused to thinking about his own well-being that he was slightly baffled when other people did so. 'Has Terri made up her mind yet between Reading and Summerton?'

Joe sighed. 'No. I think she's finding it really tough. Maybe she's worried about leaving Scarlett. Or me,' he said doubtfully. That's interesting, I thought. So if Terri took the Reading job that would mean the end of their family life, such as it was. Joe and Scarlett would not go with her. 'Look, I'm sorry Sebastian didn't get the De La Wyche fellowship,' said Joe. 'I hope you and he don't find it difficult . . . you know, being around Terri.'

'Of course not,' I lied to shut him up. I wanted to continue fishing for information, find out how much Joe knew. 'Most people would choose Summerton,' I said. 'What's in Reading's favour?' If, as Rod Firsden suspected, Terri was having some kind of an affair with this Gary Conley character, she wouldn't be able to tell her husband the real reason she was considering Reading. Or perhaps she would, and he'd continue to fetch and carry for her even with a lover.

Joe shrugged. 'The department's good, apparently.'

'Yes, but Summerton's the . . .'

'Look, we'd better be getting back,' Joe interrupted me. 'Got to get ready for tonight's feast.' Oh, great. So they were going too. That would cheer Sebastian up no end. 'Come on, Scarlett, say goodbye to Kate.' I noticed Joe was blushing, which was unusual, and that he had voluntarily cut our conversation short, which was even more unusual. Deprived as he was of adult company, Joe was normally happy to stand around chatting for the duration of several laundry cycles. Maybe he knew something about Terri's Reading/Summerton dilemma that he didn't want to tell me. I would have to have another go at questioning him at the feast.

''Bye Kate!' Scarlett shrieked up at me.

''Bye,' I said, waving at them as they scuttled out of the laundry room.

I leaned against the drying machine for a while, holding Sebastian's green sock in my hand and thinking. Then I switched off my mobile phone, so that Rod couldn't ring me when I was with Sebastian, and headed for the flat.

Sebastian was in the bath when I got back, and immediately began to interrogate me about what I'd been doing all day and how close I was to getting him the Enmity. I made a few vague but encouraging noises. I felt as if I was on the verge of some momentous discovery or event, but it was impossible to tell whether this feeling had any basis in fact, or whether the event or discovery, if there was to be any such thing, would help Sebastian in the Enmity stakes.

'Kate?' Sebastian called out to me from the bathroom as I poured myself a large whisky. 'Do we have to go to the feast? Everyone'll think I'm an impostor and a failure.'

'Yes, we do, no, they won't and if they did they'd be wrong,' I said automatically. I'd had so much practice at cheering up Sebastian that I could now rattle off reassurances faster than secretaries can touch-type.

'Kate? I don't think I can cope with life,' Sebastian said matter-of-factly. 'I mean, everything's so shit.'

'Sebastian, for God's sake. Stop being such a wimp.'

'A wi ... a wimp?' He sounded outraged. 'I'm the categorical opposite of a wimp,' he said fiercely.

'You are?' I was ready to be convinced.

'Yes. A wimp would meekly accept his fate. I protest vigorously against mine.'

'You mean you moan.'

'It's not moaning,' Sebastian scoffed at my obtuseness. 'It's a political protest. It's civil disobedience.'

I closed my eyes and prayed for a breakthrough. Something had to happen soon.

Chapter Twenty-one

The Feast

As soon as we turned into Old Court we heard the sound of voices, glasses clinking and champagne corks popping. Of all Summerton's annual feasts, the June one was traditionally the most extravagant. I parked the Micra, and Sebastian and I wandered through to Tyndsall Court, where immaculately dressed kitchen staff in black suits and starched white shirts were serving pre-dinner drinks under the cloisters. It was a warm, dry evening, and the air smelled fresh and grassy.

I inhaled deeply, trying not to think about what a happy occasion this would have been for us if Sebastian had got the Enmity. Out of the corner of my eye I could see the expression on Sebastian's face and I knew that he was afflicted by the same thoughts. We smiled bravely at each other as we headed towards the crowd that was beginning to accumulate around the drinks tables. It was another escape-from-Vidal-Sassoon night tonight, with all college members in their black gowns. I was wearing my only smart outfit, a dark-green velvet dress with a high waist and square neck, and high-heeled strappy sandals in the same colour. I hate dressing smartly, which is one of the reasons I'm suited to driving instruction as a profession; trainers, jeans, T-shirt and the obligatory packet of Benson and Hedges is the sort of attire I feel comfortable in.

'Sebastian! Kate!' Ethan Handley waved us over with his usual roguish grin. He always smiled like that, as if he had just remembered a risqué and mischievous joke. 'How are you both? Come and have a glass of champagne.' Ethan was wearing a black dinner suit, bow tie and gown like all the Summerton men. Even Damian Selinger, whom I could see leaning against a pillar talking to a tall, beefy, bespectacled man, had been forced to abandon his beigeness for the evening. 'Sorry to hear you didn't get the De La Wyche, mate,' Ethan said to Sebastian, patting him on the back. He was looking as blondly gorgeous as ever and radiating general desirability in all directions. Normally Ethan's presence was enough to spread happiness and conviviality for miles around, but Sebastian and I were feeling so gloomy that we made up a minority of two, impervious to the Ethan-radius effect.

'Not as sorry as I was,' said Sebastian, glumly. A waitress approached with champagne on an engraved silver tray. Sebastian and I took a glass each. Ethan pretended to take two and then put one back at the last minute, laughing.

'Oh, I thought you were up to your tricks, again, sir!' The waitress giggled, blushing. Ethan winked at her in a manner that made me wonder to which precise tricks she referred. I looked around for Keith Cobain, wondering where he could be. It was rare to find one component of the Keithanethan charm collective without the other.

'Do you know if Terri Skinner's going to take it?' Ethan asked Sebastian. 'She's a neighbour of yours, isn't she?'

'Yes. I've no idea.' Sebastian's tone implied that he couldn't have cared less.

'I'm afraid I've had to seat you two opposite her and her husband tonight,' Ethan confessed, frowning apologetically. 'Is that okay?' I nudged Sebastian in the ribs before he had a chance to offer his honest opinion.

'It's fine.' I smiled. Proximity to the Terri-target might be a good thing.

'Phew!' Ethan feigned extreme relief, pretending to mop his anxious brow. 'I tell you, mate, I wouldn't wish the job of steward on anyone. Seating plans for these feasts are a nightmare. You have to remember who's feuding with whom, and some of these college wrangles date back to the Fifties.' He laughed. 'You wouldn't believe how many times I have to change it all around to make sure no one's sitting next to their arch-enemy.'

'I thought you were a molecular biologist,' I said to Ethan. 'How come you have to do the seating plans?'

'Because I'm also the steward. Is it any wonder I'm suffering from executive stress,' he joked, 'having to do two jobs instead of one?' Sebastian, who had no jobs, tightened his lips resentfully.

'What does being steward involve, exactly?' I asked. 'Just seating plans?'

'Just seating plans? Just seating plans?' Ethan pretended to be offended. 'I tell you, that's only the tip of the iceberg. I have to choose the high-table wines, plan the lunch and dinner menus all year round. And on top of that I'm expected to teach genetics to undergraduates. Mercilessly exploited, I am.' He laughed the happy-go-lucky laugh of someone who not only was not exploited at the moment but was also fairly confident he never would be. 'So, how's the world of driving instruction?' he asked me. 'Those students still crashing into milk-carts and other dairy produce?' Two years ago, one of my students had crashed the Micra into a milk-cart. I had happened to mention it to Ethan at a feast and he now brought it up every time we met. I think it was his way of signalling to me that he remembered me, right down to the most trivial details of our previous conversations.

'Hi, Kate. Sebastian.' We turned round and saw the darkly gorgeous Keith behind us. 'Wotcher, mate,' he said to Ethan, who said exactly the same thing in reply. They edged towards each other until they were standing side by side. Their identical hairstyles, slicked back with just one curled lock falling boyishly on to their foreheads, and identical mannerisms made me wonder whether Summerton went in for cloning fellows in secret. 'I see you've put me next to the Master's wife.' Keith grinned wickedly at Ethan. 'Do you think that was wise?' He raised an eyebrow provocatively.

'I'm sure she'd think so, aren't you, mate?' Ethan chuckled.

'Oh, I'm sure she would. Not sure he would, though.'

'Have you seen where I'm sitting, though?' Ethan nodded suggestively.

'No. Where are you sitting?'

'Next to Professor Cavendish's wife.'

'You can tell who does the seating plans around here,' Keith smirked.

'Oh, you certainly can, mate.'

They bantered on, private jokes bouncing off their quick tongues. Sebastian and I listened politely as they chortled away happily, exchanging seduction plans for the immediate future. The crowd under the Tyndsall Court cloisters was growing and junior members of kitchen staff were sent off to get emergency supplies of champagne.

The beefy man Damian Selinger was talking to had started to shout. 'You're as bad as the fucking rest of them, Selinger,' he yelled, his glasses rising and falling with the movement of his irate nose. A few old women in evening dresses turned round in alarm. 'After everything I've done for this college! It's monstrous, fucking monstrous!' I hadn't seen Damian look so scared since Martine had attempted to attack his nether regions with a meat skewer at a barbecue they'd had a couple of years ago.

'Who's that guy?' I asked Sebastian.

'Lloyd Lunnon. He always does this. It's getting tedious.'

'Don't worry about him, Kate.' Ethan patted me on the shoulder protectively. 'Sebastian's right, this is entirely normal behaviour for Lunnon. When he stops shouting, we'll worry.' He and Keith guffawed contentedly. Damian said something I couldn't hear to Lloyd Lunnon. I got the impression he was trying to placate him. It was satisfying to see him faced with a bigger bully than himself for once.

'Don't give me that, Selinger, that's fucking crap and you know it,' Lloyd Lunnon went on, unplacated. 'I've met snails who are more intelligent than some of our esteemed colleagues!' He was shouting so loudly that no one could pretend not to be listening. 'Hey, Jack!' Lunnon whirled around angrily and latched on to Jack Collinson, the Junior Bursar, who had made the mistake of standing behind him. 'I was just telling Selinger here that I've met snails who are more intelligent than some of our council members. Do you have a view on this? Or does your loyalty to the pond life of this college prevail, yet again?' He sneered contemptuously.

'He hates the Junior Bursar,' Keith whispered to me.

'And the Senior Bursar,' said Sebastian.

'He wishes there were an intermediate bursar for him to hate as well,' Ethan quipped. 'He feels he's been short-changed.'

'What's it all about?' I asked.

'Lunnon wants to make some minor change to college rules,' said Keith. 'And no one will let him. It's all very boring.'

'I'm not discussing college business now, Lloyd.' The Junior Bursar smiled politely. 'I'm having an evening off.' Lunnon looked baffled. He clearly regarded taking time off from savaging one's colleagues as the highest form of negligence.

'This whole fucking place is off, if you ask me!' He whirled round theatrically to face Damian again. His black gown whipped the air behind him. 'It stinks to high heaven.'

'What's his subject?' I asked.

'Diplomacy,' said Ethan. 'Conflict resolution.' I looked at him and smiled, expecting to see a mischievous glint in his eye, but for once he looked serious. 'I'm not kidding,' he said. 'He's the head of the Peace Studies department. He's written a famous book, *Achieving and Preserving Consensus*. Haven't you heard of it?'

153

'No,' I said.

'It won a prize.'

'The trouble is that the Jacks of this world and the Daphnes of this world have got brains made of foam rubber!' yelled the author of *Achieving and Preserving Consensus*. 'To call them fucking retards would be an insult to spastics!'

'The college'd love to get rid of him,' Keith whispered in my ear. 'But he's the world's leading authority on conflict resolution.'

'Fucking brain-dead morons!' wailed the head of the Peace Studies department and world expert on diplomacy. 'Their mental agility can only be improved by death or a persistent vegetative state!'

I felt a tap on my shoulder and turned round. Bryony James was standing behind me. 'Hello again,' she said apologetically. I wasn't sure whether it was her refusal to answer my questions earlier or her presence now that she felt the need to apologise for. Her hair was still in a messy braid, with bits falling out at the sides and underneath, and she was wearing a crumpled blue cotton dress. She was without doubt the scruffiest woman present. 'I'm not prepared to change the way I dress for them,' she explained, seeing me eyeing her outfit. She stressed the last word resentfully. What was Damian Selinger thinking of, anyway, bringing her to the feast?

'Until two days ago you wanted to work for "them",' I reminded her, edging away from where Sebastian was still talking to Keithanethan. He didn't know what Bryony looked like and I didn't want him to find out there was yet another De La Wyche candidate present. I knew it would make him feel worse, that he would be consumed with envy, as I was, at her ability to drop out and rise above it all. 'Won't people think it's a bit odd, your being here?'

'Damian and I have decided to go public. We thought that, as I dropped out, there'd be no harm in it. Besides, Professor Fielding is so preoccupied with her feud with

Terri that she hasn't even noticed I'm here. Look.' She nodded sideways. Daphne Fielding, Joe and Terri were leaning against the wall, sipping champagne and not speaking. There was definitely a bad atmosphere between them. None of them looked particularly happy, least of all Joe, who kept shifting his gaze uncomfortably from his mother to his wife and back again. They resembled three failed wise monkeys who had seen, heard and spoken lashings of evil in the very recent past. Terri was wearing her blue silk strapless dress, the one with the 'Tim and Bettina Elworthy' label, and blue stilettos with heels that were nearly as high as Damian Selinger's whole body. I caught her eye and she smiled. I forced myself to do the same. I obviously didn't do very well because Bryony asked, 'Don't you like her?'

'Of course I don't,' I said. 'She got Sebastian's job.'

'Professor Fielding really loathes her, according to Damian,' said Bryony. 'She's dreading having her around college, seeing her every day.'

'Why did she give her the job, then?' I said crossly.

'I don't know. She wasn't the only panel member.'

'No, but Damian was supporting you, for all the wrong reasons, and Emily Lole was supporting Rod Firsden, the guy who came second. It was only Valerie who was in favour of Terri at first. If Professor Fielding hadn't mysteriously stopped supporting Sebastian some time between Wednesday afternoon and Thursday morning, Terri wouldn't have had a majority.'

'I don't know,' said Bryony. 'Maybe she thought . . . well, I mean, you can't not give someone a job just because you hate them.'

'I can't think of a better reason,' I said truthfully. I tried to catch Daphne Fielding's eye, but she persisted in staring sulkily at her champagne glass. I wouldn't have minded asking her a few questions, but only if we weren't surrounded by other people. She was quite attractive for a middle-aged woman, I thought. Her tailored black suit hung perfectly from her firm, youthful figure and her face had good bone structure. Without the slightly goofy teeth and protruding ears she would have been stunning.

'Look, do you think we've got time to . . .' Bryony began, but I waved her words aside. I could see the door of Valerie Williams's surgery opening on the other side of Tyndsall Court.

'Got to go, sorry,' I said quickly, leaving Bryony behind and striding across the grass. Valerie Williams looked up, saw me approaching, then looked very quickly to her left and right. She was wearing a brown waistless dress with blue flowers on it and white sandals.

'Looking for an escape route, were you?' I asked.

'Oh,' she said, not smiling. 'You again.'

'Yes, me again, sipping my champagne under the cloisters. Out in the open.' I stressed these last four words. 'I do prefer it when everything's out in the open, don't you?' I hoped to unsettle her by repeating the words she had used to Daphne Fielding in the conversation I'd overheard.

'I don't know what you mean.' She looked at her feet, her face turning red.

'Look, there's Professor Fielding,' I carried on in a chatty tone. 'How do you think she feels about things being out in the open?'

'Leave me alone,' said Valerie fiercely.

'Oh, don't mind me. You know how we driving instructors love to throw accusations around.' Valerie looked genuinely alarmed. I was quoting, word for word, what she had said to Daphne. 'What I'm saying rings a bell, does it?' I asked rhetorically. 'Your amnesia must have gone into remission.'

'I don't have to put up with your . . .' Her self-justification was interrupted by a loud, high-pitched shriek. 'Watch out!' Valerie shouted at me, at the exact same moment that I felt two large hands land on my shoulders and squeeze hard. 'Emily, Emily, stop!' Valerie seized the

156

wrists of her distraught patient and colleague, and the two of them tugged at each other's arms for a while, with me trapped in the middle. Emily Lole was wearing a long black rubbery dress that clung to her ample body in all the wrong places; she looked like a portly sea lion. She was crying and snarling at me. 'Have you taken your pills today?' Valerie demanded. 'Emily, have you taken your pills?'

'What are you doing here again?' Emily sobbed in my face. Evidently the De La Wyche panel members were not keen to have me around. 'Fernando's sent you, hasn't he? You know where he is, don't you? Tell me, oh, tell me.'

Valerie Williams relinquished her grip on Emily's wrists and my shoulders were clamped once more in the vice-like grip of Summerton's resident madwoman. 'Do you know where Fernando is?' Valerie asked me.

'Of course I bloody don't.' I tried to struggle free. I looked around for Sebastian and saw that he was talking to Professor Fielding, standing with his back to me. Lloyd Lunnon had launched into another loud tirade, to which most of the assembled company were listening attentively. No one seemed to have noticed that I was being manhandled by a hefty head case. 'Do something, will you!' I yelled at Valerie. 'Help to get her off me.'

'It's best to wait until she calms down naturally,' said Valerie, folding her arms and stepping back a few paces. I don't know who she thought the beneficiary of this policy would be, but she certainly didn't have my shoulders in mind.

'What do you know?' Emily bleated at me. 'What do you know about Rod Firsden?'

'What?' This took me by surprise. Had Emily seen us together in the Micra the day Rod had nearly run her over? I was sure she hadn't; she'd been in a miserable little world of her own. And even if she had, why was she so bothered about Rod Firsden? I could understand her getting agitated about Fernando, but why Rod? 'Nothing,' I said. This was no lie. I knew very little about Rod Firsden, only that I was teaching him to drive, that he liked George Herbert and

157

that he was obsessed with the Enmity and to a lesser extent – much lesser, I hoped – with me.

'You're lying, I know you are,' Emily shrieked, her hands moving up to my neck.

'Stop that right now, Emily,' Valerie said sternly and tried to grab Emily's hands again.

'Help! Sebastian!' I called out, knowing it was pointless. I could hear Lloyd Lunnon bellowing curses at the top of his lungs and stealing the show. No one was interested in us. Luckily two waiters who had been sent to the kitchens for more champagne appeared on our side of Tyndsall Court at that moment and Valerie called them over. Between them they managed to restrain Emily. They carried her back to her room, holding an arm each as she writhed angrily between them, still accusing me of knowing something. Valerie ran after them, mumbling instructions. I was sure I heard the word 'syringe'.

I took a few deep breaths, rubbed my sore shoulders and returned to the party. Everyone was so busy chatting in their little groups and/or listening to the Lloyd Lunnon Rage Roadshow that no one had noticed what had just happened to me. Sebastian was still talking to Daphne Fielding. What the hell about, I wondered. I was close enough to see the expression on his face and it was a reasonably pleasant one.

Bryony James appeared at my side. 'What I was going to say before . . .' she began.

'I've just been attacked,' I interrupted her. 'By Emily Lole, you know, one of the . . .'

'I know who she is.'

'She just attacked me, physically. No one even noticed. Why isn't she being locked up instead of being put on interview panels? This place is a madhouse.'

'I agree,' said Bryony. She unzipped her handbag and produced a small blue envelope. 'Look, read this,' she said, handing it to me. 'I want to . . . tell you the truth. There are things you need to know.'

158

I felt a leaping sensation in my heart. Someone finally wanted to tell me something. 'I thought Damian had vetoed your speaking to me,' I said, feigning nonchalance.

'He did, but I'm going to ignore him.' Bryony smiled.

'Very wise. He's a contemptible little shit.'

I started to open the envelope, but Bryony said quickly, 'Don't read it now, here. Take it to the loo, or something. Read it as soon as you can and then later . . . I'll explain.'

'Is there any point?' I asked. 'Will any of this help to get Sebastian the De La Wyche fellowship?'

'Terri Skinner got the job,' said Bryony, puzzled by my referring to it as though it were still up for grabs. I didn't see that it'd do any harm to explain. She was prepared to talk to me, it seemed, so in exchange I would let her in on at least part of my plan. The champagne had gone to my head and I was less cautious than usual; my handbrake was down. Besides, if Bryony told anyone I could always deny it.

'Terri's asked for two weeks to think about it,' I said. 'She's deciding between . . .'

'. . . here and Reading University,' Bryony chipped in.

'How do you know that?'

'Sorry, I shouldn't have interrupted. I'll explain later. It's all connected. Everything's connected.'

'Oh. Well, anyway, when I heard that, I decided to use those two weeks to get both her and the reserve, Rod Firsden, out of the way so that Sebastian could have the fellowship. I didn't need to get you out of the way because you'd thoughtfully left the field of your own accord.' Bryony smiled but didn't say anything. 'Well?' I demanded. 'Go on, tell me I'm wasting my time, there's no point, I'm living in a fantasy world . . .'

'Not at all,' she said softly. 'I'm sure you can do it, if you put your mind to it.'

'What?' I examined her expression closely, to check she wasn't taking the piss. She didn't sound disapproving, or even surprised.

'You and I have got a lot in common,' she said. Not another one, I thought, remembering Rod Firsden saying he felt he'd connected with me after having known me for less than an hour. 'When can we talk?' Bryony whispered eagerly as Damian walked towards her with quick proprietorial steps. I shrugged.

'Are you okay, darling?' He put his arm round her. I nearly laughed out loud at the enlarged vocabulary of Damian in love. I was so used to hearing him call Martine 'bitch' or, when he was feeling more adventurous, 'tweatures' (his own inspired abbreviation of twat-features), that at first I thought he'd said 'dalek' instead of 'darling'. He pronounced the word oddly, like someone struggling with a foreign language. 'Sorry to abandon you. That arse Lunnon got his claws into me and wouldn't let go. Is she hassling you?' He nodded in my direction without looking at me.

'I'm fine, Frisky,' said Bryony.

'Frisky?' I exclaimed before I could stop myself. I thought they might at least have the grace to look embarrassed but they simply giggled indulgently and stared into each other's eyes. A loud gong sounded and a ripple of movement travelled through the crowd. Several waiters appeared with empty trays to collect our glasses.

'Ah, good,' said Damian. 'Dinner.' He moved towards Great Hall, pulling Bryony after him. She looked at me expectantly as she was hauled away.

'I'll speak to you later,' I muttered. I wasn't sure how much longer I could bear this state of prolonged suspense: waiting to hear news of Rod's Reading trip, waiting for Bryony to tell me whatever it was she felt was so desperately important. I didn't think I'd be able to digest a single mouthful of food, especially not with Terri Skincrawl sitting opposite me. I decided to make a quick trip to the loo to open the blue envelope.

Chapter Twenty-two

Bryony James – Curriculum Vitae

Profile

This CV is going to be a slightly unusual one, even by my standards. It is going to be longer than the ones you've seen so far. It is going to contain dialogue. It is going to be almost like a self-sufficient short story. This is because Bryony James is an unusual person, whose circumstances merit slightly different treatment. I thought I'd put all this right at the top, in the 'Profile' section. Before I get on to Bryony, however, a word on 'Profile' sections in general. Recently, experts in CV construction (and, if areas of expertise can be viewed hierarchically, we are really scraping the bottom of a post-prolapse barrel now) decided that before name, address, age, education and employment history, every CV must sport a 'Profile' section. This should, ideally, offer the gist of the person in a short paragraph, even though the prospective employer has not yet got to the 'Name' section and has no idea who the person is. Worryingly, many people's gists can be fitted into a short paragraph. Bryony James's can't. So, don't fret when you see how different this CV is from the others. Expecting all CVs to be broadly the same leads swiftly and dystopia-inducingly to expecting all people to be the same.

Name

Bryony Helen James. Her parents wanted a boy, whom they would have called Brian. Perhaps originally Bryony was a male foetus. The difference in aesthetic quality between the names Brian and Bryony is possibly great enough to produce psychosomatic X chromosomes in a terrified embryo.

Address
Flat 6, 47 Upper Parliament Street, Liverpool, officially. For all practical purposes, however, she has moved in with Damian Selinger. This is a clear case of love not being blind, not architecturally at any rate. G12 in Summerton's Queen's Court is an infinitely superior residence to flat 6, 47 Upper Parliament Street, Liverpool, and one in which the daily cleaning, washing up and bed-making is done by a type of servant particular to Cambridge University known as a bedder, so it could be argued that Bryony was very sensible to move there. On the other hand, there might be something to be said for living in a damp and smelly bedsit, scrubbing out one's own pans and shaking out one's own duvet if the alternative is sharing an abode with the warped and self-seeking 'Frisky'.

Even leaving him aside, the squalor option has certain psychological advantages. Once you have lived in Summerton College, one of the most beautiful buildings in the entire world, everything you encounter afterwards looks like a dump. This is fine for permanent fellows, who get to live in college all their lives, but temporary fellows often find it hard to adjust after they leave Summerton. They cannot come to terms with the harsh reality of having to find accommodation for themselves, as opposed to having it given to them, complete with antique furnishings, by the Junior Bursar. And those who do manage to battle their way through the no man's land of dodgy landlords and lettings agencies are always disappointed by what they see. No more views of Trinity, King's or the River Cam. No more arched doorways or bedders. Lots of houses, flats and bungalows but no one has even heard of 'fellows' sets'. Poor ex-Summertonians, they cannot bring themselves to sign on the dotted line when the time comes because they feel sure they're entitled to something far, far better. They stand bewildered in estate agents' offices in rough inner cities, praying to be beamed up by a magic Junior Bursar. Who do you think the homeless people in Cambridge are? They're not mental health care refugees or teenage runaways as they are in most places; they're ex-fellows who simply could not bear to settle for inferior accommodation.

And flat 6, 47 Upper Parliament Street is about as inferior as you can get. There are slug trails all over the carpets and mouse droppings in the cupboards. Damian Selinger is a permanent fellow, though, so unless Bryony leaves him or he throws her out, she should be okay. Even when they move out of Summerton and into a flat – for strictly speaking only single fellows are allowed to live in college sets – it will be a Summerton-owned flat, like those in Noble House, and they will not encounter problems such as wet rot or vermin infestations. There may not be a *petits fours* home delivery service, but that will be about the worst of their troubles. Damian and Bryony are unlikely to consider buying a house. Once you've experienced Summerton accommodation you realise there is no property ladder for those foolish enough to strike out on their own, only a property snake.

Age
Thirty-six, by far the oldest of the four De La Wyche candidates.

Place of Birth
St Helens, Merseyside.

Marital Status
Single. Nearly got married once but it fell through. See Employment History/Qualifications and Education section for further details.

Employment History/Qualifications and Education
Had to leave school at sixteen and get a job because both
her parents by that stage were too ill to work. Mr James
had emphysema and Mrs James suffered from rheumatoid
arthritis, so Bryony went to work as an office junior for a
magazine that had just started up in the area, the *St Helens
Review*. The editor and founder of the *Review*, Selena
Gamble, intended it to be far more than a local rag and
hoped that it would appeal to the intellectual and cultural
élite of St Helens, a group with as much presence, arguably,
as George Kaplan in the film *North by Northwest*. As well
as the usual local news items, the magazine contained a
comprehensive What's On guide, longer articles of a
serious journalistic nature that Selena Gamble felt would
give her paper the gravitas of a national broadsheet, book,
art, cinema and theatre reviews, and an Eating Out column
that featured a different expensive restaurant every week.
Despite Selena's high ambitions for the magazine, however,
its intended readership seemed intent on shunning it. It
appeared that the intellectual and cultural élite of the
region did not want any part of a publication that had 'St
Helens' in its title, and continued to buy *Homes and
Gardens*, the *Daily Telegraph*, the *Spectator* and other such
journals that had the good manners not to remind them
that they didn't live in Hampstead. Did the editor of the *St
Helens Review* regret aiming so high? Possibly. Probably,
but who's to say she would have been wiser to aim lower?
Even the worst-off among us are capable of snobbery; the
poor and dispossessed of Merseyside would doubtless have
shunned the *St Helens Hobo*, preferring to read *Homeless
and Gardenless* and imagine they resided on the pavements
of Knightsbridge.

Nobody subscribed to the magazine, in which Selena
Gamble had invested a substantial amount of her own
money, and she was forced to start giving it away for free
like any old common muck, like the sort of paper that
sported headlines such as 'Heart-warming Hero's Headless

Corpse Horror'. It soon became clear that much money was going to be lost unless substantial revenue could be brought in from advertising. The trouble was that the *Review*'s losses, even after only four or five issues, were so vast that a lot of the serious journalism had to go in order to make way for full-page spreads of reject furniture warehouses, golf and bridge clubs, double-glazing specialists and stairlift suppliers. Even after having sold out to tacky market forces to such an overwhelming extent, more money was still being lost than made.

All of which put Selena Gamble in a mighty bad mood and she became unbearable to work with. From the start, her leadership qualities had been poor, but financial worries put an insuperable strain on her minimal management skills. Selena was unable, Bryony noticed within her first few weeks at the *Review*, to ask any of her employees to do anything. Her method of getting things done consisted of first hinting at what she wanted so obliquely that no one knew what she was on about, then yelling at staff at the top of her lungs for failing to interpret her veiled comments correctly, find the hidden instruction and comply with it.

As well as helping with the running of the office, Bryony was in charge of the travel page. This, like the rest of the *Review*, had speedily degenerated from being a round-up of exotic holiday locations to a list of local bus and train times, because the latter was cheaper. On a particularly fraught Thursday afternoon, after Bryony had been working for the *Review* for about three months, a helpful citizen phoned the office and informed Selena that she had just caught a bus home from town that wasn't listed in the magazine's bus timetable. Instead of telling the caller either (a) to get a life or (b) to be glad of the bonus bus and simply accept rather than question its bounty, Selena started to hyperventilate and grind her teeth. She summoned Bryony with a gnashing growl, and instructed her to check all the timetables and find the missing bus. The next morning,

Bryony got up two hours earlier than normal and cycled round town picking up all the relevant up-to-date timetables. She spent the whole of Friday morning altering the magazine's travel page accordingly.

Selena came in at lunchtime demanding to see what she had achieved. When Bryony showed her the new page, Selena asked, 'So where's the missing bus?'

'I don't know,' said Bryony.

'What do you mean you don't know?' Selena yelled.

'Well, the woman who phoned didn't tell us the time of the bus she got, did she?' Bryony tried to explain, smiling patiently.

'But . . . but . . .' Selena spluttered. 'But . . . it must be possible to find out which was the missing bus by comparing the new timetable with the old one.'

'But I've deleted the old one,' said Bryony, 'to replace it with the new one.'

'You've *what*? You've *what*?' Bryony couldn't believe her ears. Even her parents didn't scream at her like this – well, her dad couldn't, because he had emphysema and even breathing was an effort for him. 'I can't believe how stupid you are!' Selena shrieked like a harpie. 'How are we ever going to track down the missing bus if you've deleted the old timetable?'

'Surely all that matters is that our timetable is now correct.' Bryony kept her cool. 'What does it matter if we don't know which bus that woman got?'

'Because if we don't know which one it was, we don't know if we've got it in our new timetable!' Bryony kept thinking it couldn't get any worse and then Selena would raise her voice even higher and open her mouth even wider until it looked like the entrance to a terrifying fairground ride of the dark-tunnel variety. 'How *dare* you tell me what matters and what doesn't matter? You've had a bad attitude ever since you started here. Don't *dare* to open your mouth again; you just do what I say, you hear me? You're happy to take my money, so don't ever, *ever*

166

question what I say!'

'That's not fair,' Bryony protested, her instinctive sense of injustice triumphing momentarily over her fear of Selena. 'I don't take your money in return for never questioning what you say. I take your money in return for working for the *Review*, which I've been doing perfectly well.'

'Don't fucking lecture me, you . . . I don't want to hear another word out of you. I want you to get down to that bus station right now and make a note of every bus that arrives and leaves, is that clear?'

'But what's the point?'

'And then I want you to ring up every bus company that operates in the region, demand to speak to the boss and get a full list of . . .' On it went. Selena threatened to sack Bryony unless she went to the depot straight from work that afternoon and stayed there until the end of all bus activity for the evening. Bryony asked if she could phone home first, to let her parents know she wouldn't be back at six o'clock as usual.

'Phone home! Phone home!' Selena matched ET in vocabulary and inhumanity, but certainly not in cuteness. 'How many buses will come and go while you waste time chatting, did you ever stop to consider that? Well? Well?' Bryony was convinced Selena was deranged. She did as she was told because she couldn't afford to lose her job. When she got back home at one in the morning, her mum told her that her dad had died at eight o'clock that evening. He had asked for her, apparently – those were his last words – but his beloved daughter had been busy recording the late arrivals of both the number 132 and the number 47, owing to some confusion over driver swapping.

Several weeks later the *St Helens Review* went bankrupt, and Selena Gamble went mad and was committed to a mental hospital. According to the few members of ex-*Review* staff who confused bad character judgement with loyalty and visited Selena occasionally, she dribbled a lot

167

and muttered 'the missing bus, the missing bus, oh, dear, I've missed the bus, oh, dear, we've missed the bus' over and over again.

Bryony decided she would stand a better chance of being treated well by future employers if she acquired some skills, became an employee to be reckoned with, so she took out a large bank loan and signed up for secretarial college. Two years later she got a job as a secretary for a firm of solicitors called Walker Hall Suggs, known affectionately by its clerical staff as Wall-to-wall Slugs. Coincidentally, this job was responsible for her not being at home when her mother died. She and a group of secretarial colleagues had taken a couple of hours off work one afternoon to put up Christmas decorations. Lionel Suggs, the biggest slug of them all, became aware of this and demanded that they stay behind at the end of the day to make up the time. At four thirty, Bryony's mother phoned her to say that she wasn't feeling very well and could Bryony come home immediately. Bryony explained that if she did she would undoubtedly get fired, the mood Suggs was in, and that she and the other secretaries had to stay late to make up the deficit in their working hours. When she got home at eight thirty she found her mother dead in an armchair. She had had a heart attack. The doctor hadn't been able to say for certain whether Bryony's presence at the relevant moment might have prolonged her mother's life.

There was only one thing for it: A levels and university. No one would dare to treat an educated person the way Bryony had been treated by her bosses to date. She took out another loan, did three A levels in a year at a local adult education centre and got a place at Edge Hill University College to do sociology. Bryony had no doubts about her choice of subject. Her experience had taught her that there was something terribly wrong with society and with the world, and she thought that studying sociology might help her first to explain and then to cure it. She worked nearly fifteen hours a day, in her dingy flat on Upper Parliament

Street (her parents' house was repossessed by the council after her mother's death), and got a first. She then enrolled to do a PhD on the cultural theory of Antarctica. She was fascinated by the continent of ice because it reminded her of her own heart and psyche after the devastating losses she had suffered, although this sounded so pretentious even to her that she never mentioned it to anyone else.

Her supervisor, Blake Nevins, surprised all his colleagues at Edge Hill by falling in love with Bryony and inviting her to move in with him. It wasn't his lack of professionalism that astounded them, it was the fact that Blake had obviously seen and spoken to a supervisee for a period of time sufficient for the gestation of amorous feelings. The standard of supervision rose considerably after the Blake–Bryony news broke and other single lecturers in the department began to wonder whether they too might meet the love of their life if they allowed themselves to catch an occasional glimpse of a student.

Bryony got her PhD, started to feel almost like a human being again, and she and Blake got engaged. She was offered a lectureship in the Sociology department at Edge Hill, but Blake encouraged her to turn it down because he, at the same time, was offered a personal chair at Caldwell University in Minnesota. He promised to get Bryony a job in his department over there and left the country almost immediately, swearing to send for Bryony as soon as he'd found somewhere for them to live and sorted out a job for her.

Bryony waited and waited, but Blake never got in touch. She later heard from another graduate student at Edge Hill who, as a result of the flurry of academic mentoring Blake inspired, was sleeping with her supervisor, that Blake had met another woman on the plane and was now planning to marry her.

Bryony re-rented her old flat on Upper Parliament Street, since there hadn't been stiff competition for it in her absence, and started to apply for other academic jobs. She got as far as the interview stage relatively often, because her work was generally agreed to be brilliant, and by this point she had published numerous articles and made a bit of a name for herself, but she kept dropping at the final hurdle. After doing a bit of research, she found out that her referees at Edge Hill, two wizened and vindictive old professors, made a point of mentioning at every opportunity that she had turned down a job in their department, opting instead to swan off to America with her boyfriend. Bryony started to be brutally honest with prospective employers; she told all the universities that interviewed her her life story, hoping that they would see she was serious about her career and make allowances for her one moment of love-induced weakness, entirely understandable after the emotional traumas she'd suffered. Sadly this backfired and she got a reputation for being emotionally unstable and overly revelatory about personal matters. She did not get a job and after a while she also stopped getting shortlisted.

Other Information
You may be wondering, given what you've just read, how Bryony came to get an interview for the De La Wyche Enmity, or why she seems, in her present incarnation, to be so calm and kind, so able to fall in love with Damian Selinger. So am I, but the contents of the blue envelope indicate that the rest of this story, this unfairy tale, will have to come from Bryony herself. Meanwhile, two more things must be recorded on her CV.

First, Bryony won the pools. Doing them was a family tradition, one that Bryony had always seen as pointless, especially after she stopped believing in good luck, but she continued to fill in her pools card because giving it up would have made her feel disloyal to her father. Thank God she didn't give up, because just when her career and morale were at their lowest ebb and she was seriously beginning to consider suicide as an option, she won £750,000.

Second, she wrote a book called *Cold World*, the

170

culmination of her years of research into the cultural theory of the polar regions. She sent it off to Manchester University Press, thinking this would probably be her final act on earth, the one piece of evidence that she had existed. The press accepted the manuscript with unnerving enthusiasm; by this point Bryony had suffered so much that she found good news unsettling and didn't know how to cope with it. She was sure something would go wrong: either MUP would go bankrupt before her book came out or they would change their minds at the last minute. She decided, nevertheless, to postpone her suicide until the book had appeared. Two days before publication date she found out about her pools win. She went into severe shock, had a slight breakdown and, by the time she resurfaced, *Cold World* was not only published but receiving lavish praise in newspapers and on television and the radio. In the quagmire of her depression, Bryony had failed to notice that she'd written a major, ground-breaking work. It was only the fuss other people were making about it that alerted her to the fact that she was probably too talented to squander it all by killing herself. So she didn't.

To find out what happened next, return to present story. (If you want to guarantee you'll get an interview, try ending your CV with a cliff-hanger. Bugger what the experts say.)

Chapter Twenty-three

Underdog, Overdog

'How the other half lives, hey?' Joe Fielding grinned across the table at me as we took our seats. Great Hall looked as imposing as ever, with portraits of Summerton's former Masters lining all four oak-panelled walls. There was an ominous empty space in the middle of the far wall above the oak panelling, a painting-shaped rectangle of wallpaper that was slightly lighter than its surroundings. That must be where Grimshaw De La Wyche was, I thought to myself. At the end of the long row of faces, near the door that led out on to Tyndsall Court, there was a picture of Sir Noel Barry, the Master who had retired last year, and one of Sir Patrick Chichester, his crown-appointed replacement. They were total opposites, physically. Barry had been short, fat and bald, and Chichester was tall and thin with a full head of auburn hair.

'Mm.' I nodded half-heartedly at Joe, thinking how inconvenient it was that his other half lived at all. He had no right to engage me in an us-and-them kind of conversation; his mother was a professor here and his wife was very probably the next De La Wyche fellow, so our situations were hardly comparable. Then I remembered how excluded he was from Terri's life of career choices and libraries, trapped in the laundry room with a squawking child, and I felt guilty for counting him among the privileged.

There were twelve tables in total, long and rectangular, with twenty-six places at each one. Six large chandeliers hung from the ceiling. Every place setting comprised four forks, four knives and two spoons, one for soup and one for dessert. Five glasses, each one differing very slightly from the others in shape and size, had been set down at a fixed point north of every collection of knives. The tops of the tables, covered with starched white linen cloths, were punctuated every half-metre or so by lighted candles in beautiful ornate works of art that looked more like sculptures than candlesticks. There were bottles of sparkling and still mineral water on the table. I picked up my menu card and put it safely in my handbag, to be added to Sebastian's and my collection later. Then I picked up Sebastian's menu card and read it. It was printed, as always, on thick, cream-coloured paper and folded like a birthday card. On the front was Summerton's blue, lilac and gold crest and the name of the feast, which in this case was 'Feast of the Masters'. For some reason Summerton was very keen on giving every feast a theme, and this one was nominally a tribute to the college's late and great figureheads, including those whose portraits had vanished from the walls. Inside the card were details of the food and wine we were about to consume. There were more courses on offer tonight in Summerton's Great Hall than most universities offer in their academic prospectuses.

Before we had been allowed to sit down, Sir Patrick Chichester had said grace in Latin. At least I think it was Latin; I can't be sure, because he didn't say *carpe diem*, quid pro quo or *dulce et decorum est pro patria mori*, which are the only bits of Latin I know. Fifty-odd waiters and waitresses lurked around the perimeter of the hall, each bearing a silver tray. As soon as we were seated they began to move with apparently effortless grace around the tables, putting down a bowl of lobster soup in front of every person and pouring a glass of a wine called Martinborough Pinot Noir 1988 for each of us.

'This tastes as if it came out of a carton,' Daphne Fielding lisped to Joe after her first mouthful. She said 'carton' as if it were synonymous with 'dustbin'. She was sitting opposite Ethan Handley, who was on my left. Sebastian was on my right, facing Terri. She'd whispered 'I hope there are no hard feelings' to him during the Latin grace and he'd grunted unpleasantly in response. Someone less self-obsessed than Terri might have noticed that, with his habitual honesty, Sebastian was making it clear that his feelings on the matter were as hard as the limestone walls that protected our food from the elements, but she probably attributed his ungracious behaviour to general misogyny and the desire to introduce compulsory female circumcision as a state practice, if she was aware of his reaction at all.

'Ethan, you're the steward.' Professor Fielding leaned forward, moving a candlestick out of the way. 'This soup tastes like it's come from a packet.'

'Don't say that to the chef.' Ethan smiled. 'He'll have you for slander.'

'Well, it tastes very Bachelor's to me,' said Daphne doubtfully.

'Oh, really? And how do you know what bachelors taste like?' Ethan chuckled, winking at her. 'Or perhaps we shouldn't discuss that in front of your son. Maybe later, eh?' This was too much for Daphne Fielding to resist and she began to giggle, simper and gulp down her soup in large mouthfuls.

'You only get a hug from a Bachelor's mug,' I told her. I'd always loved Bachelor's soups and felt compelled to defend them against this barrage of professorial soup philistinism. Daphne looked at me oddly. 'What a dreadful slogan,' she said.

'It's better than "Rectify the anomaly",' I said before I could stop myself, wondering whether I'd consumed a bit too much champagne under the cloisters. My tongue wasn't usually this loose. Daphne Fielding looked offended until she noticed that Ethan was laughing heartily.

'Kate, you're a breath of fresh air,' he said. Daphne

cocked an eyebrow at Ethan, ignoring me completely. She gave him a challenging stare, as if to say that one person's breath of fresh air was another's wafted scent of blocked drain. I considered asking her why she had supported Sebastian on Wednesday and not on Thursday, but decided against it. She would never tell me, not here, with Terri and Joe within earshot. And Ethan would think it was bad form to raise a contentious issue at a feast. It would go against his charm ethic.

The soup was followed by fried goat's cheese and mixed green salad, which was absolutely delicious. Waiters swarmed around the tables with the second of the night's wines, Chassagne-Montrachet Les Chenevottes (Niellon) 1992, pouring it from bottles encrusted with cellar dust into our glasses.

'Are you going upstairs for drinks afterwards?' Ethan asked me.

'Definitely,' I said and he laughed, mistaking my enthusiasm for a desire to consume yet more alcohol. After feasts it was customary to retire to the Master's Lodge to drink spirits, but I was always too full of food and wine by that stage. Normally Sebastian and I went home pretty soon after the last course, but tonight I'd have to see to it that we went to the Lodge so that I could catch Bryony before Damian whisked her off to his boudoir.

'Are you going upstairs, Ethan?' Daphne Fielding asked.

'No, can't this time, I'm afraid. I'm meeting some friends at the pictures. We're off to see the late show of *Sliding Doors*.'

Daphne wrinkled her nose. 'I much prefer old films,' she said. 'In the days of black-and-white cinema people paid more attention to detail.'

'Ah, but I'm not an expert like you, Daphne,' said Ethan deferentially.

'I've seen *Sliding Doors*,' I said. 'Well, minus the first fifteen minutes. I got detained in the ice-cream queue. It's really good.'

Terri Skinner leaned over. 'Is that the one where it has two alternative versions of what happens to her, depending on whether she does or doesn't catch a particular tube train?'

'That's right,' Ethan and I said in unison.

'I love that idea.' Terri beamed at us. 'Doesn't it end up the same, though, whether she gets the train or not? I think that's so clever, you know, it's as though fate has things worked out right from the start, so whatever choices we make don't matter.' I wondered if she was referring to her own choice between Reading and Summerton. I hadn't realised she was the fatalistic type. Perhaps I could pretend to be a psychic, convince her that it was written in the stars that she should go to Reading. 'It's a brilliant idea,' Terri went on. 'It's so anti this whole male idea of action and change, and making things happen.'

'As if anyone could believe in that rubbish.' Daphne Fielding gave Terri a sharp stare. 'Action and change aren't male ideas.' I nodded in spite of myself. Terri's comment was, apart from its obvious sexism, plain stupid. I was in favour of changing things – in particular who got the Enmity – and I was a woman. 'Well done, anyway,' Daphne said to Terri. 'You've just ruined the film for Ethan.'

'No, no, it's fine . . .' Ethan began.

'It isn't fine,' Daphne protested quietly. 'She ought to think before she speaks.'

'God, I'm sorry.' Terri looked taken aback. 'I'm sorry, Ethan. I didn't mean to give anything away.'

'It's fine, honestly. Everyone knows what the film's about. I still want to see it.'

There was an embarrassed silence. Then Daphne said, 'Anyway, Terri hasn't even seen the film so she doesn't know what it's about. She's probably got it wrong.' Her tone implied that this wouldn't be unusual.

'I do know what it's about,' said Terri quietly, giving Daphne a puzzled stare.

'Mum,' Joe whispered. 'Stop it. Not tonight, okay?' I got the impression he was used to intervening in squabbles between his mother and his wife. I tried to catch Sebastian's eye and saw immediately that he was waiting to catch mine. He tapped my leg twice with his knee under the table to let me know he'd taken it all in. I gave him a sly grin; we would have a lot to discuss later.

After the goat's cheese and salad came the wild boar terrine and the Château Gruaud-Larose 1978. I was beginning to feel inebriated and decided to switch to water. I wanted to ask Ethan a couple of questions about the night Fernando Rose and Martine Selinger disappeared. Even though there was probably no link whatsoever between their vanishing and the oddness surrounding the De La Wyche appointment this time round, I was curious to hear Ethan's opinion, since he and Keith were the only two people who had actually been with them on the night in question.

'How well do you know Emily Lole?' I whispered into Ethan's right ear, trying to be tactful even though no one was listening to us. Daphne Fielding and Joe were talking about Scarlett's nursery school and Terri had shifted her whole body round to face the man on her left. I didn't blame her for turning her back on Daphne; much as I resented Terri, both for the way she treated Joe and for getting the Enmity, I thought Daphne had been seriously out of order talking to her like that in front of everybody. On the other hand, if I were Joe's mother, maybe I also wouldn't be able to restrain myself from lashing out.

'Reasonably well,' said Ethan cautiously. 'Why?'

'She said something very odd to me before the feast,' I said and told him about Emily's insistence that I knew where Fernando Rose was.

'Oh, don't worry about that. She's always going on about him.'

'But has she ever accused you of knowing where he is? Or anyone else, as far as you know?'

'Well, no, I must admit that's a new one. I assume you don't know where he is, then?' Ethan grinned at me.

'Of course I don't. I've never even met him.'

'Keith and I were the last people to see him, before he disappeared. And Martine Selinger.'

'Really?' I tried to appear interested without being too nosy.

'Yeah. The four of us went to the Jive Hive.'

'Did he say anything to you?' I asked.

'Well, he didn't sit in silence all night. He was a bit quieter than usual, though, I seem to remember. The trouble is Keith and I had had a few that night. We weren't able to be of much help when he went missing.'

'Sebastian said everyone thought he and Martine had run off together,' I said casually.

'What?' Ethan laughed. 'No, everyone thought he'd run off with the Noble portrait of Grimshaw De La Wyche. But that was silly, Fernando's not a thief. And Martine was making a play for Keith that night. Anyway, Fernando was far too decent to take off with another fellow's wife.'

'Maybe that was a decoy,' I suggested. 'Maybe they planned it all so that no one would suspect.'

'No way.' Ethan shook his head. 'Martine couldn't plan anything beyond her clothes and make-up. As for Fernando, it wasn't his style at all. He was a straight-forward nice guy.'

'You mean he was boring?' I asked. 'Square?'

'Well . . . he was a great bloke, don't get me wrong, I mean, I really liked him, but . . . well, yes, I suppose he was a bit square. You must have heard the spliff story.' I shook my head. 'Martine had this holiday brochure with her, right?'

'In the club?'

'Yeah. She was obsessed with holidays. She always had brochures in her bag wherever she went. Anyway, she'd got one out on the table and Fernando was messing about with it . . .'

'Aha!' I interrupted. 'Could they have been planning a secret holiday together?'

'Kate, trust me,' said Ethan. 'They didn't go off together, not unless I'm a very bad judge of character.'

'Okay. Go on. What about the brochure?'

'Fernando rolled it up and stuck it in his mouth. Keith and I thought . . . well, you know.' He raised his eyebrows suggestively.

'You thought it was a drugs-related joke,' I guessed.

'Exactly. You see, you understand. We both looked at him and laughed but he didn't seem to get it. I said something like, "Good spliff you've got there, Fernando" and he asked me, very earnestly, what a spliff was. He'd never heard the word before. He was very . . . otherworldly.'

'Hm.' I had to admit he didn't sound like the sort of person to elope with a colleague's wife in the middle of the night. 'He can't have been that much of a fuddy-duddy if he went to the Jive Hive, though,' I said. I'd been there once and found it loud, hot and tiring. By around midnight, images of my nice comfy lemon-meringue-coloured bed had started to flash before my eyes and I didn't regard myself as particularly square.

'That was his first time,' said Ethan. 'I could tell he hated it. He didn't dance or drink. He only came with us to try and relax a bit, because he'd been having trouble sleeping. But he wasn't very good at relaxing. He was so ambitious. He couldn't switch his brain off. I've never met anyone so obsessed with their work, before or since.' Ethan sighed. 'Poor Fernando. I wonder where he is.'

I wanted to ask him what he thought about the fact that Emily Lole didn't know anything about Fernando's family, or claimed not to. If she'd known the name of even one of his relatives, perhaps they could have shed some light on the mystery of his whereabouts. I decided not to mention this to Ethan, because if I did I would have to tell him I'd got the information from Valerie Williams and he would be bound to wonder what I was doing snooping around college, trying to unearth stray facts. Good point: what was I doing? Nothing seemed clear any more, in my drunken haze.

The wild boar terrine was followed by chicken breast stuffed with avocado and Stilton to the accompaniment of Chateau de Fesles 1985. Dessert was a spiral-shaped cake called 'L'âme de mon rêve' that somehow managed to stand up like a little helter-skelter on each plate. I stared at mine for a while before starting to eat it, not wanting to ruin its artistic effect. This could be our last feast, I thought. These could be our last helter-skelter-shaped cakes. The thought distressed me deeply, not because of the cakes themselves – I'm not that trivial – but because of what they symbolised: a level of quality that we weren't going to find anywhere else. Summerton was, quite simply, the best. Even if Sebastian got the Canterbury job or the Sheffield job, it would never be like this. I decided to go and see Daphne Fielding first thing tomorrow morning. She'd supported Sebastian on Wednesday; I might be able to persuade her to annul the committee's decision, reconvene the panel, open the matter up again. She clearly hated Terri, so it was in her interests to ensure she wouldn't have to work with her. I sighed, knowing this was no more than a desperate fantasy. Daphne would probably send me away with a flea in my ear, if a flea was not too plebeian a creature for her to administer.

Ethan and Daphne were now discussing how to make Oxbridge more attractive to state school pupils. 'We need to change our image,' Ethan was saying. 'Make ourselves more accessible.'

'I'm not sure they'd want to come,' said Daphne. 'They think of Oxbridge as over-privileged and élitist, and they despise us for it.'

'That's true,' I chipped in. Daphne looked at me with barely concealed contempt, evidently thinking that, breath-of-fresh-air-wise, I was reaching pneumonia-inducing levels. What did the woman have against me, I wondered. I was agreeing with her, for Christ's sake. 'I went to a state school,' I said, 'and we all thought Oxbridge was full of Hooray Henrys. We wouldn't have been seen dead here.'

'This is the sort of attitude we're up against, you see,' Daphne said to Ethan, pointing at me.

'I don't think that any more,' I added quickly, not wanting to be misunderstood.

'Exactly,' said Ethan. 'The trouble with this image of Cambridge as privileged and élitist . . .'

'Oh, no, I still think that,' I interrupted him. Everyone stared at me. I seemed to be having difficulty making myself understood. 'I mean, it's obviously privileged.' I pointed at my pudding. 'Where else do you get desserts called "L'âme de mon rêve"? What I meant was, about changing my mind, if I were seventeen again, knowing what I know now, I'd see that as a reason to go, not not to go.' I wished I hadn't drunk so much wine.

'What? I don't quite understand,' said Terri.

'It's perfectly simple,' Daphne snarled at her. Did she mean it was simple or I was?

'You've got to grab every privilege you can,' I slurred. 'Because no one gives a shit about you. Just look at Sebastian.' Everyone did so obediently, except Sebastian, who turned to look at me. 'He's brilliant, everyone knows that, and he hasn't got a job. Who's going to change that? Who's going to make everything all right for him? No one, that's who!'

'Kate, be quiet,' Sebastian said sharply. 'You're pissed.'

'I know I'm pissed. It's still true, though. If you want to attract more state school kids, just send me round to talk to them. I'll tell them that while they're busy being cool and anti-bourgeois, other people are studying for their Oxbridge exams and those people are going to pinch their jobs if they don't watch out and they'll be left with nothing.'

'Are you talking about me?' Terri looked me straight in the eye.

'Not specifically, no,' I said, as the cake plates were removed by waiters with Olympic stamina levels. Trays of *petits fours* were now in circulation, as was the Fonseca 1963. 'I'm trying to make a general point, namely that if some people are privileged and others aren't, it makes sense to try to be one who is, doesn't it?'

There was a long silence. Finally, Daphne said, 'I can't argue with that. People need to be competitive if they want to survive in the world.'

'That's horrible,' said Terri. 'I don't agree with any of this at all.'

'I feel like the speaker in the House of Commons here, trying to calm everyone down,' said Ethan amiably, in one final attempt to inject charm and banter back into the proceedings.

'The division between the haves and have-nots is . . . one of the greatest causes of misery in the world,' said Terri earnestly. 'You can't just say you want to be one of the . . . haves. What about the people who can't be? That's such a male attitude. Women should look after the underdog because most of the time we *are* the underdog.' Except in flat 3, Noble House, I thought, where there wouldn't have been room to squeeze even the tiniest poodle under Joe's rung on the status ladder.

'You bloody hypocrite! You're the most competitive person I've ever met.' Daphne scowled at her. Joe emitted a loud sigh. That was the moment at which my hatred for Terri peaked. How dared such a blatant overdog, who couldn't even take the odd Sunday off work to spend time with her daughter, who lived in the library and did everything she could to ensure that she got the best research position in the country, pretend to care about anyone but herself?

It was a combination of excessive wine and accumulated anger that made me say what I said to Terri as we walked up the stairs to the Master's Lodge for drinks. Joe and Daphne Fielding were immediately behind us, and

Sebastian and Keith Cobain behind them. 'Oh,' I began innocently, as if it had just occurred to me. 'Some bloke was looking for you the other day. I bumped into him in the road, just outside Noble House. His name was . . . hang on a sec . . .' I pretended to search my memory. 'Could it have been Gary?'

Chapter Twenty-four

A Very Modern Marriage

I regretted it the minute I'd said it. What the hell was I
doing? I hadn't thought it through at all. I should at least
have turned on my mobile phone first to see if Rod had left
a message. He might already have found out that Gary
Conley was nobody of any particular significance to Terri,
maybe just a remote family friend. In which case it was
unlikely he would turn up at Noble House out of the blue.
Perhaps he didn't even know Terri's address. She obviously
didn't know his, since she'd had to ring R English to try to
trace Gary.

'What?' Terri whispered, gripping my arm with both her
hands. Her face had turned white under its make-up.
'Gary? What did he look like?' I felt my heart leap up to the
top of my throat. She believed me. Calm down, I told
myself. Of course she believed me, why wouldn't she? She
didn't know about my residency in her wardrobe. From her
point of view, there was no way I could know about Gary
Conley unless what I was telling her was true.

'Oh . . . er . . . well, I don't know, sort of . . . erm . . .' I
muttered stupidly, playing for time.

'Tall? Dark? Green eyes? Good-looking?' Terri hissed
eagerly as her talons embedded themselves in my arm.

'Well, yeah, I suppose so.'

'When was this?'

'Oh . . . a day, couple of days ago. I don't remember
exactly.' I decided I could get away with being extremely

vague. There was no reason why the incident should have held any particular significance for me.

'Oh my God,' she gasped, still clinging to my arm.

'Are you okay, Terri?' Joe asked from the stair below, putting a hand on her shoulder.

'She's drunk,' said Daphne disapprovingly. 'Look, she can't even stand up on her own.'

'Mum, stop it. Terri, are you feeling all right?'

'She's fine,' I said. 'Come on, let's go and get a drink.' I speeded up my pace and Terri hurried after me.

'Don't say anything to Joe or Daphne,' she said, her fingers pulling at the sleeve of my dress. 'Please, I can't explain now, but you mustn't say anything.'

'Oh,' I said, feigning doubt and confusion. 'Well ... okay, if you say so.'

'What did he say? What were his exact words? How did he seem? Did he look happy or sad?' I twisted my face into a quizzical, thoughtful expression, pouring myself a large whisky from a glass decanter on the table. The whole top floor of the Master's Lodge was packed full of people, many of whom were lighting up cigarettes. What a good idea, I thought, and lit one myself. Terri and I were standing in the corner of the room, next to one end of the drinks table, which stretched the length of a whole wall. Spirits of all varieties, as well as water, orange juice, chocolates and open wooden boxes full of cigars and cigarettes, were laid out on white lace doilies on the green velour tablecloths. I should have been moving on to water, not whisky, but suddenly I was in the mood to celebrate. Terri was staring at me wildly, waiting for me to answer her questions. I no longer regretted my Gary fabrication. It had been rash, foolish perhaps, but it had worked. Terri was either very frightened of Gary, or very obsessed with him in some other way. I didn't think it would take me too long to work out which. I looked around to check that Joe and Daphne were suitably far away and eventually spotted them at the opposite side of the room, being ranted at by

185

Lloyd Lunnon. I heard him say to Daphne that anyone who believed film and media were proper subjects for academic study was a cretinous something or other.

'I can't remember,' I said after a long pause. 'I didn't take much notice of him.'

'Try.' Terri's lips narrowed and her eyes flashed.

'Well, he asked if you lived in Noble House,' I lied. 'I said you did.'

'Did you tell him what flat number?'

'No. He didn't ask.'

'Thank God.' She closed her eyes.

'Listen, Terri, if I'd realised it was this important I would have paid more attention. Should I not have told him you lived there? I mean, you seem scared of him. I didn't realise he was someone you wanted to avoid.'

'I'm scared of him coming round,' she said, 'because of Joe. Of course I don't want to avoid him, I've been . . . well . . .' Her voice tailed off. She looked over her shoulder to see where Joe was.

'Oh, I see,' I said. 'You're having an affair with him.' So Rod had been right.

'No, no,' Terri's face creased with distaste. 'Not at all. I haven't seen him for four years. This is what I can't understand. How did he know where I lived? How did he find me? I didn't even know he wanted to, I thought he'd practically forgotten me. Maybe he asked at Pembroke. They know where I live. Still, they don't normally give out that sort of information.' She seemed to be talking more to herself than to me.

'I don't get it,' I said. 'Who is he, exactly?'

'There isn't time.' Terri looked over her shoulder again. 'Joe could come over at any minute. What else happened? Try to remember everything.'

'Nothing,' I said. I was annoyed with myself for the guilt I was beginning to feel. This was a woman who treated her husband like shit, I reminded myself, a person who stood between Sebastian and the Enmity. Nobody seemed to feel guilty about Sebastian's misery, least of all Terri, so why should I care about her? Still, Gary Conley clearly meant a lot to her and here I was, coolly lying about him, recklessly messing with her life and her head, not knowing what sort of effect my words might have. I couldn't help feeling like a bit of a cow. My regret at having embarked upon this series of falsehoods began to creep back, but I could hardly opt out of the situation now that I'd created it. 'He asked if you lived there, I said yes, but you weren't usually in during the day, and he just . . . wandered off.'

'That sounds like Gary,' she whispered. Tears filled her eyes.

'I'm sorry,' I said, half meaning it. 'I didn't mean to upset you. Perhaps I shouldn't have said anything.'

'No, no.' She shook her head. 'You should, of course you should. You haven't upset me. I'm happier that I have been for . . . years.'

'Really?' This took me aback. I wished I knew what the hell was going on.

'Oh, yes.' She smiled through her tears. 'He hasn't forgotten me. He came all the way from Reading to see me. That means he must still care about me.'

'Reading?' I pretended to be surprised. 'That's where he lives? Oh, I see. I wondered why anyone would seriously consider Reading as an alternative to Summerton.'

'If I thought Gary wanted me to, I'd go to Reading like a shot,' said Terri, then quickly, aware of the implication of what she'd said, added, 'Oh, it's not what it sounds, it really isn't. It's not that I don't love Joe . . .'

'Listen,' I cut in, seeing Keith Cobain approaching us and realising I didn't have much time. 'Gary must like you a lot to come all that way. If I were you, I'd . . . well, I'd follow my heart, and if that means going to Reading . . .' I felt a stab of guilt at the thought that I was encouraging Joe's wife to abandon him and their daughter, and elope to the M4 corridor. Still, she had effectively deserted them already and it was a desertion far worse than the simple geographical kind. There was no other man and no other place involved in Terri's abandonment of Joe in its present form – it was pure, unmitigated, close-range abandonment.

'But . . . you don't even know the situation. You don't know anything.' Terri eyed me suspiciously. 'You wouldn't have an ulterior motive for saying that, would you?'

'Of course not!' I gave her my best shocked look. 'What could I . . . oh, you mean the De La Wyche? Sebastian's not even second, Terri. It wouldn't do him any good if you turned the fellowship down. Rod Firsden would get it.'

'I suppose so. I'm sorry.' I adopted a wounded expression, but only briefly. I didn't want to overdo it.

'Kate!' Keith Cobain ambled over, having refilled his brandy glass. 'Terri! How are you both? Did you enjoy the feast?'

'Excuse me,' said Terri, pushing past him. She marched up to the table and poured herself a tumbler full of whisky.

'What's up with her?' Keith asked me.

'Dunno. Daphne Fielding's been snapping at her all evening. Maybe it's that.'

'I don't know why she hates her so much,' said Keith. 'It's not going to be much fun around here next year if Terri takes the job. There are enough feuds in the college already.'

'Daphne was one of the people who appointed her,' I reminded him.

'I know. I can't believe it. She must have been outvoted by the others.' Not according to Damian Selinger, I thought, but I didn't say anything. 'Still, Daphne's very professional. She takes her position here too seriously to let personal feelings get in the way of work.' Based on what I'd seen of Daphne I was inclined to disagree, but then I didn't know her as well as Keith did. She'd been indiscreet tonight, but hadn't we all, me especially? All that champagne and wine was enough to make anyone behave unprofessionally. I hoped Keith was right; if Daphne was a sensible, fair-minded person, she'd have no reason to refuse to answer my questions when I went to see her tomorrow.

I saw Bryony waving at me from the other side of the room. I waved back, swearing under my breath at the sight of Damian by her side.

'Ah, yes, Damian's new woman.' Keith grinned lasciviously. 'I sat opposite her. She seems . . . rather nice.' I laughed at the note of puzzlement in his voice.

'Too nice for him, you mean?'

'Well . . . still, he's changed a lot. I think he and Martine brought out the worst in each other.'

'Do you think Martine ran off with Fernando Rose?' I asked. I'd put the question to virtually everyone else I'd spoken to over the past few days, so I saw no reason to leave Keith out.

'I know she didn't.' He smiled. 'Nothing was further from her mind than Fernando that night. She had the hots for Ethan.'

'Ethan says she was after you,' I said, confused.

'Oh.' Keith frowned. 'Oh . . . well, possibly. She may have made passes at both of us. In fact, I think she did. Ethan was probably too modest to tell you.'

'So where did Fernando go, if not somewhere with Martine? Where did they both go? Why isn't anyone curious, or worried about them?'

'We were . . . are . . . but they're both adults. Sometimes people move on. What could we have done?'

I frowned. This was all most unsatisfactory. It wasn't so much the unsolved mysteries that were making me feel giddy and out of my depth, even though they were increasing in number at an alarming rate. I could have coped with the idea that some facts remained unknown if only there were some kind of general consensus as to precisely what information was lacking. I seemed to be the only person who was aware that questions needed to be asked, or who cared enough to ask them. Without anyone to back up my perception of the situation, I felt lonely and paranoid.

It suddenly occurred to me that no one to whom I had spoken in connection with this whole business was what you might call a normal person. Apart from Valerie, I corrected myself, but even she was normal in a scary way. She was a bland, bureaucratic emblem of the seethingly corrupt system, I thought drunkenly. Rod was so obsessed with the Enmity that he sobbed in the cars of total strangers. Terri sewed names into her dresses and, despite having been offered the best job in the world, was considering moving to Reading to be closer to a man she hadn't seen for four years with whom she was not having an affair. Emily Lole thought I was part of a conspiracy to conceal from her the whereabouts of Fernando Rose. Damian Selinger had a history of attacking women with cricket bats, even if this tendency was currently dormant. Bryony James was in love with Damian Selinger, which was about as serious a form of abnormality as it was possible to encounter. Daphne Fielding seemed intent on publicly humiliating her daughter-in-law in a most unseemly fashion. I felt as if I was navigating a perilous course across a strange planet, inhabited by creatures so different from me that I couldn't even begin to identify with them.

I tried to comfort myself with the thought that I wasn't as much of an outcast as all that; I was pretty odd myself, sneaking around trying to achieve the impossible, making up stupid stories about tall, dark visitors and hiding in people's wardrobes.

I started to wander over to Terri but she saw me coming and moved away. 'Not now,' she hissed at me, jerking her head. I saw that Joe and Sebastian were advancing upon her from the other side.

'Shall we make a move?' said Joe.

'Not yet.' I noticed Terri's lips tighten impatiently at this suggestion. 'I ought to network a bit, in case I decide to take the job.'

'Oh. Oh, yeah, that's a good idea.' Joe nodded enthusiastically. 'Well, I'll go, then, pick Scarlett up from

190

the babysitter.'

'Can we get going too?' Sebastian asked me. 'I'm knackered.'

'I'm too drunk to drive,' I said. 'Why don't you get a lift with Joe? I'll ... stay.' I gave him a meaningful look, indicating that I had not yet concluded my investigations for the evening.

'Okay,' he said, frowning at me. 'Don't be too long.'

'I won't,' I said. 'I'll get a cab with Terri later.' Terri edged her body away from mine as I said this. She was probably regretting having told me as much as she had about Gary, suspecting – correctly, I might add – that I planned to subject her to merciless questioning at the earliest available opportunity.

'Joe, when you get back, don't forget to bring the laundry in and put the bin out,' said Terri without a trace of guilt in her voice. 'And Scarlett's bed needs changing. Oh, and don't forget to pay the babysitter.'

'Okay,' he said happily. Sebastian's lip curled into a sneer and I coughed discreetly to remind him not to say anything. Sometimes anger rendered him temporarily unable to keep his thoughts to himself.

After they'd gone I said to Terri, 'Joe must be exhausted, the amount of housework he does on top of having a full-time job.' I smiled broadly, so that she couldn't prove I was attacking her.

'Oh, he doesn't mind,' said Terri. 'He's a feminist. We have a very modern marriage. Not like my mum and dad. My dad thinks his work's so important that he shouldn't have to do anything at home. So do most men. Joe's not like that at all.'

'No,' I said pointedly. 'I've noticed.'

'He doesn't trivialise my career the way so many men do. Even when he's got a really important project on at work, like he has at the moment, he still takes an interest in what I'm doing.' Suddenly Bryony James was beside us, miraculously free of Damian.

'Are you talking about Joe's project, the Bressingham contract?' Bryony asked cheerfully. 'He's just been telling me and Damian all about it. Damian's decided to go to the Jive Hive with Keith Cobain.' This last statement was directed at me. I gave Bryony a conspiratorial look and we exchanged a relieved smile. Finally it looked as though we would get a chance to talk. 'It sounds fascinating,' Bryony said to Terri. 'Which did you tell him to go for, the orange or the black?' I had no idea what this meant; it was clearly something that only someone with a detailed knowledge of Joe's work would understand.

'Bressingham contract?' Terri looked confused and then blushed. 'Oh ... probably, yes. Erm ... I don't know really. Remind me. Orange or black ... what?'

Chapter Twenty-five

Joe Fielding – Curriculum Vitae

Name
Joseph John Fielding.

Address
Flat 3, Noble House, 14 Renshaw Road, Cambridge.

Age
Thirty.

Place of Birth
Wigan, Lancashire.

Marital Status
Dire. Domestically exploited in the name of feminism which, on close inspection, appears to be somewhat of a charade. Many sacrifices made for wife's career, meanwhile wife is making decisions about said career based, it seems, upon the whims of Gary Conley, or at least his imaginary whims, as misrepresented by neighbour with ulterior motive. One daughter who, it is taken for granted by all concerned, will stay in Cambridge whether her mother moves to Reading or not.

Employment History
Marketing Consultant for Spectrum Technology since leaving university. If you want to know what the job

entails, what Joe does on a day-to-day basis, don't ask his wife, who needs a stranger to tell her that there is a choice to be made between orange and black. 'Orange or black . . . what?' she asks. We must assume this is something to do with a particular marketing campaign, or is this underestimating our Joe? It could be orange or black suit to wear to the divorce courts, orange or black chemical dye to put into Terri's next whites-only wash. No, no, this is too optimistic. Joe shows no such promising signs of rebellion.

Qualifications and Education
BA Hons Business and Management Studies from what used to be Oxford Polytechnic. Chose this subject for future financial security and now earns a substantial salary. Terri's selective feminism does not involve objecting to economic reliance on a man.

Strengths and Weaknesses
Main weakness is naïvety about what human beings are capable of. Despite having spent thirty years in a world that contains starvation, rape, murder, biological weapons and state-hosted executions, still retains belief that most people known personally to him, and certainly all those he might meet in the Sidney Street branch of Sainsbury's, are decent sorts who would do the right thing if at all possible. Is very reluctant to think badly of anybody, apart from well-known historical figures of whom one must think badly in order to be socially acceptable. This weakness leads directly to inappropriate good behaviour and persistent failure to recognise true nature of wife. If Terri moves to Reading and shacks up with Gary Conley, the two of them will probably send their dirty laundry to Cambridge by courier, at Joe's expense, for him to take care of and send back clean, fabric-conditioned and ironed. It is conceivable that he would agree to do this.

Strengths include excellent parenting skills, a kind and helpful nature (this doubles as a weakness, depending on

194

who benefits), a cheerful and easygoing temperament, almost superhuman energy levels that enable him to do work of one sort or another from six in the morning until after midnight most days. Also, never leaves socks or underwear in washing or drying machines and ensures safe return of items left there by other less careful launderers like Sebastian. Very practical, in fact. Of all the people whose CVs have been included so far, I would be willing to bet hard cash that Joe is the only one who can do the following things:

1 Assemble an item of furniture that comes in lots of little bits with a set of instructions
2 Change a car tyre (I should be able to do this, as a driving instructor, but I'm too weak to twist the wheel nuts with a wrench)
3 Unblock a drain
4 Rid computers of viruses
5 Make a Baked Alaska

You can usually sense fairly soon after meeting someone whether he or she is a useful person or a merely ornamental person. Joe is someone who shakes off more dust than he gathers. He is to inconvenience what celery is to calories. But if Joe is celery, Gary Conley may be a chocolate éclair.

Is Gary Conley a useful person, or is he balloon-debate-casualty fodder? What can he do? Might as well bring him into it – we all have to compete with other people after we send out our CVs, so why not start at source? Imagine that: being defeated within the confines of your own curriculum vitae, before it even reaches a prospective employer. Well, Gary Conley can influence Terri's choice of job at a distance of four years – that's a pretty impressive achievement. And that's only the real Gary Conley. Who knows what my imaginary Gary, the one I pretended to meet in the grounds of Noble House, could do. I'll have to give it some thought.

Other Information

I have some other information I could give Joe, but I don't want to hurt him. On the other hand, I so, so want to hurt Terri, even though I felt a bit guilty when she got upset about my Gary lies after the feast. That was just a moment of weakness. Or was it? Am I basically a nice person trying to be ruthless or a ruthless person feigning the occasional pang of conscience? Two more unanswered questions to add to my list.

Chapter Twenty-six

Panel Beating

It was half past one in the morning and I was sitting in the Micra in Noble House's car park, having spent the past hour and a half with Bryony James. Losing Terri had proved remarkably simple. Shortly after Joe and Sebastian had left, Terri had spotted a space in the circle around Sir Patrick Chichester, the Master, and had rushed over to suck up to him. Damian had been persuaded by Keith Cobain and a few of the other younger fellows to go for a lads' night out at the Jive Hive, so Bryony invited me up to their love nest in Queen's Court where, she said, we could talk properly.

I'd found our conversation so unsettling that, in my eagerness to get away quickly, I'd driven home afterwards over the limit, which was something I hadn't been stupid enough to do for years. I often promised myself that if Sebastian ever got himself anything resembling a good income I'd make a point of driving drunkly and frivolously past lots of police stations. To risk my licence without risking starvation and penury was my idea of luxury.

I didn't go straight inside. Sebastian might still have been awake and I wasn't ready to speak to anyone yet, not until I'd had a chance to take it all in.

I was so preoccupied that I almost forgot to switch on my mobile phone to see whether Rod had left a message. I pulled it out of my bag and punched in my pin number. Within seconds the phone was ringing, green light flashing.

'You have two new messages,' said my Callback service, then Rod's voice came on the line.

'Kate, it's me, Rod. Um . . . I don't really know where to begin. Can you come round first thing tomorrow morning, Saturday? As early as you like. Um . . . I suppose I'd better say a bit more, but the trouble is I don't really know whether today was a success or not.' There were a few more ums and ahs while Rod assembled his thoughts. I drummed my fingers on the dashboard impatiently. I wished he'd sorted out what he was going to say before he phoned. If he'd left a four-hour message full of indecisive ramblings my bill would be immense. I decided to introduce him, next time we met, to the proverb 'He who hesitates is lost'. 'Well, I found him.' Rod imparted some information finally. 'I found Gary Conley. He's at the YMCA in Reading, like you said. I spoke to him for quite a while but . . . well, he was exceedingly difficult to talk to. He knows Terri, but not very well. I'm not sure whether he can do anything. Oh, and he gave me a video. Oh, this is silly, I can't explain now. Just come round tomorrow. 'Bye.'

I chewed the inside of my lip thoughtfully. Why had Gary Conley given Rod a video? From his tone of voice, I could tell Rod was dissatisfied with the results of his trip. He'd sounded particularly miserable when he said, 'I don't know whether he can do anything.' He had obviously been hoping to find Gary Conley poised to spring into action and whisk Terri away so that Rod could have the Enmity. I could have told him that was unlikely to happen, although after the evening I'd had, nothing seemed impossible. Besides, I didn't much care any more what Gary Conley could or couldn't do, being more concerned with what I could do in his name. My made-up story had caused Terri to blurt out that she would take the Reading job if Gary wanted her to, and I was confident that a couple more fake sightings would do the trick, especially if I put some convincing words into his mouth. Terri would find out I'd been lying, of course, especially once she'd moved to

Reading and confronted the man himself, but by then it wouldn't matter; she would already have turned down the Enmity. Her good opinion of me wasn't top on my list of priorities. Getting rid of Terri was the easy part. Rod would be much more problematic. Suddenly I felt incredibly sad and was pleased to be distracted by my second message.

This one was from Sebastian, who told me to hurry up and come home. He sounded baffled, as though he couldn't work out why I'd deserted him. I resolved to try to find something to dislike about Rod tomorrow. Even though I was doing it for Sebastian, I felt incredibly disloyal consorting with the De La Wyche reserve behind his back and more disloyal still because so far I'd been unable to hate Rod. He was a bit loopy, but I found him quite amusing. I laughed to myself, remembering how he'd leaped out of the Micra to rush off to Reading. Sebastian wouldn't have done that; he would have adopted a defeatist attitude and said there was no point.

I tutted at myself – there I was again, comparing Rod and Sebastian. I was nearly as bad as the De La Wyche panel. I rang our flat and got the answering machine. Sebastian had obviously gone to bed. I left a message saying I was on my way, then I switched on the Micra's overhead light and got my notebook and pen out of my bag.

When I tried to make notes about my encounter with Bryony, I found I didn't know where to begin. I decided to approach the task as I would the minutes of a meeting. I'd started off the proceedings by telling her I'd read her letter and expressing sympathy. She had then asked me what I thought of her and Damian as a couple.

She professed to want my honest opinion, so I gave it to her. 'I find it hard to get my head round the two of you being together,' I said.

'Why? Because you knew Martine?'

'No. Well, partly, maybe. I mean, she and Damian used to fight all the time and . . . try to injure each other. Has he told you about that?'

'Oh, yes. He's told me everything.' Bryony sat straight-backed on the torture chair, cupping her hands around a mug of coffee. She liked her coffee instant and strong, as I did, except she only had two spoonfuls of Nescafé where I had two and a half. 'I know he detached her retina once and nearly blinded her.' She smiled, as if we were talking about herbaceous borders or exchanging recipes. 'Things were so bad by then that they didn't know how to extricate themselves.' I raised a sceptical eyebrow. Anyone who couldn't work out how to extricate him- or herself when the alternative was retina detachment was in my view too stupid for sympathy. 'Do you know what first attracted me to Damian?' Bryony asked.

'This place?' I looked around at the gleaming polished surfaces, deep-pile carpets and high ceilings. 'The fact that the washing-up gets done by a bedder every day?'

She laughed. 'No. His bitterness.' A quote from George Herbert's 'Sighs and Groans' ran through my mind: 'put not thy hand into the bitter box'. I'd read that poem over and over since Rod first showed it to me. I almost knew it by heart. 'It wasn't a coincidence that I met Damian in the Mitre Tavern,' Bryony went on. She waited, giving me an opportunity to ask the obvious question.

'What do you mean, it wasn't a coincidence?' I said obligingly.

'I'd followed him there. I'd been in Cambridge for a week by then.' She paused and smiled, baiting me.

'What? Why?' I had never been good at playing hard to get.

'I was trying to find out as much as I could about the people on the panel. I hung around in the college bar, chatted to porters and students. By Saturday I'd gathered quite a lot of information.'

'What? You're saying you came here over a week before your interview to . . .'

'To do research,' she finished my question for me. 'Yes. It was what I always did before job interviews. It doesn't occur to most people.'

'No,' I agreed. It sounded like a mad idea to me. Being well prepared was one thing but this made no sense.

'You'd be amazed how much you can find out in a university or a college, just by gossiping with people. Within a few days I'd heard all about Professor Fielding and Terri hating each other, all about Emily Lole having a nervous breakdown after Fernando Rose disappeared. I got to know the panel members by sight and followed them around a bit. That wasn't very exciting. Valerie Williams and Emily Lole never seemed to leave college, and Professor Fielding only went back and forth from college to home. Damian's little excursion to the Mitre Tavern was exotic in comparison.' She smiled.

'Hang on a minute,' I said. 'Why? Why did you do all this?'

'I wanted to be offered the job,' she said simply. 'The De La Wyche fellowship was the thirtieth academic job I applied for, the twenty-second I got an interview for.' My eyes widened. Her record was worse than Sebastian's. An unfamiliar sensation, not unlike seasickness, rolled through my body. I was either scared or excited, I couldn't work out which. 'I considered . . . well, still do consider myself as a bit of an expert on job interviews, I've been to so many,' she went on. 'One thing I worked out pretty soon is that the best man does not always win.' I nodded eagerly. She was saying exactly what I'd thought so many times. 'And the reason he doesn't, or she doesn't, is because people are involved, people whose moods, quirks and personal histories are brought to bear, whether they know it or not, on every single decision they make. This is why I started doing my pre-interview research. Get to know a bit about the panel members as people, then you can drop things into your conversation at the interview which chime in with opinions or preferences of theirs. Do you understand?'

'I'm not sure,' I said. I thought I did, but for some reason I didn't want to admit it yet.

'It doesn't always work. Sometimes you don't find out

much that's of any use. But other times you do. For the De La Wyche interview, my plan was to stress the fact that my research proposal was inter-disciplinary, linking artistic, scientific and philosophical approaches to the Antarctic. I even said there'd be a section concerned with medicine, its cultural relevance in the battle between humanity and nature. I knew, if I did that, that all the panel members would feel important. Valerie, according to college gossip, is against any academic research that's too theoretical and doesn't benefit society. Emily's a scientist, Damian's a philosopher . . .'

'I get it,' I interrupted her. 'Go on.' I think I was waiting for her to incriminate or exonerate herself. I would have been happy with either. At the moment I was simply confused.

'I'd heard enough about Damian and Emily Lole to work out that they were both deeply insecure, damaged people. Professor Fielding had it in for her nasty daughter-in-law who'd stolen her only son. You see?' She beamed at me. 'All of them had bees in their bonnets, of one sort or another. All I had to do, I thought, was tailor my answers, in the interview, to their individual concerns, one by one, make each of them feel important and worthwhile by emphasising the vital roles played by their subjects in my proposed research.' She patted her knees with her hands. 'I've done it with loads of jobs,' she said. 'One time I found out a professor who would be interviewing me loved blondes, so I dyed my hair. Another time I knew there'd be a famous anti-nuclear philosopher chairing the committee: I wore a CND earring. It's like a game. I call it "panel beating".'

'It's a game you can't be very good at, if you've been turned down twenty-two times,' I said cruelly. It turned my stomach to listen to Bryony boasting about the sneaky tactics she'd used to try to beat the other candidates. I was also annoyed I hadn't thought of it first. Perhaps Sebastian and I could go to Sheffield and Canterbury a few days before his interviews and see what morsels of gossip we could dig up.

'I never said I'd been turned down twenty-two times. I said I'd had twenty-two interviews.' Bryony's unflappability irritated me. Nothing I said could ruffle her. 'I've been offered the last seven jobs I was shortlisted for, before the De La Wyche. I turned them all down.'

'You turned them down?' Now I really was lost. 'Why?'

'Because I don't need to work. I'm rich. My pools win . . .'

'I know, but . . . then why go to the trouble of doing all this . . . snooping and sneaking around to try and get jobs if you're only going to turn them down?'

'Revenge.' She smiled expectantly, watching me closely to gauge my reaction.

Chapter Twenty-seven

A Change of Vocation

'You've read my life story,' she said. 'After everything that happened, resentment just took over my whole existence. It was as if I had no personality of my own any more, I was just this . . . this walking grudge.' I nodded, feeling not unlike one of these myself. How long had it been since my every waking moment wasn't dominated by worry and resentment about Sebastian's lack of success on the job front? 'I used to have vivid fantasies about killing them all: Blake, my referees, Selena Gamble, Lionel Suggs, all the people who interviewed me and turned me down. If I hadn't been so convinced I was a born failure I'm sure I would have tried to murder them. That's how desperate I felt, but what were the chances of my getting away with it, when I couldn't seem to do anything else right?'

I smiled nervously, anxious not to get on the wrong side of her. She was clearly deranged, in a far worse state than either myself or Sebastian. I may have had the occasional interview panel massacre fantasy, but I confined them strictly to my imagination.

'I know what you're thinking.' Bryony chuckled. 'And you're right, I probably was mad at the time. Don't pretend you can't understand, though. I saw the state you were in when I came back and found you here with Damian. You were desperate, you had that look in your eyes. I recognised it immediately. I used to look like that, before my book came out and got rave reviews all over the place. And then

I won the money. But I'm not interested in that, really, the money or the book, I only told you about them to explain how I was able to do what I did next, to get revenge.' She leaped up and grabbed both my hands. Suddenly she was talking so quickly that I found it hard to keep up. I had evidently underestimated her desire to share with me the details of her revenge and now here I was, trapped in a tower room with a madwoman. As disturbed people went, I preferred the Emily Lole variety, those whose mental instability is immediately apparent and therefore easier to avoid. 'I knew I'd stand a good chance of getting a job, after the reception my book got, but I no longer needed one. I was rich,' she squealed. 'Suddenly I knew what I wanted to do with my life. I wasn't interested in being an academic any more, that was the old me. All the new me wanted was revenge on those bastards, on the whole corrupt system that had nearly ruined my life. That's when I started playing my game.'

'Panel beating?' I asked wearily.

'Yes. I applied for every job in my field that I saw advertised. I got interviews for nearly all of them. I'd go to the place a few days early, do my research on the committee members and try as hard as I could at the interview to say the things they wanted to hear. Every time I was offered a job, which was nearly all the time – I think there was only one I wasn't offered – I would accept and then, at the last minute, once I'd made them really want me, I'd turn them down. I always left it as late as I possibly could, right until just before the beginning of term, then I'd pull out and really drop them in the shit. The great thing was, everyone still wanted me because my book had had such an impact. People started to ask me at interviews why I'd turned such-and-such a place down, and I just smiled sweetly and said I wanted to work for the absolute best university, which of course was them, and they fell for it every time. I kept a list of all the places I'd jilted – that was how I thought of it – Leeds, York, Bristol, Swansea, Sussex, UCL, Exeter.

Summerton was going to be my crowning glory. I couldn't wait to add Cambridge's best college to my collection of victims. And then I met Damian. Do you want another coffee?'

I shook my head.

'Are you shocked?' she asked me.

'I don't think so,' I said slowly, still unsure of my feelings. 'I don't know . . . I mean, wouldn't it have been a better revenge on all the people who blocked your career to take one of the jobs you were offered? Then you'd really have beaten them, because you'd have the academic career you always wanted.' Even if Sebastian were lucky enough to win a large sum of money, I knew he would still want to be an academic. 'It seems to me they're still winning,' I said to Bryony. 'You've allowed yourself and your vocation to be sidetracked.'

'You're wrong,' Bryony flashed me a patronising, zealous smile. 'Revenge is my vocation. Damian said you wouldn't understand. Maybe you're not bitter enough yet.'

'I can assure you I am,' I said indignantly, then realised how ridiculous I sounded. I didn't have to prove myself to Bryony, nor did I want to.

'Meeting Damian – falling in love with him – really messed up my plans,' she said. 'I followed him to the Mitre Tavern, like I said. I didn't think he'd spotted me, but he had. We were standing at the bar and the barmaid came up to serve him. He looked straight at her and said, "Do you know I'm being followed by that scarecrow over there?" pointing at me. "It's been following me all day," he said. "I don't know what it wants."' Bryony laughed affectionately. 'I was wearing my retribution suit, you see – well, it's an interview suit, really.' She laughed again. 'I used to wear it every single day, until I met Damian. I called it that, because retribution was all I cared about. Do you want to see it?' I was about to say that I didn't especially, but Bryony was already half-way across the room. From a cupboard built into the living-room wall she produced a bent, rusty coathanger. 'Look,' she said, dangling a filthy maroon jacket and skirt in front of me. The jacket had what looked like a large coffee stain on the left lapel and the skirt appeared to have tyre marks on it. There were dark patches in the jacket's armpits.

'It's filthy.' I leaned away from the retribution suit. 'Ugh. It smells.'

Bryony giggled. 'I know. Isn't it cool? I used to love seeing the disgust on the panel's faces when I walked in wearing this. It was kind of like a statement: "I'm so good, I don't even have to wash my suit." I was the one in control, not them.' I frowned. 'You don't get it, do you?' She smiled patiently, like a special-needs teacher who had been assigned a particularly challenged pupil. 'I wanted to make a point. Job interviews mean pain. That's what the retribution suit reflects. It's symbolic.' Whatever it was, I wished Bryony would put it away. It smelled of a combination of gas leak and mould.

'You wore it every day?' I wasn't surprised Damian had been alerted to her pursuing presence with that stench behind him. 'Bryony, that's disgusting.'

'I felt disgusting. Why not look disgusting too?' She shrugged.

'You were saying about Damian.' I reminded her. 'He'd just accused you of following him to the Mitre.'

'That's right.' Bryony hung the suit over the door. It swung to and fro for a while, wafting its putrid scent into the air around us. 'Well, before I had a chance to deny I was following Damian, he turned on me and let rip with the most bitter tirade I'd ever heard.'

'What did he say?' I asked.

'That all the women he'd ever known had conspired to destroy him. He went through a whole long list: his mother, his sister, every girlfriend he'd ever had and Martine, of course. He accused me of being out to get him, which I couldn't deny because in a way I was.' She smiled fondly, as though she were recounting details of a romantic courtship. 'He said all women should be put in a meat-grinder.' She giggled. 'He was so full of hatred. You should have seen him. His top lip was so dry it stuck to his gums. He looked like a shark. It was at that moment I realised I was in love with him.'

'You're mad,' I said tactlessly. The effort to conceal my true attitude was becoming too much for me in my exhausted post-feast state.

'I know it sounds funny, but don't you see? No one else could touch me. For years I'd felt as if I'd been exiled from the human race. Suffering had warped me so much, I didn't have anything in common with normal people who behaved in a polite, civilised way. Every minute of my life, all I wanted to do was yell and scream and say awful things, but I was too much of a coward. I kept it all bottled up. Then suddenly there was Damian, freely expressing all the rage and hatred I felt, in a pub, in front of loads of people.' I wanted to ask her why she hadn't fallen for Lloyd Lunnon under the cloisters if she found freely expressed rage such a turn-on, but she was talking so quickly that I couldn't get a word in. 'It was such a relief. I stood there and listened to him shrieking, expelling all his fury into the air around us, and I could feel my own pain begin to drain away. It was as if a huge weight had been lifted from my shoulders. Everything he said ... well, it could have been me speaking.'

'No, it couldn't,' I said pedantically, annoyed by the inaccuracy of Bryony's thought processes. 'Your grudge was against interview panels and employers, whereas he was just being horrible and misogynist.'

'But he isn't horrible, or misogynist.' Bryony shook her head adamantly. 'I could tell he wasn't, despite what he was saying.' I said nothing. Anyone who hears a man saying women should be put into meat-grinders and concludes that he isn't a misogynist must either be exceptionally perceptive or downright dumb. If Bryony was the latter, there was no point trying to reason with her.

'Do you know what I did, when he stopped yelling?' she asked me eagerly. 'I kissed him. I walked up to him, put my arms round him and kissed him on the lips. No one in the pub could believe it. They were all watching to see what he'd do next.'

'And what did he do? Hit you?' I said hopefully.

'No. He did nothing. He just looked at me and blinked several times, as if he thought I was a hallucination. So I offered to buy him a drink. And he said yes. We sat down at a table and I told him what a wonderful effect he'd had on me, you know, with his yelling. I couldn't do it myself, you see. I'm the sort of person who bottles things up and I admired him so much. He could just go on and on endlessly, being loud and unpleasant. I know it sounds mad, but he made me feel I wasn't alone. He gave me a voice.'

'Oh, please,' I said, but Bryony didn't even pause for breath. She was full of the sort of comprehensive confidence found only in the entirely bonkers, the kind that enables a person to wear a sandwich-board without feeling like a pillock.

'You see I can just talk and talk now, and say everything I want to say.' Indeed, I thought. 'I could hardly string two words together before I met Damian, apart from at interviews but that didn't count. That was acting. I told him about my life, what had happened to me and . . . well, we just hit it off. It wasn't exactly love at first sight, but almost. That night we . . .'

'I get the point,' I said quickly, hoping to be spared any nocturnal anecdotes. I could live without hearing the origins of Damian's 'Frisky' nickname.

'No, no, I'm not talking about sex, although of course it happened.'

'Of course,' I said sarcastically. How could it fail to when the relationship had got off to such an amorous start?

'We just yelled and yelled. We broke things, most of the furniture, in fact. Damian had to ring the Junior Bursar the

209

next day for new chairs and tables and everything.'

'And he got them,' I said rhetorically. Summerton was rich enough to have plenty of spare furniture for just such an emergency. Who knew when a fellow would need to indulge in a spot of cathartic vandalism?

'Of course,' said Bryony. 'But that's not important. The point of this whole story is to explain why I dropped out. You wanted to know,' she reminded me.

'And I still don't,' I said.

'The one thing I didn't tell Damian about myself, that first night, was about my panel beating. He was all excited about me getting the De La Wyche. He said he could swing it for me and I really believed he could. But I couldn't abandon my revenge, not after all the effort I'd put in. And Summerton was going to be my big victory. Except that I loved Damian and couldn't bear to disappoint him. I'd have broken his heart if I'd knocked Summerton back.'

'Why didn't you tell him the truth?' I asked, kicking myself for the fact that I was still there, still listening. I should have put a stop to this conversation as soon as it veered off in the direction of extreme weirdness and fungus-ridden suits, instead of sitting there nodding and asking sensible questions as if I were talking to a regular, stable person. The trouble was, curiosity had temporarily triumphed over all my more noble impulses and, whatever else she was, Bryony certainly wasn't dull.

'I thought he'd try to force me to take the job if I got it. He wanted me at Summerton and . . . well, Damian's quite selfish. He doesn't like it if things don't go his way.'

'Damian, selfish?' I said snidely. 'Never!' She giggled conspiratorially, which somehow neutralised my sharp comment. I wanted to pull her hair and wrestle her to the ground, but didn't in case she fell in love with me. That seemed to be her reaction to unbridled hostility.

'I was a bag of nerves at the interview. I was so worried about what I'd do if I got the job. I think, subconsciously, I deliberately messed it up so that there was no way they could give it to me. Damian was furious with me for doing so badly. He called me a total loser, which really upset me.' Bryony said this as though it reflected a quirk particular to her, as if most people would be thrilled to be called total losers by their lovers. 'He didn't speak to me all of Tuesday night,' she went on. 'On Wednesday, when he got back from work, I couldn't hold out any longer – I had to tell him the truth. I thought he'd kill me, but he found it funny. He loved the idea of panel beating. That's one of the things I adore about Damian. He can really empathise with other people's revenges. I was expecting him to say what I'd been doing was pointless and destructive, but he was all for it, he really entered into the spirit of it. He was even more vindictive and vengeful than me. You see, he's not always selfish,' she added as an afterthought. I'm sure my mouth must have fallen open at this point. Did Bryony seriously expect to convince me of Damian's benevolence by citing his ability to enthuse about her wrongdoings as if they were his own?

'Everything would have been fine,' she said, stunning me yet again with her twisted perception of things, 'except that I felt as though I'd fallen at the last hurdle. I hated the thought that Summerton would be the one panel I hadn't beaten. But Damian – he's so brilliant – he thought of a way round it. He said the panel hadn't made their decision yet, even though they should have done, because Professor Fielding had had to leave early. He told me to phone the college and withdraw on Wednesday night, and then it would still be me rejecting them. They wouldn't be able to reject me. So that's what I did.'

'Great. I'm thrilled for you,' I said, getting up to go. 'You've got a grim boyfriend and no job. I mean, what are you going to do with the rest of your life? You can't panel-beat for ever.'

'No, it's time for a change,' she agreed. 'I'm moving on to a bigger, better revenge. It was Damian's idea. It's brilliant, even better than panel beating.' I felt a stab of fear in the pit of my stomach. I had visions of her and Frisky the fruitcake planting a home-made bomb somewhere in Summerton and reducing the whole place to rubble. Thank God neither of them was a physicist, I thought.

'What?' I asked nervously.

'Before I tell you, are you in? Will you help us? I was sure you would. You seemed angry enough the other day.'

'Of course I'm not "in"! In what, anyway? What is this plan?'

'I can't tell you unless you're in.'

'Fine. Don't tell me then.' I turned to leave, wishing I'd done so an hour earlier. The grand gesture of my indignant departure would be diluted somewhat by the fact that I'd hung around for so long.

'You'll change your mind,' Bryony trilled merrily as I marched out. 'Come back when you do.' I ran down the stairs and back to my car, feeling, as I had the last time I'd left G12 Queen's Court, like I'd escaped from an unspecified but terrible fate. I considered calling the police to ask whether the disappearance of Martine Selinger had ever been officially investigated. After the vivid portrait of Damian painted by her successor, elopement with Fernando Rose seemed suddenly to err on the side of extreme optimism as a hypothesis regarding Martine's fate.

Chapter Twenty-eight

Martine Selinger – Curriculum Vitae

Name
Martine Lisette Selinger.

Address
Unknown.

Age
Thirty.

Place of Birth
Farnham, Surrey.

Marital Status
Married to Damian Selinger, no children. She wanted children but he didn't, or at least not with her. His argument was that her genes were inferior and undeserving of reproduction. None of Martine's relatives had been to university and a close inspection of her family tree revealed a frightening assortment of plumbers, hairdressers, taxi drivers and shop assistants. While Damian was content for his wife to be of a low intellectual calibre, since she compensated for this by having large breasts and long legs, he was not keen to risk passing her intelligence deficiency on to his children. It would have been all right if there were some way of ensuring any prospective offspring would inherit his mind and Martine's looks, but as there wasn't,

and as the opposite scenario would have been disastrous, Damian insisted upon maintaining tight control over the contraceptive situation, and carrying out regular and rigorous condom checks. He became increasingly angry that Martine did not sympathise with his philanthropic desire to spare the world a succession of beige mini-bimbos. He also found himself unable to tolerate her ever-growing collection of photographs of her breeding friends' babies and made a point of drawing a Hitler moustache on each new one within a day or so of its appearance on the mantelpiece. Without consulting Damian, Martine bought a hamster as a child substitute. This, among other frictions, provided the impetus for his cricket bat attack. The hamster was small enough, of brain and body, and unattractive enough to be just the genetic disaster Damian feared, making the substitution all the more grimly plausible.

Employment History
1996 UNTIL DISAPPEARANCE IN MARCH 1997
Beauty therapist at the Jacques Duchamps shop in Cambridge. Speciality: manicures. Colleagues were relieved when she disappeared because, although she delivered top-of-the-range nail buffings, cuticle shapings, palm acu-pressure therapy and finger-joint aromatherapy massages, she tended to be indiscreet about her personal life, often alarming customers who wanted to relax and pamper themselves by regaling them with stories of her decaying marriage. A couple of clients complained to the manager that Martine's detailed descriptions of having her retina detached, her beautifully shaped and painted fingernails chopped off jaggedly in the middle of the night and her car upholstery urinated upon by her husband had given them nightmares.

Occasionally Damian would burst into the salon while Martine was busy beautifying, to continue a fight they'd not had time to conclude at home, and would feel free to comment unfavourably upon the client of the moment. 'Her hands are the least of her problems – she looks like a fork-lift truck,' he once said in front of a customer, reducing her to tears. 'She's a double-bag job.' This was his nickname for women who were so unappealing that intercourse with them would demand bags over the heads of both parties in order to be tolerable. Martine avoided being sacked by crying on the shoulder of the manager, who was forced to agree that she shouldn't be penalised for her husband's bad behaviour. The fact was that, having employed her in the first place, it was easier for the manager to let her stay than to get rid of her, even if this meant squandering a percentage of the shop's profits on beauty treatment vouchers given out as compensation to mortified clients.

I feel sorry neither for Martine nor the manager. She should never have married Damian, but since she did, she should at least have had the good manners not to mention him in the aesthetic haven of the Jacques Duchamps shop. Damian Selinger's soul is a direct affront to the beauty industry; it is an instance of ugliness that no amount of sea kelp elbow gel or blueberry muffin eyelash softener can hope to combat.

The manager deserved everything he got for taking Martine on in the first place. Among the five women interviewed for her job, there was surely at least one who knew what was and what was not a suitable topic of beauty parlour conversation, and who did not have a beige menace of a husband, but this did not come to light until it was too late, which neatly illustrates the inadequacy of the interview procedure.

Before moving to Cambridge, Martine was briefly, so she told me, an orange-faced perfume sprayer in a department store in Oxford. Here Damian succeeded in getting her fired by coming in and demanding sex in the middle of the working day. When Martine refused, he pulled her knickers down on the shop floor and stuck his head up her skirt, causing her to lose her balance and accidentally expose herself in front of a crowd of horrified shoppers.

Qualifications and Education
Diploma in Beauty Therapy from the James Leach Adult Education College in Farnham. Five CSEs: English Language, Maths, Home Economics, General Science and Childcare. After leaving school, Martine rarely thought about the subjects she had studied. Memories of her childcare course occasionally surfaced when she and Damian had one of their procreation rows, or when she was in the company of Ethan Handley, who was the sort of man Martine had imagined settling down and having children with when she was a teenager. The sight of Ethan Handley's face and of the beautiful Handley hands (Damian's were knobbly and chafing) alerted her to the fact that something somewhere had gone badly wrong.

Strengths and Weaknesses
Strong enough to survive nine years with Damian Selinger. We must assume she did survive since her body, as if to compensate for its ostentatious behaviour in the Oxford perfumery, is keeping itself well hidden and has not turned up to prove otherwise. It is impossible to assess Martine's strengths and weaknesses without knowing what happened to her. Did she leave Damian, or did he chop her into little pieces and dump her in the Cam? She may not have been an intellectual, but she had the common sense to desire Ethan Handley. She might have realised he was out of her league and settled for Fernando Rose as a substitute, employing that persuasive hamster logic again and demonstrating yet more common sense.

Physical Appearance
Hasn't made one for over a year. When last seen, she was tall with long, blonde, loosely permed hair. Long legs, large bosom. Hideous feet, covered with bunions and blisters

216

from years of wearing pointy-toed high-heeled shoes. Well-maintained fingernails, never unpainted. Wore make-up day and night, even while asleep, according to Damian. Green eyes with fake lash attachments. Eyebrows which went missing long before their owner, to be replaced by thin eye pencil arches drawn over the raw, red areas she plucked every day with tweezers. Sun-bed tanned skin. All in all, Martine put far more effort into her appearance on a daily basis than Bryony James, or 'Scarecrow' as Damian called her when he first met her, has in her entire life. And look which one of them doesn't get hit over the head with a cricket bat.

This is why lazy, unambitious people should be admired, as I often tell my learner drivers. They know human efforts are so rarely rewarded that we might as well not bother. In this context, effort itself becomes degrading. A black kohl semicircle painted over the site of an ancient eyebrow looks all the more desperate when everyone knows that beneath it lurks a once-detached retina. Most people fail gracefully at life and everyone respects them for it.

Chapter Twenty-nine

Lenin's Flute

I was woken the next morning by the sound of Sebastian shouting in the hall. 'What the fuck is this? What the fuck is this?' he bellowed. I tumbled out of bed clumsily and ran towards the source of the noise. Today wasn't the first time I'd had this sort of alarm call. Sebastian always woke up before me and went to get the post, and on days when a letter arrived telling him he hadn't got a particular job he would almost bring Noble House down with his high-volume rage.

I tried to work out which one it could be this time as I pushed open the lounge door. As far as I was aware he hadn't applied for any lectureships recently apart from Canterbury and Sheffield, and he hadn't yet been interviewed for those. Was his failure going to reach new levels, I wondered, with interview panels being so eager to reject him that they couldn't even restrain themselves until after the interview? 'What is it?' I asked, rubbing sleep out of my eyes. Sebastian, in crumpled paisley pyjama bottoms that threatened to fall down at any minute, looked like a sleepwalker trying to escape from a frightening dream.

'It's a letter from Scholars Press. Read this. I can't believe it, I just can't believe it!' He thrust the letter into my hands. My throat and stomach muscles tightened ominously. Scholars Press were publishing Sebastian's book on Lenin; that was one of the few things that had gone well for him since he finished his PhD, one of the things I always reminded him of when there was no prospect of a job on

218

the horizon. Not only had the thesis been accepted for publication straight away, the social sciences editor, Venetia Curran, had said it was one of the best manuscripts she'd read in years.

Judging from Sebastian's outraged expression, this letter was bad news. Surely Scholars couldn't back out, not after they'd signed the contract. I didn't see how we could go on if they'd changed their minds. Extreme thoughts flooded my head: Sebastian would be so distraught that I might have to kill him to put an end to his suffering, then kill myself.

I began to read, sick with fear.

'Dear Dr Nunn,' the letter said.

I am writing to introduce myself to you, as one of our valued authors. As Venetia Curran's temporary replacement, who has taken up a position with Macmillan publishers, I would like to officially welcome you to our list.

I stopped and reread these first two sentences. Since the letter was signed 'Camilla Pearson, Editorial Assistant', I assumed the valued author referred to was Sebastian and that the person who had taken a job with Macmillan was Venetia Curran. This was at once reassuring and disturbing; if Sebastian was being described in these terms, Scholars were unlikely to renege on the publishing deal. On the other hand, insofar as the book was now in the hands of a grammatically confused person, there might be cause for worry of a different kind.

I read on.

I have just finished reading your manuscript and I think it is generally excellent. There are, however, a few changes I would like to ask you to consider making. Most of these relate to Lenin himself, as the overall structure and plot I think are great, as are all the other characters. The revolution is brilliant!!!

Lenin as the main character in the book needs to be made more sympathetic. At the moment he comes across as selfish, power-crazed and a bit of a tyrant. I realise he needs to be a strong leader for the rest of the story to be credible, but the reader will find it easier to identify with him if you give him a more 'human' side, as it were. I know he has his political ideals but that's not enough, it needs to be balanced out. It will be hard for readers to like someone so obsessed with a political party – (bit dreary!).

Could you perhaps give him a more sensitive side? For example, if he were to play the flute (not necessarily that, that's just an example) or do something maybe more artistic?

Another thought: a few moments of self-doubt wouldn't go amiss. At the moment he seems so sure that his opinions are right, and I'm worried he'll appear arrogant to the reader. Maybe it might be an idea to insert a few passages here and there where he thinks something like 'Hang on, a minute – what if I'm wrong about this socialism lark? Who am I to think I know best how the world should be run?' Let's face it, most of us don't know what's right for ourselves, half the time, let alone whole societies.

So: more insecurity, more vulnerability, more creativity is an absolute must, I think. Also, if Lenin is made more 'lovable', there will be a sharper contrast between him and Stalin (who's fine just as he is – a total baddy!!!).

Finally one more suggestion is that do you think really *so* many people need to be killed, peasants, etc.? Less is sometimes more, as it were.

I do hope you'll give serious consideration to these revised areas and I look forward to working with you.

Best wishes,

Yours faithfully,

Camilla Pearson

I burst out laughing.

'It's not funny.' Sebastian snatched the letter out of my hand as I clutched my stomach. 'Have you seen what she wants me to do? She must be insane! I mean, how can I make Lenin more lovable? What's all that shit about him playing the flute? What the fuck is she, some sort of revisionist?'

'Sebastian . . .'

'What if I refuse to make these changes and she pulls the plug on my book?'

'Sebastian!' I dried my eyes. 'Don't be a fool. Of course you can't make the changes, she doesn't know what she's talking about.'

'I can see that much!'

'No, I mean, it's a misunderstanding. Don't worry, it's easily remedied. She'll be so embarrassed when you tell her, she won't dare to make another suggestion about a manuscript as long as she lives. She thinks it's fiction.' I giggled.

'She . . . what?' Sebastian read the letter again, breathing deeply. I could see his eyes widen as it dawned on him. 'Oh, Christ,' he muttered, a smile slowly spreading across his face. 'What a fucking idiot I am. I just read it and . . . panicked.'

'You were probably half asleep,' I said. 'And, let's face it, we're so used to expecting the worst. This is just another example of someone getting a job they don't deserve. She thinks it's all a story you made up. Your manuscript probably ended up in the wrong department. Looks like you're going to have to give Camilla Pearson some history lessons. You'll have to ring her first thing Monday morning, before she has any more bright ideas, like the tsar break-dancing on street corners.' We both gave way to hysterics.

'I'm going to ring and demand they sack her,' Sebastian said breathlessly, trying to compose himself. 'The woman's a complete fool. She probably comes from one of those small Cambridgeshire villages where everyone is their own dad.'

'Oh, come on, she made us laugh, didn't she?'

'Kate, she's a liability.'

'Oh, don't be so harsh,' I said, suddenly in a good mood. 'We haven't had such a jolly morning in ages. Usually we wake up, you say something about what a failure you are and how shit everything's going to be, I try to cheer you up, you get cross with me for being unrealistic and we're both miserable before the day's even started.'

'Is it that bad?' he asked sadly. 'I wouldn't blame you if you left me, you know.'

'Sebastian, I have no intention of leaving you. I love you, you idiot. Stop looking so gloomy. I'm going to get dressed and go out now, carry on with my task of getting you the De La Wyche fellowship. This letter has given my confidence a real boost.'

'I'm so glad you're pleased that a moron is trying to sabotage my book,' he muttered sarcastically.

'Look, yesterday I had a long conversation with Bryony James. She's also a moron. Damian Selinger's one too. Don't you see? Everyone's a moron. Cambridge is supposed to be a world centre of excellence, but it's okay because everyone's a moron! Sebastian, I know we can beat them!' I was grateful to Camilla Pearson for changing my outlook on life. Last night I'd come home feeling weak and vulnerable, my head full of macabre images of Damian murdering Martine, of Bryony setting fire to Summerton like some sort of bluestocking Bertha Rochester. Now, in the comforting light of day, I saw things for what they really were; I was surrounded not by menace and villainy but by complete buffoonery.

'But what are you actually planning to do?' Sebastian asked. 'I don't know whether to believe you about this De La Wyche business.'

'What if I told you I could persuade Terri Skinner to turn it down?'

222

'I'd ask how, then I'd say, what about Rod Firsden, the second choice?'

'Just leave everything to me,' I said, running back to the bedroom to get dressed. No matter what he said in his darker moods, I knew Sebastian liked me to be optimistic, or unrealistic as he called it. If he'd married someone with as negative an outlook as his own, he wouldn't have been half as happy to be a misery.

As I drove to Rod's house on Sterling Road, I considered Sebastian's question: what about Rod Firsden, the second choice? Since my lies about Gary Conley seemed to have been almost sufficient to make Terri decide to take the Reading job, I wondered what story I could dream up that would persuade Rod to change his mind about the Enmity. If only he were superstitious and could be made to believe it was cursed. He already knew about Fernando Rose's disappearance and he didn't seem at all spooked by it. Could I come up with some self-empowerment claptrap along the lines that he should reject Summerton before they had the chance to reject him?

I sighed. I could see no way to deflect Rod from the course of his obsession. I'd have to approach the problem from another angle. Perhaps I could persuade a panel member that, for some reason, Rod was unfit to be a Summerton fellow. They hadn't yet made him a formal offer. I didn't know for sure but I was prepared to bet Rod didn't have it in writing that he was second choice; Summerton had made no firm commitment to take him if Terri turned them down. I felt my brain begin to speed up. Yes, of course. Why hadn't I thought of this before? I felt a pang of regret about the fact that I had to behave like this. If my plan, once I'd formulated it, held water, if I carried it out, I would be responsible for depriving Rod of what he most wanted in the world. Maybe that was why I'd taken so long to think of the Summerton angle of attack: because deep down I didn't want to betray someone who liked and trusted me.

I was so distracted that I forgot to torment Vincent Strebonian by parking in front of his driveway. Instead, I pulled up on the opposite side of the road outside Rod's house. Mr Strebonian wouldn't even have entered my thoughts had he not made a point of rushing across the road and rapping on my car window with his bony knuckles. I couldn't get over the fact that he never failed to detect my presence in the street. Did he have a surveillance camera hidden in his bushes, videoing all Sterling Road's traffic action? He was wasting his talents as a plastic surgeon; he should have been a spy. I wound down the window, thinking he might have come over to call a truce, since for once I'd behaved myself and displayed good parking etiquette.

'Morning,' I said politely.

'You have exactly three minutes to remove your vehicle,' Vincent Strebonian barked. 'If you don't, I shall go and get a tin of purple paint and write exactly what I think of you across the side of your car.'

'What? But I'm not even blocking your driveway,' I said, loathing him. 'I'm nowhere near your house. Look, I'm outside Rod's house.'

'Who?' He scratched his head, looking confused, and I cursed my bad luck. If he'd forgotten who Rod was, why the hell couldn't he forget me? Why couldn't I be the one to benefit from his selective senility? I wondered whether Vincent Strebonian was related to Lloyd Lunnon, Summerton's diplomacy expert. In the final heat of the World's Most Confrontational Man contest, those two would be pretty evenly matched. 'Do you like having a white car?' he went on, after a brief pause. 'Because if you do you'd better move it. I've got enough paint to paint your whole car purple.'

'But I'm not doing anything wrong,' I protested, bemused.

'Kate!' Rod yelled out of his ground-floor window, which he had opened hastily in an attempt to rescue his neighbour. 'How dare you speak to Mr S like that? How can you be so cruel?' Within seconds he was out in the road, patting Vincent Strebonian on the back and muttering soothing words. He walked him across the road slowly, ushering him back into his house.

I decided I'd had enough of this pantomime; from now on I'd arrange to pick up Rod somewhere else. I told him this as soon as he got into the car, speaking in a monotone through tight lips. Next time I felt guilty about Rod and the Enmity, I thought, I would remind myself of how he always took Strebonian's side and acted as though I were the aggressor.

Instead of being chastened by my unfriendliness as I'd hoped he would be, Rod seemed determined to outsulk me. 'We won't be having any more lessons,' he said frostily. 'In fact, I won't speak to you ever again unless you stop being so nasty to that poor man.' He managed to sound simultaneously like a little child and an old woman.

'Good. Suits me fine.' I folded my arms and stared out of the window. If Rod was intent on being so unreasonable that he and I fell out, I wouldn't have to worry about doing the dirty on a friend when I told Daphne Fielding he was a child molester, or whatever story I decided to go for.

'You have no idea of what he's been through. You deliberately wind him up by parking in front of his . . .'

'I didn't!' I yelled. 'Look where we are. Are we blocking his driveway? No, we're bollocsing not! He's in the wrong, not me, and I don't want to have anything to do with you if you can't even stick up for me when your mad neighbour attacks me for no reason.'

'He's got a reason!' Rod shouted back. 'His wife died because someone parked there.'

There was a brief silence. '*What*?' I asked.

'I shouldn't have told you,' said Rod quietly. 'He told me that in confidence, but I had no choice, the way you were carrying on. Don't you understand, even if you *are* across the road, every time he sees you it reminds him of his wife's death?'

'Don't I . . . don't I *understand*?' I shrieked, frustration and anger taking over my whole body. 'How the buggering hell am I supposed to understand when I didn't know a single fucking thing about it? How was I supposed to know his wife died? How did she die, anyway?' My temper was so out of control that I momentarily suspected Rod of inventing this story just to make me feel guilty. 'Was she lying on the pavement and someone drove over her? Was that it?'

'She had a heart attack. She was still alive. She could have lived.' Rod sighed. 'Mr S phoned an ambulance, but for some reason it didn't arrive. When he went to get his car out of the garage to drive her to hospital himself, a lorry was parked in front of his driveway. He couldn't get out and . . . she died.' There was a long silence. 'So now you know why he's so sensitive.'

'She might have died anyway,' I snapped, closing my eyes tightly to avoid crying in front of Rod. 'And it's not my fault. I didn't know. Why didn't you tell me?'

'I'm sorry. I should have done, but . . . well, it's his private business.'

'You've allowed me to keep upsetting him, when you could have told me the first time it happened. You're the one to blame for all this,' I said vindictively.

Rod started to cry unexpectedly, which made me even angrier. For once I was the officially upset one and I didn't want him muscling in on my territory. 'It's secrets that are to blame,' he sobbed. 'I hate secrets. Why can't everything be straightforward? Oh, I hate this life!' Tears dripped from several points along the line of his chin, so that he resembled a chandelier. He seemed so upset that I eventually began to forget about my own ill-treatment and started thinking of ways to cheer him up. He wasn't nasty, just a bit moronic at times, like everyone else. 'I hate secrets, oh, why can't there be no secrets?' he whined, still weeping.

'Tell me about Gary Conley,' I said. Rod's tears began immediately to subside at the mere mention of the name. It was as if Gary Conley were a new way of saying Abracadabra, a magic phrase with the power to change the mood of anyone who heard it. Maybe if I said 'Gary Conley' to Vincent Strebonian, I could undo all the harm I'd unwittingly done him over the past few days.

Chapter Thirty

The Difference Principle

It was only then that I noticed Rod was holding a rectangular brown paper bag with something in it, about the size of a brick. 'What's that?' I asked.

'Gary Conley gave it to me,' he said, wiping his eyes. 'It's a film. Terri gave it to him as a Christmas present. He didn't want it. He told me to take it back to her.'

'But you don't know her.'

'I know,' said Rod. 'I told him that, but he just shrugged and handed it to me anyway. Honestly, Kate, I wish I could explain what this man's like. It's impossible to have a conversation with him.'

I pulled a videotape out of the bag. For the third time in three days, I found myself face to face with Marlene Dietrich. '*Witness for the Prosecution*,' I said.

'Have you heard of it?'

'It's one of my favourite films. Haven't you seen it?'

Rod eyed the tape dubiously. 'I don't like films,' he said. 'I don't regard them as a proper art form.'

'That's silly,' I said. 'You should watch it. Have you got a video?'

'Yes,' Rod admitted reluctantly. 'But I never use it, apart from to record literary programmes.'

'Watch it,' I said, handing him the tape. 'It's brilliant. Anyway, it was a play by Agatha Christie before it was a film, so it is literary.'

'Agatha Christie is hardly what I'd call literature,' said

Rod sniffily.

'Well, aren't we snobby today? Okay, I'll have it if you don't want it. I was planning to buy a copy anyway.'

'No, I'll watch it.' Rod held on to the tape. 'If you say I should see it, I will. I respect your opinion. Kate . . . ?'

'What?'

'I'm really sorry, you know, about Mr Strebonian. I should have told you.'

'Forget it,' I said. 'Just tell me about Gary Conley.'

'No, no. I will in a minute, but first . . . I don't know how to say this. I really like you, Kate. I was wondering if I could take you out some time.' He rubbed his beard nervously, squeezing his chin between his forefinger and thumb. It didn't make him look very attractive.

'Rod, I have to be honest,' I said, preparing to do the very opposite. 'I like you a lot, but you're so obsessed with this De La Wyche thing and Summerton that . . . well, anyone you got involved with would have to take second place.'

'What? But I haven't even got the De La Wyche fellowship.'

'Whether you get it or not's irrelevant. You're the sort of person who puts his career above everything. You're so ambitious and that's good, I'm not criticising it, but . . . it's not the sort of life I want. I want someone who's going to put me first, just a regular bloke who's happy to be ordinary.' I laughed to myself as I said this. No one could be less reconciled to ordinariness than Sebastian, with his scathing views about bun shop jobs. I was relying on Rod being enough of an intellectual snob to find this viewpoint plausible, coming from a driving instructor who liked Agatha Christie film adaptations. 'You know, I'll probably end up marrying someone who works for Kwikfit,' I embellished further.

'Marry?' Rod looked alarmed. 'Hold on a minute, I didn't mean . . .' His face started to redden beneath its cocoa butter sheen. 'Well, I only meant, you know, a date.'

'You see? You're scared of committing yourself,' I said,

beginning to enjoy the role I was playing. I would never have been so clingy and demanding as myself, but it was quite fun to allow my adopted persona to say such outrageous things. Of course, no man could reasonably be expected to commit himself to marrying his driving instructor after only three meetings. Still, the sort of woman I was pretending to be wouldn't care about anything but getting a ring on her finger. I realised there was already a ring on my finger, a wedding ring at that, but fortunately Rod hadn't noticed. If he did, I could always say – honestly for once – that I'd bought it for myself. Sebastian had been skint, as always, when we'd got married, so I'd had to buy both our rings. 'I'm not interested in a relationship that's not going anywhere,' I continued. 'This is exactly what I mean about the sort of person you are. You're happy to pledge your troth to Summerton College – you've even said you'd stay there for ever if you could – but not to a woman. You'd always put your career first.'

'No, I wouldn't.' Rod looked confused. 'Not necessarily.'

'Okay, then, prove it.' I giggled girlishly. I felt like one of those women in movies – the sort Rod would never watch – who hinders her man's attempt to save the world from aliens/prevent a nuclear war/uncover a governmental conspiracy by whingeing about how he never makes time to go on family picnics any more. 'Promise you'll turn down the De La Wyche fellowship if Terri drops out,' I said.

'What?' Rod was rightly horrified. 'Kate, you're mad. I can't work at Kwikfit. I can't even drive. I'm not a practical person. I want to . . . write about poetry, I mean, that's what I want to do with my life. It's not that I'm scared of commitment, but . . . well, isn't all this a bit premature? We haven't even been out together once yet.'

'Nor will we, then,' I said stubbornly.

'But Kate, I thought you understood!' Rod seemed to be on the verge of tears again. He was one of the most tearful men I'd ever met. That would never do at Kwikfit; you wouldn't catch Zac Hunt sobbing over a broken exhaust pipe, composing an ode on the subject of its decline. 'I want the De La Wyche more than anything. How can you ask me to give it up?'

'I'm not,' I said. 'I'm just trying to show you how incompatible we are. You're obsessed with your career, whereas I think too much ambition is bad for a person. I mean, look how much harm it's doing you. You're too sick from stress to work, aren't you?'

'I suppose you're right,' Rod muttered anxiously, and for a minute I thought he was about to agree to drop out of the competition. 'But, Kate, what about Reading and Gary Conley? Why did you encourage me to go if you now want me to drop out?'

'I don't want you to drop out,' I said. 'I'm just explaining why I think we should be friends and nothing more. As a friend, I'm happy to help you get the fellowship.'

'But not as anything else,' Rod concluded sadly.

'That's right,' I said, feeling sorry for him. In a way, I thought my husband-seeking persona had a point. If Rod hadn't spent so much time obsessing about his career, he might have learned enough about people to know that any woman who spouted the kind of garbage I just had was to be avoided at all costs.

'I can't change, Kate,' he said. 'I really can't. There's no way. I've put everything into getting the De La Wyche, you've got no idea.'

Oh well. I should have known I wasn't the sort of woman for whom men made large sacrifices. I'm not pretty or fragile enough. For God's sake, you're a driving instructor, I reminded myself. Perhaps if I'd been a russet-haired princess imprisoned in a tower that might have appealed to Rod's poetic imagination. 'Fine,' I said. 'So, let's be friends. Well, we already are.'

'Won't you even go out with me once?' Rod pleaded. 'I could cook you dinner. We could watch *Witness for the*

Prosecution.' He gave me a timid, hopeful smile. 'Oh, please say yes. I feel I . . . I *need* to spend an evening with you.'

'There's no point, Rod. What about everything we've just said?' If he hadn't stressed the word 'need', I would have said no immediately.

'I know,' he said unhappily. 'But can't you forget all that for one night? Evening,' he corrected himself quickly, blushing.

I laughed. Not only did I like him, I also felt sorry for him. For a second I wondered whether my role in life was to act as consolation prize to everyone who didn't get the Enmity. 'All right then,' I said. 'When?'

'Tonight?'

'I'm not sure I can . . .'

'Oh, please!' He clasped his hands together in a praying motion that, for some reason, I found hard to resist. My weakness annoyed me; I'd always been told desperation was off-putting, but it never seemed to work like that in practice, at least not for me.

'Okay, tonight. What time?'

'Eight o'clock,' said Rod, with a sudden formal stiffness. 'You know where I live, the ground-floor flat. Please don't be early. I'll need lots of time to tidy up.' He sounded as if he was in a trance. Perhaps he wasn't accustomed to having guests or, even worse, had never had one before. I could see how he might not have an action-packed social life, with his one-track De La Wyche mind and sudden crying fits.

'Fine,' I said. 'Now, come on. Gary Conley.'

'Oh. Yes.' Rod snapped back into the present. 'Where should I start?'

'From when you got to Reading.'

'Right. Well, I found the YMCA and asked if he was living there. He was. And he was in, so that part was easy. I introduced myself and asked him if he knew Terri Skinner . . .'

'Hang on,' I interrupted him. 'How exactly did you

introduce yourself? Didn't he find it odd, your turning up out of the blue? Did he ask why you wanted to know about Terri?'

'Kate, he was too odd himself to have a definition of oddness. And he was exceptionally stupid. He reminded me of a few boys in my secondary school, the ones who were locked up in the Unit, so thick they were unteachable.'

'The Unit? Charming.' I laughed. 'What sort of school was this?' I'd assumed Rod, with his Oxbridge aspirations, had been educated privately, but apparently not. What mother would pay twelve grand a year to have her child dismissed as unteachable and locked in a place called the Unit?

'I thought we were talking about Gary Conley, not me,' Rod said crossly. 'Stop interrupting.' I apologised. Where Sebastian was moody in a long, gloomy depressions and general curmudgeonly outlook sort of way, Rod was ecstatic one minute and crotchety the next. I didn't know which was worse. Here I am, comparing my two men, I thought, faintly amused. 'I got the impression he didn't care who I was,' Rod continued. 'That's one way of telling when someone's stupid, when they have no curiosity.' This made me smile. Rod had hardly asked me anything about myself since we'd met. Self-obsession, as well as stupidity, could lead to a lack of interest in others. 'I told him my name,' said Rod, 'where I was from, and that I wanted to ask him a couple of questions about Terri Skinner. He just nodded blankly.'

'How odd,' I said. 'But . . . he can't be that thick if he's Terri's friend.' Remembering that, as far as Rod knew, Terri was a stranger to me, I added. 'If she's clever enough to get the De La Wyche fellowship . . .'

'He isn't her friend, though. He says he hardly knows her. They met when he was working as a waiter at Pembroke College in Oxford. I managed to work out that this was about four years ago. Gary isn't good with dates, so it took us a while to get that far. He actually asked me if

1993 came before or after 1994, can you believe that?'

'No,' I said bluntly. This was the man for whom Terri was considering leaving Joe?

'She was a student at Pembroke when they met. Apparently they . . . he . . . well, his exact words were "I pulled her one night". What do you think that means?' Rod frowned earnestly. 'I assumed it meant he kissed her or something.'

I laughed. Only in Cambridge would you meet a person of Rod's age who didn't know what pulling was. 'It means they copped off, got together in some sexual manner,' I said. 'I would guess that more than kissing was involved, but I could be wrong. Naughty Terri, anyway. She was married by then.'

'How do you know?'

'Oh, er . . .' I improvised hastily. 'I had a snoop around when I broke into her flat,' I said. 'She's been married for seven years.'

'Good grief!' said Rod. 'You're amazing. Did you train as a spy?'

'Self-taught,' I said. 'Go on. He pulled her and then . . . ?'

'Well, according to Gary, that's all that's ever happened between them. She wanted to see him again but he couldn't be arsed, as he so delicately put it, so he . . . what was his expression? Oh, yes: he "binned her off". And that's basically it.'

'What do you mean? What about *Witness for the Prosecution*?'

'Oh, yes. Every Christmas since then, she's sent him a card and a present.'

'Why, though, if it was all over between them?'

'Gary said he thought she was still trying to pull him,' said Rod. 'He didn't seem at all keen on her. He said she was "in his face". I found it very confusing, all this talk of pulling and binning. Oh – I found out who R English is. It's his stepfather. Gary thinks even less of him than he does of Terri Skinner. He called him a bastard wanker.'

'How did Terri know his name and where he lived?'

'He also used to work at Pembroke. That's how Gary got the job.' Rod laughed. 'He said English was the catering manager and that Terri called him the mandible. He meant manciple, of course. It's what they call the head of the kitchen staff in Oxbridge colleges.'

'I know,' I said indignantly. 'I have lived in Cambridge for years. I'm not some hick from the sticks.'

'Sorry.' Rod grinned sheepishly. I wondered whether I believed him about Gary's stupidity. Coming from someone like Rod, this could mean ignorance of the poetry of George Herbert and not knowing what a manciple was. But if it was true that Gary Conley had been unsure whether 1993 preceded or followed 1994, and I couldn't see why Rod would make it up, there was clearly something wrong with him, mentally.

'Did you talk to him about NEG?' I asked. 'Remember, Terri asked R English if he still worked there?'

'Yes, I did. It was some courier place, deliveries. They sacked him, as did Pembroke College. He's on the dole now. Oh – and he's leaving the YMCA next Wednesday. The council have found him a flat.'

'Sounds like you did quite well,' I said. 'You got a lot out of him.'

'With the greatest of effort, I assure you. And anyway, where does it get me? Nowhere nearer to getting the fellowship. He's not interested in Terri, even if she would move to Reading for him. But, Kate, this is what I can't make sense of. Why on earth would she be willing to give up a Summerton fellowship for someone like him? Why would she cry over . . . over *him*?'

'I don't know,' I said truthfully. 'Was he attractive?'

'Yes, but he was a . . . well, if you'll pardon my political incorrectness . . .'

'Hang on,' I interrupted him. 'How attractive was he, exactly?'

'I don't know.' Rod sounded bemused. 'He's a man.'

'Well, what type is he? Does he look like anyone famous?'

'Like who?'

'Anyone on telly? Any film star?'

'I told you, I don't watch films. I suppose he's attractive enough to be in a film.'

'So that's it, then,' I said. 'It's a physical thing.'

'But he's so dim-witted,' said Rod. 'No intelligent person could be attracted to someone like him.'

'Of course they could,' I said, amazed at his naïvety. 'Haven't you ever heard of sex?'

'I find stupidity repulsive,' said Rod, bypassing my question. 'The most important question I asked him, the one I could really have done with getting a decent answer to, was too much for his one brain cell.'

'What was that?'

'I told him about Terri's job offer from Reading. I asked him if he thought her decision might depend partly on him. He didn't understand. The question was too speculative for him. He could only answer factual questions and even those only with great difficulty. I rephrased it several times – did he think Terri liked him enough to move to Reading? Did he think she would consider moving to Reading if he were somewhere else? – but he couldn't grasp the concept of interpretation, of hypothesising. It was the word "if" he seemed to have most trouble with.'

'Jesus,' I said. If this was an accurate description of Gary Conley, how could Terri have believed even for a minute that he had tracked her down in Cambridge, made the effort to come and look for her? Because that was what she wanted to believe, I answered myself. I guessed Conley was pretty stunning to look at, or exceptionally good in bed. Even then, would Terri honestly want to trade in the useful, Alaska-baking and child-rearing Joe Fielding for someone who found the chronology of the years a struggle and was phased by the word 'if'? Apparently so, in which case she was even more of an idiot than Gary, because she was intelligent enough to know better. Stupidity wasn't a necessity for her, it was a lifestyle choice.

'It's the difference principle,' I said aloud.

'What's that?' asked Rod.

'Cleverness is Terri's natural environment,' I explained. 'Maybe she finds imbecility exotic – it's her way of escaping.'

'No one could be so mad, surely?' Rod seemed to want me to say something comforting. I shrugged, not wanting to shatter his world-view. I tried not to think of our impending date. I should have followed Terri's example, acted upon the difference principle myself. There wasn't much to choose between an evening spent reassuring Sebastian at home and one spent illicitly reassuring Rod in his flat on Sterling Road.

Chapter Thirty-one

Gary Conley – Curriculum Vitae

Name

Gary Brian Alan Conley. You can tell a lot about parents from what they choose to call their children. Gary Brian Alan is the choice of people who hope their son will be a famous footballer or a pop star or, failing that, something solid and manly like an electrician or bus driver. I don't know whether Gary has any brothers or sisters and this did not emerge from Rod's excursion to Reading, but if he does they might be called Gavin or Michelle. They are unlikely to be called Sebastian or Emily. It is possible to infer (correctly) from the fact that I have two sisters called Lucy and Hannah that my parents are incorrigible *Guardian* readers with sanded parquet floors. Sebastian has one brother called Dominic; his parents are lapsed-Catholic *Guardian* readers with sanded parquet floors.

With a name like Kate, I was determined not to end up shopping at Laura Ashley and working in an art gallery. It's good to keep the categorisers on their toes. If Sebastian ever does become a tramp, this will be the pinnacle of name–occupation incompatibility and will therefore carry with it a certain panache.

Address

YMCA in Reading, although moving out shortly. The council has found him a flat. Councils are to the under-privileged what Junior Bursars are to privileged

Summertonians: providers of accommodation. The irony is that fewer people complain to the former than the latter about their abode's view, state of repair, cleanliness, location and general level of comfort. Gary has been waiting so long for his flat that all he wants it to be is his.

Age
Physical: twenty-four; mental: considerably younger, probably somewhere in mid to late teens.

Place of Birth
Reading. Sees no reason to move further afield, as there is nothing he requires that he can't get in his home town. Soon he may need to get away from Terri Skinner, but it still may not occur to him to leave Reading. As far as he is concerned people who don't live in Reading live either in Wokingham or Bracknell, both of which have inferior nightclubs and video shops. It was bad enough when he had to commute to Oxford to work at Pembroke College. Gary didn't like Pembroke and had complained to R English, his stepfather and Pembroke's manciple, that it didn't contain his sort of people. This was only partly true. Many of Pembroke's fellows had speech and memory problems that were remarkably similar to Gary's.

Marital Status
Single and intends to stay that way for a good long while, he told Rod. However, anticipates that at the age of thirty his opinion on the matter will change and he will want to settle down and have kids. His natural father has told him that at thirty, men change from young and horny to old and boring, and as Mr Conley is a man who practises what he preaches, being unusually decrepit and tedious for his age, it does not occur to Gary to disbelieve him.

Employment History
Worse than Sebastian's. Sacked from over thirty jobs,

including Pembroke College, NEG courier service, Legoland, McDonald's, Burger King and a BP filling station. Just as Sebastian cannot disguise for more than about three weeks his contempt for any job he considers to be beneath him, Gary is unable to conceal from employers the fact that he cannot do anything. The only thing he wants to be is a hero with medals. He's seen such people in films and likes the look of it.

Qualifications and Education
None of the first and little of the second.

Physical Appearance
Must be good, or else what does Terri see in him? Perhaps he resembles a fish's tooth. From what Rod said and what Terri let slip I have cobbled together an image of a tall, dark-haired, green-eyed person with an athletic body. If Gary is not irresistibly gorgeous, the only other possible explanation is that Terri is turned on by male failures because they enable her to realise the dream of female superiority in her own personal life. And, of course, Grumpy Skinner would loathe Gary.

Strengths and Weaknesses
Such extreme weaknesses that they could almost be counted as strengths. Poor thought and speech quality, appalling social skills, lethargy, unemployability, coldness, aggression.

Other Information
Likes going to raves, going to the cinema and watching videos. Has probably seen as many films as Daphne Fielding, although he has formulated, on the basis of his experience, a theory which is radically different from hers. Gary divides all the films he watches into the good, the okay and the shit. He is pleased with this classification system. *Witness for the Prosecution* is undoubtedly shit

because it commits the unforgivable twofold sin of being black and white and about posh people, and Gary was quite happy to send it back to Cambridge with Rod Firsden who, as a posh-sounding person himself, was bound to have more use for it.

Chapter Thirty-two

Fernando's Envelopes

Bizarrely, I felt excited about my date with Rod Firsden. It was so long since I'd experienced that mixture of fear and romantic possibility. Evenings with Sebastian hadn't made me nervous for a long time, unless we were waiting to hear the result of one of his job interviews and that was hardly a pleasurable form of anticipation. A night with Rod might be, if not entirely fun, at least interesting. I tried to tell myself that my motivation for spending time with him was merely Enmity diligence, but I was worried there was slightly more to it. It made no sense for me to fancy Rod – he was every bit as emotionally demanding as Sebastian and not nearly as good-looking. Not that he was un-attractive, exactly, just a bit other-wordly. I could imagine him – with his pointy beard, shiny face and posh, fussy voice – making a good absent-minded professor one day. I wished I could imagine Sebastian as a professor, of any kind. Perhaps this was the slight pull of attraction Rod had for me: disloyally, I could more easily picture his success than my own husband's.

Feeling guilty, I switched on my mobile phone to ring Sebastian and check he was okay before I went to see Daphne Fielding, but my messaging service got to me first. I listened patiently as the anonymous, calm female voice told me I had two new messages.

The first was from Bryony James. Her voice sounded soft and eerily breathless as she explained to me that I had missed the point of our conversation the night before and failed to understand the necessity of revenge. She still wanted me as an ally, if I was ready to be 'true to myself', as she put it. 'Oh,' she added as an afterthought, 'in case you were worried about violence, it's nothing like that. It's ... what Damian and I are planning is ... well, it's appropriate to the situation. What I mean is, it's not excessive. You don't need to worry that we're going to do anything silly. You know, Kate,' she murmured in a preachy tone in between gusts of breath, 'one thing I've learned is that you can't begin to fight on the inside unless you fight on the outside.'

'Ugh, how vile,' I said aloud, hoping my second message would be less offensive. I was growing to dislike intensely Bryony's peculiar blend of new-age self-helpery and unhinged vindictiveness.

When I heard Valerie Williams's voice I sat up straight in the driver's seat. I certainly hadn't expected her to ring me. 'Dr Valerie Williams here,' her recorded voice said briskly. 'As I think you guessed last time we spoke, I wasn't entirely honest with you. At the time, I thought I was doing the right thing, with a few reservations, but I don't believe in dishonesty and I've decided not to continue with it any longer. Lying, in the end, only damages the liar. I'll feel better if I tell the truth.' She said all this in a detached, businesslike manner.

'Selfish bitch,' I muttered into my phone. I've always been highly suspicious of people who want to do the right thing because it makes them feel better, rather than for the effect it will have on others. Let's face it, if doing the right thing made you feel worse, you wouldn't even contemplate it. There's no virtue or sacrifice involved, it's just whatever turns you on. Valerie Williams obviously got a kick out of honesty the way I got a kick out of perverting the course of appointment procedures.

'It was your visit that brought things to a head,' Valerie explained. 'I don't know how much you know, but judging from your behaviour you clearly know something. Anyway, I'll be in the surgery this afternoon so if you could drop in, we can discuss the matter then.'

'This afternoon!' I wasn't sure I could wait until then; I might go mad in the meantime. I drummed my fingers furiously on the steering wheel. The agony I felt was almost physical. So much for Valerie's desire to do the right thing. Was it right to put me through this ordeal of waiting, knowing I would have no idea whether good or bad news lay in store for me? No wonder Valerie loved rules. Like many people who subscribe to a rigid moral code, she was almost entirely devoid of imagination, neither perceptive nor sensitive enough to assess each situation on its individual merits. My stomach swilled with nauseous tension.

I didn't phone Sebastian because I didn't trust myself not to blurt out this new development. I didn't want him to have to go through the same emotional turmoil I would have to endure until two o'clock. I decided to kill time by going to see Daphne Fielding as I'd originally planned. I suspected she wouldn't be thrilled to learn of Valerie's intention to tell me about whatever misdemeanour had taken place, not that I had any intention of mentioning it. The argument I'd overheard between the two of them through Daphne's window in Old Court must have been about this very issue. It was too much of a coincidence otherwise – they were both Enmity panel members and dishonesty had definitely been the subject of their row.

I struggled to remember as much of it as I could. Valerie had wanted everything – whatever that might be – out in the open, whereas Daphne, although she didn't say so directly, seemed more in favour of continuing with the cover-up. I agreed wholeheartedly with whichever of them held the view that enhanced Sebastian's chances, whether it was truth or lies that got them there.

I parked in Old Court, in what I now thought of as 'my' space, in front of a stripy wooden bollard that protruded from the ground for no apparent reason. As if to remind me that the bollard was far from being Summerton's most useless accoutrement, Emily Lole appeared from an arched doorway beside me as I got out of the car. There was no way I could avoid her eye. I think I must have ducked or flinched or something, because she said, 'Don't worry, I won't hurt you. I'm much more in control of myself today.' I tried to look suitably grateful at the same time as keeping a safe distance between us. 'I'm glad you're here,' Emily went on. 'I wanted to talk to you, to apologise for what happened at the feast.'

I was about to ask, sharply, precisely what aspect of the feast she wanted to apologise for – the disappointing range of *petits fours*? the scratches on the cutlery? – but I restrained myself. She seemed more *compos mentis* than usual and I didn't want to miss the opportunity to see how she reacted to a few more of my searching questions, so I nodded and smiled. All the same, I made a mental note of the manner of her apology. People who say sorry for 'what happened' or 'that business the other night' are usually engaging in pyschological hypocrisy. They aren't quite ready to face up to what they've done, so they cop out by glossing over the offence with abstractions.

I put on my fake forgiveness face, remembering my sore neck, and resolved to nurture my grudge against Emily until she saw fit to include in her declaration of contrition the words 'attempted strangulation'. 'Forget it,' I said.

'Have you got a few minutes?' she asked. Her voice sounded almost normal, neither close to hysteria nor sedatively slow, and her blonde, wavy hair looked as if it had been combed for once. A brown plastic clip held it back on one side. Her face was blessedly mucus-free and even her clothes looked as though an iron had sauntered across their folds in the recent past. Still, all this could be a ruse to lull me into a false sense of security. 'Really, don't worry,' Emily took a step towards me. 'I'm feeling much better today. I won't . . . be difficult, I promise. I really could do with talking to someone and you . . . seem like the right person.'

I shrugged and followed her to her set in Tyndsall Court. The curtains were closed as they had been when I visited yesterday, but Emily must have been feeling more co-operative because this time she threw them open immediately, saying, 'You like the daylight, don't you?' She made it sound like a weird fetish of mine, and I subdued the urge to point out that I was perfectly normal and it was she who was in the minority, along with a few vampires and marijuana zombies.

The Fernando Rose shrine looked even more sinister in the light. There were nineteen – I counted – framed close-ups of his moonly features in Emily's lounge. 'Wouldn't you stand a better chance of getting over him if you didn't have all these?' I asked, indicating the pictures. I was still on my feet and ready to run if a psychotic attack seemed imminent, but Emily's mood remained mercifully stable.

'I'll never get over him,' she said, as if this were obvious and I shouldn't need to have it pointed out to me. 'Now, how about a nice cup of tea? Oops!' She laughed and it seemed as out of character as Gandhi rolling up his sleeves in preparation for a bar-room brawl. 'Don't tell Damian Selinger I said that – he hates people who say "a nice cup of tea". He can't stand the word "nice". He despises people who drink tea,' Emily went on, her eyes clouding over at the thought of Damian's disdain. 'He says they're depressing and unimaginative.'

'I'd love a cup of tea,' I said brightly, trying to reverse this sudden change of mood.

'Damian says tea . . .'

'Forget Damian. He's an arsehole. There's nothing wrong with tea.' I tried not to show my impatience. I had better things to do than defend the honour of a hot drink.

'I have to get my life back on track,' Emily suddenly announced. 'I'm going to stop taking pills. Valerie keeps giving me the wrong ones anyway. I want you to help me.'

246

'How?' I asked reluctantly. Emily struck me as the sort of person whose preferred mode of assistance would be designed to cause maximum inconvenience to the helper.

'Help me find Fernando.' She sank down into an armchair. 'I've got to find him. I know he's . . . around, somewhere.'

I sat down next to her, resigning myself to prolonged thirst. She'd obviously forgotten all about the nice cup of tea and I was reluctant to change the subject. 'I don't know how much I can help,' I said, 'but . . . well, presumably you've contacted some members of his family?'

'I don't know anything about his family, their names, where they live, nothing,' Emily said tearfully. Despite her considerable distress, she was still far more in control than I'd ever seen her before. 'Fernando wouldn't talk about them. He wasn't in touch with them, hadn't been for ages. All he ever said about his family was that he preferred to pretend they didn't exist. He must have had an awful childhood. I didn't press him for details because . . . well, he was so sensitive on the subject. I didn't want to upset him. After he went missing I wished I had insisted. It might have helped me find him.'

'I doubt it, not if he has nothing to do with them,' I said. 'Emily, I know this is an upsetting suggestion, but I have to ask . . . do you think anything bad might have happened to him? You know, I mean, seriously bad?'

'You mean do I think he could have been abducted and murdered?' Her voice shook, but I got the impression this idea wasn't new to her. 'I did, until a couple of months ago. I just couldn't believe Fernando would disappear by choice. He loved Summerton.'

'What about you?' I asked, surprised by the way her sentence ended.

'I don't know whether he loved me. He said he did, but I suppose sometimes people say that, don't they? When they don't altogether mean it. Oh, I don't know! I hope he loved me, but he couldn't possibly have felt as strongly about me as I did about him. I think I might have pressurised him into pretending he did, though. Oh, God.' She covered her eyes with her hand. 'I was so needy, so neurotic. I'm sure I drove him away.' I agreed, but didn't say so. Her use of the past tense in her description of herself was encouraging, I thought, and indicated that she really did mean to try to pull herself together. When she spoke lucidly like this, I could almost see the human being behind the psychological condition. 'But Summerton, I *know* he loved Summerton,' Emily went on. 'He was passionate about the place. He would never have left before his fellowship was finished, not by choice. That's why I thought something terrible had happened to him until . . .' She blushed and looked away, sighing deeply.

'Until what?' I asked. I wished the fellows of Summerton could get their acts together and tell me what I wanted to know more quickly. Whatever Valerie had accidentally prescribed for Emily, it certainly wasn't speed.

'Do you remember when you first came to see me? You were asking questions about Fernando and I thought you knew where he was?' I nodded. 'Well, that was because . . . I thought he'd sent you. I thought you were another one of his messages. He's been sending me things, you see.'

'What? What things?' I rushed to get the words out.

'Photographs.' She got up and opened the door to her bedroom, which adjoined the far end of the lounge. An unpleasant musty smell wafted towards me. As Emily sifted through one of her desk drawers, I noticed that the curtains in her bedroom were closed and guessed that they hadn't been drawn for months. My first impression, from what I could see through the narrow doorway, was that the carpet was navy-blue like the one in the lounge, but with an irregular pattern of large pink flowers. Then I realised the flowers were crumpled pieces of tissue paper that Emily had dropped on the floor. I counted five of them, all of which must have been used and discarded today, since no Summerton bedder would have left them there. I imagined the whole of Emily's substantial body to be made up of individual teardrops – lots of little pear shapes in one big one.

It was almost ten minutes before Emily slammed her desk drawer shut and came back into the lounge carrying two salmon-coloured envelopes. I couldn't believe it had taken her so long to find them, that she didn't know the exact location of all Fernando-related objects. Maybe she had wanted to censor the pictures before showing them to me.

She handed me one of the envelopes and sat down, holding on to the other with both hands. 'That was the first lot he sent,' she said. I turned it upside-down and shook out the contents eagerly. When Emily had first said Fernando had sent her photographs, I'd assumed she meant photographs of him, to add to her collection. It didn't take me long to realise that what I had in front of me was infinitely stranger than a few snapshots.

There were six photographs altogether, each one more mystifying than its predecessor. The first was a close-up of an Oxo cube, beef flavour. 'What the hell . . .' I muttered, moving on to the next one, a blurred shot of lots of trees. 'Emily, what *are* these?'

'I've no idea,' she whined. 'I was hoping you could tell me.' After the trees there was a picture of a pile of magazines on a coffee table. The one on top was called *Literary Review*. 'Fernando used to read the *Literary Review* religiously,' said Emily, leaning forward. 'Those are his magazines, that's how I know he definitely sent the photos. You see that biro mark on the top one?'

I looked carefully and noticed a small blue squiggle in the bottom right-hand corner of the cover, taking in at the same time that it was the February 1997 issue. The month before Fernando Rose disappeared. 'Yes. What about it?'

'Fernando made that mark, trying to get his pen to work. I was there when he did it.'

I nodded, flicking through the rest of the photos. There were three more. One was an arty, angled shot of a packet of Nurofen, the headache tablet. If I'd seen it in an art gallery I would have assumed it was just another example of the sort of ah-but-you-didn't-think-of-it-did-you? art that wins all the big prizes these days, but in this context I could only see it as evidence that Fernando had had some kind of nervous breakdown. Why else would an allegedly intelligent person vanish in the middle of a job he loved and send photos of stock cubes and painkillers to his abandoned girlfriend?

I was about to say as much to Emily when the last two photos distracted me. One was of Ethan Handley, slumped in an alcove in some nightclub or other. His face looked almost white under the not very flattering strobe lighting. His eyes were closed and his mouth was half open in what looked like a groan. He was clutching his stomach.

'I was there when Fernando took that photo,' said Emily. 'It was in the college bar. Ethan had really dreadful food poisoning. He was sick immediately after the photograph was taken. Keith and Damian said it was drink at the time, but it turned out that the squid had been slightly off that night at dinner and Ethan was really ill.'

'Emily, this is ridiculous!' I snapped, frustrated by my lack of comprehension. 'Why has he sent you these pictures? What do they mean? You must know. I mean, look, this last one is of Peter Ustinov!' I yelled. Emily cringed, backing away from me. I took a deep breath and lowered my voice. 'Peter Ustinov, standing next to a pyramid. In the dark.' This had to be the most far-fetched of all the pictures. Fernando couldn't have taken it himself, not unless he knew Peter Ustinov and had been on holiday with him to Egypt at some point. That seemed most unlikely, although perhaps no more unlikely than the idea that someone would send his ex a photo of an Oxo cube.

'That's from the film *Death on the Nile*,' said Emily. 'You know, the Agatha . . .'

'I know what it is,' I interrupted her. 'What I don't know is why he's sent it to you. Did *Death on the Nile* have any

250

particular significance in your relationship?'

'No!' she wailed, looking bemused. 'I don't know why he sent them, I don't know anything.' She clutched the curtain that she had used as a handkerchief substitute yesterday with such force that the curtain rail sprang from the wall on one side and swung back and forth in mid air. She emitted a feeble howl.

'Emily, calm down. I'm not accusing you of anything, I just . . . I don't understand this. Did he send a note with the photos?'

'No, nothing,' she said defensively. 'Just two envelopes full of photos. The ones you've seen came about two months ago and then last week these arrived.' She handed me the second envelope.

This time I was prepared for Fernando's sheer non-sensicality and was therefore not remotely surprised to see, in this order, an old man wearing glasses, a stained-glass image of Jesus, a photo of Summerton's Great Hall, candle-lit and full of people in gowns, a bottle of orange squash, a car door with a large patch of rust under the window and, finally, one of those supermarket cartons of Tetley's bitter. When I got back to the one of the bespectacled man I held it up. 'Who's he?' I asked Emily. 'Another member of the *Death on the Nile* cast?'

'Don't be silly, that's James Pickles,' said Emily, as if this should have been obvious.

'Who?'

'You know, the judge. Judge James Pickles.'

'You can repeat his name all day and I still won't know who he is.'

'Oh. I thought everyone had heard of him. He's a judge. Remember the "She's no angel" case? It was on the news.'

'Oh, yeah. I remember that. I didn't know his name, though. Is this definitely him?'

'Yes.' Emily nodded.

'Emily, are you sure these were sent to you by Fernando? I mean, if there was no note with them, nothing . . .

couldn't someone else have sent them?'

'No!' Emily's eyes filled with tears. 'I told you, those are Fernando's *Literary Reviews* and I saw him take that photo of Ethan in the college bar. And these are his envelopes! Fernando always used these orangey-pink envelopes.' Hysteria had crept into her voice.

'Okay, okay,' I said soothingly. 'I'm sure he did send them.'

'They're his envelopes,' Emily insisted. 'And before you suggest someone may have kidnapped him and be using his things to show me they've got him . . .'

'What? That hadn't occurred to me,' I said, trying not to laugh. John Donne scholars were not frequently kidnapped, and kidnappers, in my televisual and literary experience, rarely behaved in such a cryptic manner. Indeed, sending the captive's loved one a photo of an Oxo cube rather than a demand for loads of money would be a sure sign that the kidnappers recruitment panel, like so many panels before them, had appointed the wrong person for the job.

'Well, it's occurred to me,' said Emily. 'I've thought of every possibility. But no one knew Fernando used those envelopes except me.' This conversation reminded me, as everything seemed to these days, of *Witness for the Prosecution*, in which Marlene Dietrich's letters are identified as being hers specifically because of the writing paper she uses.

'And, presumably, everyone else at Summerton that he ever wrote to,' I said.

'No!' Emily contradicted me indignantly. 'I'm not a complete imbecile! Everyone here uses e-mail for business stuff, well, for everything really. Fernando didn't need to write to anyone in college.'

'Oh. Okay.' I gave in, exhausted. Without warning, Emily sprang out of her chair and fell to her knees at my feet.

'Please help me find him,' she begged. 'You've got to, you

must know something, the pictures must tell you something, some clue . . .'

'Emily, they mean nothing to me. I'm sorry,' I said truthfully. 'Why did you think they would?' As far as I knew I didn't have a reputation in Cambridge for being a weird-photograph decoder. She shrugged morosely. 'Have you shown them to anyone else?' I asked.

'No. I know it sounds funny but . . . I knew Fernando didn't want me to tell anyone. I knew he wanted the photos to be private, just between us.'

'How did you know?'

'I just did. I can't explain it.'

'Right,' I said sceptically. The handbrake in my head hauled itself up a notch. 'So why did you show them to me?'

'Because you came round here, asking about Fernando and Rod Firsden and . . . I don't know, I thought maybe you knew something.'

'Why did you support Rod so strongly for the fellow- ship?' I asked. This was one of the many unanswered questions on my list and the mention of his name reminded me.

'No reason,' said Emily quietly, shuffling away from me.

'No reason? You supported him for no reason?'

'No. Yes, I mean.'

'Oh. So you didn't think he was the best candidate?'

'Yes, of course. Yes, that's why I supported him, obviously.'

'So there was a reason,' I said pedantically.

'Yes, there was that reason.' She sighed heavily. 'But there was no *other* reason.'

'Right,' I said. I was fascinated by this other reason that there allegedly was not. 'Listen, Emily, can I take these photos?'

'Oh, I knew you'd help me!' She beamed at me.

'I don't know whether I can help,' I said, 'but I'd like to have a better look at these and a chance to think about . . .'

'Oh, thank you, thank you!'

'I'm not promising anything.' I picked up both envelopes. 'I'll bring these back in a day or so.' It was only once we'd said goodbye and Emily had shut the door of her set that I realised how little I deserved her confidence in my powers of strayed-boyfriend detection. I hadn't even thought to check the envelopes for postmarks.

Chapter Thirty-three

Suspicion (The Sentiment Not the Handbrake)

A quick inspection revealed that there was no postmark on either envelope, which meant they must have been delivered by hand, to the porters' lodge, to one of the college's internal postboxes or directly to Emily's set. Whatever Emily said, I still wasn't convinced Fernando had sent the photos, or that no one else knew he used salmon-coloured envelopes; she couldn't possibly say what other people did or didn't know.

If Fernando had walked into college to post them, somebody would have seen him, unless he'd done it in the middle of the night. Even then, one of the porters on night duty could easily have spotted him. I doubted he'd have risked it, not if he'd disappeared from Summerton of his own free will. Which meant that either someone else had sent the pictures or Fernando had a sidekick, someone in the college who knew where he was and why, and who was willing to help him communicate in this bizarre fashion with Emily.

I went back to the car and got out my notebook and pen. Taking the photographs out of the two envelopes again, I made the following list:

Photos sent to Emily Lole (possibly by Fernando Rose)
FIRST ENVELOPE (SENT TWO MONTHS AGO)
1   A beef Oxo cube
2   Some trees

3 A pile of *Literary Reviews* (which Emily says belonged to Fernando)
4 A Nurofen carton
5 Ethan Handley with food poisoning (Emily says Fernando took this one)
6 Peter Ustinov and a pyramid (from *Death on the Nile*)

SECOND ENVELOPE (SENT LAST WEEK)
1 Judge James Pickles
2 Stained-glass window of Jesus
3 Summerton Great Hall, some feast or other
4 A bottle of orange squash
5 A patch of rust on a car door
6 A box of Tetley's bitter cans

I found the photographs just as puzzling the second time round and stuffed them angrily back into their envelopes. I was about to get out of the car and head for Daphne Fielding's office when I caught sight of her in my rear-view mirror, walking out of the building and across Old Court. She was smartly dressed in a brown trouser suit and had swept her hair up into a French knot. I beeped my horn to attract her attention. When she didn't respond, I leaned out of the window and yelled, 'Professor Fielding!' She turned round but made no move to approach the car, so I got out and ran over to her.

As I got nearer, she looked pointedly at her watch. 'What is it?' she asked. 'I'm in a hurry.'

'I just wanted to have a word with you about the De La Wyche fellowship,' I said, feeling the effects of smoking upon my lung capacity. Daphne Fielding looked at me disapprovingly. I suspected she was angry with herself for allowing an out-of-breath driving instructor to waylay her. 'I just wondered . . . could you tell me why you decided not to give it to Sebastian?'

'Sebastian should ask me himself,' she said.

'He wouldn't. He's too proud. I said I'd ask. I am his wife.' I tried to sound self-righteous.

'The panel felt he wasn't the best candidate. Which isn't to say his work isn't good, but, as you know, the standard is so high . . .'

'But on the Wednesday you were supporting him,' I interrupted her flow of platitudes served with a garnish of lisp. 'And then, by the time the panel met on Thursday morning, you'd changed your mind. You voted for Terri Skinner. I just wondered why that was.' I smiled sweetly, to give the impression that I confidently expected there to be a perfectly innocent explanation.

'How do you know that?' Professor Fielding fiddled with the top of her ear, which protruded as usual from her hairstyle. A patch of pink appeared at her throat above her shirt collar and started to spread upwards.

'Other panel members have told me,' I said, no longer caring if I caused trouble. As long as I didn't name any one person, there wasn't a lot she could do.

'Well, then they misunderstood. I didn't "support" anyone, as you put it. I simply discussed, as we all did, the relative merits of each applicant's case.'

'Oh. That's definitely not what I've heard.'

'Really.' She smiled coolly with her mouth only. Her eyes were full of contempt for me and my questions. 'What have you heard, exactly?' I was tempted to quote a line from one of Sebastian's favourite films, a Western called *Shane*, and say, 'I've heard that you're a low-down Yankee liar.' I could then test her cinematic expertise by asking her to guess where the line came from. What stopped me wasn't instinctive politeness – I don't suffer from that particular affliction – but the knowledge that, in order for the phrase to come out sounding right I would have to fake an American accent and risk embarrassing myself.

'That you argued strongly in favour of Sebastian on Wednesday, then adjourned the meeting, even though that's against the college rules, and then argued strongly in favour of Terri on Thursday. I'm sure you had your reasons and were doing what you thought best, but I just would love to know why, that's all.'

'My, my,' said Daphne, smiling nastily. 'You have been misinformed, haven't you? I don't know which of Valerie, Emily and Damian you've been talking to, but in this case it doesn't matter because they are all, in their different ways, completely unreliable.'

'In that case, they shouldn't have been on the De La Wyche panel,' I said angrily.

'I quite agree, but don't blame me for that. I didn't select the panel. But I'll tell you one thing: I never have wanted and never will want Terri working here. It's bad enough that she's married to my son. I think her work's substandard and her personality's worse, and I sincerely hope she'll go to Reading and inflict herself on them instead of us.' She folded her arms defiantly, but I was too confused to feel intimidated. Damian had quite unambiguously said that Daphne had supported Sebastian on Wednesday and Terri on Thursday. I didn't for a minute doubt that he was capable of lying, but why would he, in this case? What did he have to gain from pretending Daphne had suddenly and inexplicably switched her allegiance?

'So let's get this straight,' I said. 'You never supported Terri Skinner's application? You never argued that the fellowship should be given to her?'

'I argued as vociferously against her as I possibly could without seeming unprofessional,' said Daphne. 'If you must know, your husband was my first choice. Emily Lole wanted Rod Firsden, Damian wanted to appoint that Antarctic girl he's now dating and Valerie fell for the old "scientists are useful" myth and voted for Terri. Now, I'm afraid I really must go.' She looked at her watch again, then sighed and swung her arms back and forth like a sulky teenager. I didn't believe much, if any, of what she'd said. If Sebastian had really been her first choice and she'd been thwarted, that meant we were on the same side. Wouldn't she, in that case, have been more friendly and conspiratorial with me?

'Hang on,' I said. 'I won't take up much more of your time. Supposing I accept what you're saying . . .'

'I don't care whether you accept it or not.' She sniggered, tucking a stray strand of hair behind her enormous ear. There was something about Daphne Fielding that reminded me of a nasty schoolgirl. 'I'm just telling you what happened.'

'Is it at least true that you adjourned the meeting on Wednesday? I was told that you kept looking at your watch, like you're doing now, but that you didn't explain to the other panel members why the decision had to be postponed till Thursday.'

'I don't have to listen to this.' She shook her head in disgust and began to walk away. I ran after her, grabbing the sleeve of her jacket. 'Kindly take your hands off me!' she bellowed.

'Okay, I'm sorry,' I muttered. 'But please tell me why the panel met again on Thursday.'

'Because I wasn't feeling very well, all right?' She stopped walking and swung round to face me. The patch of red had now spread across her entire neck and the tips of her ears had turned an alarming shade of burgundy. She reminded me of that line from Rod's favourite George Herbert poem, 'Sighs and Groans', the one that refers to 'vessels full of blood', meaning people. Daphne Fielding was the sort of thin-skinned person whose blood lay very close to the surface, a mosquito's idea of a slap-up meal.

'I made it clear to the rest of the panel that I was feeling sick and that that was my reason for ending Wednesday's meeting,' Daphne went on indignantly, 'so whoever's said otherwise is telling you a pack of lies.' She flounced off, her high wedge heels smacking the concrete of Old Court.

I concluded with uncharacteristic pessimism that all four panel members were lying to me. Soon the truth would be so thoroughly submerged under all their deceit that I'd never be able to unearth it. I went back to the car and stuffed the two salmon envelopes into the glove compartment, wondering whether Emily was mad enough and sad enough to have taken the photos herself and made up the whole story, in the way that children invent imaginary friends.

I drove into town, parked on a double-yellow line and had lunch in McDonald's. Since I had an hour to kill before I could see Valerie, I was probably unwise to have a fast food lunch, but I was in one of those moods where only a cheeseburger and large fries would do. By quarter to two I couldn't stand the suspense any more, so I drove back to Summerton, hoping I wouldn't bump into either Emily or Daphne.

As I turned the corner from Old Court into Tyndsall Court, I collided with Lloyd Lunnon, the peace studies don. 'Watch where you're fucking going! Are you visually impaired?' he yelled.

'Sorry,' I said, trying to shuffle past without drawing further attention to myself.

'Hey!' Lunnon shouted after me as I headed towards Valerie's surgery. 'Who the fuck are you anyway? Are you one of these new female fellows whose arrival we're constantly being told we should be happy about?' I couldn't help being flattered by the suggestion that I might be a Summerton fellow.

'No, I'm a driving instructor. I'm the wife of . . .' I stopped, realising Lunnon might not have heard of Sebastian, a mere graduate student.

'Evidently a memorable chap, whoever he is.'

'Sebastian Nunn,' I said. 'He did his PhD here.'

'Oh, I know Sebastian.' Lunnon smiled unexpectedly. 'Wasn't he up for the De La Wyche this time?'

'That's right,' I said. 'He didn't get it.'

'No, some skirt got it, I believe. The question is, is she well-endowed up top? I have no objection to the presence in college of the female persuasion, as long as they haven't

260

got chests like ironing boards. I don't think that's too much to ask, do you?'

'She is,' I said. 'And she wears revealing clothes.'

'Marvellous, splendid,' Lunnon chortled. 'Although I'm sure your husband is a superior intellect.'

'He is!' I blurted out, praying Lunnon would offer to put the full force of his belligerent personality behind remedying the situation forthwith.

'Well, then not coming here is the best thing for him. The place is full of baboons. He's had a lucky escape.' Lunnon looked me up and down. 'Your chest tends toward ironing-boardery,' he said amiably, 'but you're very pretty.'

'Thanks,' I said, ignoring the insulting part of his remark because I'd had an idea of how I could make most efficient use of Lloyd Lunnon. As someone who had had nothing to do with the De La Wyche appointment and who was in the habit of speaking his mind, he would have no reason to lie to me. 'Can I ask you a question?' I said.

'I'm not giving you and your husband any money, however destitute you are,' he said huffily. 'Whatever's wrong with prostitution?'

'I don't want money.'

'Good. Most people do.'

'I want to ask your opinion – your honest opinion, uncensored – of the De La Wyche panel members.'

'Almost definitely low, I would have thought,' said Lunnon. 'Remind me precisely which of the college's laughing stocks were involved.'

'Daphne Fielding, Valerie Williams, Damian Selinger and Emily Lole. They're all telling me different things about the De La Wyche business and I don't know who to believe.'

'Oh, none of them,' said Lunnon cheerfully. 'Daphne Fielding fucked her way to a personal chair and has kept her knees tightly shut ever since. If we'd known that would happen ... well, regret gets us nowhere, as eminent thinkers such as Frank Sinatra and Sid Vicious have pointed out. She and Selinger are devious, self-seeking,

261

manipulative snakes, and Valerie Williams and Emily Lole get laid too rarely to be trusted. They only come into college so that they can rub themselves up against the corners of tables.'

'Right,' I said wearily. Lunnon's extreme nastiness was beginning to irritate and depress me.

'I can see you're not finding my comments very helpful,' he said. 'All right, then, let me be serious for a moment. Emily and Valerie would be more likely to tell you the truth, or at least their tight-fannied, lunatic interpretation of it. But Fielding and Selinger are cleverer, and would make better allies. There, is that better?'

'Slightly,' I said.

'For Christ's sake, stop dithering, girl,' said Lunnon sternly.

'I've never dithered in my life,' I said indignantly.

'Yes you are. If you think you smell a rat – and, might I point out, you are ideally situated so to do – then go to the Master! Go to the press! Bring us down, drag Summerton's name in the mud. What's wrong with young people these days? The young are supposed to fight. Fuck and fight, that's what the young should do. You wouldn't care for a quick fuck, I don't suppose?'

'No, thanks,' I said, keener by the second to get away from him. 'I've got an appointment with Valerie Williams.'

'Suit yourself,' said Lunnon, backing off. 'If you change your mind, I'm in B4 Queen's Court.' He sauntered away with his hands in his pockets, humming a tune. Furious at being labelled a ditherer, I marched straight to Valerie's surgery and banged on the door. She opened it immediately, looking even more disapproving and hostile than she had the day before.

I refused the chair she offered me and stood in the middle of the room with my arms folded. 'Well?' I said. 'What's this thing you've got to tell me?' Valerie also seemed reluctant to sit down. She pottered around the surgery, picking things up and replacing them.

'Tell me the truth,' she instructed me. 'How much do you know about the ... attempted deception of the De La Wyche panel?'

'Absolutely sod all,' I said.

'You're not going to like it.' She sat down heavily in the chair behind her desk. Her large bottom spilled over on both sides. 'But I'm going to tell you anyway. I'm sick of this whole silly business. It's better that you know.'

'I agree,' I said.

'On Wednesday, as you know, Professor Fielding ended the meeting before an appointment had been made . . .'

'Why?' I interrupted. 'Because she was feeling ill?'

'I don't think so, no. Did she tell you that was why?' Valerie looked suspicious.

'Yes.'

'Well, she was lying. She didn't say anything about feeling ill. I wasn't at all happy about the proceedings being delayed – it's totally against college rules, but there was nothing I could do. I came straight back here after the meeting ended. There was an envelope on my desk. I opened it. It contained . . . a rather unpleasant anonymous note.'

'Was the envelope a sort of salmon-pink colour?' I asked quickly. Perhaps Emily wasn't the only person with whom the absent Fernando had started to communicate.

'No, it was brown,' said Valerie. 'Why?'

'Never mind. What did the note say?'

'Wait.' Valerie inhaled deeply. 'The note wasn't all that was in the envelope. There were two letters from Daphne Fielding to your husband.'

'*What*? What sort of letters?' As far as I knew Sebastian had never received any correspondence from Daphne Fielding. 'Have you still got them? I want to see them.'

'I don't think that would be appropriate. But I'll summarise their content for you. They referred to a plan to discredit Terri Skinner. It was clear that Daphne and Sebastian . . . well, there's no nice way of putting this. It was clear that they were trying to cheat.' This last comment had an unmistakable undertone of triumph. Valerie was in her morally self-righteous element.

'That's impossible,' I said. 'Sebastian would never lie or cheat. You must have got the wrong end of the stick. What exactly did these letters say, word for word? I want to see them. Are you sure they were from Professor Fielding?'

'Positive. I know her handwriting well,' said Valerie. 'In the first letter, she told Sebastian that, as they'd agreed, she'd altered Terri's references, added some critical comments that cast doubt on her ability and character, in the subtlest possible way. She also said she'd added a few choice comments to Sebastian's references, favourable comments, which should swing things in his direction.'

'But . . .' I could feel tears pricking at the back of my eyelids. 'Sebastian would never do that, I know he wouldn't.'

'The second letter was to wish him good luck before the interview,' Valerie went on mercilessly. 'And she added something like, "After our little reference adjustments, it should be in the bag." And that is almost word for word.'

'What did the anonymous note say?' I gritted my teeth.

'That these two letters had been found on Daphne's desk and the writer, whoever he or she was, thought I should see them. I think it must have been one of the bedders. Or a student.'

'Hold on a minute,' I said, detecting a flaw in Valerie's reasoning. 'If those letters were really from Daphne Fielding to Sebastian, written before the interview on Tuesday, as they must have been if she was wishing him good luck in one of them, why would she have left them lying around on her desk? Why wouldn't she have sent them to him?'

'I have no idea.'

'No. No!' I felt as if I was suffocating. 'This is just not possible. I'm telling you, Sebastian knows nothing about this. Someone – I don't know who – has set this up to sabotage his chances.'

'I'm afraid not, Kate,' said Valerie sanctimoniously. 'As soon as I got the letters I went straight to Daphne's rooms and confronted her with them. It made sense, it all rang horribly true. She'd been supporting Sebastian all day, and the references she'd read out, for Terri and Sebastian, fitted in with what she'd said in her letters. Terri's were a bit iffy and Sebastian's were practically calling him a genius.'

'He is a genius,' I said automatically, feeling dizzy and nauseous. 'Anyway, surely she couldn't rig the references even if she wanted to? Don't you all get copies of them?'

'No, we don't,' said Valerie, with a sort of smug regret. 'The chair of the panel, Daphne in this case, assembles all the references and reads them out to the rest of us after the interviews. That's in the rules. Unfortunately it would have been as easy as anything for her to tamper with them.'

'What did she say when you confronted her?' I asked numbly.

'She admitted it. She had no alternative, I had the evidence in my hand. I accused her of having an affair with Sebastian and trying to get him the fellowship for that reason. Daphne has . . . a bit of a reputation in that department.'

'What did she say?'

'She denied it.' I breathed a sigh of relief. Of course Sebastian wouldn't have an affair. 'According to Daphne, she was simply terrified of Terri coming to work at Summerton and she was willing to bend the rules a bit to ensure that didn't happen. She suggested this plan to Sebastian, whom she genuinely believed to be the best candidate, and he agreed.'

'She could have fiddled the references without telling him,' I said, struggling to keep up with the emerging horrors. 'Why didn't she just do that? Why involve Sebastian in this . . . this plan?' Valerie looked away. 'You think they are having an affair, don't you?' I guessed, correctly, judging by the way she tightened her lips until they formed a tiny circle, like the neck of a drawstring bag.

'I didn't entirely believe her when she denied it,' Valerie said finally. 'People who can cheat professionally can cheat personally.'

'So what happened then?' I asked, ignoring this latest slur on Sebastian's character. 'Did you threaten to grass her up?'

'I made it plain I thought something had to be done,' said Valerie with palpable pride. 'Daphne begged me not to go to the Master. She knew she would lose her job over something like this. I agreed, out of loyalty to the college. I felt it was my duty, in the circumstances, to try to right the wrong without damaging Summerton's reputation. If the scandal became official the press would be all over us. I told Daphne Sebastian couldn't possibly be appointed, not after he'd tried to cheat, and she agreed. She said she would make it clear in Thursday's meeting that she no longer supported him and she wouldn't oppose Terri's being appointed.'

'Which was what you wanted all along,' I said, remembering what Damian and Daphne had told me.

'Yes, I did, because I believed she was the strongest candidate. In return, I agreed not to take the matter of the cheating any further.'

'It sounds to me like you blackmailed Daphne into supporting your candidate.'

'I did nothing of the sort!' said Valerie. 'I've done absolutely nothing wrong.'

'Neither has Sebastian,' I snarled. 'I'm telling you, you've got it wrong. Either you're lying or Daphne Fielding's lying, but Sebastian is an honest person.'

'Kidding yourself won't do you any good, in the long run,' said Valerie in her best doctor's voice.

'Where are these letters, anyway? Why won't you show me them?'

'Because I don't approve of voyeurism. This business is sordid enough already.'

'I think you're making all this up.'

'Reading them would only upset . . .'

I didn't hear the rest of what she said because at that point I was so close to tears that I had to leave. I ran out of the room, slamming the door behind me.

I'd really paid the price for my persistence now, hadn't I? All the way back to the car I kept insisting to myself that I knew Sebastian hadn't conspired with Daphne Fielding behind my back, that he would never have an affair, but ninety-nine per cent sure and a hundred per cent sure are miles apart. As soon as I got home I would have to ask Sebastian about it, however much I dreaded his response.

Chapter Thirty-four

Daphne Fielding – Curriculum Vitae

Name
Daphne Cynthia Fielding.

Age
Fifty-four.

Address
8 Newton Road, Cambridge. Could have opted to live in college, as a single fellow, but was reluctant, according to college gossip, to allow any of Summerton's bedders to observe the steady traffic through her bedroom, since many of those present between her sheets would not be entirely unknown to college staff.

Place of Birth
Wigan, Lancashire.

Marital Status
Has never been married. It could therefore have been argued, if Joe Fielding were not so reluctant to argue, that to give Scarlett the surname 'Fielding' would have been the more proper feminist course of action, since it is the surname of a maternal rather than a paternal grandparent.
Does the antipathy between Daphne and Terri date back to Terri's rejection of the Fielding surname, or does it have its origins in Terri's exploitation of Joe? Joe would never

have told tales to his mother, but surely it cannot have escaped her notice. And mothers are very protective of their sons. This might explain why Daphne gave Terri, whom she loathes, a key to Summerton's library: to get her away from Joe for as much time as possible. Poor Joe, if his mother has deliberately engineered his wife's elopement with a collection of learned tomes.

Joe is Daphne's only child, although – how can I put this without being crude? – he was not her only pregnancy. Daphne fell pregnant twice after Joe was born, once when he was five and once when he was nine, but opted for termination on both occasions, despite Joe's constant pestering for a sibling, because pregnancy was not a condition she had enjoyed the first time round. In terms of discomfort and all-round inconvenience it rivalled punt-launching, the hellish chore I heard her complain about to Valerie Williams.

Employment History
1992–PRESENT
Professor of Film and Media Studies at Summerton College, Cambridge.

1986–1992
Senior Lecturer in Media and Film Studies at Anglia Polytechnic.

1980–1986
Lecturer in English Literature at Manchester Polytechnic.

1972–1980
Lecturer in English Literature at the Cheffing College of Further Education in Wigan.

Qualifications and Education
BA Hons (III) in English Literature from Preston Polytechnic.

Publications

Lots of articles published in journals edited by sexual partners or ex-partners pre-1992. Three books: *Fantasy and Femininity: Deconstructing Dietrich* (Scholars Press, Cambridge and New York, 1997), *The Popcorn Polemic: Class and the Cinema* (Scholars, 1996) and *Shades of Grey: The Ambiguity of Black-and-White Cinema* (Scholars, 1994). No sleeping with editors was necessary for these three volumes – Daphne was a Summerton professor, so the publishers naturally put their unintelligibility down to intellectual sophistication.

Strengths and Weaknesses

Not many people would have had the necessary stamina, determination and talent for – let's put it politely – 'networking' to get from a third at Preston Poly to a chair (in Daphne's case it should be called a bidet) at Summerton. Even now, at the pinnacle of her profession, Daphne still goes in for strategic screwing. Sleeping with one's own students is not a sackable offence at Summerton as it is in some of the Oxbridge colleges. The rule book says only that if you bed a student you must declare it and you will thereafter be forbidden to mark that student's work. Daphne, who has always hated marking, quickly realised that it was in her interests to seduce, and declare the seduction of, as many students as possible. She didn't much care what any of her colleagues thought of her, but as it turned out she needn't have worried. The general consensus was that she was a post-feminist icon, valiant reverser of discriminatory roles. Any criticism levelled against her was immediately trampled upon by every women's society in every college and the word 'witch-hunt' was spread liberally across campuses nationwide.

Is there anything wrong with screwing your way to the top? Isn't it simply a more extreme version of the more innocuous connections that so often get people the jobs they want? Earlier this year Sebastian had an interview for

270

a job at Kennett College, Oxford. He and the four other candidates were sitting in the waiting room before the interviews and the panel members came out to introduce themselves. They shook hands with Sebastian and three of the other candidates, asked their names and where they had come from and said how nice it was to meet them. When they got to the fifth candidate, instead of shaking hands they waved casually and said, 'Hi, Jim.' Guess who got the job? Jim may have kidded himself that he got it on merit, that his knowing the interviewers did not affect their objectivity, but he will have been wrong.

Strangely, Daphne's stamina does not seem to extend beyond the bedroom. As the official college punt-launcher, she finds her responsibilities onerous in the extreme. When a new punt is built, she has to think of a name for it, spill champagne over it in a mock christening ceremony and push it on to the river. She suspects, correctly, that her colleagues do not understand how gruelling the life of a punt-launcher truly is. Many of Summerton's punts, incidentally, are named after actors and characters from *Witness for the Prosecution*, Daphne's favourite film. The first time Sebastian and I went punting, our punt was called *Tyrone* after Tyrone Power, otherwise known as Leonard Vole, the husband Marlene Dietrich pretends to hate. Summerton also has punts called *Marlene*, *Dietrich* and *Witness*.

Chapter Thirty-five

Les Amants

I sat in my car near Rod's house, trying to decide what to
do. I was nearly half an hour early for our date. Rod had
instructed me not to be early and I hadn't planned to
disobey him, but when Sebastian had ordered me out of the
flat a short while ago, I'd had nowhere else to go.

I'd parked on Raymond Road, a couple of minutes' walk
from Rod's. If I hadn't been feeling so weak and miserable
I would have parked on Sterling Road, in a blameless
parking space far away from Vincent Strebonian's gateposts, and made a point of seeking out the widowed plastic
surgeon, in the unlikely event of his failing to appear as if
by magic at my car window, to apologise for any distress
I'd caused him over the past few days. Tonight, though, I
couldn't face it. I couldn't really face an evening with Rod
either and would have pushed a note through his letter-box
cancelling our date if I hadn't been too scared to go home.

After speaking to Valerie, I had driven straight back to
Noble House, trying to think of an inoffensive way to ask
Sebastian if what she had said was true. I decided not to
mention her affair theory, so convinced was I of its
impossibility. For a while, I considered not mentioning
anything at all, ignoring everything Valerie had told me and
hoping it would go away, but tempting though it was on
one level, I knew I wouldn't be happy until I'd heard
Sebastian's version of events. There was also the chance
that if Valerie had broken her silence by telling me, she

might not stop there. What if she went to the Master, or the papers, with her story and somehow word got around the academic community that Sebastian was a cheat? There was no alternative; I had to ask him. Whatever he told me, however awful it was, I would stand by him.

My rehearsed phrases deserted me as soon as I walked through the door. Sebastian was lying on the sofa – I hate to say 'as usual', but the fact was that I almost always found him lying on the sofa when I came in. None of the washing-up from the previous day, this morning or lunchtime had been done, and the bin was overflowing. Crumpled sheets of lined A4 paper were scattered all over the floor, reminding me of Emily Lole's discarded tissues. 'Sebastian!' I moaned in dismay before I could stop myself. 'Why is the flat such a tip?' I then listed all the domestic tasks he had omitted to do. I knew this sort of nagging drove Sebastian wild with rage, but I provoked him nonetheless. In hindsight, I think I might have welcomed the distraction of a safe row, one we'd had many times before. Anything to postpone the horror of what I had to ask him.

'I've been writing an article for a journal, that's why,' he snapped at me, turning up the volume on the TV. 'Perhaps it's escaped your notice, but academics these days – not that I am an academic, I'm just a nothing, a nobody – but anyone who wants to be an academic has to publish, publish, publish, in the hope that some mediocre university department will give him an exploitative one-year job and use his publications shamelessly to improve its research rating. I know it's shit, I know it's deeply depressing, not to mention soul-destroying, but that's life.' His voice rose steadily until it was a shout. I'd clearly caught him at his most sensitive. 'If I want to stand any chance of getting any job, ever, I have to write articles. No interviewers are going to be impressed to hear that I take the bin out every morning. I can't put doing the fucking washing-up or the hoovering on my CV, now, can I?'

273

'Okay, calm down,' I murmured, seeing his point. I regretted mentioning the state of the flat. Now I'd put him in a foul temper, which made the prospect of discussing Daphne even more scary. Still, he'd probably been in a grim mood long before I got back; being at once an expert on Lenin and unable to take that expertise any further than one's own sofa would be enough to blacken anyone's spirits.

'If you're so bothered about dirt and mess, why don't you do some housework yourself?' Sebastian yelled at me. 'How long have we lived here? Four years? Have you ever once picked up the hoover? Have you ever once cleaned the bath or the toilet?'

This is a new one, I thought, trying to cobble together a hasty defence. 'Well . . . I don't really remember . . .' I lied.

'You just assume that because I'm at home all day and you bring in all the money, my work doesn't count. It's okay for me to interrupt my writing – which no one thinks enough of to employ me, after all – to cart stinking bin bags full of mouldy bread and fag ash . . .'

'Sebastian!' I put up my hand to stop him, but he paid no attention, continuing in a similar vein for several more minutes. I covered my ears and hummed loudly, ignoring him. It was too painful to listen to Sebastian going on like this, as if I were one of the enemy, one of the people who ignored or undermined his work. 'You know I don't think any of that,' I said when he'd finally stopped ranting. 'I hardly ever put any pressure on you about housework and I don't expect you to do everything. I know you've got to spend most of your time writing and I've always encouraged you. Well, haven't I? It's just that . . . today the flat looked such a mess, I couldn't help mentioning it. But, I mean, usually I don't say anything, do I? When was the last time I complained?'

'You don't complain because you know bloody well that I do most of the housework that gets done around here. I should be the one complaining. Why should I do more than you? Do you think that's fair?'

'Well ...' I prepared, unwisely, to offer my honest opinion. 'I don't think it's all that unfair for you to do a bit more than me, given that I'm ... well, the breadwinner and out at work all day.' I held my breath, knowing that yesterday I would never have used the word 'breadwinner' in Sebastian's presence. I was punishing him, I realised, for conspiring with Daphne behind my back, for leaving me out of something so important.

'Oh! Oh, it's like that, is it?' Sebastian bellowed furiously, marching up and down the lounge. 'So I'm just a servant now, am I? You bring in the money and in return I skivvy for you. Who am I, Joe fucking Fielding, some fucking feminist's slave?'

'The situations aren't even remotely comparable,' I said resentfully. 'What's so bad about the Joe and Terri situation is that he does all the housework as well as working full-time while Terri just ...'

'So it's all right for me, a mere unemployed person, to do all the housework, is that what you're saying?'

'No!' I wailed in frustration. 'I wish I'd never started this discussion.'

'But you did,' said Sebastian, who was just warming up. 'And I want to know, since you've brought up the subject, when you're going to start doing your fair share.'

'Sebastian, I don't have time, I work every single hour I can because we need the money and ...'

'Look, it's not my fault I've got no money,' Sebastian roared at the top of his voice. 'It's not as if I haven't tried to get a job – no one will give me one! But if you're going to take advantage of the fact that I'm at home all day being an unwanted failure by treating me like a servant then I might as well get a job in a fucking bun shop, like some brainless pleb.' I couldn't understand how Sebastian managed to be modest to the point of self-abuse at the same time as being one of the most arrogant people I'd ever met, but he somehow achieved it.

'Well, would it really be so bad?' I yelled back at him. Now that I'd started, now that Sebastian was no longer the person I thought he was, I might as well say all the things I hadn't previously dared to. 'Most people just accept that, at certain points in their life, they have to do something unfulfilling or boring, or even downright degrading, *just because they need the money*! But not you, oh, no, not the great Sebastian Nunn, the great intellectual can't get his hands dirty, oh, no . . .' Where were these words coming from, I wondered as I ranted. I didn't really believe all this, or indeed any of it. I was trying to hurt Sebastian and it seemed to be working.

'But . . . how can you say that?' He looked horrified. 'What about all that stuff you used to tell me about how if you have a crap job, you should do it craply?'

'I know,' I said wearily. Sebastian was quite right: I was the person who had told him never to do a job he didn't like. I had never resented supporting him financially – after all, I liked my job, so it wasn't as if I was suffering to keep him in socks – and I didn't think he should do more of the housework because he wasn't earning any money. If truth be told, I rarely thought about housework at all. I had blurted out the first thing that sprang to mind to divert attention away from my own domestic inadequacies. 'I'm really sorry,' I said. 'For everything. I know it's hard for you and of course you have to write articles instead of taking the bin out . . .'

'Why don't you take the bin out, then?' Sebastian asked suspiciously, as if to check that my apology was genuine. 'If I'd got the De La Wyche fellowship we could have afforded a cleaner,' he added mournfully and I felt hideously guilty.

'We can afford a cleaner,' I said emphatically. 'I'll sort it out tomorrow.' This was one good thing that had come out of our row, at least. It would be a great relief to have a cleaner. I liked cleanliness, I realised, in the abstract. If I didn't have to create it myself. For the time being, however, the bin stayed in. 'Sebastian . . .' I said tentatively.

'What?'

And then I asked him. And the row that followed made our housework altercation seem as benign as a barn dance. Two hours later Sebastian was still demanding to know, in icily subdued tones, how I could possibly believe such a thing of him.

'I *don't* believe it,' I said and it was true. It was true now. I hadn't been sure when I first brought it up, which was why I'd had to bring it up at all, but I'd been thoroughly convinced as soon as I saw the look on Sebastian's face. Since then I'd been trying to repair the damage my doubting him had done to our relationship. 'I had to ask once Valerie had told me, Sebastian, you must understand that. What was I supposed to think?'

'You could have suspected her of lying,' he said stonily. His coldness terrified me. I was used to Sebastian yelling and fuming, but not this hard, steel-eyed contempt. 'Why wouldn't she show you the letters? Oh, right, because that would be voyeuristic. Not, of course, because they don't exist. So instead of concluding she was a liar, you concluded that I was.'

'I didn't,' I shouted in exasperation. 'I just wanted to check. I believe you, Sebastian, totally. I just couldn't think of any other explanation.'

'It didn't occur to you that Valerie or Daphne, or both, were lying?' he continued with his expressionless interrogation.

'Yes, but . . . I overheard that argument in Daphne's office,' I told him for what must have been the third time. 'Daphne was accusing Valerie of wanting to tell tales and Valerie was saying she wanted things out in the open. When Valerie told me about the letters, it all seemed to make sense. Except . . . the bit about you.'

'The bit about me,' Sebastian repeated, nodding gravely. 'The bit about me, your husband, whom you've known for years, conspiring with a Summerton professor to embellish my references and sabotage another candidate's. If you thought, even for a minute, that I would do something like that, then you don't know me at all.'

'I do know you,' I insisted pathetically. 'I got confused. I've had such a weird few days, nothing makes any sense. We're always going on about how unfair it is that the best people never get the jobs, I just thought that if I were in your position, I might have fiddled things a bit . . .'

'Well, you may be a cheat and a liar, but I'm not.'

'But Sebastian, you know I'm trying to get you the fellowship . . . you don't disapprove of that.'

'Oh, for fuck's sake, shut up about that stupid rubbish. I never believed that, not really. How the hell are you going to get me the fellowship, Kate? Oh, I see. You were planning to lie and cheat, were you?'

'Maybe a bit, yes,' I said truthfully. 'In a good cause. What did you think I was going to do?' I thought back over the past few days and asked myself if I had done anything that was morally reprehensible. I had suspected the panel of peculiar and possibly pernicious behaviour, and I had asked questions accordingly. There was nothing wrong with that, as I was sure Sebastian would agree. But what about hiding in Terri's wardrobe, listening to her private conversations? What about the story I'd fabricated involving Gary Conley and his imaginary visit to Cambridge? What about – my heart flattened like a sink plunger – arranging a date with Rod? What the hell was I thinking of?

'I don't know,' said Sebastian. 'I thought you might talk to people. Certainly nothing that wasn't entirely legitimate. Obviously I was wrong. Anyway, I don't want you to do anything for me, not now that you've shown how low an opinion you have of me. In fact, get out.' His tone was alarmingly lethargic. 'I don't want to see you for a while, not until I've had a chance to think.'

'But . . . Sebastian, I live here. Where am I supposed to go?'

'I don't care,' he said. 'All I know is, I don't want to have to look at you.'

278

So I'd driven to Rod's as planned, wondering why Daphne or Valerie – or both, as Sebastian had suggested – had made up this particularly nasty story about my husband.

I got out of the car, walked round the corner to Sterling Road and rang Rod's doorbell. I hoped Vincent Strebonian wouldn't recognise me with my back to him and without the car. 'Come on,' I muttered when Rod did not respond. Finally the entry phone conveyed his distorted voice to me.

'Who is it?' He sounded suspicious. His front-room curtains were closed so I couldn't peer in.

'It's me, Kate,' I said.

'Oh. You're twenty-five minutes early. I said don't be early. I haven't finished tidying up yet.'

'I don't care,' I said crossly.

'Hold on, then.' Nearly five minutes later, just as I was beginning to get really angry, Rod appeared at the door. His face was shinier than I had previously seen it and he reeked of cocoa butter. A globule of the offending lotion that he had neglected to rub in rested on his beard in the shape of a teardrop. 'I'm not ready yet,' he said. 'Why are you so early? What's wrong? You look livid.' He was wearing his usual black polo neck and black jeans. Perhaps he would have changed into evening wear if I hadn't cut short his preparation time; I would never know.

'An abusive driving pupil,' I lied.

'I'm sorry. Oh, dear. Come in,' he said, and I followed him along the short passageway, past the foot of the staircase that led up to the residences on higher floors and into his flat, which was shaped like a fat cross. From the house's communal hall we walked straight into the kitchen, which was not merely tatty in its decor but piled high with washing-up, I noticed, feeling even more guilty for having criticised Sebastian, who only ever left dirty crockery for a day at most. I didn't have a chance to observe further details about the kitchen because Rod, probably ashamed of his mound of unwashed plates, steered me quickly

279

through to a small, square hall. He reached over my shoulder and pulled the kitchen door closed behind me, creating a rather claustrophobic effect, since each of the hall's four walls contained a doorway and the other three doors were also closed. 'The bathroom's there.' Rod pointed to his right. 'The bedroom's straight ahead and the lounge is through here.' I wondered whether he always kept internal doors closed or whether it was a precaution he'd taken to prevent me from witnessing whatever crimes against hygiene the other rooms were committing.

Rod pushed open the door on his left, and ushered me into a dark and extremely untidy room with pale-blue walls and brown fake-leather furniture. Clothes, most of them black, were scattered all over the sofa, armchair and carpet, and books about George Herbert and poetry led the way across the floor like stepping stones. Rod had the same edition of Herbert's *Collected Poems* that I'd bought, but his had a large coffee stain on its cover and looked considerably more battered. There were a few Athena posters attached to the walls with drawing pins, the only one of which I knew being *Les Amants* by Magritte. Every visible surface, from the top of the television to the bookshelves to the coffee table, was covered in a thick film of dust. A few small squares, semicircles and rectangles formed little islands of cleanliness on the shelves and mantelpiece. These stood out in sharp contrast to the blanket of dust that covered most of the room; perhaps when I arrived Rod had just begun to move a few objects in order to do some dusting and polishing. I'd only been half an hour early, though, and unless he had Mary Poppins stashed away in the bedroom, there was no way he could have made the place sanitary, let alone presentable, in half an hour.

'Sit down. Move some things, just throw them on the floor or something' said Rod nervously, flapping his arms about. 'I'm sorry it's so messy. I was planning to do some clearing up, but . . .' He looked at my face, which distracted him from his apology. 'What did this abusive pupil do?' he asked, concerned. 'He wasn't . . . violent, was he?'

'No. It was my own fault,' I said bitterly, thinking about what had really happened. I was angry with myself more than with Sebastian. I should have trusted him. I loathed being in the wrong and since I didn't get a lot of practice, I didn't deal with it very well.

'Why, what did you do?'

'I suddenly got it into my head that . . .' I swallowed, 'that someone I know really well was a different person altogether.'

'What do you mean?' Rod pulled me down on to the sofa. I could feel something hard biting into the back of my thigh. I guessed it was a fork, a filthy one, probably. 'This is most distressing. Please explain.' Rod had gripped me by both shoulders and was staring searchingly into my eyes.

'I'd really rather not discuss it,' I said wearily.

'You must tell me!' He raised his voice. 'Stop playing games. I'm in a terrible enough state without you adding to it.'

'Oh, leave me alone.' I pushed him away. 'It's nothing to do with you, you don't know the person from a bar of soap. I don't want to think about it any more.' Rod put his head in his hands and began to murmur tearful apologies. Another mood swing. Rod was so full of contradictions that I found it hard to keep up with him. He came over all houseproud, then it turned out his flat was a hazardous cesspit. He could shout at you one minute and cry the next.

'Why are you in a terrible state?' I asked him.

'Oh, the usual.' He sniffed. 'And now I've annoyed you and . . . I feel so inadequate. No wonder you'd prefer a real man who can fix cars.'

'Don't be silly.' I couldn't help laughing.

'I've got nothing. I can't have you. I probably won't get the fellowship. It's all been worth nothing.'

'You might get the fellowship,' I said and for an instant I almost forgot I hoped he wouldn't. As to his having me or not, I decided to avoid the subject altogether. 'Look, don't forget what Gary Conley told you about how Terri won't leave him alone. If she's that obsessed, she won't pass up the chance to move closer to him. And then you'll get it, Rod. But . . . you know you can't keep it.' I tried to inject a note of reality into the proceedings. 'After three years you'll have to leave and then . . .'

'I might not have to leave,' Rod snapped.

'What? Why not?'

'There's a new Master at Summerton, Sir Patrick Chichester. As George Herbert said, "Well, I will change the service and go seek some other Master out."' Rod laughed bitterly. 'Chichester's less traditional than Noel Barry, the previous Master. I've heard he's not averse to changing college rules when he thinks there's a strong case to be made. If I get the fellowship and . . . convince him of how dedicated I am, how much better than everyone they've had before . . . well, he might change it from a temporary position into a permanent one.' Seeing my incredulous expression, Rod added, 'He might!'

'But he might not,' I pointed out gently. This was an interesting difference between Rod and Sebastian. Sebastian wanted the Enmity for the three years of money and luxury it would give him, and for the benefit to his CV long after his time as a Summerton fellow was over. But more than that, he simply wanted an academic job, anywhere – he didn't have the same mad obsession Rod had with this position in particular. 'What's so great about Summerton?' I asked him. 'There are plenty of other places, other colleges in Cambridge, even. I mean, have you considered applying for a fellowship at Trinity or St John's or King's?'

'"God help poor Kings,"' said Rod quietly and I suspected he was quoting again. 'Oh, why don't you get out of here and leave me alone? I was wrong to see you as a . . . kindred spirit.'

'Well, if you will make snap judgements about people

282

you've known for less than a week . . .'

'That's right, twist the knife.' He smiled bitterly. 'Twist the knife in the open wound of rejection.'

'What are you on about, Rod?'

'I love you, Kate.' He raised his face so that it was level with mine. Several teardrops perched on his shiny cheeks like rain on a turtle-waxed car bonnet. 'I want you. I want something no one can take away after three years or . . . or any number of years!' he shouted. I was so alarmed by this extreme appeal, and the possibility that Rod might be becoming obsessed with me in earnest, that I opened my mouth to protest. Before I knew what was happening, Rod's lips were pressing down on mine, his beard rubbing uncomfortably against my chin.

Chapter Thirty-six

Coming out in the Wash

I wrestled free. 'Get off me!' I yelled.

'Kate, I've had a good idea,' Rod said urgently. 'I can't pretend I don't want the De La Wyche more than anything and I know you don't reciprocate my feelings for you, but can't we have one night together? I mean, just one night?' I had to restrain myself from snorting. Of course Rod didn't love me; he merely wanted to have sex. I doubted he was capable of loving anyone properly, not if the main difference he could see between me and the Enmity was that I was less likely to run out after three years. I couldn't believe I'd been soft enough to let that comment pass. 'I need you,' Rod whimpered.

'Tough,' I said firmly. 'Don't be ridiculous. If you intend to carry on like this, I'm off.'

'No, no, please! Please don't go!' Rod backed away with his hands in the air, like a robber who had just dropped his gun. 'I'd do anything to make you happy, maybe even give up the De La Wyche. Look, let's just watch *Witness for the Prosecution* and I'll cook you dinner as I promised I would.'

'Okay,' I said uncertainly. Had he really said that, about the Enmity? Before I had a chance to ask him if he'd meant it, he was in the kitchen banging pans around. 'I just need to wash up before I cook, all right? Will Chicken à la King be okay?' he called out cheerfully. I felt as if I'd entered a frighteningly surreal world. One minute Rod was earnestly declaring his love, the next he was chatting about recipes. He was as mysterious and confusing as the Magritte poster on his wall.

Rod's cooking was nowhere near as good as Sebastian's and I quickly made my mind go blank to prevent further comparisons. Rod produced *Witness for the Prosecution* from beneath a pile of old, yellowing books and we sat chastely on the sofa, with a good two inches between us, eating and watching the film. Rod enjoyed it more than he'd expected to, I could tell, because he asked me to pause it while he took the plates through to the kitchen. When he came back with another bottle of wine, he sat down next to me and took hold of my hand. 'Do you know what I wish?' he said.

'What?'

'That we could start this evening again. That you'd come round on time, happy instead of angry and that we could just . . . be normal with each other. Like a proper couple.'

'Rod, please don't refer to us as a couple. We aren't . . .'

'Let's watch the rest of the film,' he interrupted me with false jollity. 'I can't wait to see what happens.' I sighed and let him clutch my right hand. It seemed petty to wrestle it free.

'That was good,' he said when the film had finished.

'Mm,' I said distractedly. I hadn't really been able to concentrate properly. 'Did you guess that the woman at the station was Marlene Dietrich? It's a bit of an as-if, isn't it?' I couldn't help thinking about Sebastian's criticism of most thrillers: 'Too many as-ifs and why-bothers,' he often said. 'There's no way you could disguise yourself that well in real life.' Rod was staring past me, towards the curtains. 'Rod?'

'What time is it?' he asked me briskly.

'I don't know. Look at your watch,' I said, since he was wearing one and I wasn't.

'Oh, right. Yes. Erm, Kate, I think you should go. Look, about before, when I tried to kiss you . . .'

'Let's pretend it never happened,' I said.

'Right. Good. Well, I'd better be getting on with some . . .' He paused, as if searching for the right word. 'Chores,' he said finally. I stood up and picked up my bag. I was as embarrassed as he was about our ungainly kiss, but I couldn't help thinking he was behaving a bit immaturely about it. He wouldn't even meet my eye and only minutes ago we'd been holding hands.

'Right, then,' I said. 'So, what about your next driving lesson?'

'Um, I don't know. I'll phone you.' He shuffled from one foot to the other, keeping his hands in his pockets. When I moved towards the door he sighed with what sounded like relief, then proceeded practically to frogmarch me out on to the street. I turned to say goodbye, but he was already closing the door. I couldn't understand why he was so keen to get rid of me, unless it was embarrassment at having referred to us as a couple, only to be corrected by me in no uncertain terms. That can't have done much for his confidence.

I walked to Raymond Road where I'd left the car and drove back to Noble House, hoping that by now Sebastian might have calmed down. As I walked up the driveway I noticed that the light was still on in the laundry room. Joe Fielding waved at me through the window and I waved back, hurrying past. I was anxious to get home and see if I was still as unpopular as I'd been when I'd left a few hours earlier.

I unzipped the pocket of my handbag where I kept my key and sighed heavily when I realised it wasn't there. I must have forgotten to pick it up in my state of agitation. I rang the bell, normally at first and then long, repeated presses. There was no response. Sebastian was either deeply asleep or ignoring me.

I wandered dejectedly back down the path, thinking that Joe would talk to me even if Sebastian wouldn't. I can't have been looking my best because as soon as I appeared in the laundry room Joe said, 'Kate, what's wrong? Is everything okay? Where's Sebastian?'

'We've had a row,' I said, seeing no point in lying.

'Oh, dear. Nothing serious, I hope?' Joe sounded alarmed.

'So do I,' I said.

'Do you want to talk about it?'

'Not really. Anyway, it's late, Terri'll be waiting for you.'

'She's not back from the library yet,' he said with a trace of embarrassment. 'I only just got back myself. Tonight was my work's night out. I was about to go and pick Scarlett up from my mum's.'

'Oh. Weren't wives invited?' I sniffed.

'Well, yes, but . . . Terri was busy with her research. She came to the feast last night and . . . well, you know how it is.' He sounded tired.

'How?' I asked, wondering if I was being slow off the mark.

'Well, she doesn't like to go out on Friday and Saturday nights. It interferes with her research too much. Actually, she doesn't really like to go out at all.' Joe sighed. I tried to gather my faculties. I had a feeling he wanted to elaborate, so I tried to look alert. 'Kate . . . I've been wanting to say something to you for a while and now seems like a good time.'

'What?'

'I'm really sorry we've never invited you and Sebastian for dinner. I know I keep promising to and it never happens and . . . well, you must think we're so rude and unfriendly.' I started to deny this, but he interrupted, 'No, no, don't tell me it's okay. It isn't okay. It's . . . well, the thing is, it's Terri.'

'What about her?' I asked, half expecting him to say that she hated me and Sebastian, and refused to have us in the flat.

'She won't . . .' He paused and shrugged. 'She doesn't seem to care if we have no social life whatsoever. Her work is everything to her. It . . . it gets me down sometimes.'

'Oh? But . . . you always seem so cheerful,' I said, fishing for more information.

'I try to make the best of things.' Joe nodded. 'What else can I do? But I don't know how much longer I can keep it up. I hope you don't mind me telling you this.' He looked at me cautiously, trying to gauge my reaction.

'Of course not,' I said quickly. I was so astounded by this revelation that I completely forgot about my row with Sebastian. 'But . . . I had no idea. I mean, how serious is it?'

'I don't know. I know it sounds horrible but . . . in a way I wish Terri would take the job in Reading. Then I wouldn't have to do anything. She'd move to Reading, me and Scarlett would stay here and . . . things would probably fizzle out.' Seeing my stunned expression, Joe added, 'It's not sudden, you know. I've felt like this for a while.' I nodded and shivered. Normally I would have lapped up this information, but the last thing I wanted tonight was further evidence of the frailty of marriages that, only a short while ago, seemed perfectly solid.

Since Joe was being so forthright, however, I decided to do the same. 'I did think it was a bit odd the way you didn't seem to mind doing all the housework as well as working full-time and looking after Scarlett,' I said.

'What was I supposed to do?' Joe looked sad and defeated. 'I kept hoping things would get better. But they didn't, they got worse. I mean, Terri used to let me have people round for dinner occasionally, even though . . .' He stopped and looked away.

'What?' I prompted.

'I'm embarrassed to tell you. It sounds so ridiculous. Kate, this conversation, I mean, please don't mention it to anyone, even Sebastian . . .'

'Sebastian and I aren't on speaking terms,' I said grimly.

'You'll sort it out,' said Joe. 'You and Sebastian have got . . . a proper relationship.' I knew what he wasn't appending to the end of that sentence and he knew I knew.

'So what were you going to say?' I asked.

'Terri always used to kick up a fuss if I wanted to have

anyone over for a meal, a drink, anything. She resents any time spent away from her work. Sometimes, if I really went on at her, she'd allow me to make an arrangement, but then on the relevant day she wouldn't turn up. It was so embarrassing, Kate. Our guests would be there, we'd all be waiting to eat, and then Terri would phone and say she wasn't coming. She did that maybe six or seven times. It got to the point where I couldn't risk inviting anyone. So . . . I made a deal with her. This was when she'd just finished her PhD and, well, she hadn't got a job, so she'd got no money apart from what I gave her. I started to bribe her. I told her that if she let me invite people round and actually turned up and participated like . . .'

'Like a normal person?' I suggested.

'Yes, exactly. Well, I said if she did that, I'd buy her something. A present, something special. It worked for a while. She'd fulfil her part of the bargain and in return I'd buy her a designer dress. It had to be a dress every time as well, she'd never let me off with anything cheaper, like a scarf. She was so . . . cold about it, it was scary. She even . . . oh, God!' He sighed heavily.

'What?'

'She'd make labels, and write on them the names of the people that I'd invited round, that I'd forced her to spend the evening with, and the date, the night she'd had to sacrifice, and then she . . . she'd sew the label into whatever dress I'd bought her.' I restrained myself from shouting 'Aha!' as one of the many mysteries of the past few days was solved. 'I had to buy the clothes before the particular evening, "upfront", as Terri called it. She insisted on that, otherwise no deal.' I shook my head, astonished. 'The minute the guests left, she got out her stupid label kit and started sewing, glaring at me resentfully as if I'd put her through some terrible ordeal.'

'Joe, that's positively twisted! How could you put up with that?'

'I couldn't, not for very long. Keith Cobain and Ethan

Handley were the last straw. I met them at a Summerton feast . . . well, Terri and I both met them. They seemed like fun guys, so I suggested to Terri that we invite them round. I thought that, just that once, she might let me off the dress-buying. I mean, she'd applied for the De La Wyche fellowship, so I thought she might regard spending an evening with a couple of Summerton fellows as . . . well, as a good career move.'

'God!' I winced.

'I know, it's appalling.' Joe looked ashamed. 'But that's how Terri's mind works. She spends every second of every day thinking of ways to further her career.' Apart from those she spends fantasising about Gary Conley, I thought. I guessed that Joe didn't know about Terri's obsession with Gary, or else he would surely have mentioned it. An unfaithful wife was arguably less embarrassing a fact to share with the neighbours than one who hired her company out to her husband at the rate of one dress per evening.

'Do you know what she said?' he continued bitterly. 'That, since neither Keith nor Ethan was on the fellowship committee, they couldn't directly affect her chances. Therefore they counted as a social event and I had to buy her another dress. That was when I decided it was too depressing, I couldn't do it any more. It would have bankrupted me if I'd let it go on. So since then we haven't seen anyone. I feel like a hermit, it's driven me half mad. I don't know what I'll do if she doesn't go to Reading.'

'It shouldn't depend on Reading,' I said. 'Why don't you leave her? You've put up with a lot more than most people would.'

'I can't.' He looked away. 'I'm not that sort of person. And I might not need to, I mean, she's giving Reading serious consideration. I never thought she would. I thought Summerton would look so much better on her CV, but – thank God! – apparently the department at Reading's brilliant.'

'Does she know you wouldn't go with her? Are you sure

290

she wouldn't want to take Scarlett?' I let the brilliant department myth go unchallenged. Joe had enough to be miserable about without my adding to his grievances.

'She knows,' he said cynically. 'She says we could see each other at weekends, which of course means me and Scarlett would have to go there, not her come here, and then amuse ourselves while she worked all day and night. She certainly wouldn't want Scarlett with her during the week, getting in the way of her work. Terri doesn't care about anyone but herself, Kate. You'd be shocked if you saw the inside of our flat.' I cleared my throat nervously, hoping I didn't look guilty. 'There are photos of her all over the place, she's set up a sort of . . . a sort of shrine to herself and there's not a single picture of me or Scarlett in the whole lot, not a single one.' He seemed on the point of bursting into tears. 'And she's put a nameplate she used to have when she was a kid on our bedroom door that says "Terri's room". As if I don't exist.'

'Is that why your mum hates Terri?' I asked. 'Because she knows how miserable you are?'

'No.' Joe looked confused, as if I'd reminded him of something he had puzzled over but failed to work out. 'I've never said a word to anyone until now,' he said. 'I don't know why Mum's got it in for Terri. They got on fine until quite recently.'

'Maybe she suspects,' I said.

'I don't see how she could. I've made an effort to hide how bad things are.'

'So what are you going to do?' I asked. 'I mean, even if Terri goes to Reading, she'll expect you to visit her. You'll have to tell her, at some point, that as far as you're concerned it's over. Joe?' He shrugged. 'Come on, you have to,' I insisted. This is why I would make a terrible therapist. I don't go along with all that listen-supportively-and-let-them-make-their-own-decisions nonsense. If I ever took up counselling I'd have to introduce into the profession a new ethos of maximum interference and coercion.

'I can't face it, Kate,' said Joe sadly. 'I know I should, but . . . I don't know, maybe we can drift apart gradually. And at least if she moves to Reading I'll have the whole week to myself. It'll be a lot better than it is now.'

'Yes, but . . .' I was about to point out that 'better' was a relative concept and that anyway Terri might not go, and what would he do then, but Joe grabbed his wrist unexpectedly and gasped.

'Oh, shit, I've got to pick Scarlett up. Mum'll be wondering where I am, it's a quarter to midnight. I said I'd be there at eleven thirty. Shit! Look, I'd better go. Kate, you couldn't do me a huge favour, could you? Ring her and tell her I'm on my way? Her number's . . . oh, Christ I can't remember it!' He frowned, massaging his forehead. 'Terri put it on the memory button ages ago. It's so long since I've dialled it. But it's in the book, the address is 8 Newton Road . . .'

'I can't ring her, Joe.' I stopped him. I could imagine only too well Daphne Fielding's reaction to receiving a call from me in the middle of the night. 'We . . . had a bit of a clash today.' Mentioning this to Joe didn't seem as inappropriate as it once might have, given the personal nature of our discussion so far.

'What sort of clash?' Joe asked. 'Where?'

'I was at Summerton today,' I explained. 'Joe, can I ask you something without offending you? It's to do with your mother. Someone . . . told me something about her, I mean, they may well have been lying, in fact it's almost certain they were, but . . . you might be able to confirm that Daphne would never do the thing this person is saying she did.'

'What? What are you talking about?' Joe sat down again, frowning. He clearly didn't like the thought of his mother being the subject of gossip, but it was too late to retract what I'd said, so I decided to take the plunge.

'Somebody – one of the other panel members – told me that Daphne altered Terri's references, made them worse, to try to stop her getting the De La Wyche. The same person said that . . . she made favourable adjustments to Sebastian's references to fix it so that he *would* get it, and that she and Sebastian had concocted this scheme between them.'

'Oh my God.' Joe slumped forward and covered his face with his hands. 'That's insane. If she did that, she was risking her job. But . . . anyway it didn't work,' he added, as if he had just remembered Terri was, in fact, offered the Enmity. 'Who told you this?' I noticed that at no point had he expressed a belief that his mother wasn't capable of such deviousness.

'Valerie Williams,' I said.

'Your row with Sebastian – it was over this, wasn't it?'

'Yes,' I admitted. 'I made the mistake of asking him about it. But he totally denies it and I believe him.'

'I don't,' Joe said glumly. 'I'm sorry, Kate, but it sounds horribly plausible to me. My mother has a gift for getting her hooks into men and making them do things they wouldn't otherwise do. I've seen it happen time after time.'

'But Sebastian would never never lie,' I said feebly.

'Look, I'd like to talk more, but I've got to go and collect Scarlett.' Joe sighed and stood up slowly. He paused when he reached the door. 'She . . . She's the only thing that keeps me going,' he said.

Chapter Thirty-seven

Scarlett Skinner – Curriculum Vitae

Name
Scarlett Skinner. Joe said the choice of her first name was inspired by Scarlett O'Hara, Terri's favourite fictional character. This should have worried Joe, because few literary heroines have wreaked as much havoc in the lives of those around them. It's lucky Terri's favourite novel isn't *Heart of Darkness*, or Joe's head would by now be on a spike in the middle of some remote jungle area.

Age
Three.

Place of Birth
Oxford.

Employment History
None, but fortunately she is still at the age when this is not an embarrassment, unlike Sebastian, who has done almost as little paid work as Scarlett in a life nearly ten times as long.

Education and Qualifications
No qualifications. Has attended the 'Little Sweethearts' nursery school on Lathen Road for nearly a year, despite Terri's initial reservations about the name. Terri suspected that any nursery that was so called would be bound to go

in for serious gender stereotyping, but the school's director, a Mrs Gill Baish, managed to convince her that the term 'little sweethearts' was intended to include boys as well as girls and, neglecting the wood (imagination) in favour of the trees (ideology), Terri was satisfied with this and did not think to ask any further questions, such as whether the nursery was a front for a kiddie dating agency.

Gill Baish is concerned about Scarlett's education – in particular her slowness to learn, antisocial behaviour and general apathy – and is constantly summoning Terri and Joe for concerned chats. So far, only Joe has been concerned enough to attend. He cannot understand why Scarlett appears to be so dim-witted and puts it down to emotional problems caused by inadequate mothering. He does not say this to Gill Baish, though, because he's either a gentleman or a complete mug, depending on how you look at it, so together they shake their heads and wonder how a child with two intelligent, university-educated parents can have such trouble mastering the basic cognitive skills that other children acquire so easily.

Physical Appearance
Glossy brown hair in ringlets like her mother's. Small, pretty and fragile-looking. Green eyes.

Other Information
Hobbies include playing, eating, sulking and crying.

Chapter Thirty-eight

Players

After what I'd just told Joe, I reckoned that only someone with exceptional self-restraint, in his position, would be able to resist mentioning it to the accused and seeing how she answered the charges.

I felt the blood rush to my head as I stood up suddenly. I had a stake in this as well. I decided, on the spot, to go to Daphne's house, wait until Joe and Scarlett came out, and ask him what she'd said. He had told me where she lived: 8 Newton Road, only five minutes away from Noble House by car. I could have waited for him in the laundry room, since he'd have to pass it on his way home, but I didn't want to take the chance of Terri returning from the library and interrupting us.

I drove along Brooklands Avenue, down Trumpington Road and on to Newton, following the wide, bumpy left-hand lane around a soft corner. Number 8 was at the far end near Bentley Road, a large, red-bricked, detached house with a big garden and a barrel-shaped gravel parking area at the front. It had a pillared porch and two bay windows, neither of which was lit. I would have thought the house was empty, except that the Terri-ferry was parked on the gravel alongside an S-reg silver Audi.

I parked on the road, on the other side of a small garden fence that was topped by a thick rectangular hedge. I knew no one inside the house would see me if I stayed there, so I put a tape on my car stereo, stretched and leaned back in my seat to wait for Joe. I was about to reach into the glove compartment for my cigarettes when I saw a white hand sliding down the car window. It was small, thin and made a horrible sucking noise. I screamed and leaped up like a one-woman Mexican wave, banging my head on the sunroof.

Then a face appeared and I recognised Scarlett Skinner. 'Scary fucking brat,' I muttered to myself, winding down the window. There was no sign of Joe.

'Hello, Scarlett,' I said. She ignored me. 'Where's your dad? Where's Daddy?' She sucked her mouth in and rolled her head around. 'Scarlett, it's me, Kate Nunn. You know, your neighbour.' I wasn't sure I'd perfected the art of conversation with small children. Babies and adults I could do, but I could never seem to find that happy medium between gurgling and debating the finer points of the highway code.

'Joe inside,' she babbled suddenly. So she called him Joe, not daddy. How very Terri, I thought, not doubting for a minute that she was responsible. Another brave act of defiance in the face of tyrannical nuclear-family role impositions. 'Joe fight with Daphne.'

'Oh?' I tried to look like a trustworthy grown-up. 'What about?'

'Glabbywaaah!' Scarlett exclaimed.

'I'm sorry?'

'Baaamellobom.' I was unable to translate either of these words into anything Joe and Daphne might conceivably be fighting about.

'Sebastian?' I suggested hopefully. Scarlett giggled and started to jump up and down on the spot. She stuck both her thumbs in her nostrils and stretched the corners of her eyes with her index fingers.

'It's not safe for you to be wandering out here on your own,' I said. 'Come and sit in the car with me.' Joe must have been extremely preoccupied if he'd failed to notice Scarlett's absence. Normally he'd go running after her if she strayed more than a couple of feet from him, as if he had some sort of internal radar that detected Scarlett-distance.

She ignored my invitation and I didn't repeat it, since by this stage I'd realised that I wasn't keen to have a snotty, incoherent child in the Micra. Wearily, I climbed out of the car, grabbed one of her mucus-encrusted hands and headed for Daphne's house. I would have to say I was 'just passing' and happened to notice Scarlett in the road, even if neither Joe nor Daphne believed me.

I tried to walk towards the front door but Scarlett planted her feet wide apart and forced us to a standstill. She pointed to the side of the house. 'Back door!'

'Right.' I nodded and she began to gibber nonsensically again. I was puzzled by her tendency to appear lucid one minute and deranged the next, as if intelligence and density were fighting for territory in her little brain. We walked across the grass and around the corner, and suddenly I could see shafts of light and hear faint voices. I could have sworn I heard the word 'Reading'. We crept closer. I realised that Joe and Daphne were in a room at the back of the house with the window and curtains open. I gestured to Scarlett to be quiet and hoped she understood. Eavesdropping now seemed a far better idea than asking Joe later what his mother had said. I clamped my hand on Scarlett's shoulder to stop her from advancing. I knew she could withstand a bit of manhandling – or personhandling, as Terri would be bound to call it – because I'd seen Sainsbury's bags, laundry bags and briefcases land on her head on several occasions when Joe had too much to carry.

I heard a male voice, but the sound of the night wind rustling the trees in Daphne's garden made it difficult to follow the sense of what he was saying. I half cajoled, half coerced Scarlett into a seated position, gathered together some twigs and stones, and put them in front of her. 'Here, play with these,' I said.

'Lego!' she protested.

'Look, these are better than Lego.' I picked up a twig and

waved it in front of her face. 'People used to play with these before Lego was invented.' Scarlett scowled, but took the twig from my hand. Terri could thank me later for introducing her daughter to ecological and non-consumerist toys.

I tiptoed closer to the part of the garden that was streaked with light, stopping a few feet short of a beam. I heard Daphne say, 'I can't be expected to know these things if you don't talk to me, Joe' and crouched down against the wall to listen. I hoped they couldn't hear my pounding heartbeat through the wall.

'All this time,' Joe said slowly. His voice was quieter than usual, but sounded furious. 'All this time, you've been bitching about Terri, acting as though you hate her, making life really difficult for me. . . . The way you went on at the feast last night! And the feast before that! Taking me for a complete fucking mug.' I frowned to myself. I'd never heard Joe say 'fuck' before. The disadvantage of being an eavesdropper is that you can't ask people to explain themselves as and when you feel it's necessary. I couldn't see how Daphne being horrible to Terri constituted taking Joe for a mug. Anyway, he'd known about the animosity between his wife and his mother for ages; it was old news. Why, tonight, was he so angry about it?

'Same old self-righteous Joe.' Daphne laughed. 'You've been doing exactly the same thing in reverse, taking *me* for a mug, pretending all's well between you and Terri. How was I to bloody know you wanted her to go to Reading? She told me you loved her.'

'Well, she would say that, wouldn't she?' Joe's voice rose in volume. 'Terri thinks everyone loves her. Anyway, it's not the same.' He sounded outraged. 'I'm not obliged to tell you, or anyone, if my marriage is falling apart. And even if everything was fine between me and Terri, there's no excuse for what you did, Mother. It's unforgivable. And to implicate Sebastian Nunn as well! What's the poor guy ever done to you? You should see Kate, Mother, she's distraught. They've had a huge row about it, for God's sake. It's all your fault.' I held my breath. Was Sebastian innocent, then? Joe seemed to think so.

'I wasn't to know bloody Kate would start meddling. That woman's too nosy for her own good.' I couldn't feel too hard done-by on hearing this, since my present position and activity, crouching on all fours beneath Daphne's back window listening in on a private conversation, rather bore out her analysis of my character. 'I'm sorry if I misjudged the situation.' Daphne tried to sound conciliatory but succeeded only in sounding false and despicable. I wondered whether this was just my personal reaction to her crawling, oily tone or whether Joe saw through it as well. 'I honestly thought you'd want her to get the De La Wyche. But, look, it turns out she might go to Reading anyway. And, you know, the whole thing started out as a joke. Terri and I added the Sebastian touch because we thought it'd be funny, because he's absolutely the last person who'd ever do anything like that. We needed a Max. Oh, come on, don't give me that shocked look. If Kate doesn't trust him that's her problem, not mine.'

So Sebastian had done nothing wrong. It was satisfying at least to have that confirmed. But why was Daphne saying 'Terri and I' as if they were old pals? And what the hell did 'We needed a max' mean? I tried to fend off a strong, unpleasant feeling that I can only describe in one way: it's what I call the lateral-thinking-puzzle feeling, a fear of impending revelation. When I was at secondary school, my friends and I used to be obsessed with these puzzles. They would start with a description of an apparently mysterious situation and the guesser would have to ask questions, which the setter could only answer with a straightforward yes or no until the full truth of the situation was revealed. Whenever I was the person guessing, I would start to panic as soon as I felt I was close to getting the answer and beg the setter to put me out of my misery. I couldn't bear the suspense. That was how I felt now. I wanted to shout out,

'Just tell me what's going on, please!' More than that, I wanted to rush back to Sebastian, who now seemed like the one island of safety in my life of floating, undefined dangers, and climb into our comfortable bed, curl up next to his warm body.

The word 'max' rang a distinct bell. I knew I'd heard it, and recently too, but I couldn't think where or when.

'You disgust me,' Joe said. 'I wish you weren't my mother. I know that's a terrible thing to say, but it's true.'

'Oh, lighten up.' There was evident amusement in Daphne's voice. 'It was a misunderstanding. I had no idea you wanted rid of Terri and neither does she. Well, there you go. It's rather like a French farce. Let's blame it on Marlene.' I frowned, leaning closer to the window. What was Daphne talking about? Before I had a chance to think further about this, I heard a new voice, a Cockney accent. 'I'll give you something to dream about, Mister. Wanna kiss me, Duckie?' The Cockney voice had a pronounced lisp. Loud guffaws followed. I froze as I recognised Daphne's impression of Marlene Dietrich, disguised as the Cockney woman at Euston Station in *Witness for the Prosecution*. And I knew where I'd heard 'max' – it was at Rod's flat earlier tonight, when we were watching the same film. Max was the non-existent lover Marlene Dietrich – or rather Christine Vole – fabricated, to whom she wrote the love letters that she later, posing as somebody else, gave to her husband's barrister. Just as an unthinkable hypothesis was beginning to form in my mind, Daphne started to speak again.

'It was more Terri's idea than mine. Gripe at her, not me. We were watching *Witness for the Prosecution*. It was one night when you weren't there for some reason, I can't remember why. When it got to the bit where Marlene Dietrich says nobody would believe a wife who testified in her husband's defence, Terri started to laugh and said, "Why don't we do a *Witness for the Prosecution*?" She said people would be suspicious of me if I supported her for the

301

De La Wyche fellowship because she's my daughter-in-law. If I argued against her, on the other hand, and was then revealed as a liar . . . Honestly, it started as a joke. But then the more we discussed it, jokingly, the more we started to wonder if we could get away with it.' I bit my lip to stop myself from screaming.

'And you thought you'd give it a try,' said Joe angrily. 'Fake letters to Sebastian Nunn giving the impression that the two of you were cheating and poor little Terri was the victim.'

'And then make sure those letters fell into Valerie's honest hands, yes. Easy as anything, it was. I wrote them, stuck them in an envelope with an anonymous note and sent them to her on Wednesday morning. I ended the meeting before a decision had been made to allow Valerie to discover the letters on Wednesday evening. I knew I could rely on her not to make a big fuss – all that loyalty to the college bullshit she constantly spouts. I let her think she'd got me right where she wanted me and then offered her a deal: I wouldn't oppose Terri if she would keep her mouth shut about what I'd done, or rather, what Sebastian and I had done.' Daphne giggled girlishly. 'Valerie agreed. So we both went in on Thursday supporting Terri and pushed it through. Bryony James had dropped out by then, Sebastian was out of the question because of his, er, attempt to cheat and only Emily Lole wanted the other man and no one takes her seriously. So Terri came up trumps. Our plan worked.'

'I hope you don't expect me to congratulate you,' said Joe coldly. 'I wish you hadn't told me. Why tell me now, Mother? Is it some kind of sick joke?'

'Oh, don't be so po-faced. What choice did I have? You were yelling at me about what you thought Sebastian and I had done. If I must be yelled at, it might as well be for the right thing. You weren't supposed to find out and you wouldn't have done if Kate Nunn hadn't started prying into college affairs, putting the wind up Valerie. I knew you'd be

302

like this if you found out. Anyway, Terri had a point, you know. If I'd been upfront about supporting her, people would have thought it was nepotism and probably resisted giving her the fellowship, even if I genuinely believed, as I did, that she was objectively the best candidate. I mean, that would hardly have been fair, would it?'

'And you did all this behind my back, pretending you'd fallen out and hated each other. Didn't you care how that might affect me? Or Scarlett?' Joe's voice vibrated with rage. I looked over my shoulder to check Scarlett was still there and she gawped back at me, dribbling. 'Suddenly her mother and grandmother are at each other's throats for no apparent reason. What sort of effect do you think that had on her?'

'Oh, she'll be fine,' said Daphne dismissively. 'Kids are more resilient than people think. Come on, Joe, we could hardly let you in on it, could we? You'd have been a spoilsport.'

'Damn right I would. Will, rather. If you think I'm keeping quiet about this, you're wrong. I think Kate Nunn's got a right to know, before you ruin her marriage and her husband's career.' I nodded approvingly.

'Oh, Sebastian's doing a perfectly good job of ruining his own career,' Daphne said flippantly. 'He's a bumbler. In order to succeed in academia these days you have to be a player, like Terri.'

'A liar, you mean. A sneaky, manipulative fraud.'

'I wouldn't say anything about this if I were you,' Daphne said nastily. 'Imagine the effect it would have on Scarlett if both her mother and her grandmother were publicly disgraced and branded as corrupt. She'd be ostracised at playgroup.' Daphne chuckled at this prospect. 'If you keep your mouth shut we'll all get through this intact. Kate Nunn won't go public with what she thinks she knows. She'll want to protect Sebastian.' I remembered the poster on Damian Selinger's door advertising a seminar entitled 'Is Evil a Valid Concept?'. I felt as if I was doing some primary research into that area right now and the answer was a resounding yes. I thought Joe was holding up remarkably well. I would have committed suicide if I thought I shared any genetic material with that monster. 'It would get into all the papers, Joe,' Daphne went on. 'They're all desperate to dig up any dirt they can on Oxbridge in their stingy attempt to deprive us of our extra millions.'

'You're such a bitch,' Joe shouted. 'And as for Terri . . .'

'As for Terri, what is all this Reading nonsense?' Daphne interrupted him. 'I mean, we played our trick, it got her the job, so why the hell isn't she taking it? When I ask her she just hums and hahs. I'm convinced there's something she's not telling me.'

'She'd better not take it,' said Joe quietly. 'I won't be able to stand the sight of her after this. I may not be able to expose the two of you, for Scarlett's sake, but I don't have to live with that creature.'

'No, you're quite right, you don't.' Daphne sounded bored. 'There you go, then, I've done you a favour. If I hadn't told you about our little game you might never have plucked up the courage to leave her. What did I do to deserve such a spineless son?'

'Where's Scarlett?' Joe asked suddenly. 'Scarlett? SCARLETT!' I could imagine him looking around the room wildly. As quietly as I could, I tiptoed back to the car, putting my finger over my lips as I passed Scarlett to indicate that she shouldn't mention having seen me. I'd just got back into the driver's seat when I heard Joe's footsteps outside and his exclamations of relief as he spotted his daughter.

'Where have you been?' I heard him ask her sternly. 'I've told you not to wander off, haven't I? Come on, let's get your coat.'

'Home!' Scarlett shouted.

'No, we're going to stay with William and his family. You know William, from nursery? Won't it be nice to see him?' Scarlett started to whine loudly.

I waited for the sound of them going back inside, then wound up my window and started the car, still numb from what I'd heard. So Joe was serious about leaving Terri. Good luck to him, I thought. I decided not to ask him what Daphne had said. I didn't want to put him in the position of having to lie to me. It was understandable that his priority was to protect his daughter from the scandal that would inevitably result from this being made public.

I, on the other hand, didn't give two hoots about Scarlett Skinner's reputation at nursery school. There was nothing I would have liked more than to see full-page spreads in every broadsheet and tabloid detailing the shameful, unforgivable behaviour of Daphne and Terri. The trouble was, I didn't have any proof. If I tried to take it further, Daphne could deny ever having said the things I'd heard and Joe, for Scarlett's sake, might back her up.

I more than doubled the speed limit driving home, desperate to get back to Sebastian. I knew I couldn't tell him what I'd overheard because he would be his usual impetuous self and act without first thinking it through, indignantly launching himself straight into the centre of a national academic scandal.

I swerved recklessly into Noble House's car park and heard running footsteps as I hauled my exhausted body out of the car. I looked into the darkness expectantly, convinced that Sebastian had heard the Micra's engine and was rushing outside in his eagerness to put things right between us. I ran across the car park hopefully, and collided instead with a tearful and yelping Terri Skinner. Her hair was sticking out in strange places and make-up was running down her face. 'Joe's gone,' she wailed, grabbing me by the lapels of my jacket. 'He just phoned! He's left me. He's taken my daughter. They've gone to the Flemings. You've got to help me!'

Chapter Thirty-nine

The Scarlett Letter

'Scarlett is Joe's daughter too,' I said unsympathetically. 'I have no intention of helping you. I know what you and Daphne did, how you tried to stitch up Sebastian and rig the De La Wyche fellowship.' I was amazed at my ability to say this calmly, without ripping her hair out of her scalp in clumps.

'What?' Terri's front teeth were smeared with red lipstick. Her face was horribly contorted in the ugly expression I'd seen, fleetingly, before, but this time no quick smile replaced it; it stayed put. She was wearing a shiny silver dress with a matching sequinned purse on a string around her neck. If she'd worn that outfit to the library, she had more serious problems than a deserting husband. I diagnosed a terminal case of sartorial Tourette's.

'You heard. I know about your *Witness for the Prosecution* idea.'

'But it was Daphne's idea, not mine,' Terri said indignantly. 'Oh, God, you've got to let me explain. I never meant to hurt Sebastian, or you. My life is . . . such hell!'

'I don't care,' I said. 'You'd just better turn the De La Wyche fellowship down.'

'I will.' She sobbed pathetically, still clinging to my lapels and trying, periodically, to hug me. 'I have to go to Reading to be with Gary. I have to find Gary, now that Joe's left me. Oh, he can't leave me, he can't! He can't take my daughter.'

306

'She's his daughter too.'

'No, she isn't, she's Gary's daughter,' Terri wailed. 'Scarlett is Gary's. Joe doesn't know, you mustn't tell him. It'd destroy him. Oh, I've got to go to Reading and find Gary, I've got to go now. Kate!' Her eyes widened as if she'd only just noticed me. 'You could drive me there, we could go now.'

'Fuck off,' I prised her fingers off my jacket. I wished she hadn't told me about Scarlett being Gary's child. It made me feel ill, especially when I thought about what a good father Joe was. It didn't surprise me, though. 'Why should I help you after what you've done?'

'Oh, leave me alone then, leave me to rot. Everyone hates me. Even my own father has always hated me. Oh God, it's all Gary Conley's fault!' she shouted, looking up at the sky as if that was where she thought he might be. I started to walk away, leaving her fumbling in her sequinned purse. It was nearly one in the morning. I felt as if today had dragged on for long enough already.

As I approached Noble House's porch I heard a key click in a lock behind me. I looked over my shoulder and saw that there was now a square of light on the lawn opposite the laundry room window. I had never known Terri to venture in there before and I couldn't think why she was bothering. I turned to go inside when a gruesome noise stopped me. It sounded like the drying machine after possession by the devil. I sprinted towards the door. The thumping and hissing got louder as I approached. I pushed, but Terri had locked the door from the inside and I didn't have our laundry key with me. I ran to the window and saw something grey, pink and black going round very quickly in the drier. It took a few seconds and a quick flash of a hand in the round convex glass of the machine's door for me to realise that it was Terri in there.

I took off my shoe and banged it as hard as I could against the glass in the door. It cracked but didn't shatter, so I hit it a few more times. Finally, it fell to the floor in shards.

I reached inside and turned the handle, taking care not to cut my hand or wrist, and ran to the drier. It was set at the highest possible heat level. I pressed the off button and pulled the machine door open. Terri's top half fell out. She was mumbling incoherently. She'd sweated so much in the machine that she was now completely wet, as if she'd stepped out of a bath. I tried to help her out of the drum, but she wouldn't, or couldn't, stand up and instead fell to the floor in a heap.

'You should have let me die,' she moaned. 'I want to die.' I pulled her into a standing position and then propped her up on the wooden bench, wondering whether Noble House's modest little laundry room had ever before experienced such an eventful day. First it got to hear me and Joe discussing our marital difficulties in depth, then it nearly became the site of the strangest kamikaze known to man. It was becoming nearly as integral a venue as the ladies' toilets in *Cagney and Lacey*.

'Kate, I've got to explain, I've got to tell you everything,' Terri began to babble. 'I would never have done that thing with Daphne – never! – if I wasn't in such a state about Gary. I just . . . I *had* to be offered the De La Wyche, I couldn't risk not getting it because of . . . what might be seen as nepotism.'

'But what's the De La Wyche got to do with Gary?' I asked, suspecting the drier had frazzled her brain. 'If you took it, you wouldn't be able to go to Reading.'

'Even if I don't take it, I needed to be offered it,' Terri whimpered. 'For my self-esteem. Gary's so indifferent to me most of the time and I needed a comfort, something to hold on to.' She wiped her eyes. 'Anyway, Daphne and I hatched our plan before I knew about the Reading job. I didn't apply there, you know. The job offer came out of the blue.'

'Oh?' I winced with resentment. No one ever offered Sebastian jobs for which he hadn't applied.

'Yes. My supervisor from Pembroke got a personal chair

there and asked me to join the department. I couldn't believe it. It seemed like destiny, what with Gary living there. Do you mind . . .' She looked at me out of the corner of her eye. 'Do you mind if I tell you about me and Gary? From the beginning? I've never been able to tell anyone, in case it got back to Joe, and it would be so good to tell somebody. It's been driving me mad, going round and round in my head, year after year, having no one to talk to . . .'

'If you must.' I could hardly tell her that I had already heard Gary's version of events from Rod. Terri's story resembled Gary's only in so far as the basic facts were the same: they'd met at Pembroke when she was a graduate student and he was a waiter in the college dining hall, they'd had sex once, and she had sent him a Christmas card and present every year since then. But whereas Gary had made it sound like a one-night stand followed by an uncalled-for amount of hassle, to Terri it was a doomed romance of tragic dimensions. According to her, the college had fired Gary because they'd found out about what she called their 'love affair'. Any sort of sexual liaison between students and staff was regarded as highly inappropriate, and Terri was sure someone had found out and reported them. From what Rod had told me about Gary's stupidity and lack of social skills, I thought it was just as likely that he'd been sacked for general uselessness, but I kept this to myself.

Shortly after their one-night stand, Terri found she was pregnant. She knew the baby was Gary's because she had been too busy working to allow Joe any opportunities to impregnate her. She wanted Gary to be the father in any case because she was convinced he was 'The One'.

'What do you mean?' I interrupted. She spoke like a member of a religious cult, full of respect for its leader.

'You know, The One. The love of my life.' Terri's tone implied that this should have been obvious. 'Don't you feel as if Sebastian's The One for you?'

'Well . . . yes, I suppose so. But if I'd never met him, I would have met someone else and thought he was. I mean, there are probably lots of people who are potentially The One and it just depends who you meet.'

Terri shook her head. Perhaps tiredness had impaired my powers of perception, but she looked different now that she was finally telling the truth, more like a real person. 'No. I don't believe that. There can only be one One. Don't you believe in fate?'

'No. Of course not.' It would have pissed me off in the extreme to think that some supernatural force already knew, had known for ages, who would end up with the Enmity and all my efforts to change the outcome had made no difference whatsoever. 'Surely you don't either, being a scientist,' I said.

'I do. Gary is the other half of my being, I've always felt that. We're meant to be together, we always were and we always will be. Don't mock me,' she added quickly, just as I was preparing to do so. 'My dad always mocks my opinions about everything and I've . . . I've just had enough of it, okay?' I restrained myself from asking how Terri's narrowly avoided death by drying machine would have affected her and Gary's romantic destiny. People who believe that sort of rubbish have an answer for everything. No doubt it had been written in the stars that I would come along and rescue her at an opportune moment.

'Where does Joe fit in?' I asked sternly.

'Joe's just . . . Joe. I married him to escape from home but . . . I have grown to love him in a way. He just isn't . . .'

'The One?'

'Yes. But he's been good to me and Scarlett. I love Scarlett too, but . . . I can't stand to be around her. She reminds me of Gary so much. I . . . I have to avoid her.' I couldn't think of anything to say to this. 'Joe doesn't know she isn't his, so please don't say anything.' Terri added this last request hastily, as if she was reminding me of a little white lie we had both agreed it would be politic to tell. 'He

310

doesn't know anything about Gary. That isn't why he's left me. It's this . . . well, he found out about the De La Wyche business. How did you know about that?' She looked at me suspiciously.

'I've been looking into things,' I said enigmatically. I didn't feel I owed her an explanation.

'It's all destiny, you see.' Terri nodded wisely. 'Joe finding out, you finding out. Gary coming to Cambridge to look for me. Joe leaving me. Now I'll have to turn down the De La Wyche, and go to Reading and be with Gary. I wanted to, anyway, I just didn't know if Gary would want me to. But now I know it's my fate. I feel so calm and . . . appropriate. Isn't it funny to think I wanted to die before?'

'Side-splitting,' I said. I couldn't work out whether I hated Terri, admired her or just thought she was a nutter.

'I suppose I just panicked. I've never had to look after myself, you see. Joe did everything. The journey has taken so long,' she went on, 'but this is how things were always going to turn out. You know, in a way I'm glad all this has happened. I feel free, really free. You've got no idea what it's been like. Four years of lying to Joe, working almost twenty-four hours a day to block out my feelings, trying to make Gary realise how much I loved him. He's been so confused. I think he's tried to keep away from me, to pretend he doesn't love me, just to save my marriage. He's so self-sacrificing.'

'Mm,' I said sceptically. 'Does he know Scarlett's his?'

'Yes. I wrote to him and told him, but he didn't reply. I'd written to him before and he'd never responded, but I thought after the letter about Scarlett he might be different. He still didn't get in touch, though. It must have been such a shock for him. I think he's scared to admit how he really feels. He's . . . he's basically left me alone for four years. Sometimes I wondered whether he cared about me at all. But then you told me he'd come here, that he'd been looking for me!' She clutched my sleeve. 'Oh, Kate, you've no idea how happy I was then. That was the turning point.

And now everything seems so clear.' I nodded uneasily. All this talk of fate was beginning to get to me. What if my lie about Gary's visit had interfered with some grand plan? Then I told myself I couldn't have too much to fear from a force of destiny too feeble to withstand the tamperings of a mere driving instructor.

Chapter Forty

The One – Curriculum Vitae

Name

Can be anything. If it's unusual, you'll repeat it to yourself over and over again and decide it's the best and most unique name in the world for the best and most unique person in the world. Bryony James will have enjoyed doing this with the name 'Damian Selinger', imagination-defeating though it is that anyone would enjoy doing anything with that creep. Emily Lole will have chanted the name 'Fernando Rose' like a mantra, thinking it made the most beautiful noise known to human ear, savouring its metrical neatness. She may even have based a little verse or two around it. *Where d'you suppose/Fernando Rose/Has gone, or goes?/Nobody knows.* No, Emily would never invent a rhyme like that. This is somebody who studies microscopic worms. Still, Terri works with fishes' teeth and look at the unscientific behaviour and beliefs of which she is capable. Conclusion: it is simply impossible to know what anybody is really like. Most people's characters are totally inconsistent.

In fiction, it is easy to recognise Ones. There is the pretty One (normally the sister or close friend of the clever One – oh, what potential for contrast, I would never have thought of that). There is the heartless-but-handsome-womaniser One (usually called something like Calvin Nightmare-Fletcher) always to be found in close textual proximity to the also-quite-handsome-loving-reliable-but-strangely-

313

unappreciated-for-three-hundred-pages One.

Address
Yours, if you're lucky (and Terri says I am). Which raises an interesting point about why I needed Terri to tell me Sebastian is my One: it could be that I don't fully appreciate this fact because I'm married to him and take his Oneness for granted. Maybe separation brings one's One into sharper relief, just as people who have jobs cannot imagine that the desire to be in fulfilling, lucrative employment, to leave the house in the morning and return to it in the evening, can become an all-consuming passion.

Age
Could be any age. Date of birth is more important. You will never forget the date of birth of The One. This is interesting from the point of view of ascertaining whether there is only one One, as Terri claims, or whether it's possible to have several over the course of a lifetime – how many exes' birthdays do you remember? But if there's more than one One out there, it must be possible for two to come along at the same time. If you can have serial Ones, why not concurrent Ones? Perhaps it depends on whether your personality changes over time but is, at any given point, a consistent, united whole, or whether you have a fragmented character with a big split in the middle, each half requiring a different sort of One.

Marital Status
Again, this depends on whether The One is the person you would be happiest living with for ever, or the grand passion of your life. Does Oneness mean contented togetherness or continued yearning? When Meryl Streep fails to go off with Clint Eastwood in *The Bridges of Madison County*, it isn't because of any selfless duty she feels to her husband and family; it's because she knows that ten years on she'd probably find Clint as mundane as her husband. Separation

from The One is the only way to preserve the perfection of the feeling.

I suppose the ideal marital status of The One would have to be married to you or single. And not merely single, but, if possible, single with no previous romantic or sexual history, no jealousy-inducing baggage. Gary Conley complies, or appears to comply, with these requirements. If he did not, Terri would be forced to abandon the ideal of sisterhood and instead espouse the twin causes of hair-pulling and eye-clawing. On the other hand, she could settle the personal–political dichotomy in the way most people do: by being a total hypocrite.

Employment History

Whatever The One's occupation, you will find it not merely fascinating, but also sexy. Martine Selinger once told me that Damian used to object strongly – violently even – to her coming home and telling him stories about her work, things that had happened to her during the day. 'It's so fucking tedious,' he used to yell. 'What do I care what condition some fat bitch customer's nail cuticles are in?' This is a sure sign, ignored for too long by both Damian and Martine, that she was not The One for him.

Education and Qualifications

Neither will help you withstand the powers of The One. Look at Terri. Or Bryony.

Physical Appearance

Irrelevant. People do not become each other's Ones by virtue of attractiveness. Some Ones are hideous, in fact, but there are ways round this. A scarred and pock-marked complexion becomes rugged. Fat becomes something to get hold of, boring becomes shy, selfish becomes a free spirit. At least for the duration of the Oneness. I forgot to ask Terri whether she thinks there can be an end to it, but I suspect she would have said no. Once The One, always The

One seems to be her philosophy. But this doesn't explain why as many people fall out of love as fall in.

Strengths and Weaknesses
Will be exaggerated and overlooked, respectively.

Other Information
In many ways, the specific qualities of The One are irrelevant. No one can ever really know another person properly, let alone him- or herself. All we can do is choose the face or body or behaviour pattern to which we can most easily attach our favourite fantasies, our preferred image of ourselves, at any given time. Many people will opt for an ugly One because it makes them feel secure, or a nasty One because they think they deserve to be punished for their failings. This is nice and democratic, and ensures that even total grimsters get a bit of romantic action.

Chapter Forty-one

The Turned Vile

As I drifted out of a hyperactive, disturbed dream and into consciousness on Sunday morning, I struggled to work out where I was.

I opened one eye and saw George Herbert's *Collected Poems* on my bedside table before I saw anything else. Then, one by one, I noticed my clothes in a pile on the floor, the rest of my bedroom and Sebastian lying next to me, still asleep. The sequence of events quickly righted itself in my head. I had gone home at about three in the morning. Sebastian, who by this point had woken up and started to worry about me, let me in and forgave me immediately. He was excessively relieved to see me safe and well; being a pessimist he had naturally assumed I'd reacted to his hostility by impaling myself on a nearby spike and dying a gruesome death.

I fell asleep quickly and spent the next eight hours fending off frenzied dreams. Now it was eleven o'clock in the morning. I'd only just woken up but I already felt exhausted.

I crept out of bed as quietly as I could and tiptoed to the kitchen to make some coffee. I wanted to sort things out in my head before Sebastian woke up. I hadn't told him anything, as usual. He was blissfully unaware of Daphne's attempt to frame him and ruin his reputation at Summerton. Thinking about that bitch made me grit my teeth involuntarily. *Oh, do not fill me with the turned vial of thy bitter wrath*. Like Rod's neighbour Vincent Strebonian, Terri had been turned vile by the sheer force of misery, whereas Daphne, from what I could gather, had had no particular hardship or suffering in her life; she was simply a nasty person. Morally, they were worlds apart.

Once I had a cup of coffee in front of me I pulled my mobile phone out of my bag and switched it on. I couldn't risk exposing Daphne publicly in case she tried to pin all the blame on Sebastian, but I could certainly mention it to Bryony James, the self-professed revenge expert, and see if she had any advice as to a suitable come-uppance. I was so determined to strike out at Daphne in some way that I no longer cared about distancing myself from Bryony's madness.

I was just about to dial the number of Summerton's porters' lodge and ask to be put through to Damian's set when my phone started ringing. I looked at its small square screen and read the words 'Call from Callback'. It was my answering service. 'You have a new message,' it said. 'Please hold the line and you will be connected to your messaging service.' I waited for a voice I knew, drumming my fingers on the table. It was bound to be my parents, making their customary weekend call to ask whether Sebastian had got a job yet.

'Kate, it's me, Rod.' I sighed. 'Listen, something astounding has happened. I must see you. I have to talk to you. Terri Skinner isn't taking up the De La Wyche fellowship. She's said no. The college just phoned me. They've offered it to me, Kate, you've no idea how strange it felt when they said that. Wanting something so much and then it happens, it's almost an anticlimax . . .'

'Get to the fucking point,' I muttered under my breath. 'Did you say you'd take it?'

'You've got to come round as soon as you get this message, I've got to talk to you,' Rod went on, oblivious of my impatience, still not giving me the information I most wanted. 'Kate, I'm really sorry about throwing you out last night. I wasn't myself at all. I could understand if you never wanted to see me again but . . . oh, please come round. I've got to talk to you about what to do about the De La Wyche.' A jolt of energy hit my brain as I heard this last sentence. That must mean he hadn't given them an answer. I could hear noises coming from the bedroom; Sebastian was getting up.

'Come on, finish,' I hissed at the message.

'Where's my pissing Armani jumper?' Sebastian shouted grumpily.

'In your jumper drawer, under the black polo neck,' I yelled back, missing a few of Rod's words. I didn't think this would matter too much, since he was so profligate with them.

When I tuned in again, he was saying, 'I've realised how important you are to me, Kate. You're the only person who's ever broken through. If there's a chance . . . oh, I really need to talk to you, Kate.'

'So you keep saying,' I murmured wearily.

'I can't quite bring myself to make any sort of decision, really. It's like . . . I've come to an impasse in my life . . .'

'Morning,' Sebastian lumbered into the kitchen, knocking the edge of my chair. 'Any coffee left?'

'Yeah.' I quickly switched off my phone and put it back in my bag. I missed the end of Rod's message but I was sure I could live without whatever directionless waffle it contained.

'Who were you talking to?'

'Oh, no one. Just listening to my messages.'

'Anything interesting?'

'No. People trying to arrange driving lessons.'

'If I get either Sheffield or Canterbury, you'll be able to do less teaching,' said Sebastian. At first I didn't have a clue what he was talking about and when I worked it out, it annoyed me. How dare he mention those piffling red-brick jobs when I was so close to getting him the Enmity? Terri had said no and Rod hadn't said yes. He was waiting to talk to me, which had to mean that I could sway his decision if I went about it in the right way. 'Still, I won't get them,' Sebastian added gloomily. 'For some reason I don't ever get jobs. Everyone else gets jobs, except me. Obviously I appear untouchable, in some way. Contaminated.'

'Sebastian, stop moaning.' I felt faint, as I always did when he unleashed his despondent streak.

'Why? At least moaning is something everyone acknowledges I do well. I might as well use my one undisputed talent. Anyway, I can't help it. This is what I'm going to be thinking about and worrying about every second of every day, until I get a job. Oh, I might pretend to be happy occasionally, just to make you feel better, but it'll be a lie. Really, deep down, I'll be feeling like this.'

'Sebastian, don't!' I felt my throat constrict. I told myself that it was good that this was happening. I'd been so busy running around after Summerton types over the past few days that I'd almost forgotten how it had all started, why I had been so determined to get Sebastian the Enmity in the first place. This was why, this sort of conversation. I would have to endure outbursts like this and worse ten times a day every day until someone employed Sebastian.

'You'll get a job,' I said in my auto-reassurance-pilot voice, trying to pacify him and at the same time focus on my Rod dilemma. Should I go round and see him or not? He seemed to want me to tell him what to do. On Thursday when he'd first climbed into my car, I would have given my dual control pedals to be in this situation. Now all I wanted was to shy away from the responsibility. Rod had become too much of a person in my mind; I knew him too well to treat him so instrumentally.

'You don't really believe that,' said Sebastian. 'You're only saying it to shut me up. You know I'll probably be unemployed for ever, a permanent burden to you, a drain on your resources . . .'

'Sebastian, what do you care more about, me or getting a job?' I asked.

'What? Why are you asking me that?'

'I just wondered. I mean, let's say if you had to choose between losing me but getting the De La Wyche, or staying with me but not getting it, which would you choose?'

'The De La Wyche,' said Sebastian with his customary tact. I was about to have a hysterical fit when he added, 'If I chose you and no job, I'd make you miserable, I'd ruin your life. Whereas if I chose the job and no you, I'd only be making myself miserable.'

'No, you wouldn't.' I fought back tears. 'Sebastian, if I didn't have you I'd be distraught. Don't make out that I'd be better off without you. I love you, whether you've got a job or not.'

'Yes, but you can't deny I make you miserable. Look, you're crying now.' He poured himself a cup of coffee.

'Oh, this is ridiculous. Look, I've got to go out.'

'See! You can't even stand to be around me.'

'Yes I can, I just . . . I've got a driving lesson. Look, please stop being so negative. You'll get a job, okay? I promise.'

'We'll see,' he said gloomily. 'Oh, by the way, this arrived yesterday.' He pulled a small, square card off the cork notice-board above his head, sending two drawing pins flying through the air. Neither of us picked them up.

'"Scholars Press invite you to the launch of *Me, Me, Me: Embracing Selfishness* by Dr Damian Selinger. Monday, 8 June at 7 pm, Heffers Bookshop, Trinity Street, Cambridge. Refreshments will be provided,"' I read aloud. 'Do you want to go?'

'Turn it over,' said Sebastian. On the back of the card, Damian had scrawled, 'Do come – you never know, my success might prove contagious – D.'

'What an arsehole!' I said, deciding not to phone Bryony after all. Her willingness to love the Selinger weasel could not be overlooked, however good the cause.

'I have to go.' Sebastian scowled. 'If I don't, that bastard Selinger will think I'm sulking, or feeling inadequate.'

'Does it matter what he thinks?'

'Yes.' Sebastian stood up, sighing. 'As it is, I'm probably regarded as a joke at Summerton. I don't want to make it any worse. We don't have to stay long, just put in an appearance.'

When Sebastian had turned his back I pulled a face. I knew from previous experience that the entire fellowship always made a point of attending any Summerton book launch. Daphne Fielding would certainly be there and I would have to restrain myself from attacking her with a large hardback.

The phone rang in the lounge. For a confused moment I feared it might be Rod, but he didn't know our home number. Hardly anyone did. Sebastian didn't get very many phone calls and most people who wanted to speak to me used my mobile number.

'Hello?' Sebastian picked it up. He listened for a few seconds, saying 'Right' a couple of times, then made a strange twitching gesture in my direction with his forefinger and thumb.

'What? What does that mean?' I whispered loud enough for him to hear me.

He put down the phone and stared at me in utter bemusement. 'That was Valerie Williams,' he said. 'Apparently Skincrawl's going to Reading. She's not taking the De La Wyche.'

'Oh. God.' I tried to sound appropriately surprised. 'But . . . why did she ring to tell you that?'

'Because they've offered it to the reserve, Rod Firsden, and he's not definitely taking it either. Valerie says if he doesn't, I get it automatically because I'm the only one left. I don't believe it, Kate.' He blinked with shock. 'I'm still in with a chance.'

Chapter Forty-two

Snap

'Oh. Wow.' That was the best I could manage. My brain struggled to keep up with events.

'She's a fucking weirdo,' said Sebastian.

'Who, Terri?'

'No, Valerie. She sounded almost angry with me. She said something like "count yourself lucky", as if she was ticking me off.'

'Oh, just ignore her,' I said evasively. If Rod said no, Valerie would find herself in the dubious position of having to offer the Enmity to someone who in her eyes was an undeserving cheat. Still, what could she do apart from tell all and allow her precious college to be attacked by the press? Valerie would never do that. It wouldn't suit her high moral image to work for an institution that was known to be corrupt.

'Oh, God, this is awful!' Sebastian pulled at his hair and swayed from side to side. 'This is even worse, if I don't get it now. Why did she ring and tell me that? Why couldn't the stupid bitch have waited to see what this Firsden guy does, before raising my hopes?'

'It's probably in the rules,' I said. 'You're now officially the reserve, so they have to alert you to the fact. Look, I must go, I've got ... lessons. I'll see you later, okay?' Sebastian wasn't listening. He was prowling up and down the lounge, mumbling to himself through white lips. He had never been able to handle pressure.

I ran to the car. I had no idea what I was going to say to Rod, but I knew I had to get to him as quickly as possible. Maybe I could tell him the truth, everything, and beg him to let Sebastian have the Enmity, out of sheer goodwill. I could try to convince him that Sebastian's need was greater than his own. As if that has ever convinced anybody of anything.

I parked on Raymond Road again and walked round the corner to Sterling Road. I still wasn't ready to face Vincent Strebonian. Rod's lounge curtains were closed and probably had been since I'd left last night. I rang the doorbell and waited. Nothing. I rang again, pressing my finger down for longer. He had to be in, I thought, since he'd left a message instructing me to come round straight away. Unless he'd had another radical change of mood, which was eminently possible.

I stepped back a few paces on to the pavement and felt something hit me on the back.

'Would you mind watching where . . .' a stern male voice began, stopping only when I turned round. It was Vincent Strebonian. His wrinkled skin changed colour when he registered who I was. Purple and white mottled patches stood out from the rest of his face. 'You,' he said dully.

'Mr Strebonian, look, I'm really sorry about everything. I didn't realise about your wife. I'm really, really sorry. I didn't mean to upset you.'

'My wife . . .' He looked past me, into the distance. 'Yes. My wife.'

'Mr Strebonian, you haven't seen Rod, have you?'

'Who?' He squinted at me.

'Rod,' I repeated. 'You know.'

'Rod.' He shook his head. Perhaps it had been unwise of me to mention his wife directly. It seemed to have had a strange effect on him. 'Do excuse me, I must be off,' he muttered, starting to cross the road. I shrugged. At least he didn't seem angry any more.

I still couldn't believe Rod wasn't in. My mobile had

been switched on since I'd left home, so if he'd had to go out, or even if he'd changed his mind about seeing me, he could have left a message. There was a small passageway between the side of the house and the wall. I didn't think it would be too rude of me, in the circumstances, to go round to the back and try tapping on the window. I worked out, from what I remembered of the inside of Rod's flat, that the bedroom would face on to the back garden. Perhaps Rod had fallen asleep. I smiled at the thought. He had so much nervous energy, it was hard to imagine him sleeping. A vague recollection of him telling me he was an insomniac lurked in the corner of my mind.

I walked around the building, trampling on the overgrown grass that spilled over on to the narrow path from both sides. I passed a wheelie bin with its lid half open that reeked of many forms of unpleasantness. It made me think of Sunday morning bad breath after a heavy Saturday night. A woman stared at me from a top floor window as I approached Rod's bedroom. I could see that the curtains weren't shut, but not much more than that because light was bouncing off the glass. I looked up at the woman and gestured reassuringly, pointing towards Rod's flat and smiling. This was intended to signify that I was not a burglar, but in fact on friendly – indeed intimate – terms with the resident of the ground-floor flat. She twitched her upper lip at me suspiciously and withdrew.

I shielded my eyes from the sun and pressed my face up against the glass. I saw Rod's bed straight away, and noted that he wasn't in it. The duvet was half on the bed and half trailing on the floor, the sheet was crumpled and the long thin pillow was twisted in the middle, so that it resembled one of those bow-shaped bits of pasta that you can buy from highbrow supermarkets. It looked as if Rod had spent hours wriggling and writhing, either from insomnia or general agitation, then leaped out of bed, unable to take any more, without bothering to smooth over the traces of his troubled night.

A couple of polo-neck jumpers lay on the floor near the window. Seeing them made me wonder whether Rod possessed any other sort of top, and how he avoided getting swelteringly hot wearing polo-necks in June. I couldn't see much else, apart from a few shelves full of books.

Rod's window was slightly open. I put my mouth next to it and shouted his name loudly. Perhaps he was in the shower and that was why he couldn't hear me. I moved a few yards to the right, to get a new angle on the room, and saw a little cabinet at the foot of the bed. Its top was about one and a half square feet in size, and covered with tiny picture frames. I wasn't close enough to see any of the photos, and in any case light was reflecting off the small squares, circles and rectangles of glass. It didn't surprise me that Rod should have a collection of little tricksy frames like this, the kind you'd buy in shops called 'Trinket Town' or 'Gifts Galore'; it seemed to go with his fussy nature. For the first time, it occurred to me that he might be bisexual, or homosexual but desperately trying to be bi. I didn't know many straight men who wore cocoa butter lotion and had such cutesy photo frames.

I shouted Rod's name again, but there was no answer. I looked at the window, and decided that it would be easy for me to slip an arm in and open it to its full extent. Rod might be sick and need rescuing, I told myself. The shock of being offered the Enmity might have brought on a stroke. For all I knew, he could have been lying unconscious on the bathroom floor. It was my duty as a citizen to check that this was not the case. I squeezed my right forearm in and fiddled about until the window creaked open. Checking that the woman upstairs had not returned to gawp at me, I put my left knee on the windowsill and planted my right foot in Rod's bedroom, surprised by my lack of nervous reluctance. Still, this wasn't the first time I'd broken and entered; this was nothing, after the endurance test of Terri's wardrobe.

I pulled the rest of my body through the window and

closed it after me. My eyes were immediately drawn, as if by a magnetic force, to a small face that stared up at me from an ornate oval frame on the bedside cabinet. Damian Selinger. I felt myself retch, although I couldn't understand why; my mind hadn't yet caught up with my body. What was Rod doing with a photo of Damian? He'd never mentioned to me that he knew anyone at Summerton.

I soon located the source of my dread, the unformed fear that had made bile rise in my throat: it was the thought that Rod might be sleeping with Damian Selinger. But that was ridiculous. A photo does not necessarily imply a sexual relationship. I knelt down beside the cabinet to examine Rod's other photos, hoping to reassure myself. I was quickly disappointed. I retched again and this time put my hand over my mouth. I didn't want to tarnish Rod's bedroom by being sick in it.

Apart from the photo of Damian – which, on close inspection, I could see had been taken in the Summerton College bar – there were four other framed pictures on the cabinet top. One was of Keithanethan in what looked like Queen's Court, with their arms slung laddishly across each other's shoulders, each holding a can of lager in his free hand. Then there was another photo of Summerton's bar, a long-distance shot of one of the long wooden tables. Around the table, facing the camera, were Keithanethan, Damian, Martine, Emily Lole and various other people, including Sebastian, who was smiling and waving at the camera. Emily Lole was also smiling, maybe even laughing. It suited her. My heart was thudding harder and harder as I took all this in. I felt as if it was expanding to fill my whole body, taking over more and more territory, pushing my lungs up to right under my chin. It was the lateral-thinking-puzzle feeling again, only fifty times more severe.

I had to think quickly; for all I knew Rod could appear at any moment. What was he doing with a photo of Sebastian? Did it mean that he knew about me, that I was Sebastian's wife? Why hadn't he told me that he knew all these people from Summerton? If he had photos of them in his bedroom, that meant they were his friends. Maybe he hadn't wanted me to know in case I suspected he'd only got as far as he had in the Enmity competition because of who he knew, not what he knew.

The fourth photo, in a little round frame, was of Fernando Rose and Emily Lole sitting side by side on Emily's sofa. She was smiling again in this photo; I couldn't get used to seeing a happy expression on her face. This certainly wasn't the Emily Lole I knew and tried not to get strangled by. Fernando was frowning slightly, sitting with his arms folded behind his head.

I couldn't believe this. Why hadn't Rod told me he knew Fernando Rose? Maybe he also knew where Fernando was. I tried to think back over all my conversations with Rod. He may not have said, directly, that he didn't know Fernando, that he wasn't friends with several of the younger Summerton fellows, but he had certainly misled me.

I sat cross-legged on the floor, feeling faint. There was something deeply not right about all this. It wasn't just the nepotism and favouritism, although both had clearly reached epidemic proportions at Summerton, what with the Daphne–Terri scam and now Rod and his mates; it was Rod himself who bothered me, and having to adjust to the knowledge that he had lied to me about his connections to Summerton. He was so convincing as an eccentric loner who had no friends that I simply couldn't bring myself to believe that wasn't the real Rod.

I pulled my mobile phone out of my bag and dialled Summerton's porters' lodge. They took ages to answer and I bit my nails impatiently until there was a click and a deep male voice said, 'Summerton College, how may I help you?'

'Ethan Handley, please,' I said.

'Thank you, ma'am. Putting you through.'

I heard a ringing tone again and Ethan picked up the phone. 'Ethan Handley,' he said charmingly. I wanted to hit something. No one should have been allowed to feel or sound laid back until I also could.

'Ethan, it's Kate Nunn.'

'Kate! How are you? Hey, I hope you're not using your mobile phone while you're driving. Can't have you driving instructors setting a bad example, you know.'

'Ethan, do you know Rod Firsden?'

'Heard of him,' said Ethan casually. There was not even a hint of guilt or subterfuge in his voice, but then what did I know? I'd trusted Rod. I'd suspected Sebastian. And if Ethan Handley was a liar, he'd obviously be a brilliant one, just as he was a brilliant everything else. 'He's our reserve candidate for the De La Wyche, isn't he? Never met him, though. Why?'

'Ethan, I *know* you've met him, please tell me the truth. You know him.'

'I don't know him, Kate. What are you talking about? I've never met the man in my life.' Ethan sounded puzzled but amused.

'I'm in Rod Firsden's bedroom at the moment,' I said stiffly. 'Looking at . . .'

'What, and you a married woman?' Ethan laughed. 'I don't know whether you should tell me what you're looking at.'

'There's a photo of you and Keith on Rod's bedside cabinet. In a frame.'

'What?' He sounded surprised. 'Are you sure?'

'Of course I'm sure. I'm looking at it.' I yelled in frustration.

'Well, that's mighty peculiar,' said Ethan. 'I mean, photos of Keith aren't exactly rare on the bedside cabinets of Cambridgeshire, but . . . well, I can't think why this Rod chap would have one. Can you describe . . . ?'

'Wait!' I hissed. 'I heard something. Ethan, I can't talk now. 'Bye.' I snapped my phone closed on the beginning of his next puzzled enquiry and crawled under Rod's bed. I wasn't sure exactly what I'd heard, but I didn't want to take any chances. The dust under the bed blocked my throat almost immediately and I wrinkled my nose in horror at the thought that I was almost certainly inhaling not only Rod's dead skin cells but those of several former residents as well. I found myself face to face with several yellowing sheets of newspaper and saw the name Vincent Strebonian. Rod appeared to have several articles about the death of his neighbour's wife under his bed. My feelings of unease grew. I folded the articles and stuffed them into my pocket to read later.

When I hadn't heard anything for a few minutes I crawled out and brushed my clothes down. Clouds of dust billowed out into the room, clearly visible in the sunlight, then slowly fell to the floor and settled. I considered ringing Keith Cobain, to see if I could get the truth out of him, but Ethan was bound to have phoned him already and alerted him to my suspicions if any sort of deception was going on.

An unpleasant feeling crept into my consciousness, distracting me. Sebastian was implicated in this. He'd told me he met Rod for the first time at the Enmity interview. Whenever he'd mentioned him since, it had been in the terms one uses to refer to a stranger, but here he was in this photo, framed, in Rod's bedroom. He had to know him. So did Damian and Emily. Maybe the photographs she'd given me were part of some trick. I tried to fight extreme paranoia but failed. The evidence suggested that everyone was in league against me.

Damn, where were Emily's photos? I thought I'd put them in the Micra's glove compartment but I made a mental note to check. I wanted to have another close look at them in the light of my new conspiracy theory.

I took one last look at the bedside cabinet, and headed for the window, thinking about Damian Selinger. He was hardly the soul of discretion; if there had been any element of nepotism in the choice of Rod as first reserve, why wouldn't he have told me? As soon as I'd asked myself the question, I thought of the answer: Bryony. The one thing

330

that might put her off her beloved Frisky – where being a boorish bullying egomaniac had failed to do the trick – was the knowledge that he'd been involved in perverting the course of appointment procedures, wiping out her chance of getting the Enmity by favouring Rod in some way. With a chip of Harry Ramsdenesque proportions on her shoulder about interview panels, she might have regarded this as an unforgivable offence.

I climbed out of the window and into the garden, staying close to the wall in case the woman upstairs had returned to her staring post. I crept around the side of the house, trying to look casual and innocent as I strolled back out on to Sterling Road.

I was stopped in my tracks by a sight even more alarming than the pictures on Rod's bedside cabinet. I gasped involuntarily and ducked down behind Rod's garden wall. No, it can't be, it can't be, I told myself. Slowly I raised my head until I could see the road again.

It had been and it still was. My throat was as dry as paper. Across the road, in front of Vincent Strebonian's gateposts, in the exact space that yellow paint decreed should never be blocked by man or machine, stood Rod and Vincent Strebonian. They were only inches apart. Rod's feet were on the yellow 'No' and Strebonian's on the 'ing' of 'Parking'. They were as close as Rod and I had been the previous night. They were as close as characters in low-budget soap operas who put their faces side by side in order to have conversations because the camera can't cope with wide-lens shots. I held my breath. People only ever got that close for one reason. They were about to kiss. In the middle of the road, in broad daylight.

Vincent Strebonian took a further step towards Rod. Now he was standing on the 'Par' of 'Parking'. I narrowed my eyes, wanting to see what happened so much that I could hardly bear to watch. Slowly, with great concentration, Vincent Strebonian raised his left hand and began to caress Rod's cheek.

331

'You're too old for him!' I wanted to yell, but didn't. I watched Rod raise his right hand and move it towards his face. Everything seemed to be happening in slow motion. I shut my eyes for a second when the lateral-thinking-puzzle feeling became too overpowering. When I opened them, Rod's hand was on top of Vincent Strebonian's and he had moved even closer, on to the 'o' of 'No'. I steeled myself to witness a major necking incident. Instead, Vincent Strebonian disentangled his left hand, put his arm round Rod's shoulders and led him up the driveway and into his house.

I fell down on the grass, panting with shock. So Rod was bisexual. No wonder he'd always defended Strebonian so ferociously. I lay flat on my back on the grass, no longer caring whether Rod's upstairs neighbour saw me. How could I have been so stupid as to imagine I was close to a virtual stranger? I knew nothing about Rod; he was always so cagey. Now I could see why.

After a few minutes I dragged myself up off the grass and hobbled – or at least that was how it felt – back to the Micra on Raymond Road. I lit a cigarette and looked through Emily's photos again: Ethan Handley looking very, very ill. A stock cube. Some trees. A pile of *Literary Reviews*. It helped to concentrate on small puzzles like this; the prospect of grappling with my larger worries was too horrific to contemplate for the time being.

A packet of Nurofen painkillers. Peter Ustinov in *Death on the Nile*. Judge James Pickles. Jesus. Summerton Great Hall on the occasion of some feast or other. A bottle of orange squash. A rusty car door panel. A box of Tetley's bitter.

A bitter box, I thought, hearing an echo in my mind. *Put not thy hand into the bitter box, but oh, my God . . .*

'Oh my God,' I whispered.

Chapter Forty-three

Vincent Strebonian – Curriculum Vitae

Name
Vincent Nigel Strebonian.

Address
1 Sterling Road, Cambridge.

Age
The articles I found under Rod's bed say he's sixty-five, not as old as he looks. The late Mrs Strebonian was a sun-worshipper, who refused to go on any sort of holiday other than the badly-burn-on-a-beach variety. The Strebonians became, as a result, an excessively leathery couple. Mrs Strebonian took full advantage of the fact that she was married to a cosmetic surgeon, and had her wrinkles removed as and when they appeared. Her husband, believing himself to be the best in the field and unable to operate on himself, decided to settle for the wrinkles. On a plastic surgeon wrinkles could be seen as cool, an attempt to 'out-casual' one's patients, to give a sort of 'Hey, I could get rid of these in five minutes, but who's got time?' impression.

Place of Birth
Leatherhead, Surrey. Honestly. Could Terri Skinner be right about the existence of destiny after all? No, destiny would be more accurate: Leatherface, Surrey. Still, it might

be worth finding out if Lloyd Lunnon was born in Yelling.

Marital Status
Married the painter Edna Strebonian (née Glover) in 1955 and remained married to her until her death as a result of inconsiderate parking in 1996. Edna Strebonian was internationally renowned for her paintings of her husband's patients before, during and after surgery. Many of these can be found in famous private collections and galleries including the Saatchi Gallery, the Tate and the National Portrait Gallery. Some of Vincent Strebonian's richer patients were able to buy their pictures; all were greatly flattered to have the subcutaneous layers of their skin immortalised in art. Vincent Strebonian hasn't driven since Edna's death. He has turned the garage into a gallery for her work. Her paintings hang from all four walls around the central exhibit of the filthy, unused car. Vincent calls the garage 'The Life and Death of Edna Strebonian'. All of which means, presumably, that he was a late convert to homosexuality.

Employment History
Worked first as a doctor, then as a surgeon, then as a plastic surgeon for the National Health Service. Went private twelve years ago, to make it easier for Edna to draw his clients. His colleagues at the Gallwoodey Hospital in Cambridge tended to get a bit sniffy about Edna hanging around the operating theatre with her sketchbook.

Qualifications and Education
FRCS (Federation of Royal College of Surgeons), MB B.Chir. Clinical Medicine from Chathams Hospital, Stafford, MA (BA) Human Biology from Keele University.

Strengths and Weaknesses
Must be a good cosmetic surgeon if he can afford that huge house. Apparent versatility in choice of romantic partners.

Not many people would feel happy about switching, in only two years, from a leathery (although cosmetically lifted) old female painter to an earnest, bearded, poetry-loving young man. Weaknesses might include amnesia (saying 'Who?' when I mentioned Rod was a bit off, even if it was a codgerish rather than a caddish 'Who?') and unnecessary unpleasantness towards those who park in front of his driveway. I know I escalated the situation by parking there a second time to wind him up, but there is no doubt that he was unduly harsh with me during our first encounter. This is a forgivable weakness, though. He has been made harsh by misery. The question is, if he is still so distraught at the loss of Edna that he savages anyone who blocks his driveway, how can he have enough free emotional energy for an affair with Rod?

Chapter Forty-four

Closer to Fernando

I leaned against the wall of Tyndsall Court and smiled at a passing porter. As soon as he had disappeared, I banged on Emily Lole's door, bruising my knuckles. I didn't care if I scared her. I knew for a fact that she had lied to me; all that remained for me to find out was how much.

'Who is it?' Emily murmured timidly from behind the door. I banged again, too angry to co-operate with any visitor-screening shenanigans. 'Is that you, Fernando?' she asked hopefully.

'No, it isn't Fernando, it's Kate Nunn,' I said impatiently. Emily opened the door. I saw that she was crying. 'Sorry to disappoint you,' I said caustically.

'I really thought you were him. That's how he used to knock,' she sobbed. I walked through to her lounge without waiting to be invited. 'Have you brought my photos back? Did you work out what they meant?' Emily gulped, following so close behind me that her toes bashed my heels with every step we took.

'If you really wanted me to work out what they meant,' I said, sitting down on her sofa and spreading my arms out as if I owned the place, 'why didn't you give me all the photos?'

Emily stopped crying. She grabbed the door with both hands and hunched up her shoulders. 'What do you mean?' she asked, looking ready to run away.

'There was one photo you didn't give me, wasn't there?

It arrived in the second envelope, in the same batch as Jesus and the rusty car door. Well? I'm right, aren't I?'

'I need to go to the loo,' said Emily, still clinging on to the door.

'Fine. Go,' I said. 'But when you come back, I want an answer.' I already knew the answer; it was clear from her reaction that I had guessed correctly, but I wanted to hear Emily say it.

While she was in the bathroom, my mobile phone rang. I waited until it stopped ringing and then phoned Callback to see if whoever it was had left a message. It was Rod and he had. 'Kate, where are you?' he whined. 'Did you come round before? I had to nip out for a few minutes. I should have left a note. Kate, I know you're probably furious with me and that's why you're staying away . . .'

'I'm not furious with you,' I whispered, stroking the phone.

'. . . this is probably some sort of test, isn't it? You don't want to give me any advice, isn't that right? You think I need to make the decision myself. Kate, I've realised how much I love you. I'm . . . different since they offered me the fellowship, everything's changed.' There was a pause of a few seconds while Rod swallowed and cleared his throat.

'Please don't cut him off,' I muttered.

'What?' Emily had reappeared in the doorway.

'Nothing,' I said quickly, switching off my phone. 'Just talking to myself. So. What's the story?'

'How did you know? About the other photo?' she asked, sitting down on a chair opposite me.

'What was the other photo of, Emily? I want to see it.'

'I thought you knew.'

'I do know, but I want you to tell me.'

'No.' Her voice shook. 'You say.' She sounded like a shy three-year-old.

'Okay. It was a photograph of Rod Firsden, wasn't it?'

'Yes!' she panted eagerly, as if relieved to have been found out. 'Yes, it was. I'll get it.' She went into the bedroom and came out a few seconds later with the missing picture, the one she'd withheld. I fought the urge to cry as I stared at this close-up of Rod's face. He was smiling earnestly, looking right at the camera. His glasses had slipped half-way down his shiny nose. 'How did you know? How did you guess?' Emily droned in the background. 'Do you know where Fernando is? Did he tell you? Are you in league with him?'

'Of course I'm not in league with him.' I watched her reaction carefully. 'I could ask you the same question.'

'How can *I* be in league with him?' She started to weep again. 'I don't even know where he is.'

'Why didn't you give me this photo when you gave me the others?' I asked sternly.

'Because . . . then you'd have known why I supported Rod Firsden. In the De La Wyche committee. You might have . . . reported me. I could have lost my job.' She was almost cringing with fear as she said this.

'I still don't know, Emily. Why did you support Rod? Please explain it to me. Look, I promise I won't report you to anyone. I just want to understand what's going on.'

'Fernando sent me these photos,' she stammered between sobs. 'I didn't know why. All I knew, from the envelopes, was that Fernando had sent them, so they had to mean something. He had to be trying to tell me something. I didn't know who Rod Firsden was when the second envelope arrived, I'd never seen him before. I nearly died of shock when he walked into the interview room. It was like . . . a sign from God!'

'Of what, exactly?' I asked.

'Of . . . the fact that Fernando was trying to communicate with me. He must have known, somehow, that Rod was on the De La Wyche shortlist. He was trying to tell me that he wanted Rod to get the job. That was why I supported him. Fernando was testing me. I thought that if Rod got the fellowship, I'd have passed the test and . . . Fernando would be pleased with me, maybe get in touch again. Maybe . . . come . . . back.' Tears cascaded down her cheeks.

'Emily, how did you know, how could you be sure, that Fernando sending you a photo of Rod meant he wanted Rod to get the job?' I asked carefully, almost certain she was telling the truth.

'What else could it mean?'

'Why would Fernando want Rod to get the De La Wyche fellowship?'

'I don't know!' Emily wailed. 'Maybe the photo didn't mean that, I don't know. The one thing it definitely meant was that Rod was connected – somehow – to Fernando and that was a good enough reason for me to support him. I know it doesn't make any sense. I only listened to what my instincts told me. I thought eventually Fernando would come back and . . . explain everything.'

'Okay, let's assume that Fernando did want you to support Rod,' I said calmly. 'That explains why he sent that photo. But what about all the other photos. What do they mean?'

'If I knew that, I wouldn't have asked you, would I?' Emily snapped, wiping her eyes and nose with her chubby hands. 'Sorry. I don't mean to be rude.'

'Don't worry about it,' I said. 'Emily, did Rod Firsden interview well?'

'I don't remember.' She sniffed. 'I was in a complete state that day. I couldn't concentrate. I just stared at him and thought, this is the person Fernando sent me a photo of. I was so excited and nervous. I felt . . . closer to Fernando than I had since . . . well, since he disappeared. I know it sounds ridiculous . . .'

'Not at all,' I said.

'. . . you have to make do with these scraps, these tenuous links, when the person's gone. It's all you've got left. Sometimes I go and stand outside Fernando's old rooms, just to feel close to him . . .'

'Emily,' I interrupted her. 'Did Rod give you a poem

339

during his interview?' She looked at me blankly. 'Did he hand out a poem, to all the panel members?'

'Oh . . . that. Yes. It was called "Sighs and Groans". I remember the title. I didn't read the poem, I was too preoccupied.'

'Did you read it later?'

'No. I threw it away. I don't like poetry. It's too . . . misleading.'

'What do you mean?' 'Sighs and Groans' was a fairly straightforward poem in my opinion. Even I understood most of it.

'Oh, you know. Poets don't just say what they mean. It annoys me.' Emily dismissed a major art form in a sentence. 'What does all this mean, Kate?' she whimpered, picking skin from her top lip. 'How did you know Fernando had sent me a photo of Rod Firsden?'

I should have prepared an answer to this question, but I hadn't. Total honesty seemed, momentarily, to be an attractive option, but then the moment passed. I wasn't sure Emily was strong enough to survive the truth, the whole truth and nothing but the truth; she might sink into a shock-induced coma and I didn't want to have to try to revive her.

'I've got to go,' I said, standing up. 'I'm sorry, Emily. I can't discuss this any more.'

'But I told you what you wanted to know!' she said indignantly.

'No you didn't. I'd already guessed.' I headed towards the door.

'Do you know where Fernando is?' Emily chased me down the hall. 'Do you know? Have you spoken to him?'

'No,' I said, because anything else would have been too difficult.

Chapter Forty-five

The Launch

There were few things I wished to do less, on Monday evening, than attend the launch of *Me, Me, Me: Embracing Selfishness* by Damian Selinger. I got dressed in silence, nodding and making appropriate noises when Sebastian seemed to be talking to me. I was physically present in the bedroom with Sebastian, dressing to go out, but mentally I was somewhere else. Worries about what Rod Firsden might do next had set up camp in my mind and I couldn't seem to evict them. It was now over twenty-four hours since he'd left his first message on Sunday morning, telling me to go round there straight away. Since then he'd left three more and his love for me, oddly, seemed to grow between phone calls. In his most recent message he'd said he'd be willing to die for me if he had to.

I couldn't bring myself to tell the authorities at Summerton what I now knew. I would have to tell Rod it was over between us and allow him to accept the Enmity. It made my head spin to think how much had changed in twenty-four hours. If someone had asked me yesterday, I would have said there was nothing I wouldn't do to get the Enmity for Sebastian.

'Let's get a taxi to Heffers,' I said. 'If we have to listen to Damian reading smugly from his how-to-be-a-git manual we can at least get hammered on free wine.' I could picture Rod pacing the streets of Cambridge in a frenzy, looking for my car. Driving it tonight was too much of a risk. If Rod saw us, he would be bound to accost us and make a scene. The prospect was too monstrous to contemplate.

'You know he's got a photo of himself on the front cover?' said Sebastian. 'A big mugshot of him, with a slimy, arrogant grin on his face.'

'Really?' It sounded not unlike the photograph I'd seen on Rod's bedside cabinet. 'Will you have your photo on the cover of your book?' I tried to joke.

'No, I think a picture of Lenin would be more appropriate. But then, my book isn't called *Me, Me, Me.*'

'He should have had three photos of himself,' I said. 'To embody the repetition of the title.'

'Covers don't have to be that precise,' said Sebastian. 'You're so pedantic.'

I knew it was going to be a bad evening – admittedly I underestimated precisely how bad it would be – as soon as our taxi pulled up outside Heffers. The whole front window of the shop was full of showcards advertising Damian's book, so the first thing we saw was thirty-odd copies, in varying sizes, of the slimy, arrogant grin Sebastian had so accurately described.

As we walked into the shop, a young woman in a Heffers T-shirt waved two empty wineglasses in front of our noses and said, 'Red or white?' We took a glass of white wine each and wandered over to the crowd of Summerton people that had assembled around the till. It occurred to me that the definition of 'Summerton people' changed, depending on where you were. In the college itself, Sebastian and I would have been seen as – and felt like – outsiders, but in Heffers, where there were only two kinds of people, the Heffers kind and the Summerton kind, we joined the latter group by default.

'Selinger, you smarmy fucker, why didn't you just have a photo of yourself wanking on the cover of your book, hm?' Lloyd Lunnon enquired loudly. Damian blushed and Bryony glowered protectively. Their great love was evidently still going strong and had defied all those cynics who said it couldn't last, such as myself, by running to a second week. Bryony was dressed from neck to toe in beige, which I found deeply worrying. Couldn't she love Damian without contracting his beigeness? They looked ridiculous standing side by side – like a pair of camels. Bryony waved at me and grinned, but I pretended not to notice.

I spotted Daphne Fielding talking to Sir Patrick Chichester, Summerton's Master, in the hardback fiction section. Even at a distance of some feet I could see she was flirting with him. She held a glass of red wine in her left hand and ran her right index finger around its rim as she spoke. Deliberately, I moved into her line of sight. She saw me and looked away sharply. I moved even closer and watched her for a few more seconds. I could tell she was aware of my presence from the way her flirting technique deteriorated. She slammed her glass down on a shelf and folded her arms. The sight of me had spoiled her romantic mood. I didn't think it would affect her chances of becoming the Master's mistress, however; Sir Patrick was too busy staring at her cleavage to notice her twitching lip.

I sipped my wine in silence and breathed in a calm, controlled way. No one who saw me would have guessed I was fantasising about attacking her. Daphne took Patrick's arm and tried to lead him away from hardback fiction and towards horror. I strolled over to where they had been standing and picked up Daphne's wineglass. It was only considerate to take it over to her, since she'd clearly forgotten it. I walked right up to her and handed her the glass. 'You forgot your brandy, Sir Wilfrid,' I said, which is the last line of *Witness for the Prosecution*. Or maybe it's the other way round: 'Sir Wilfrid, you forgot your brandy.' Either way, Daphne's throat started to ripple with shocked gulps, like clay on a potter's wheel. I smiled and walked away.

'Kate!' Ethan Handley wandered over to me, one hand in his trouser pocket. 'That was an interesting phone call

343

yesterday. Been in any other good bedrooms recently?' He was wearing an immaculate dark-grey suit that perfectly complemented his enigmatically gorgeous blondness. If I'd seen that suit on anyone else I would have concluded that it must have cost a packet, but in this case it was more likely that one of the salesgirls at whatever designer shop it came from had fallen in love with Ethan and risked her job by stealing it for him. Things like this happened to Keithanethan all the time.

'Sh,' I hissed, looking around to check Sebastian hadn't heard.

'Oh, I see.' Ethan winked. 'Well, well.'

Keith appeared behind me, looking like an alluring Italian gangster. He had slicked back his hair and put on a black suit, as he often did for special occasions. Keithanethan did not seem especially interested in the release of *Me, Me, Me: Embracing Selfishness*; I suspected it wasn't the book launch aspect of the evening that made the occasion special for them so much as the prospect of embracing some busty blond (Ethan's type) or Carmen-like brunette (Keith's type) at the end of the night. They kept their affairs strictly colour-coded, never trespassing on each other's territory. This was how they had been able to remain friends and pulling partners for so long.

'What's this Ethan tells me about that Rod Firsden bloke having photos of us in his room?' asked Keith loudly. For a second time I looked guiltily over my shoulder. Sebastian was on the other side of the shop, talking to the Junior Bursar. I saw Valerie Williams and Emily Lole arrive together and hover tentatively near the wine table. They both looked miserable. Perhaps Valerie hadn't wanted to come, but had been ordered by the Master to act as Emily's personal medical escort for the evening. Just as I turned back to Keithanethan I heard Emily call my name in a mournful tone.

'Emily wants you,' said Ethan. 'And the second Mrs Selinger is waving at you as well.'

'Engage me in conversation,' I pleaded with him. 'I want to avoid them both.'

'Very wise,' said Keith. 'So what about these photos?'

'I was wrong,' I said flippantly. 'Forget it.' Keith nodded his best laid-back nod, but Ethan wasn't going to let me off the hook so easily.

'Wrong in what way?' he asked. 'About whose bedroom you were in, or about who was in the photos? Or do you mean you were wrong about seeing the photos at all? Did it turn out to be a hallucination?' He chuckled.

'I was just wrong,' I said. Ethan looked dissatisfied, as well he might, and opened his mouth to ask me another question. I was deeply grateful to Sebastian for choosing that moment to wander over with a blonde of unparalleled bustiness in a short, tight skirt.

Ethan instantly forgot whatever he had planned to ask me and turned his attention to the new arrival. 'Hello. I'm Ethan Handley.' He held out his hand and the woman giggled and shook it. 'Summerton. Molecular Biology. Hi, Sebastian. Good to see you, mate.'

'This is Camilla Pearson from Scholars Press,' said Sebastian. 'She's Damian's editor, and mine, now. This is Keith Cobain and this is my wife, Kate.' He nodded at me in a not very subtle and obviously significant manner, to remind me – as if I would have forgotten – that this was the woman who had thought Lenin was a fictional character. Camilla Pearson looked at Keith, then at Ethan, then at Keith again before finally settling on Ethan. She giggled, blushed and turned to me. 'Hi. God, it's so great to meet you,' she said. I didn't believe she really meant it; she was just buying herself some time to think of what she could say to Ethan that would inspire him to propose to her. 'You must be so proud of Sebastian. The book's so great, isn't it?'

'The bits I've read are good,' I said. 'I haven't read it all. I don't know much about the Russian revolution.' And neither do you, I nearly added, before Camilla beat me to it.

345

'God, I didn't even know about it at all!' She giggled, wiggling her bum in Ethan's direction. 'I didn't realise that Lenin and Stalin and Trotsky were real people. I thought Sebastian had made them up.' Her breasts wobbled up and down as she laughed. Ethan seemed to find her admission of ignorance hilarious and even went so far as to describe it as 'brilliant'. Camilla was so taken aback at this compliment, so unable to believe her luck, that she opted for the safety of talking to me again while she worked out a response. 'So, are you a writer too?' she asked.

'I'm a driving instructor,' I said, interested to see whether Camilla Pearson would pretend to find this interesting or not.

'Oh. Cool.' She sounded distinctly underwhelmed.

'Have you heard of the Red L driving school?' said Ethan. 'That's Kate.'

'Oh, wow!' Camilla's eyes widened. All of a sudden my occupation was fascinating; it had been ratified by an Ethan mention. 'I've seen that loads of times. Is that really you? God, you'll be such a famous couple once Sebastian's book comes out!' She twisted a strand of hair around her finger and looked at Ethan.

'What's your book called, Sebastian?' asked Keith.

'*Lenin: The Sealed Man.*'

'Oh my God! Oh my God!' Camilla shrieked.

'What's the matter?' Ethan rushed over to her in true gentlemanly fashion, putting his arm round her shoulder.

'No, no, I'm fine. I've just had a wonderful idea! Why don't we call your book "Red L"?' she squealed at Sebastian. 'Like your wife's driving school! L for Lenin and – didn't you say he was left-wing?'

'Yes, he was,' said Ethan. He and Keith exchanged a quick smile, which I interpreted as a silent but unanimous verdict of dense-but-eminently-shaggable.

'There you go then. It's perfect!' Camilla beamed at us all. Sebastian had gone grey in the face. '"Red L"! It's so much more snappy than . . . what was it again?'

346

'Lenin the Sealed . . .' Sebastian began hopefully.

'You can't call it "Red L",' Keith laughed. 'No one will take it seriously.'

'I think it's a cool title. You know, memorable. Not too wordy. Easy to say.' Camilla looked at Ethan for support. He looked away. 'What do you think Sebastian? Don't you love it?'

'No,' said Sebastian. 'I loathe it.'

'And we can have an L-plate on the cover, with a big red L!' Camilla bleated on, oblivious. 'I never liked the photo of that bald guy.'

'Lenin,' said Sebastian through clenched teeth.

'An L-plate would be miles more fun,' said Camilla.

'But the book's about Lenin, not learning to drive,' Sebastian snapped.

'Covers don't have to be that precise. Don't be so pedantic,' I muttered mischievously.

'No way,' said Sebastian. 'I'd rather burn the thing.'

'Oh. Gosh.' Camilla laughed nervously. 'Well, we can discuss it later. Do give it some thought, though. Your title sounds so stuffy. I suppose I'd better get the ball rolling with this launch. CAN I HAVE EVERYONE'S ATTENTION PLEASE!' she yelled, nearly shattering the eardrums of those of us who had the misfortune – and it was by no means only an aural one – to be standing near her. 'Can everyone please gather round and Damian will read from his new book, *Me, Me, Me: Embracing Selfishness*. Then afterwards he'll sign copies – make sure you buy loads – and we can all have some more wine! Cool! Latecomers at the back, come to the front, quickly, the reading's about to start.'

Everyone turned to watch as the latecomers crept forward guiltily. One of them was Rod Firsden. I was so shocked that I nearly dropped my wineglass.

'That's Rod Firsden.' Sebastian elbowed me in the ribs. 'That bastard! I bet he takes the job, just so that I can't have it.'

347

'Where is he?' Ethan looked up. I gave him a desperate nudge and he winked at me, to reassure me that he knew Sebastian wasn't supposed to know I'd been in Rod's bedroom. 'That guy with the beard and glasses? He looks familiar but I've never met him.' I looked away, hoping that the sight of Rod wouldn't reawaken Ethan's curiosity about my phone call and the photos.

Rod and the other late arrivals appended themselves to the top right-hand corner of the crowd. Mercifully, because I was on the other side of the shop, he didn't see me. I hid behind Ethan, where I would be safe at least until the end of Damian's reading. It wasn't what you might call a flawless plan, but it was the best one I could come up with. I toyed with the idea of pretending to feel violently ill and leaving, but I didn't think I could manage to get out of Heffers without Rod spotting me. With everyone standing in awestruck silence waiting for the Beige Oracle to speak, any small movement was bound to attract attention.

'I'd like to introduce with great pleasure Dr Damian Selinger!' Camilla cheered loudly. She sounded like a Radio One DJ. 'Reading from his amazing book.'

Damian shuffled forward, brandishing a copy of *Me, Me, Me*. 'Thank you,' he said, staring into Bryony's eyes. 'I'm not reading anything until I get a refill,' he barked at Camilla, jerking his head towards the empty wineglass at his elbow. Bryony, I noticed, was visibly trembling and her eyes were shiny with tears. I decided she was suffering from a most unsavoury brand of loopiness. I could easily imagine her taking part in – even presiding over – ceremonies in which virgins were sacrificed on village greens, which is never a good sign.

'I'm not going to read for very long because I'd rather get pissed,' said Damian cheerfully.

'Selfish git,' someone yelled from the back of the room.

'Precisely,' said Damian. 'We're all selfish gits, which is, in essence, the subject matter of my book. I'm going to read from the introduction, because that's the only bit most of you will be able to follow. The arguments become rather sophisticated later on.' He cleared his throat and began to read:

It is the norm, in Western society, for a distinction to be made between selfish and unselfish behaviour. Allow me, immediately, to define those terms. Selfish behaviour means any action a person performs solely or mainly for his or her own sake, irrespective of how it will affect others. Unselfish behaviour, in contrast, means putting other people's needs and feelings before one's own. The former is, broadly, regarded as good and the latter as bad. A person whose behaviour falls into one of these categories more frequently than the other is labelled, accordingly, as a selfish or unselfish person. Unselfishness, it is generally agreed, might lead one to sacrifice something one wants very much for the sake of someone else.

I tried to keep calm. I felt immensely grateful to Damian for taking the time and trouble to tell us all what we already knew, and hoped he would continue to define concepts as obvious as selfish and unselfish, because the longer he read, the longer I would have to make some kind of life-saving plan. Resisting the urge to surrender to panic, I assured myself that this situation – me, Sebastian and Rod all in the same bookshop – was only potentially disastrous, not necessarily disastrous. I went through various possible courses of action in my head.

Damian went on:

In this book, I aim to prove – indeed, I believe I succeed in proving – that our consensus with regard to the distinction between selfish and unselfish behaviour is a false one, and that all behaviour, the behaviour of all human agents with free will, is in fact selfish. I am aware that this view will not achieve instant popularity and I

349

would be foolish not to anticipate a certain amount of criticism. Some of this criticism will come from moral philosophers who disagree with the logical premises and premises of evidence upon which I've based my thesis – and let me say at this stage that I am confident I can answer all their questions more than satisfactorily – but more criticism, I suspect, will come from those who are reluctant to accept my argument because of the threat this would pose to their self-image.

This needn't be so. The word 'selfish' has negative connotations only in the current moral language of our society, where its polar opposite, 'unselfishness', provides an illusory virtuous contrast. In this book I will argue that, since all human behaviour and decision-making is selfish, and since this is beyond our control and will continue to be so for the foreseeable future, we should liberate the term 'sefishness' from the moral baggage it carries, from its present ethically loaded usage.

As Damian spoke, I shuffled slowly sideways, away from Sebastian and Keithanethan, towards Rod. I'd made a plan and its execution involved being in exactly the right position when Damian finished reading. No one noticed me move; they were all gripped by the wisdom of the Beige One. A few people shook their heads and muttered about barbarism.

Damian turned a page and read on:

Put simply, my thesis is as follows: that in any situation in which a person is faced with several choices of how to act, every human being, without exception, will choose the course of action they most want to choose, the one that most pleases them and most thoroughly satisfies their instinctive desires. It is important to point out at this stage that this book is not concerned with the consequences of actions, only the motivation behind them. Obviously a person who continually satisfies his instinctive desire to burgle and swindle his neighbours can be said to be more harmful – and, in a practical sense, more in need of being locked up – than one who continually satisfies his instinctive desire to help the poor and do work for charity. We can all agree, I hope, that the latter would make a more productive and co-operative citizen. The thesis of this book, however, is that his or her actions are equally selfish, in the sense of having their origins in what most pleases the actor. I am satisfied that I have proved, through detailed research and extensive interviewing of what our society calls 'doers of good' and 'doers of wrong', that no human being ever puts the needs of others before his or her own by acting in a way that is contrary to his or her own wishes.

'Selinger, that's the biggest load of fucking arsewipe I've heard in all my born days!' Lloyd Lunnon shouted and a few people giggled.

'It isn't time for questions yet,' said Camilla anxiously, looking at Damian.

'It's okay.' He smiled superciliously at Lunnon. 'I was expecting interruption and I was expecting outrage.'

'You won't be disappointed,' someone behind me mumbled.

'Let's have some audience participation.' Damian rubbed his hands together in glee. He clearly enjoyed being under the spotlight. Bryony glowed with pride, beaming at him adoringly. 'Hands up anyone who thinks they've ever done something truly unselfish, put someone else's needs before their own?'

'I have,' a defiant female voice announced. The front half of the crowd, the half that contained Rod, turned round to see who had been brave enough to rise to the Selinger selfishness challenge. I ducked behind someone tall so that Rod wouldn't see me; I hadn't bargained for head-turning at this early stage in the evening. 'I have,' Valerie Williams repeated. 'In fact, I often do.'

'Give me an example,' said Damian.

'Well ... I once cancelled a holiday that I was really looking forward to because my best friend's husband left her the day before I was due to go. I was desperate to go away and bask in the sun, I hadn't had a proper holiday for years, but I cancelled it. And lost my deposit as well.' There were a few half-admiring, half-sympathetic murmurs from the crowd.

'Why did you do that?' asked Damian.

'Because my friend needed me,' said Valerie. 'And I put her needs before my own.'

'That's not true. You may think it's true, but it isn't. You're seeing it as a choice as follows: either (a) have a nice holiday in the sun or (b) stay at home listening to your friend whining and sniffling. If that was the real choice and you chose (b), I'd agree that you'd acted unselfishly.' Damian paused dramatically. 'But that wasn't the real choice, was it?' He wagged his finger at Valerie, as if she were a naughty schoolgirl. 'The real choice was between (a) have a nice holiday in the sun or (b) be a good friend. You may have wanted to go on holiday, but you didn't want it as much as you wanted to be a good friend. If you'd ignored your friend's needs and gone away regardless, the knowledge that you'd been a bad friend would have ruined your holiday. Your friend would have felt rejected and you would have lost her friendship. Therefore, what you were really thinking was: what would I be unhappier about losing, this opportunity for a holiday or a long-standing friendship? Missing a holiday might be annoying, but it's hardly a tragedy. You can go on holiday any time. Whereas a ruined friendship, particularly when one is the responsible party, is much harder to get over. You would have had to live with the guilt and you would have lost a potential crutch for when you had any problems of your own. Therefore, you made a rational, self-interested choice based on what would make you happier in the long run.'

'But she put her friend's needs before her own!' yelled a thin woman in large red glasses.

'No, she didn't,' said Damian patiently. 'What she wanted and needed, above all – what a lot of us want and need above all – is to think of ourselves as good, moral, unselfish. For many people that's a prerequisite to happiness. They may be doing good, in so far as their actions have a positive effect on others, but they're still basically just satisfying their own urges and instincts by doing what they want.'

'Are you saying, then . . .' Sebastian began, raising his hand, 'that there is no moral difference between someone who, say, wants to murder people and does, and someone who wants to help people and does?' His tone made it clear that, should this turn out to be the argument that Damian was putting forward, he for one wouldn't think much of it.

'There's a difference in terms of the harm they do, but one is not more selfish than the other, or more disciplined in terms of control over behaviour,' said Damian. 'It just so happens that some people want to do good and some people want to do evil. And to the extent to which our instincts are not of our own choosing, but simply there whether we like it or not, to that extent it could be argued that, no, the murderer is not more blameworthy than the do-gooder. It only makes sense to blame a person for giving in to instinct if it can be proven that it is possible to act contrary to one's instinctive desires. And I don't believe it can. People are incapable of acting contrary to their instinctive desires, be they do-gooders or killers.'

'Utterly monstrous bilge!' shouted Lloyd Lunnon. 'Master? Where are you, Master?' He whirled around until he caught sight of Sir Patrick Chichester. 'If you're experiencing an instinctive desire to hurl this reprobate into the dole queue, I suggest you succumb to it instantly.'

'Well, talking of do-gooders,' Camilla said nervously, 'I think another glass of wine would do us all good. Let's have a fifteen-minute break and then we can have more questions and Damian'll be happy to sign copies of his book.'

'He can sign my arse,' said Lloyd Lunnon.

In the general mingling that followed it was easy to slip through the crowd unnoticed. I walked over to Rod, making sure to approach him from behind. When I reached him, I put my hands over his mouth and whispered, 'Sh, it's me' in his ear. 'Don't make any noise and don't make a scene,' I instructed him. Once I was sure he wasn't going to yell, I let go.

He turned round. 'Kate!' he whispered excitedly. He looked thrilled to see me, which made me feel considerably worse about what I would have to say to him. 'Why all the secrecy? What are you doing here?'

'Listen, we have to talk, but not here. Meet me in the Blue Boar down the road in five minutes.'

'But . . . what are you doing here, at a Summerton launch?' he asked.

I looked around to check that Sebastian was still safely far away. 'What are *you* doing here?' I asked.

'Valerie Williams invited me when she rang to offer me the job. Kate, why haven't you been to see me? Didn't you get all my messages? I need to give Summerton an answer about the De La Wyche and I can't do that without talking to you.'

'The Blue Boar. Five minutes.' I tried to walk away.

'Why the Blue Boar? I want to talk here, now.' Rod's voice was rising.

I only knew one way to shut him up. 'Rod, I know about you,' I said. 'And you need to know about me. That's why we can't talk here. I promise you, you won't want any Summerton people to hear what I've got to say.' His face turned pale beneath its cocoa butter sheen. He rubbed the sides of his nose and adjusted his glasses. 'Are you short-sighted or long-sighted?' I asked him.

'Wha . . . what?'

354

'Neither, right? It's just ordinary glass in those frames, isn't it?'

'No,' he said, starting to sweat profusely. 'I'm short-sighted.'

'Let me try them on,' I said.

'Why? No.' He took a step back, away from me. 'What did you mean', he whispered, 'when you said you knew about me?'

'I meant', I said, taking a deep breath, 'that I know you're Fernando Rose.'

Chapter Forty-six

Rod Firsden – Curriculum Vitae

Name

Changed to Rod Firsden for all practical purposes in March 1997. Legally he is still called Fernando Rose. Was planning to change his name by deed poll if and when he got the Enmity as Rod, and once the monthly donations from Summerton College stopped arriving in Fernando Rose's account, come the official end of his three-year fellowship on 1 October 1998. Chose the name Rod because the George Herbert poem 'Sighs and Groans' contains the quote 'Thou art both Judge and Saviour, Feast and Rod, Cordial and Corrosive'. One of the things Fernando Rose loved most about being at Summerton was attending the lavish college feasts. When he made his plan and realised he would need another name, he picked the one that was inextricably linked in his mind with the word 'feast'.

Address

Flat 1, 58 Sterling Road, Cambridge. Opposite Vincent Strebonian, with whom he is not, nor has he ever been, having an affair. Their relationship is strictly a surgeon–patient one. The hand that turned Fernando Rose's face into Rod Firsden's was the very same one that painted 'No Parking Here' on the pavement with the yellow paint that had been left over after his late wife Edna had finished her painting 'Pus on a wound'. When I witnessed Vincent

Strebonian stroking Rod's cheek, I mistook the professional touch of a cosmetic surgeon for the caress of a lover. The reason Rod wasn't in when I went round on Sunday morning was because his skin felt tighter and drier than usual, despite its immersion in cocoa butter (he had taken to moisturising his face regularly after his operation, so paranoid was he about the side effects of surgery), and he panicked and ran, first to the chemists to buy some better skin cream, then to Vincent Strebonian's for some expert advice. Vincent Strebonian inspected Rod's face closely on the street (this was what I saw) and more thoroughly in his surgery, and reassured him that everything was fine.

Vincent Strebonian deserves to be called an expert. He is, dead-wife-hang-up notwithstanding, an extremely shrewd and intelligent man, and his mind is as clear today as it was fifty years ago. His reaction to my mentioning Rod's name ('Who?') had nothing to do with reduced brain cells and everything to do with being preoccupied, and calling and thinking of his youngest client by his original name, Fernando Rose. Rod did tell him what his new name was going to be at the time of surgery but as Vincent Strebonian has never used it, it frequently slips his mind.

Rod's operation had been perfectly safe and successful, but he still had a paranoid fear that his entire face would shrivel up and fall off one day, like the skin of a tomato as it boils in water, leaving only a mess of undefined, raw flesh. Vincent Strebonian understood this and Rod understood his surgeon's equally irrational terror of people parking in front of his gateposts. Rod was obsessed with the De La Wyche Enmity; Vincent Strebonian was obsessed with watching Sterling Road through his net curtains, ready to pounce on miscreants. The two men respected each other's foibles and had become close friends.

Just as his Enmity predicament was becoming unbearable, Rod (or Fernando, as he was then) read about Vincent Strebonian's predicament in the *Cambridge*

Evening News, in an article with the headline 'How bad parking led to heartbreak for plastic surgeon'. Vincent Strebonian was quoted in the article as saying 'I'll never forgive that driver as long as I live. If I could, I'd kill him. I don't care if they'd send me to prison for it.' Vincent Strebonian's pain reminded Rod of his own and generated a new, non-specific awareness of plastic surgery as a profession.

When he had the whole plan worked out in his head, Fernando went to see Vincent Strebonian. He described his misery in lurid detail and begged for an operation. Vincent Strebonian sympathised strongly, as a fellow sufferer of extreme anguish, but said he couldn't possibly carry out the sort of surgery Fernando wanted for less than sixty thousand pounds. Fernando nearly collapsed when he heard this. He had two thousand pounds in a building society account and he'd assumed this would be sufficient. He trudged back to Summerton, desperately unhappy. At dinner in hall that night he couldn't eat a thing. He stared at the portraits of all the masters, especially the one of Grimshaw De La Wyche, whom he loved for his legacy of the fellowship and loathed for making it a fixed-term position with no possibility of renewal.

That was when the final part of the plan fell into place. Fernando went to see Vincent Strebonian again the next day and offered him this painting in lieu of payment. Edna, as a painter, would have preferred an original Edmund Noble to any amount of money, he argued. Vincent Strebonian agreed tearfully. Fernando announced his intention to steal the painting, having no idea how, precisely, he would do this, since Great Hall was never left unlocked. Vincent Strebonian was impressed by Fernando's determination and promised never to show the painting to anyone and, of course, to perform the required surgery. Edna would finally be able to rest in peace, he said, if she knew an original Noble hung in the garage, beside her own paintings.

Fernando wanted a new nose and chin with no trace of moonliness about them. He wanted as different a face as possible. Vincent Strebonian promised that by the time he had finished, only the eyes would look the same. Fernando wasn't taking any chances – he decided to grow a beard (which was patchy at first, because of the skin grafts, but became healthier as time went by), wear glasses he didn't need, change his hairstyle and hair colour, and his voice. He spent hours practising clipped BBC vowels to replace his working-class Guildford accent.

A week before his operation, Fernando noticed a 'To Let' sign outside a flat on Sterling Road, opposite Vincent Strebonian's surgery. He took it immediately, knowing he would find it comforting to have his cosmetic surgeon on hand in case of future emergencies. So when the time came to escape from Summerton in the middle of the night, after a nervous evening at the Jive Hive, that was where he went.

Age, Place of Birth, Education and Qualifications
See Fernando Rose's CV.

Employment History
See Fernando Rose's CV for pre-Summerton employment.

Fernando's insomnia (which later became Rod's) had started almost as soon as he took up the position of De La Wyche fellow. The only reason he had accompanied Keithanethan and Martine to the Jive Hive on the night of 21 March 1997 was because he had been having trouble sleeping. His pleasure at getting the fellowship, which was the summit of all his dreams and ambitions, had lasted for approximately a week. Then he started to think about the temporariness of it, how he would soon be disowned and disinherited (this was how he thought of it) by the family that had taken him in and welcomed him so warmly. Worse than that, they would replace him with someone else, and lavish all their attentions on that impostor: his rival, his supplanter.

Fernando's fear that his ruse would be discovered should not be confused with guilt. He never felt guilty about trying to break the De La Wyche rules. He knew he belonged at Summerton, that it was his destiny to be the one and only De La Wyche fellow, and that once the college had given him the job he was entitled to keep it. He was opposed to the idea of all good things coming to an end and thought that for Summerton to give the Enmity to lots of people temporarily amounted to torture, since it meant that every three years some poor soul was doomed to lose the best thing he or she had probably ever had and suffer the emotional consequences. The Enmity was certainly the best thing Fernando had ever had. He told himself that torturers had to be resisted, by every means possible.

Being an English literature scholar, Fernando didn't know much about property theory, but he was sure someone – Damian Selinger, for example – could argue convincingly that after a certain length of time the Enmity became his property rather than the college's, from a moral and philosophical point of view, because he had mixed his labour with it. Fernando mentioned this to Damian – on the night when he also took the photos that ended up on Rod's bedside table – and Damian agreed. Most things, said Damian, cannot be taken away from their owner after three years, so why should the De La Wyche be different? It wasn't as if Fernando had signed a contract; only the permanent fellows had contracts at Summerton. The De La Wyche fellow simply received a letter saying he or she had been appointed for a three-year period and instructing him or her to let the college accountant have the relevant bank details to facilitate payment of the monthly donation. Damian said that since the college had asked for no reply to this letter, and since Fernando had never written back and explicitly accepted these terms, he could argue that he had never consented to the part about leaving after three years.

Fernando cheered up when he heard this, until Damian added that this argument would only work on the most abstract philosophical level. In practical terms it would prove utterly useless, he said, and certainly wouldn't stop Summerton from appointing a new De La Wyche fellow in October 1998 and discontinuing their donations to Fernando.

Fernando became more abject with every day of his fellowship that went by. Temporariness tormented him. Sometimes he sat in his rooms with no lights on and the curtains closed, saying 'tick-tock, tick-tock' loudly to himself, as the seconds of his Summerton time ticked away. He worked as hard as he possibly could, and was more friendly and co-operative than any of his De La Wyche predecessors, in the hope that somebody, some influential college dignitary, would suggest that he be made permanent. It never happened.

So he went to see the then Master, Sir Noel Barry, and suggested it himself. Barry told him it was against the De La Wyche rules, as set down all those years ago by Grimshaw De La Wyche. Fernando asked Sir Noel – begged him – to consider changing the rules. The Master refused, on the grounds that the changing of rules was an unacceptable practice, whatever the circumstances. 'I shall be retiring at the end of this academic year,' he said with great relief, 'and no doubt my successor, Sir Patrick Chichester, will be unable to resist the temptation to bugger about with all our customs and traditions in the way that these young, modern chaps do, but while I am still Master I can assure you there will be no changing of rules.'

The little lime-green sign on the fellows' notice board was what finally pushed Fernando to the limits of his endurance and forced on him the need to make a plan. It appeared on 18 October 1996, just over a year after Fernando became the De La Wyche fellow, when he still had two years to go. He saw it one day when he was on his way to Great Hall. It was typed and headed 'De La Wyche fellowship, 1998–2001'. 'Soon the search must begin for a successor to Fernando Rose,' it said. 'Would fellows please start to keep their eyes open for graduate students of the highest level of excellence and let the Master's secretary have their names? The deadline for applications is not until next October, of course, but we should at least start to think about it now. Thank you.' This horrifically offensive exhibit was more than Fernando could bear. Now his temporariness tormented him in public as well as in private. Everybody who walked past that notice board would know about – and, what was worse, would probably be indifferent to – the temporariness of Fernando Rose.

Marital Status

In a feeble attempt to cheer himself up, Fernando embarked upon a relationship with Emily Lole. For their first date, they went to the Warner Brothers cinema in Cambridge to see some terrible film of the wizard-and-goblin ilk that Emily had insisted upon, and there was an advertisement before the film for a plastic surgery hospital. 'Breasts, noses, faces,' it said. 'Laser treatment for wrinkles.' Fernando remembered the article he'd read about the death of the painter Edna Strebonian, whose husband was a plastic surgeon. An arrow of light speared his heart. He must have spent the next two hours planning. He hardly noticed the film and was unable to comment on it afterwards when Emily asked him what he thought. By the end of the evening he had it all worked out in his mind. He would disappear from Summerton, have his face rebuilt and reapply for the De La Wyche as another person. It was only November 1996 and the deadline for applications wasn't for another year. He could easily muster a few publications under another name in a year, especially as he wouldn't be able to leave the house for a few months after his surgery, until all traces of the operation had vanished, all swellings had subsided and his new persona was ready for presentation to the world. The quality of his work was so high that he knew most journals would take it, even from an unknown name. He would submit a research proposal on the poetry of George Herbert and fake the best references imaginable from a couple of randomly selected top literature heavyweights at Oxford. Summerton sent out reference forms with the De La Wyche application pack; it was the responsibility of each applicant to send those forms to his or her referees and ask that they be filled in and returned. Would anyone know if Fernando filled in his own? Would anyone check? He thought it unlikely. Most of the senior Summerton fellows he knew brought out the smelling salts at the mere mention of Oxford. He couldn't see them going so far as to sully the college's purity by entering into any sort of dialogue with that noxious institution.

The main problem was how to guarantee he got the Enmity a second time. The competition might be stronger for this one and there was the added problem of repetition; Summerton had just had a poetry person and might well favour a bit of variety. But Fernando couldn't quite bring himself to believe that any of the other candidates, whoever they might turn out to be, could really be better than he was. Whatever his other insecurities, Fernando had an extremely (and justifiably) high opinion of his own work. And if the panel were not sufficiently impressed by him, they couldn't fail to be impressed by George Herbert. No other candidate's research topic could trump Herbert, of that Fernando was certain.

And if he succeeded there would be a new Master appearing on the scene as well, one who, according to Sir Noel Barry, was amenable to rule changing. Fernando began to feel almost optimistic about his future.

Emily was a problem, though. Fernando realised as soon as he had made his plan that he would have to get rid of her, and quickly. If he was about to disappear, the fewer ties he had the better. But when he tried to finish with Emily she became hysterical, and said she loved him and couldn't live without him. She demanded to know how he could do this to her after everything they'd been through. Fernando frowned and wondered whether he'd missed something; to his knowledge they had been through nothing more than an evening at the Warner Brothers cinema in the Grafton Centre. He tried again to lose her, several times, at first tactfully and later less so. She refused to accept her dismissal and relentlessly forced herself on him. She followed him around college wailing and snarling during the day and climbed into his bed wailing and snarling at night. At first Fernando continued to have sex with her, because it was easier than not doing so, but he soon withdrew his sexual favours in an attempt to rid himself of Emily once and for all. Far from getting the message, she went around telling all their colleagues they were engaged. She threatened to kill herself, which furnished Fernando with a glimmer of hope, but then omitted to carry out the threat.

Fernando couldn't risk his private life becoming too gossip-worthy in case people deemed him interesting enough to be looked for in a serious way when he disappeared. If Emily was seen crying behind him too often, he would acquire a reputation as an object of unrequited love, and possibly join the exalted ranks of the legendary Keithanethan. If those two were ever to vanish, the female population of Cambridgeshire would be more united than the colours of Benetton in their attempts to find them. So Fernando steeled himself and settled into a boring relationship with Emily because it was the only way to stop her from dragging them both into the Summerton spotlight.

Fernando fended off all Emily's questions about his family, background and past life. He didn't want to leave any clues behind when he went, no little snippets of information that she could use to track him down. As it was, he was pretty much estranged from his family and had been ever since he'd decided to go to university, contrary to their wishes. He phoned them occasionally but hadn't seen them for years, so there was no need for them to find out that he had disappeared from Summerton and had had plastic surgery, as long as he made sure there was nothing to lead Emily to them. If she turned up at his parents' house screaming about his mysterious absence his mother might get worried and start to look for him, which he didn't want.

As long as only Emily cared enough to look, he figured he was safe. Her hysteria would make her ineffectual and everyone would at least suspect, if not be fully convinced, that her craziness had driven him away.

Stealing the portrait of Grimshaw De La Wyche was easier than Fernando had expected. In the early hours of 22 March 1997, after leaving the Jive Hive, he went back to Summerton, let himself into the catering office with his fellow's key and opened cupboards and drawers until he found the manciple's spare set of keys. He knew immediately which one was the key to Great Hall: the chunky grey one. He'd seen the manciple use it on several occasions. He unzipped his jacket and produced a huge Eaden Lilley carrier bag, the one he'd been given when he bought his duvet for the Sterling Road flat, and transported Grimshaw De La Wyche out of college along with all his possessions. Then he flagged down a taxi on Summerton Lane and off he went to become Rod Firsden.

The theft of the painting was reported to the police, who failed to locate it. Perhaps they would have looked for Fernando more actively if they had known that he and the portrait went missing on the same night, but Fernando's bedder, a lazy woman with no sense of loyalty to the college, decided to lessen her workload by keeping it to herself that one of the fellows for whom she bedded appeared to have moved out. When Fernando's colleagues finally realised he'd gone, and that the last night he was seen was also the last night Grimshaw De La Wyche's portrait was seen, they considered phoning the police to give them this piece of information but decided against it. It seemed somehow disloyal to Fernando and no one could bring him- or herself to believe he'd taken the picture. He was such a decent sort, everyone said.

The one consolation for the fact that Fernando was having to sacrifice his last two years at Summerton while he gambled on winning three more (maybe even more than that, maybe as many years as he lived if Sir Patrick Chichester could be persuaded to change the De La Wyche rules) was that he no longer had to endure Emily. This was such a great benefit that it constituted more of a silver king-size double duvet than a silver lining, and was Fernando's only source of happiness while he prepared to go under the Strebonian knife, then later while he recovered and wrote articles as Rod Firsden, and later still as he put together his fraudulent application for the De La Wyche Enmity and waited.

Publications
'Herbert, Heaven and Hell' (*World Literature Review*, 1997); 'Figurative Imagery in George Herbert's Poetry' (*Journal of Literary Studies*, 1998); 'Remorse in the work of George Herbert' (*Poetry Affairs*, 1998).

Physical Appearance
Substantially different from Fernando's, with the moon-profile nose and chin gone, and some new accessories thrown in – beard, glasses, posh accent. It's amazing how much a few small, specific alterations can change the overall effect. Before the operation, Rod had been worried about not looking different enough. People would instantly recognise him, he thought. But he didn't even recognise himself.

Other Information
Shortly before he disappeared, Fernando found out that Emily would be among the panel members for the next De La Wyche Enmity. At first this bothered him. If anyone would recognise him, she would. She was bound to notice that his eyes were the same. On the other hand, how could she guess? How could the possibility even enter her head?

If she did say something, he would deny it and people would believe him because the truth was so unlikely. All the other panel members would cough with embarrassment and apologise on behalf of their deranged colleague.

Fernando quickly saw a way of turning Emily's involvement in the proceedings to his advantage. He devised the photograph-sending plan, the one which eventually gave him away, to me at least.

And now that I knew what Fernando/Rod had tried to do and was in a position to get him instantly disqualified, what was I doing? Nothing. Attending a book launch. Why? Because part of me recognised that, after the great sacrifice he had made, Rod or Fernando or whoever he was deserved the Enmity more than Sebastian did.

Chapter Forty-seven

Nothing But the Truth

'Read this.' Bryony James pushed a small piece of paper into my hand. She had managed to corner me in the education section of Heffers. I sighed and began to read, quickly, not taking in much apart from the fact that the typeface was peculiar. I was supposed to be meeting Rod in the Blue Boar at this very moment and I could imagine how anxiously he awaited my arrival. In the background I could hear wine being poured, and people laughing and arguing. I felt as if I was only barely clinging on to the world they were in. 'Read it,' Bryony insisted, so I did:

> Applications are invited from senior academics for the 1999 Lanpevenger Bursary. The bursary will cover the cost of a senior academic salary for five years and allow the successful candidate to pursue his or her own research for that period. The bursary may be attached to any academic institution in the UK and Ireland. Applicants should send a CV, letter of application, a list of publications and references to: The Lanpevenger Bursary, PO Box 43, Cambridge, CB1 4LJ by 31 January 1999.

'Well, I'm afraid it's all academic.' I smiled weakly and gave it back to her, thinking privately that it couldn't be a coincidence that the word 'academic' was synonymous with irrelevant, entirely pointless. 'Sebastian can't apply, he's not even junior, never mind senior.' I thought that was why she was showing it to me.

'No, it's not real,' she hissed. I nodded politely and tried to sidle away. The oddness of what she had said didn't register. Nothing seemed particularly real to me at the moment. I just wanted to get to the Blue Boar and Rod. 'It's me and Damian,' Bryony went on. 'Look at the name of it. Lanpevenger. What's that an anagram of?'

'I don't know.'

'Revenge plan,' she whispered in my ear. 'This is it. Do you like it? Damian said not to tell you but I couldn't resist showing off. We're going to put this in the *Guardian,* see, and the *Times Higher* and . . .'

'What? What do you mean it's you and Damian? Are you saying there's no bursary?' This new fact slammed into the pile-up of surprises my brain had become.

'Of course not. Listen, it's brilliant. You know I won that money? Well, Damian and I have set ourselves up as the Lanpevenger Trust, opened a high interest account and put the money in, so that we look all official, yeah? Now all we have to do is put this advert in the papers and wait for the applications to come rolling in.'

'And then what?' I asked, not seeing where the revenge element came in.

'Every professor and senior lecturer in the country will apply for this. And when they do, we'll be there to lead them on right up until the last minute, build up their hopes and dreams, then smash them, drop them without an explanation just when they think they've got it in the bag.' Bryony's lips curled into a satisfied snarl.

'You can't do that,' I said.

'Yes, we can,' she crowed. 'Our company, being the provider of all funds, can reserve the right to withhold the bursary at its discretion. It'll work. But you've got to promise not to tell anyone. Promise.'

'Yeah. Whatever.' I started to walk away. I couldn't have cared less about Bryony and her bursary. Soon it would be time to go home and Sebastian would start to look for me. I had to get to Rod quickly.

I ran down Trinity Street to the Blue Boar. Rod was hunched over a table, looking miserable and gaunt. He hadn't even bought a drink. I wanted to hug him and forget all about the conversation we had to have. 'I suppose you've told them,' he said.

'I haven't said anything.'

'Why not? If you know I'm . . . I used to be . . . Fernando Rose, then you know I'm trying to cheat. Don't pretend you love me enough to protect me, because I won't believe you. I've been kidding myself. You don't love me at all, and certainly not the way I love you. Why are you toying with me?'

Saying anything in response seemed to be a physical impossibility. My feelings for Rod had changed considerably since I'd found out what he'd done. He was no longer the ludicrous, snivelling pedant for whom I felt some affection but not much more. He was a brave, heroic figure, a person who had been willing to sacrifice a job that he loved, his identity, his face – his entire life, in fact, to stand a chance of getting the De La Wyche Enmity again.

Whereas previously I had not found Rod especially attractive, now I was filled with a mute burning lust for him. Knowledge of what he had done made him irresistible. His shining face and the smell of cocoa butter were no longer repellent but somehow sacred. There was simply nobody else like Rod Firsden. I realised at that moment that he was The One.

This was not to say that he was the person with whom I could live happily for ever; I doubted I could live with him for five minutes. Sebastian was my One, in that sense. But Rod was the romantic ideal, the symbol of perfect love. Now I knew for sure that it was possible to have two Ones: the One for reality and the One for dreams and imagination. I didn't think I could risk telling him any of this. It wouldn't have been fair.

370

'Rod, I'm married,' I said eventually. 'To Sebastian Nunn, one of the other De La Wyche candidates. I'm sorry I didn't tell you sooner.' We sat in silence for a few minutes.

He nodded slowly, like someone in a trance or drugged up to the eyeballs on Valium. 'I met him before the interviews. So . . .' – I could see the wheels start to spin in his mind – 'if I turn the fellowship down it'll go to him, right?'

'Right.'

'No wonder you were so keen to help me get Terri Skinner packed off to Reading. I suppose I was next. Well? Wasn't that the plan?' He sounded hurt but not angry.

'I never really had a plan,' I said. 'But that was why I carried on seeing you, yes. At first. But then I got to like you. I did, Rod, honestly. Why do you think I'm not grassing you up?'

'I can't imagine. So how did you find out? About . . . Fernando,' he added uncomfortably, and I realised that he had severed all mental ties with his former self.

' "Sighs and Groans",' I said. 'You told me you gave a copy to each panel member at your interview, to prove that the interview panel had replaced God in our society. Remember?'

'I remember doing it. I don't remember telling you.' He took off his glasses and dropped them carelessly on the table. I'd never seen Rod do anything careless before and it frightened me. I speeded up my explanation.

'Well, you did. I knew Emily Lole through Sebastian's connection with Summerton. He did his PhD there, and we still get invited to feasts. We went to a feast recently and she was going on about you – well, about Fernando – and she told me he – you – had sent her these photos.' I was condensing the story considerably in order to get to the point. Rod didn't need to know that I had spent the past few days conducting a full-scale enquiry into everything Enmity-related; I felt I looked callous enough already.

'What photos?' he said dully.

'How did you expect Emily to make the connection?' I went on, ignoring his denial. 'She's not even interested in poetry. It was the box of Tetley's that occurred to me first. I looked at that photo and thought "into the bitter box", and then everything else fell into place.'

'I don't know what you're talking about,' said Rod sadly.

'You sent Emily photos of different bits of "Sighs and Groans",' I said, 'knowing she wouldn't understand what they meant and would puzzle over them. You deliberately put them in envelopes that she would know were yours. You sent the first batch of photos a couple of months ago and the second batch more recently, as the interview date was approaching.' Rod looked away. 'Envelope one contained photos of earlier parts of the poem, from the first few stanzas. "Oh do not urge me/For what account can thy ill steward make?"' I quoted. 'For ill steward, you enclosed a photo of Ethan Handley, Summerton's steward, feeling sick. It was taken in the college bar. "I have abused thy stock, destroyed thy woods" – for stock, you sent Emily a picture of a beef Oxo cube, for woods, one of some trees. A wood.'

'You can't prove I sent any photos,' said Rod. 'I could deny it. I could deny being Fernando Rose.'

'Rod, I'm not going to tell anyone,' I said. 'You can tell me the truth. Or at least let me tell you. "Sucked all thy magazines",' I went on. 'Magazines: a pile of *Literary Reviews* that you knew Emily would be able to identify as yours. That was another thing that convinced me I was right, once it had occurred to me that you had to be Fernando Rose. Ethan told me that on the night he, you, Keith and Martine went to the Jive Hive, Martine had a holiday brochure with her that you rolled up and put in your mouth. Ethan thought you were making a spliff joke, but you weren't. I bet you always sucked magazines when you were nervous, maybe because of the George Herbert line, in the way other people smoke,' I said, knowing I was right. Rod looked away. 'Sebastian told me, when I asked him about the interview and the other candidates, that he

372

and you were in the waiting room together and that you were sucking a copy of the *Spectator*.'

'How the hell could you know that? That's one of my little madnesses. But . . . it was partly the joke aspect of it that I found comforting. You see, Herbert didn't mean it in that sense. The word "magazines" . . . ' his voice tailed off. 'How did you work that out? Are you psychic?'

I could hardly tell him that, now that I knew about the sacrifice he'd made to get the Enmity, I felt as if our souls were woven together. That was one of my little madnesses. '"My head did ache."' I reverted to the safety of quotation. 'For headache, you sent a picture of a Nurofen carton. "I have deserved that an Egyptian night/Should thicken all my powers" – for Egyptian night, Emily got a photo of Peter Ustinov in *Death on the Nile*.'

'Very good,' said Rod bitterly. 'And the second envelope?'

'That contained images from the last verse only. "Thou art both Judge and Saviour, Feast and Rod/Cordial and Corrosive. Put not thy hand/Into the bitter box, but oh, my God/My God, relieve me!"'

'You recite it very well,' said Rod, who looked on the point of tears.

'Judge: James Pickles,' I said mechanically. 'Saviour: Jesus. Feast: a picture of some Summerton feast or other . . .'

'Audit feast,' said Rod helpfully. I couldn't be expected to know everything.

'And Rod.' I looked him in the eye for as long as I could bear. 'You sent Emily a picture of yourself. Weren't you scared she'd recognise you?'

'No. Not by then. It's funny. People don't recognise you, generally, when they expect you to be a different person. If you know what I mean.'

'Cordial: orange squash, corrosive: a patch of rust on a car door. And then the legendary bitter box – the bumper pack of Tetley's.' I smiled. Only Rod could dream up such a mad plan. I didn't tell him that Emily had witheld the photo of him when she gave me the others, or that I had guessed, as soon as I worked out what Rod had done, that if there was a photo of Judge and one of Saviour, a photo of Cordial and one of Corrosive, then there would not be a photo of Feast without one of Rod. I knew the sender of the pictures was too thorough for that.

'Emily didn't figure it out, did she?' Rod said angrily. 'I sent her the photos in envelopes that were clearly mine, I gave out a copy of the poem at the interview. I thought that as soon as she read it, she'd know. Just seeing those words – ill steward, cordial and corrosive – well, I thought that was bound to be enough of a clue. I even read out the last stanza in my interview and looked pointedly at her as I said the relevant words.'

'But Rod, even if the words did ring a bell, even if she had made the connection between the words and the photos, it's a big step from that to . . . realising that you actually are . . .'

'Sh,' he hissed, looking around.

'That you are . . . were . . . Fernando, and that you had plastic surgery and became Rod Firsden. I mean, I only realised because I had a few extra clues. I knew you knew Vincent Strebonian. I saw him stroking your face, for God's sake!'

'You did?' Rod looked annoyed. 'Oh, well. I always knew Cambridge was a bad place to disappear. It's so small. Everyone sees everything, everyone knows everyone else's business,' he muttered. 'Did you know on Saturday? When we watched the film and . . .'

'No,' I interrupted him quickly. 'No, I only worked it out on Sunday morning, when I saw you and Strebonian in the street.'

'Do you remember, after we'd watched *Witness for the Prosecution*, when you said there was no way you could fool people who knew you into thinking you were a different person?'

'Yes,' I said, and then, realising the significance of this,

'Yes! But I was talking about Marlene Dietrich in the film. But . . . you thought I meant you, didn't you?'

Rod nodded. 'I thought you were trying to drop a hint. I didn't know how you could have guessed, but I got paranoid. I do, quite often. It's only natural, given my situation. That was why I threw you out suddenly. Then later I realised you must have meant the film and I was overreacting as usual.'

'Rod, what did you hope to achieve by sending Emily those photos?' I asked.

'I've just told you,' he said impatiently.

'No, I mean, I know you wanted her to read the poem and connect it with the photos, but . . . what then? If she had guessed, as you hoped?'

'Then she would have realised exactly what was going on and argued my case as persuasively as possible. Emily knew how much I wanted to stay at Summerton. Everyone did. If only she'd been intelligent enough to make the connection, she would have known exactly why I'd had surgery and applied for the De La Wyche as someone else. But she was too dim to put two and two together.'

'That's a bit unfair,' I said. 'It's hardly obvious. Anyway, she supported you even without guessing. She knew you had to be something to do with Fernando.'

'I suppose I'm glad she didn't guess,' said Rod. 'Now I can take the fellowship without being lumbered with her. If she'd worked out that I was Fernando I would have had to . . .' He paused to wince. 'I would have had to be her boyfriend, or else she would have gone running to the Master to tell tales on me.'

'You stayed with her before, though.'

'Only under duress,' he said with distaste.

'Well . . . as you say, now you can take the fellowship and have nothing to do with her.' I glanced at my watch. Sebastian would start to look for me soon. I had to get back to him. I had to start preparing him for his Sheffield and Canterbury interviews.

'How can you say that?' Rod's voice sounded hollow with shock. 'Do you really think it's that simple? I don't want the De La Wyche any more. I want you.'

'But . . . but . . . I mean, I'm not a job,' I said stupidly. 'I'm married, and . . . I mean, the fellowship . . .'

'I'm incapable of wanting two things at once. You're what I want now. Oh, I wouldn't mind the fellowship. I probably will take it, I might as well, after the trouble I've been to. But it doesn't matter to me in the way it once did.'

'Rod, I'm married. To Sebastian. I can't leave him,' I said, before Rod had a chance to suggest it. 'He's devastated about not getting the fellowship.'

'He can have it if I can have you,' said Rod. 'I mean it, Kate. Come away with me and I'll give up the De La Wyche.'

Rod's willingness to sacrifice the Enmity for me made him even more perfect. My heart and brain reeled with the possibilities. I could get the Enmity for Sebastian, but only by leaving him. Was that the truly unselfish thing to do? I pushed thoughts of Damian's stupid book out of my mind. If I went away with Rod, the knowledge that our being together had meant sacrificing the Enmity would ruin things for us. How could it not? And Sebastian would probably rather have me than the Enmity, if he were given the choice, despite what he'd said to me.

'Rod, I can't.' I cleared my throat. 'If I agreed to what you're suggesting, you'd be bound to end up resenting me.'

He said nothing for while. Then slowly, under his breath, he whispered, 'I know.' We stared at each other, defeated. It was unbearable, but I could see no way round it. The only way we could preserve our love for each other was like this, with Rod being willing to give up the Enmity for me and me not allowing him to do so. And besides, I really didn't want to leave Sebastian. He was, after all, my other One.

'I don't want to see you again, in that case,' said Rod. I nodded sadly.

We walked back to Heffers in silence and sneaked in. Sebastian was arguing with an old Summerton duffer about Lenin. He saw me and waved. He hadn't noticed my proximity to Rod, thank God, or if he had, he hadn't made any ominous connections.

Camilla Pearson, Damian's editor, shouted, 'Okay, just a couple more questions and then we'll have to finish.'

'I've got a question for you,' yelled a voice I recognised but couldn't quite place. It came from the shop doorway, behind me. I turned to inspect the yeller.

'My question is, why is anyone interested in publishing or listening to a single word my stupid, small-cocked husband has to say?'

Chapter Forty-eight

The Boys to Trust

Everyone's eyes fixed automatically on Damian's beige flies. 'Martine,' Bryony said in a loud, stony voice, the same one she'd used when she'd mistaken me for Frisky's wayward wife. She walked towards Martine, parting the crowd as she went.

Martine came forward to meet her. 'Who are you?' she demanded.

'I'm Damian's girlfriend. Bryony James. You're not welcome here, particularly if you're going to make comments like that.'

'You can't deny I'm right, though, can you?' Martine smiled snidely. 'He has got an exceptionally small cock.'

'Not at all.' Bryony tilted her head haughtily. 'You're probably just . . . slack and loose.' The crowd parted even further, leaving Bryony and Martine to form a little island of hostility in the middle of the shop. Some of Summerton's more faint-hearted fellows looked as if they wanted nothing more than to climb in between the pages of the latest P D James and hide.

The two women faced each other across the new paperback fiction table. 'Girls, don't fight over me,' said Damian amicably. 'Anyway, Martine, Bryony's right. You always were a bit of a bucket, weren't you?'

'Damian!' Camilla Pearson whispered loudly, blushing. 'It's not good publicity for our authors to say things like that.'

'I know they say you can have too much of a good thing,' continued Damian, ignoring Camilla and looking disdainfully at Martine, 'but I wouldn't apply that maxim to your absence. Where have you been? Why have you come back?'

'I've been staying with friends in Colchester,' said Martine. 'I came back because one of my ex-colleagues from Jacques Duchamps told me your launch was tonight and I just had to check I was right.'

'About what?' Bryony snapped.

'About Damian being a loathsome little reptile,' said Martine. 'I've come to ask for a divorce.'

'Music to my ears.' Damian grinned broadly. 'I must say I'm impressed that one of your ex-colleagues from Jacques Duchamps can actually read.'

'You're foul. How could I ever have loved you?' Martine looked around, as if hoping for a suggestion from the floor. We all waited and watched, holding our breath.

'Right, you've asked for a divorce and Damian's agreed,' said Bryony. 'So now you can go.'

It could just have been bad luck – it probably was – but at the time it felt like fate turning his iron wrath on me. Martine looked right at me and smiled conspiratorially. 'What do you reckon, Kate? Should I walk away and leave my husband in the hands of this pasty-faced, shapeless frump? Oh, what the hell. Let's go and have a drink and catch up on the gossip.' I couldn't understand why she'd picked on me, unless it was because I was standing nearby. We'd been acquaintances, but never friends. In other circumstances I would have liked to have a drink with her. She seemed more confident, more of a proper person than she used to be. But here and now, with Bryony glowering at me, the last thing I needed was to be selected for special pallyness by Martine.

I saw Bryony's mouth open and heard her gasp. I shrugged and tried to look innocent, but I knew it was too late. Bryony James was full-blown mad. I felt as if time had slowed down and everyone in Heffers was staring at me with big, cereal bowl eyes. 'You bitch!' she screamed at me. 'You've been in league with her all along! You've told her our plan. You've spoilt everything.'

'What's she talking about?' Martine asked me and at first I couldn't answer. The Lanpevenger Bursary had seemed so preposterous to me, so like a child's silly game, that I'd half forgotten it already.

'Calm down, sweetie, calm down.' Damian put his arms round Bryony protectively. 'Nothing's been ruined.' I could tell Martine was startled to see that Damian was capable of caring behaviour. Her chin wobbled slightly.

Bryony shook Damian off and started to walk slowly towards me. She pushed the table between us out of the way, sending dozens of books tumbling to the floor. Behind the wine table, two members of Heffers staff exchanged a resentful, raised-eyebrow look. They'd be the ones who'd have to clear up the mess later on. These Oxbridge types, they were all the same, never cleaned up after themselves, physically or emotionally.

I could have run away from Bryony, but that would have looked undignified, and I knew both Rod and Sebastian were watching. I also assumed – naïvely – that in a bookshop full of people she couldn't do me any serious harm. I had forgotten that the people the bookshop was full of were mostly academics (synonymous with useless, entirely pointless). Kwikfit fitters, led by Zac Hunt, would already have intervened. Bryony carried on walking until she was standing inches in front of me. 'Have you told her about our plan? You have, haven't you?' I could smell red wine on her breath. The dark hole of her mouth looked like the entrance to a life-endangering ride at a funfair, the kind that are called things like 'Maim-master'.

'No,' I said. 'Martine's only just walked in, Bryony. I haven't spoken to her for over a year.'

'Liar!' Bryony's hands grabbed my neck and started to squeeze. I tried to pull them off but it was hard; her grasp was too firm and I was getting dizzy. I could see people running towards us: Rod, Sebastian, Martine, Damian, Keithanethan. The next thing I registered was that I was suddenly free and Bryony had turned her attention to Martine, whose neck appeared to be my neck's understudy. I sat down on the floor, next to piles of displaced books, and massaged my sore windpipe. Around me, limbs flailed and people shrieked. Daphne Fielding and the Master were still sipping their wine in a corner, looking grumpy and embarrassed respectively. Daphne was probably sorry Martine hadn't succeeded in strangling me. Valerie Williams was hugging a whimpering Emily Lole. Lloyd Lunnon was the only person who seemed to be enjoying the show. He chortled merrily and helped himself to some crisps from a bowl on the counter.

Suddenly I heard Martine say, 'Fernando.' She didn't shout it, sob it or screech it, which was why it caught my attention. I leaped to my feet. The group of flailing limbs disentangled itself and widened out into a circle of people: Damian, Sebastian, Bryony, Martine, Rod, Keith, Ethan. Martine stared at Rod. 'Fernando,' she said again. 'It is you, isn't it?' Rod looked at me for help, but I was useless (not an academic, but academic nonetheless). 'That's Rod Firsden, you pillock,' said Damian. 'You don't know him.'

'But . . . he's got Fernando's hands.' Martine grabbed Rod's arm and held it up. Beads of sweat seemed to spring from the pores on his forehead. Emily Lole ran forward before Valerie could restrain her. She seized Rod's other arm and started to rub his hand, turning it over and examining it from all angles. 'And Fernando's eyes,' said Martine, growing paler by the second.

'No,' Emily whispered. 'What do you mean?'

'Are you Fernando Rose?' Martine asked Rod. He didn't answer. 'Look, he won't deny it.'

'That's because he's been stunned into silence by your immense stupidity,' said Damian. 'How can he be Fernando? He's got a different face, for God's sake.'

'I know about hands,' Martine insisted. 'It's my job.'

'Give us a hand-job, then,' said Lloyd Lunnon merrily.

'She's right,' said Emily, still clutching Rod's right hand. 'These are Fernando's hands.' She looked at his face, blinking with disbelief. 'And eyes.'

Rod shook his arms free and stepped back. 'And voice,' he said, in an accent I didn't think of as his, presumably his original Guildford one.

'Jesus!' Daphne Fielding marched towards him. 'What the hell . . . ?'

'I've had plastic surgery,' said Rod, reverting to his clipped BBC Rod voice.

'But . . . but . . .' Daphne was unable to finish her sentence.

'For Christ's sake,' Ethan muttered.

'Weird!' said Camilla Pearson.

'You've had *plastic surgery*,' said Lloyd Lunnon. 'Why, for fuck's sake? You were no more repulsive than the rest of us.'

'So that I could stay at Summerton,' said Rod stonily. 'So that I could keep my fellowship. You lot wouldn't let me stay as Fernando Rose.' He swung round to include everyone in his accusation. 'I would have been out, after my allotted three years. I wasn't prepared to accept that. So I became Rod Firsden, applied as Rod Firsden. And yesterday I was offered the fellowship as Rod Firsden. I accept, incidentally.' Emily Lole was mumbling to herself, playing with her hair and staring at her feet.

'Don't be ridiculous,' Sir Patrick Chichester said coldly. 'If this is true, it's obscene. You can't just . . . change your face and become someone else. You're still the same person. It's a temporary fellowship. You can't hold the position twice. God, man, it's revolting what you've done, if it's true. Is it true?'

'Yes,' said Rod. 'I'm not ashamed of it. The way I saw it, I had no alternative.'

'Well, I think we should give him the De La Wyche

fellowship,' said Lloyd Lunnon. 'I've never heard anything so grotesque in my life, but if he's willing to go to such lengths to stay within the third circle of hell that is Summerton, he's earned his right to be there, if you ask me.'

'I didn't ask you,' said Sir Patrick.

'I can't believe this,' said Sebastian. 'Fernando ... is it really you?'

Emily Lole started to scream. 'Oh, shut up!' Rod said wearily. The Heffers staff, I noticed, had separated themselves from the rest of us and were huddled together in a corner at the back of the shop. Valerie rushed over to Emily with a bottle of pills and threw a couple into her wide-open mouth. She gulped as they fell into her throat and continued to scream: waves of noise, washing up only the occasional distinguishable word: 'AAAaboutmeEEE-AAAIIIUUUleave me!' She picked up an empty wine bottle from the wine table and smashed it against the hardback fiction shelf.

'Could everybody please leave the shop!' shouted a woman from the Heffers gang at the back.

'You left me,' Emily wailed at Rod. 'You left me and ... did this to yourself. How could you? How could you?'

'I don't love you,' Rod told her. 'I never did.' He turned to Sir Patrick Chichester. 'I would just like to reiterate that I accept the fellowship.'

'It isn't yours to accept or refuse,' snapped Sir Patrick. 'The offer has been withdrawn.'

'In that case, I'll go home and not bother you any more,' said Rod. I could feel tears rolling down my face, dropping on to my blouse. Rod looked at me briefly, then turned and walked away. Emily grunted and rolled her head around. Whatever drugs Valerie had given her seemed to have taken immediate effect. We all stood in silence.

'Where's Fernando?' Emily whispered.

'He's just left, you stupid bitch,' said Damian.

'No!' Her body jerked awkwardly, as though something

had sent a bolt of electricity through her. 'He can't go. He can't ... GO!' She ran out of the shop, still holding the broken wine bottle. Keithanethan and Valerie ran after her. The rest of us panted and reeled with shock.

'Come on,' said Sebastian after a while. 'We can't just stand here. They want to close the shop.' I burst out laughing. *They want to close the shop.* It struck me as hilarious because it was so normal. They would have wanted to close the shop by now after any book signing. Sebastian's comment had totally and comically failed to capture the extent to which the Heffers staff's desire to lock their doors must have been magnified in this instance.

Sebastian started to walk slowly towards the door and we all followed him, falling into line like a crowd of sleepwalkers. 'Where are we going?' asked Damian, but nobody replied. Our destination was obvious. All we had to do was follow Emily's screams.

'She's heading for college,' said Sebastian. He didn't call it Summerton, just college, as if there were only one. The One. For him and for Rod Firsden.

We walked down Trinity Street towards Summerton Street, then up Summerton Lane. Nobody spoke. When we arrived in Old Court, we simply stood still. It was as if we all knew events would not play hard to get. We didn't have to find them; they would come to us.

Through the arches I could see a cluster of porters in Tyndsall Court. They seemed to be talking frantically. Two of them, one tall and one short, ran towards us. 'Dr Nunn! Master! Professor Fielding, Dr Selinger!' the taller of them said with great relief. 'Thank goodness you're here. Dr Lole's on the roof. She and a chap. There's screaming and yelling and all sorts. Dr Handley and Dr Cobain just went up there an' all.' In my confusion it took me a while to work out that he meant Keithanethan.

'How did she get on to the roof?' Sebastian asked.

'Through the door at the top of O staircase,' said the shorter porter. 'She's not right in the head. She might fall off.'

'Fernando's rooms were in O staircase, weren't they?' said Daphne Fielding. I didn't know the answer to that, but it made sense. Where would he run to in an emergency – and being pursued by a bottle-wielding worm worrier was surely one of the situations for which the term 'emergency' had been invented – if not the place he had been happiest, felt most at home?

Panic hit me like a stone from a catapult. 'Oh my God! She's chased Rod on to the roof.' I shouted. 'She could kill him!'

'Or herself,' muttered Sebastian, attributing my concern for Rod to a general aversion to the idea of people falling off roofs. 'Come on, let's go.' We all ran towards O staircase, following each other up the spiral steps: Sebastian, the Master, Damian, Bryony, Martine, Daphne, Valerie and me.

'Keith and Ethan are up there, everything'll be fine.' Martine was confident. 'They won't let any harm come to anyone.'

'Shut up, bucket face,' said Bryony. I wondered whether it was wise to add those two to the rooftop ensemble.

'Yes, this is all your fault, Martine. If you hadn't turned up and started blathering on about hands we wouldn't be in this predicament now. And I would have sold more books.'

'Oh, fuck you.' Martine sounded more bored than angry.

Sebastian opened the small wooden door and we trooped out into the night. The soundtrack to hysteria wafted towards us on the evening breeze. I looked down at Tyndsall Court. Porters scurried to and fro, pointing up at us. I heard thudding footsteps and turned to see Keith running in our direction. 'Careful, don't slip,' Valerie Williams called out.

'Help Ethan,' he gasped, pointing behind him. 'Emily's trying to push him over the edge.' I've never seen a group of people move as quickly as we moved then, either before or since. Even those of us who were immune to Ethan

Handley's charms on the sexual–romantic front (the Master, Damian, Sebastian, Keith) knew that the very essence of Summerton was at stake. Ethan was the human embodiment of its perfection. Nothing could be allowed to happen to him.

'Where's Rod?' I yelled at Keith.

'I don't know, he's vanished,' Keith panted back at me. 'But Emily keeps calling Ethan "Fernando" and trying to kill him.'

We ran around two corners of the top of Tyndsall Court to where Ethan was struggling with Emily. 'Calm down, just take deep breaths,' he was saying gently, while she gnashed her teeth and spat at him. 'Keith, did you find Fernando or Firsden, whatever he's called?'

'No sign of him,' said Keith.

'Yeah, well, find him quickly. He can't have gone far, he must be up here somewhere.' He held Emily by the wrists, pushing her away from him and the edge of the roof at the same time. 'If she sees him, she might stop thinking I'm him.' His blond hair looked attractively dishevelled. There weren't many people who could succeed in looking gorgeous while being nearly thrown off a roof, but Ethan Handley managed it.

Sebastian and Sir Patrick overpowered Emily eventually and dragged her away from Ethan. 'Go and get . . . a syringe full of something,' Sir Patrick instructed Valerie. 'Anaesthetise her.'

'Even better, put her down,' Damian muttered.

'Evil bastard,' said Martine.

'Bucket,' Bryony countered. Valerie scuttled off.

'That's Ethan!' Sebastian shouted into Emily's face. 'Ethan Handley. It's not Fernando. Do you understand. It's not Fernando.'

Oh, do not urge me. For what account can thy ill steward make?

'She could be forgiven for a degree of confusion.' Lloyd Lunnon's ironic tones reached us before he did. He had arrived late at our roof party. 'Distinguishing those among the fellowship who are Fernando Rose from those who aren't grows harder by the hour.'

'Where the fuck is he?' Ethan demanded. 'Look, some of us had better look for him. There were a few minutes before Keith and I arrived when the two of them were up here alone. Together. God knows what she might have done to him.' He and Keith ran off to start the search.

'I don't altogether care,' said the Master to the rest of us. 'After the way he tried to cheat.' He loosened his grip on Emily's arm for a couple of seconds, distracted by his anger at the way the college had nearly been duped. It was long enough. Emily wrestled her left arm free and ran towards the edge, dragging Sebastian in her wake.

'Let go, Nunn,' shouted Lloyd Lunnon.

Sebastian turned round to look at him, but kept hold of Emily's arm. 'I can't, she'll jump,' he shouted, as Emily pulled them both forward with all the force of her substantial body. Sebastian staggered and lost his balance. Emily hauled him along a few more yards. I screamed. A few of us – Damian, I think, and Martine and I – tried to get hold of Sebastian's feet, but succeeded only in pulling off one of his shoes. We were no match for Emily's hysterical strength.

'Oh, how absurd,' said Lloyd Lunnon. He stepped forward and, extending one finger, tickled Sebastian just below the armpit of his outstretched arm, the one that still clung on to Emily.

'Aah!' Sebastian cried, jerking his arm back to his side instinctively. I collapsed in a heap at his side. I heard footsteps, followed by the sound of Emily screaming as she fell.

'Watch out!' Sir Patrick yelled down at the porters. There was a loud, flat thud as Emily landed on the grass. Sebastian and I stood up and walked tentatively towards the edge, where the others were already lined up. The aerial view of the scene looked like something by Magritte: a sprawling body surrounded by a circle of bowler hats.

On the other side of the roof the little wooden door flew open and Valerie and Keithanethan emerged from O staircase. Valerie was holding a syringe, which she dropped when she saw Emily's broken body on the ground.

'Any sign of that Rose scoundrel?' Sir Patrick asked Ethan later, as we sat in the parlour and waited for the police to arrive.

'None,' said Ethan. 'He must have made a run for it.'

'We can sue him for fraud,' said Sir Patrick. Daphne Fielding began to nod supportively, stopping only when I shot a meaningful glance in her direction. 'He might be hiding in the college somewhere. I'll have the porters comb the place straight away.'

And comb the place they did. But all they found of Fernando Rose, or Rod Firsden, were the photographs in Emily Lole's set.

Chapter Forty-nine

Sebastian Nunn – Curriculum Vitae

Name
Dr Sebastian Gregory Nunn.

Address
Flat 1, Noble House, 14 Renshaw Road, Cambridge.

Age
Twenty-eight.

Marital Status
Married to Kate Nunn (née Cahill) since February 1994.

Employment History
De La Wyche fellow of Summerton College, Cambridge –
October 1998 to present.

Also by Sophie Hannah

gripless

WHEN YOU LOSE YOUR HEART . . . YOU LOSE YOUR GRIP

Belinda Nield knows what she wants. She wants Tony Lamb, a beautiful but silent stranger who has been foisted on the school where she teaches for the duration of the summer play. But she isn't the only one who wants him. Her teenage pupils are also madly in love with Tony, which leads Belinda to formulate a plan for emotional survival that brings only far deeper trouble.

Meanwhile the principal and his wife are making lewd passes at the music teacher and rehearsals for the play begin before a script has even been written: it's time to get a grip.

Exploring the darker and lighter sides of love, *Gripless* is a wicked tale of lust, love, laughter and lies, of wanting everything and learning nothing.

'Hannah's first novel is a prize contender' *The Times*

'A fantastic modern British farce with devilish humour and a fresh take on the idea of romance' *Scotsman*

'Hannah has a wonderfully down-to-earth style . . . This book is sure to be loved by all those out there who love a good love story' *Irish Times*

'A comic heroine so possessed by lust that she makes Bridget Jones look listless' *Observer*

'Funny, audacious, well written – guaranteed to breathe life into your day' *Prima*

OTHER TITLES AVAILABLE IN ARROW

☐ Gripless	Sophie Hannah	£5.99
☐ Truth or Dare	Sara Sheridan	£5.99
☐ Concerning Lily	Sally Brampton	£5.99
☐ Seesaw	Deborah Moggach	£5.99
☐ Straight Talking	Jane Green	£5.99
☐ Chloë	Freya North	£9.99
☐ The Gun Seller	Hugh Laurie	£5.99
☐ Trading Reality	Michael Ridpath	£5.99
☐ The Last Don	Mario Puzo	£5.99
☐ The Liar	Stephen Fry	£5.99

ALL ARROW BOOKS ARE AVAILABLE THROUGH MAIL ORDER OR FROM YOUR LOCAL BOOKSHOP AND NEWSAGENT.

PLEASE SEND CHEQUE / EUROCHEQUE / POSTAL ORDER (STERLING ONLY) ACCESS, VISA, MASTERCARD, DINERS CARD, SWITCH OR AMEX.

EXPIRY DATE .... SIGNATURE ....

PLEASE ALLOW 75 PENCE PER BOOK FOR POST AND PACKING U.K.

OVERSEAS CUSTOMERS PLEASE ALLOW £1.00 PER COPY FOR POST AND PACKING.

ALL ORDERS TO:

ARROW BOOKS, BOOKS BY POST, TBS LIMITED, THE BOOK SERVICE, COLCHESTER ROAD, FRATING GREEN, COLCHESTER, ESSEX CO7 7DW

NAME ....

ADDRESS ....

....

Please allow 28 days for delivery. Please tick box if you do not wish to receive any additional information ☐

Prices and availability subject to change without notice.